THE

TWENTY-FIRST

CENTURY

Publishers Note: THE TWENTY-FIRST CENTURY was written by Bruce Schwartz during the 1990s (see acknowledgments at the back of the book). It was slated to be published in 2001, but with the bombing of the World Trade Centers it was thought to be too controversial a subject at the time. Park Avenue Press is proud to finally present this prophetic work so the world can ask itself: What will happen if a terrorist group decides to attack America? We now know that anything can happen in this day and age, and we pray that the events portrayed in this novel never become reality.

Aaron Gershon, Publisher

THE

TWENTY-FIRST

CENTURY

a   novel

BRUCE SCHWARTZ

PARK AVENUE PRESS

New York

Published by Park Avenue Press
303 Park Avenue South #1223
New York, New York 10010

Visit our website at www.parkavenuepress.net

First public printing September 2003
Printed in Colombia by Imprelibros S.A.

Library of Congress control number 2003104247
Schwartz, Bruce.
    The twenty-first century / Bruce Schwartz. – 1st ed.

ISBN# 0-9729076-0-2

1. Politics - fiction. 2. Fiction. 3. Saddam Hussein - fiction. 4. Novels
5. African-American - fiction. 6. War - fiction. 7. Civil Rights – fiction.
8. Presidential elections – fiction. 9. Revenge – fiction. 10. Iraq - fiction.
11. Riots – fiction. 12. Washington. D.C. – fiction. 13. Women in politics
– fiction. 14. Political thrillers – fiction.
        I. Title

For Cheri,
who always stood by me, believed in me,
and made sure I never stopped dreaming.
You are my heart and soul.

PROLOGUE

Baghdad, Iraq
May 1991

The Presidential Palace was quiet. Somber. Saddam Hussein was pacing the floor of his dining room. Seated at the table was Sayyid Kassim, his closest friend and most trusted advisor. The President looked at the sad man and felt his pain. America's infidels had murdered Sayyid Kassim's only son in early February after they had crossed the ocean and invaded their land. All because of George Bush, the master CIA spy and oilman. It was why Saddam had set more than 700 of Kuwait's oil wells on fire those last few days of the war. If he couldn't have them, then neither would George Bush.

He turned to the window and looked out at his Iraq. The hulks of planes and tanks decorated the landscape. Oil refineries, factories, and power stations were in ruins. Dozens of bombed bridges had fallen into the Tigris and Euphrates rivers. And tens of thousands of Iraqi sons, and countless civilians, were dead. Slaughtered in the streets of his once-beautiful country. Reports were that gasoline lines were hundreds of cars long; there was little electricity or fresh water; sewage was overflowing into the streets; and food prices had soared out of control. Saddam took a deep breath. Thankfully, he and his Baath Party had eliminated all of his internal rivals. A coup was not likely. He turned back to Sayyid. "Are you sure your numbers are accurate?"

"Yes," Sayyid answered. "More than twenty percent of our aircraft and forty percent of our tanks have been destroyed, along with almost sixty percent of our artillery." Whereas, before this war, Iraq had the world's fourth largest army, now it was minuscule in comparison. As was the economy. Sayyid continued: "But, even with all we have lost, we still outnumber our neighbors. Saudi Arabia has only 550 tanks, Iran about 500, and Jordan 1,100."

"And we?" the President asked as he paced, worried about the answer.

"We still have more than 2,500."

Saddam stopped by the window again and looked out at the devastation. He twirled his thick, black mustache between his thumb and forefinger and thought about the Al-Qiyamah, his covert plot to right this terrible wrong. "And what is our air capability?"

Sayyid Kassim told him. "Saudi Arabia and Iran have about 190 combat aircraft each. We have that many hidden in Iran alone, and more than 250 hidden in bunkers, ready for any attack, along with our long-range nuclear capability. Much of our artillery, almost 1,500 short range missiles and chemical shells, are intact."

"And your conclusions?"

"We have the power to strike strongly and deeply against

any of our neighbors, but not against the United States."

Saddam thought about it and drank his mistaki. It burned his throat as it slid down, comforting him. He let the draperies fall closed. "As long as the West believes man can shape his destiny, and we in Islam believe it is God who controls our destinies, we are destined to win."

"Allah akbar!" Sayyid Kassim answered.

"Allah akbar!" God is Good.

Saddam sat down at the head of the table, with Sayyid to his left. The staff served their dinner. The President took a last mouthful of the potent drink and began eating his muscouf. He noticed Sayyid was nibbling at the fish. His son's death had made him give up hope. It was time to tell him what he had planned. It would give his friend a reason to live again. "Al-Qiyamah!"

"Pardon?" the grieving father asked.

"We must honor your son and the martyred sons of all Iraqi fathers." The President looked into Sayyid Kassim's eyes and smiled. "Al-Qiyamah!" The Rising of the Dead!

Twenty-five years later …

BOOK ONE

BEWARE THE ENEMY WHO BECOMES YOUR FRIEND ...

CHAPTER ONE

Tuesday, November 1st
Seven days before Election Day

The limousine approached Baltimore's HOPE City, and Jane Weisser looked out at the mass of supporters awaiting the candidate. What was once the poorest, most dangerous section of the city had been miraculously transformed years ago into a Mecca of opportunity for the city's forgotten people. All because of Sam Howard, the man sitting next to her, the man she loved without question. Jane looked at him and felt her heart beat an extra beat. He was forty-seven years old, handsome, and had a commanding, yet gracious presence. As his campaign director, Jane had brought him to where he was today, to the door of the Oval Office. She had molded him into the perfect candidate.

At least she believed he was the perfect candidate. The polls, however, were not in agreement.

Jane saw the archway leading into HOPE, and she

wondered what she could do to turn things around. She thought about their years together, about their beliefs and principles, about their vision for the future.

Sam turned and smiled at her, and Jane melted. Although everyone viewed her as always in command, Jane Weisser was powerless under Sam Howard's spell. It had always been that way, ever since their days together at Yale.

The limousine slowed, and the Secret Service agents jumped out of their cars and surrounded the area. Jane stepped outside and looked around. Not a cloud was in the sky, making it feel like a spring day. The cheers and applause for the candidate was thunderous, and it gave Jane a chill, as it always did. Everyone was in a celebratory mood. They believed their Sam Howard was going to be the next President of the United States. Jane noticed the children in the crowd happily eating their Halloween bounty. Last night, they had swarmed the countryside like armies of ants, hoping not to get any tricks. They obviously hadn't. Jane smiled at them as the procession was led through the archway into Baltimore's HOPE City.

Life was indeed a treat.

At exactly 4:00 p.m, five-hundred perfectly-timed bombs devastated America's twelve HOPE Cities. What had taken twenty years to build was gone within minutes. Thousands of innocent people, struggling to survive while bettering themselves everyday because of HOPE, died instantly. Flesh and bone flew in every direction, mixed with wood, brick, metal, and glass, all colored blood-red. Thousands more were unfortunate enough to have to view this holocaust a little longer before hundreds of refurbished tenement buildings, stores, and new businesses crumbled on top of them, sending them to an agonizing final peace.

In all the cities, those who weren't in any of the stores or hi-rise apartment buildings ran through the streets. They didn't know where to go. Hide. Fire was everywhere. Everyone was crying. Screaming. Many were in shock and just stood there, watching in disbelief. Mothers clutched their children to their bodies, and fright, utter panic, filled everyone's faces. Those who were able to crawl out of these shambles would have been better off remaining there to quickly die. Some were armless and legless, and some were on fire. Some were naked, their clothes completely burned off, and a sickly shade of wet crimson-red covered their entire bodies.

It seemed to anyone lucky enough to survive this Armageddon as if a war had erupted. They looked up to the skies and saw no warplanes. No bombs dropping down on them from an enemy they could see.

It could only be the end of the world.

Jane Weisser, along with Sam Howard and the rest of the campaign team, stood inside the entranceway of the Baltimore HOPE City. She tried to run for cover, but fear had paralyzed her legs. She saw brick, wood, and blood fly in every direction, splattering and shattering everyone and everything in its way. The force of the explosions was so painful to Jane's ears that she had to cover them. In its wake, the sounds of churning metal and roaring fire, the gut-wrenching screams of little children, pierced her eardrums anyway.

Jane's eyes focused on the horrific landscape before her and she saw the Baltimore HOPE City sucked into the bowels of Hell. Before she could accept the reality of what was happening, something hard hit her on the side of her head and she lost consciousness.

"JANE! JANE!" Sam Howard yelled.

She opened her eyes and noticed she was on her back. The

sky was orange, and the heat from it felt as if it was frying her skin like it did every summer at Ocean City.

"Speak to me!" Sam Howard knelt by her side and lifted her in his arms.

Jane regained her bearing a moment later. The McCormick Spice Company was nearby, and the acrid smell of chili powder, along with the smoke and dust, burned her throat. "Oh, my God," she tried to shout as she looked around, "those poor people. We have to help them, Sam."

"No! We have to get out of here!"

"But, those people ..."

"We can't stay ..."

"... need our help!"

"I know, Jane, I know ..."

"We can't just walk away from them. We have to do something."

"We have to get out of here. Now!" Sam insisted.

Jennifer Stewart, an intern at The Weisser Organization, was sprawled out on the pavement no more than ten feet from her. Her eyes were pleading for help, but her body was still. Tears ran down Jane's cheek. Just last month she had met Jen's mother when she came to Washington to visit her daughter. Now ... she had no daughter. It was a scene Jane knew she would never forget. There were Jen Stewarts everywhere.

"MOMMY! MOMMY!" a lost child of five or six screamed in terror.

Jane heard it. Her heart dropped into her stomach with a speed and weight so great that she had to take repeated deep breaths to stop from losing it. She thought about all the dead children, all the children gripped in panic. It forced her mind back to the time she lost her eight-year old brother, Michael. Dizzy with emotions she couldn't deal with right now, Jane forced herself to concentrate on the moment. If she didn't get up, she'd be trampled to death. Feet were stepping on her, kicking her, falling on top of her. She hurt all over.

It took every bit of strength and mobility, but she was finally able to stand. Against the tide, Jane pushed herself through the crowds of hysterical people rampaging toward the city's opening archway. It was like swimming upstream; it took every muscle to move. She squeezed through the avalanche, lifted the bloodied child, and hugged her to her body. The little girl clung to her, her arms and legs wrapped tightly around her, as if begging Jane not to let her go. "It's okay, baby," she tried to assure her, "you're going to be okay."

"JANE, PLEASE, YOU'RE NOT SAFE HERE," Sam screamed as his Secret Service agents pulled him away. "SOMEONE GET HER, FOR GOD'S SAKE!"

Concrete fell all around them, fire engulfed everything, and thousands of shrieking voices made it almost impossible to hear him. Jane tried to comfort the frightened child. "Let's go find your mommy," she whispered in her ear. She saw an old man laying on the ground. Blood was pouring from his torn-off leg. He was jerking back and forth, screaming unintelligibly. Next to him, a woman in the last trimester of pregnancy lay dead. Jane's knees became rubbery and her stomach flipped.

"Allison. Oh, my baby, my baby!" A woman grabbed the child from Jane's hands and ran off. The reunion made Jane's eyes tear. She thought about her mother and how she had never had the chance to rescue her child from such fear. Her heart rebounded to her throat. Jane's mind returned to the disaster before her. She saw a young boy crawl out from beneath a building. His jaw hung open in a grotesque angle from the rest of his torn face. Nausea swept over her.

Jane tried to swallow, but her throat was dry from all the

dirt and smoke. She rushed over to help him. As she did, one of the Secret Service agents assigned to Sam Howard grabbed her right arm and spun her around. "Senator Howard is a presidential candidate, ma'am. If someone is trying to assassinate him, we have to get him to safety."

Someone knocked her down to her knee. "Oww!" She had to do something, damn it, only there was nothing, she knew, she could do. The agent reached down and helped her up. Jane stood there, frozen, gaping in horror at the enormity of the disaster. Sirens from police, ambulances, and fire engines got closer and added their wails to the mass hysteria.

The agent offered her his handkerchief, and Jane pressed it against her bloodied head. "You gonna be all right, Dr. Weisser? Maybe we should get you to a hospital."

"No, I'll be fine, thank you." Jane looked at everything around her as if it were a scene in a movie. It was too much for her. She turned away and walked toward Sam's limousine. If they had arrived on this campaign stop a few minutes earlier … Jane Weisser felt a sickly force enter her body and clutch her heart. Was someone trying to assassinate Sam Howard? And would they murder thousands of men, women, and children to achieve that? Dear God, how could something this terrible happen seven days before the election?

Sam Howard had spent his entire inheritance from Howard Oil to build his idea of the future city, and in twenty years he had made the future the present. Winner of the Nobel Prize for Peace, a U. S. Senator for twelve years, and, soon, he hoped, President of the United States, America had changed for the better because of these 'new cities.' Race relations had improved dramatically, and a sense of community had returned. Thriving families no longer on welfare filled the twelve HOPE Cities.

Along with the hi-rise tenement buildings refurbished inside and out, Sam Howard had transformed all the stores surrounding these apartment complexes into name-brand discount outlets. He built Monorail systems to transport the visitors, and theme parks, amusement centers, casinos, multiplex cinemas, and theaters for live concerts and stage productions, along with hotels, and restaurants quickly followed. For consumers from the area, it was a full-day family event. For visitors traveling long distances, it was a family vacation, affordable and safe. The city was again the main attraction, and with it came self-sufficiency as suburban and rural money fed its economy. What made it such an amazing success - dramatically reducing crime, vandalism, and welfare - was that Sam Howard had given the thousands of families who lived there no-money-down mortgages on their apartments. Each family also owned a small part of the business they worked in. In return, their children had to stay in school and out of trouble until graduation, and every parent had to attend classes offered in courses such as money management, effective parenting, and interpersonal communication taught by volunteer professors from area colleges. At the completion of each course (a minimum of one to a maximum of three each year), a pay raise would follow.

Every administration that had occupied the White House since the turn of the millennium had agreed that Sam Howard's plan to rebuild America's inner cities was accomplishing just that. He had given back the poor their dignity and pride. With jobs and decent housing, society had finally answered its own problem. The formula was simple: With Housing and Opportunity comes Prosperity and Equality - HOPE! 'Uncle Sam,' as everyone called him since his first HOPE City opened in Bridgeport, Connecticut, was an innovator. To those he helped he was a Messiah. Because of Sam Howard, the poor and underprivileged finally had their hope. Finally had something to be proud of.

Something to live for.

But, now, all that was gone. There were no more HOPE Cities. No more businesses, tourists, attractions, apartments, families. Dreams! It had all become a fiery ruin, and all that remained were the prayers and cries for 'HELP!' as death and despair once again reared its prejudicial head.

Some unidentifiable enemy had taken away the peoples' HOPE.

Sam Howard was talking on the portable videophone inside his limousine, and U. S. Representative William S. Lawson (R-Texas), his fifty-eight-year old Vice Presidential running mate, was sitting across from him. Jane got in and sat next to the congressman. Sam's heart stopped pounding. He didn't know what he would have done if she had stayed there. He put the call on hold. "Are you okay?"

"I'm fine, just a headache."

"You're sure?"

"I'm okay, Sam, really!"

Sam stared at her and his heart started pounding again, only for a different, more enjoyable reason this time. Jane was the personification of beauty. He noticed droplets of blood had discolored her white scarf. It had also matted her long, dark hair on the side of her head. He felt queasy. What if she'd been killed? It was too terrible a thought, and Sam suppressed it. He returned to the call. "WHAT?" he screamed into the hand-held videophone a few seconds later. His body arched forward, as if a wind, an unseen force, had knocked him off balance. Trembling, he looked at Jane and Bill. "All twelve HOPE Cities have been bombed!"

"NO!" Jane gasped.

"Lord have mercy!" the congressman whispered.

After asking questions and giving orders, Sam disconnected the call and lay his head back against the leather headrest. The horrible deaths he'd just witnessed made him remember the murders of his parents and sister the day he graduated from Yale. It was the worst day of his life, a day he couldn't forget. The flashback ended this time much like it did every time, with his little sister in his arms and two bullets tearing into him, shattering his left shoulder and right hip.

Sam opened his eyes from the painful memory and tried to shake it off. It always left him breathless and weak. He saw Jane press the handkerchief against the side of her head. "We have to get you to a hospital."

"No, I'm all right, Sam. I'll go downstairs and see Dr. Benjamin when we get back to the office."

"But, you may have a concussion."

"Sam, I'm fine!"

She said it with an authority all too familiar to him. When Jane Weisser made up her mind, nothing could change it. "If Dr. Benjamin feels you should go to the hospital, you will. Okay?" He stared her down, like she had always done with him. Then, he smiled.

And she smiled in return. The matter was settled.

Sam looked at her ripped stockings. Jane's legs were long, thin, and shapely. Being a runner didn't detract from them; if anything, it made them even more attractive. Although she had gained some weight this past year, she was still a centerfold to Sam. He turned away from her and saw the planes taking off from Baltimore International Airport. His driver had called ahead and instructed the pilot to have the jet ready for immediate takeoff.

Sam watched the engines spewing heat and turning the air

around them into a hazy sea of waves. As they drove up to it, he thought about Jane and the first time they had met. It was during his junior year at Yale when he was starring in MACBETH. She had come to his dressing room after the performance. Her explosive blue eyes and dimpled smile, her long brown hair and those perfect legs - it was love at first sight. Although they were the opposite of each other in every way: he rich, she from a middle-class family; he Protestant, she Jewish; champagne and caviar versus schnapps and chopped liver, it didn't matter. Love was love. There was no use fighting it.

Sam closed his eyes. He remembered the time in college when they were talking politics in bed after a heavy night of drinking. She had been as relentless in her opinions as in her consumption. Whereas he was always calm and sedate, Jane was always anxious and excitable.

"You can't look me in the eyes and tell me Ronald Reagan was a great president, Sam. That 'no new taxes' bullshit of his was a con job just to get him reelected, and we're still paying for it today. He mortgaged the country's future with his 'buy now, pay later' mentality."

"But he was the Great Communicator. The people trusted him like no other president. Personality, Jane. It brought the people together."

"And drove the classes apart. Jesus, Sam, wake up. Your Great Communicator spent almost four-trillion dollars on the global confrontation with the Soviets and added more to the national debt than all previous administrations back to George Washington *combined*. To feed his own ego and obsessive need for popularity, the actor hypnotized us and played us into near national bankruptcy. A business that spent its capital so foolishly, with nothing to show for it, would be in Chapter 11 by now. And the CEO would be thrown out on his ass - or in jail!"

He didn't know enough about politics to argue, so he listened. And learned. As the heir to Howard Oil, he had never thought about his family wealth and the power it wielded until Jane had taught him the value of a dollar. It had made him think seriously about what he could do with it.

Before Sam could think about that carefree time anymore, Jane's soothing voice woke him from his daydream.

"Sam?" she called out softly, leaning into the limo and shaking his shoulder.

Sam Howard looked into the eyes of the only woman he'd ever loved.

"Are you okay? We're ready to board."

He smiled and stepped out of the long car.

Jane took command, as always, and Sam was thankful, as always. "C'mon everyone," she shouted above the whir of the jets, her arms waving in the air as if directing traffic, "we have to get back to the office. There's still a lot of work to do. And only seven days to do it in."

She was amazing!

Jane Weisser received four stitches in her head from the Senate physician, then returned to her office inside Sam's suite in the Hart Senate Office Building. Six months ago, she had moved from her own offices on Massachusetts Avenue, with a select staff of ten. There, she would remain until the election was over. Paco Ramirez, seated at the conference table between Jane's desk and the wall screen on the opposite end of the room, was waiting for her when she walked in. He looked up at her, and, immediately, Jane saw the fear in his eyes. Paco was a product of Bridgeport's HOPE City. He was an example of how Sam Howard was saving the urban youth. Because of Sam Howard, Paco had been able to attend college. With a Master's degree in

Public Relations and Advertising, he had sought out Jane at TWO, The Weisser Organization. Now, eight years later, Paco Ramirez was Jane Weisser's first assistant in Sam Howard's campaign for President of the United States. Jane felt sorry for her friend. Not only was his home destroyed, but ..." Oh, my God, Paco, your family! Have you spoken to them yet? Are they all right?"

The tears in Paco's eyes fell down his cheeks. His parents still worked and lived in Bridgeport's HOPE City. "I tried to call, but I couldn't get through."

"Jesus, man, get back on the telecomp and keep trying. What are you waiting for?" As Paco punched in the number on the keyboard on Jane's desk, she asked, "Has Sam talked to the press yet?" She had had to fight her way through the dozens of reporters, telecomp cameras, and photographers outside the glass doors of the suite after she left Dr. Benjamin. Sam must have had the same problem earlier. Hopefully, he made a statement.

"No," Paco told her. "I was at the front desk when he arrived, and all he said was, 'I'm sorry, I can't talk right now.'"

"Damn it! Sam's probably waiting for me to prepare a statement for him." The media were like a pack of buzzards; if you didn't feed them, they would soon feed on you. It was imperative she placate their hunger and have Sam speak to them and to the America people, now. "Keep trying until you reach your parents, Paco. I'll be back in a few minutes."

Jane left her office and hurried past the reception desk, the other offices, the copy room, and the many speech writers, typists, campaign staff, and researchers busy at work for the candidate. She ignored Jackie, Sam's secretary, and walked into his office. He was at his desk, reading intently.

The room was large, with royal blue carpeting. Windows along the opposite wall of the door looked out to the Capitol.

Sam's desk was on the left side, and two sofas, with a coffee table between them, occupied the other half of the room. A wall screen faced the senator's executive desk. Two Chippendale chairs were between the desk and the sofas. Even sitting, his presence was overwhelming. From his tall and broad-shouldered physique, to his salt and pepper hair and suede gray eyes, he was … perfect!

"How could something like this have happened, Jane?" he asked after she closed the door behind her.

Dr. Jane Weisser was an expert in the psychology of public relations and the media. She was the one responsible for getting Sam Howard elected to the U. S. Senate and then reelected to a second six-year term while he spearheaded the legislation which built and financed new HOPE Cities around the country. They were a team, each with their own magical touch. "Sam, I think we're going to have to forget about the election for a few days and get out to those cities and start helping. I'll prepare a statement for you to read to the press."

He removed his half-lens glasses and rubbed his eyes.

"Sam?"

"I'm sorry, Jane. I was just thinking about the effect this might have on the election. What do you think?"

Jane didn't know how to answer him. "It all depends on the public's reaction. Sympathy, of course, will be on your side. How that translates into points, well - it's just too early to tell. By now, telecomp crews have most likely assembled in all twelve cities. They, as you well know, can determine the pulse of the people faster than anyone." Jane saw how upset and worried Sam was and her heart ached. Their love was private. It had been so for the last six years, ever since Sam's wife died in a tragic car accident near their home in Fairfax, Virginia. They expressed their passion for each other at Sam's Maryland hide-away (until fourteen months ago when he announced his bid for the presidency) in a clandestine way that even the CIA would laud. Jane's heart ached because she knew Sam's heart ached. What a compassionate man, she thought, so loving, so caring. He's going to be a great president.

The possible future President of the United States turned to the keyboard on his right. He punched in SS and the buttons marked CBS, NBC, ABC, FOX, C-SPAN and CNN on the telecomp. The large screen in the wall opposite the senator's desk lit up. From each sixth of the split screen, the networks were reporting live, feeding in video from the devastated HOPE Cities across the nation. He touched another button on the keyboard. "Jackie, no more calls. I need a break."

Sam viewed the mass carnage and destruction while Jane opened the liquor cabinet behind his desk and poured herself a double Scotch. "I think you should talk to the country immediately, Sam. Maybe your voice, since you were the architect of HOPE, will calm them."

Sam thought about it for a moment. "No, Jane. It wouldn't be ethical if I spoke before the President did. I don't want the press accusing me of being an opportunist, of trying to take control of this nation before my time. We have no choice but to wait, I'm afraid."

"But if your words can restore order and help saves lives, why wait? It's your duty to speak to the people."

"I have to do what is right, Jane. And what is right is to let the Commander-in Chief address the country first." He turned his beleaguered face back to the wall screen.

The networks were reporting that President Charles Price was in the White House being briefed by his advisers and the joint chiefs of staff. The day's events were threatening to panic the American people. No one knew what to expect. The networks were standing by, waiting to broadcast the president's words to an anxious nation.

Jane had to think. Sam wasn't going to talk to the press. How would they construe that? Avoidance of the media always breeds speculation, and speculation always breeds innuendo. That's tantamount to suicide in a campaign. She had to come up with a spin.

Jane returned to her temporary office to find Paco Ramirez sitting transfixed behind her desk. "Did you find out anything, Paco?"

"The lines are still down. There's no way to get through."

"Well, there's still hope." Immediately, the double entendre made Jane cringe.

"Is there?" he asked. There was an uncomfortable pause for a moment for them to think about it. Then, Paco changed the subject. "Have you talked to Taryn, yet?"

"Dear God!" Jane reached for the telecomp keyboard and tapped in the number of her daughter's dorm room at Georgetown University. She received a recorded message to try again later.

The six panels of the wall screen opposite her desk were displaying continuous news reports. Suddenly, Paco leaped for the keyboard. He pressed the key for CNN, and it filled the entire screen.

There it was, live for them to see first hand: Bridgeport, Connecticut. The south end of the city, from I-95 to the beaches of the Long Island Sound, was in ruins. The entire HOPE City in between looked like a war scene. Blocks of flattened housing and businesses were up in flames. Sirens blared, ambulances raced to and from, and dozens of hook and ladder fire trucks spewed arcs of water onto buildings that were no longer buildings. The scene evoked a certain strange beauty, like synchronized fountains. But, knowing there were hundreds, maybe thousands, of lifeless bodies in the smoldering debris under this waterfall made it a sickening sight to watch.

"I know that street," Paco said, pointing to the aerial shot. He walked up to the large screen. "That's where my parents' building is." Only, it wasn't. The home Paco Ramirez had lived in from the time he was fifteen, the one place that had truly made him feel like an American - like there was HOPE - was now a mountain of brick, metal, and burning wood. He held his hands up to his face.

Jane put her arm around the slight man's shoulders. She felt him shaking, and she tried to steady him by holding him closer to her. "Your parents were probably in their souvenir shop on the boardwalk, Paco. Most of the destruction looks located throughout the hi-rises. The recreational and entertainment areas by the beach look less damaged."

"What will I do if they're … DAMN IT! I'M SO MAD! Who could have done this? Why would someone do this?" he sobbed.

"I don't know, Paco. It's insane."

"Let me tell you, Jane, it's not going to end here. You don't give people something, especially something they've deserved and demanded all their lives, and then have them see it destroyed. Madre de Dios, this is going to spark an even greater fire storm."

"I'm just as worried about that as you are, Paco. It's going to be disastrous." The two friends stood there, unable to move. It was just too painful to talk about anymore.

In New York City, a fire storm hit Harlem. What had been a terrible few hours of looting, shooting, and rampant destruction had blown into a full-fledged battlefield. Thousands of people swarmed the streets, and the police couldn't tell who was doing the shooting. Snipers sprung up at random only to disappear and appear elsewhere. It was a theater of war, with a haggard defense pointing their automatic weapons at an enemy they couldn't see. Armored trucks rolled onto 125th Street with guns aimed, and helicopters patrolled from the sky with their high resolution cameras and searchlights. The lights made it even more difficult to see. The smoke from the burning buildings, along with the tear gas being thrown into the crowds, blanketed the sky but didn't deter the gunshots. Like every other city of poverty and color across America, just as many people were fighting in the streets as were hiding from the fighting in the streets.

It was anarchy!

And it was unstoppable.

The Reverend Dr. Moses McBride, with the help of his friend, Sam Howard, had been elected president of the National African Caucus after the archaic NAACP folded the year before. He had succeeded this past year in unifying his people into one voice, and that voice was backing Sam in his bid for the presidency. Now, inside his first floor Harlem apartment, Moses watched what was happening outside. Bullets were flying, fires were roaring, and buildings were exploding. The man who preached educational warfare rather than violence, the man of God, was heartsick. Whites were killing Africans (they had recently dropped the American half of their title), and Africans were killing whites, but, worse, Africans were killing Africans. This is not the way, Moses thought to himself. Lord Jesus, what do I do? Moses McBride rubbed his hands through his receding hairline. He turned away from the window and looked at his wife and sixteen-year old daughter. They were sitting on the couch, listening to the news. Nothing else was on.

Moses focused his attention on his daughter, DaNell. For the last few months, he had been trying to help her beat a drug and alcohol problem. Now, her eyes had a glazed look to them.

What was happening outside had obviously scared her enough to take something. Moses felt his heart tear. He thought he had found all her hidden stash. He looked out the window. People were running for cover, for their lives.

The preacher walked to the closet. He put on his black overcoat over his trademark purple shirt and black tie and turned to his family. "I have to go to church. I have to be there in case anyone needs me."

"In case anyone needs you?" his wife asked. "Your family needs you, Moses!"

"Please, Jessie, you have to understand. Like President Price, I have a responsibility to this community. People are depending on me at this time."

"We're depending on you, too, Moses. Look outside. Will you be safe out there?"

Moses McBride had made up his mind. "I'll be back shortly, Jessie. No more than an hour. I promise. In the meantime, stay away from the windows." He stared at DaNell. She was in another world.

"Please, Moses?" There were tears in her eyes.

The reverend understood his wife's fear, but, nevertheless, he had to do what his heart and his conscience were dictating. He kissed his girls and held them for a while.

Moses exited the apartment onto 123rd Street, turned right, and cautiously made his way west for two blocks until he came to the First Abyssinian Baptist Church. Before he opened the front door, he heard another explosion in the distance. Flinching, but not turning around, he closed his eyes. "Please, dear Father in Heaven, give me the courage and the strength to help my people."

Moses walked into the peacefulness of his Lord's home. The place was dark and desolate; no one had dared venture out with all this fighting going on. Good, he thought, now I can go back home. Moses McBride loved his wife and daughter more than life itself. Maybe even more than God. As he walked back in the direction of his apartment building, that thought, that admission, shocked him. The smile on his face, as he dreamed about Jessie and DaNell, made him forget the terror around him. What was the meaning of life? The answer was simple: Family.

The sounds of whooshing flames, burning wood, and crackling glass reverberated in his ears and ricocheted to his nerves, making him forget his pleasant thoughts. If this was what Hell felt like, he was thankful he was in God's good graces.

Suddenly, Moses saw his worst nightmare before him. His apartment building was an inferno. All six floors had flames darting from every window. He dropped his Bible. "NO-O-O! Please, dear God, NO-O-OO!"

Moses charged through the many people lucky enough to have escaped and flew in through the front door. Flames were everywhere, blinding him. He couldn't breathe. It didn't matter; he had to get to Jessie and DaNell.

Moses reached his first floor apartment door. He tried to open it. The metal doorknob was hot, and locked, and he didn't have his key. Without any thought, he battered his two-hundred and sixty-pound body into the wood until it cracked. Smoke filled the dark hallway, and sweat poured from his face. He heard his wife screaming his name inside their apartment. "I'M HERE, JESSIE!" he screamed back. "I'M HERE!" Moses heard the roar of fire coming from inside. He plowed into the door more forcefully, ramming it over and over again with his left shoulder. With a final, desperate lunge he broke through, splintering the door into jagged daggers. Although bloodied from the entry, his only thought was to get his family out of there. Fire was everywhere, singeing his hair to his scalp as he tried to see into the smoke-filled room.

"Moses." Her voice was softer, weaker.

"JESSIE! WHERE ARE YOU?" His body shook, his brain felt like it was going to explode, and, for an instant, he felt paralyzed. But, then Jessie spoke again.

"Moses, help me."

"KEEP TALKING AND I'LL FIND YOU!" There was so much smoke and heat that he had to hold his breath as much as possible. As he made his way farther into the room, he tripped over his wife and fell down by her side. "WHERE'S DaNELL?" There was no answer. Moses lifted the thin woman in his arms. She was convulsing in shock. "DaNELLLLL!"

He carried her to the front door. His left hand grabbed the handle and was instantly blistered by the hot metal. "DEAR JESUS! HELP ME!" There was a large hole in the door, from when he burst in moments before, but, now, pointed shards of burning wood were jutting in at him forming a wooden ring of knives and fire. Without a second thought, Moses pressed Jessie's face to his chest and crashed through the opening into the hallway.

Outside, the heavyset man fell to his knees. He lay his wife down and rolled back and forth on top of her until he extinguished the flames attacking their bodies. Moses got up and ran back to save his teenaged daughter. When he reached the hallway of the old apartment building, he couldn't get through the wall of flames now blocking the entrance. "DaNELL!" He screamed in guilt and in agony. "NO-O-OO!" He tried to run in a few times, but the fire shot out at him like a blow torch. Four of the men standing in the crowd of survivors bolted for him and grabbed him from his suicidal mission. "DaNell," he cried. "My baby! What have I done?" He loved his little girl. By leaving them to go to his church he had killed his little girl. "NO-O-OOO!" he cried, punching his face in frustration and punishment. "WHAT'VE I DONE?"

He refused to do nothing. Without another thought, Moses McBride ran through the flames into his apartment. He had to save DaNell.

He found her unconscious in the hallway leading to the bedrooms. Moses scooped her up in his arms, her hot skin burning into his. He dashed through the fire and thick smoke, crashed into a wall, reversed direction, and scrambled blindly to the fresh air outside. Some neighbors ran toward them from across the street and doused them with buckets of water.

In the middle of 123rd Street, with sweat pouring from every pore, Moses tried to breathe his own life into his only child. "LIVE! YOU GOTTA LIVE!" he screamed into her mouth. He looked up to Heaven. This had to be a dream. A nightmare.

It wasn't.

Moses remained still for a few moments as neighbors took DaNell from his arms. He looked at Jessie being tended to by friends and felt an anger growing inside him. He then did something he had never before done, or had ever thought he would do, in his fifty years as God's child.

For the first time in his life, Moses McBride questioned his belief in his Lord.

A tension-filled dinner of Chinese food delivered from Mickey Chang's churned in Jane's stomach as she sat back on one of the twin sofas and waited for President Price to address the country. Sam, sitting opposite her, was watching the TC and the many news reports showing what was happening in America's inner cities. Congressman William S. Lawson, seated next to him, with his hands clasped on his lap, was dozing lightly. It had been a long and emotionally draining day for everyone. Jane stared at the Vice Presidential candidate. She liked Bill. He was sincere and sweet. Not many like that in Washington anymore, she said to herself. She looked up at Ronnie Ekart. The Republican National Committee chair had just finished the last of the Pork Lo Mein and was back to his customary pacing and plotting. The strategizing never ended.

"And now the President of the United States."

"Here it is," Sam said. He reached over to the glass coffee table and punched CNN on the keyboard, relegating the other networks to small windows on the bottom.

"My fellow Americans, my heart is heavy on this, one of America's darkest days. As your president, I must ask you to remain calm. We are taking every measure to bring the current situation under control.

"When you elected me to represent you, I vowed to get this country out of its depression and back working again. You put your faith and trust in me, and together we defeated spiraling unemployment and skyrocketing inflation." The white-haired, sixty-two-year old President smiled at the telecomp cameras before him in his most fatherly, most assuring manner. "We succeeded because we came together and worked as a family. Once more we find ourselves at the crossroads of instability. Once more I have to ask you for your help. We cannot allow our emotions to ruin what we have accomplished these last four years. We must stand as one and defeat those who have wrought havoc upon our people and our land. Our family. Fighting each other in the streets will only divide us. And division will only weaken us. We must fight this evil foe together."

"What evil foe?" one of the cameramen yelled, stunning the President into silence. "You are behind this, Mr. President. This is just another attempt by your administration to keep the poor from rising in class."

"WHAT THE HELL?" Jane jumped up, amazed. The ice rattled in the glass in her hand, and the anesthetic splashed onto her fingers. Her heart was beating wildly.

White House Secret Service agents grabbed the cameraman, a dark-skinned man with a slight accent, and dragged him out of the Oval Office. However, everyone listening to the live broadcast heard the man's last words loud and clear. "Do you think by wiping out the HOPE Cities white America will reelect you?"

The President sat in shock before the world. He was speechless for a few seconds. "To think that I, or my administration, had anything to do with today's catastrophe is an absurdity. Winning this election means nothing to me if it means the loss of human lives. My fellow Americans, I guarantee that before I accept reelection as your president, I will find whoever is responsible, and they will be held accountable!" He said it powerfully, and with conviction, but as soon as he made the promise, everyone saw the President's face change color. Having broadcast the political gaffe of his lifetime, President Charles Price quickly ended his speech. "My administration and I will not sleep until this crisis is brought to a justifiable end. Thank you, my friends, and may God bless us all."

"I don't believe it!" Chairman Ekart said. "The President's gone on worldwide TC and hanged himself!"

"What does this mean, Miss Jane?" Congressman Lawson asked.

"It all depends on how Sam handles it, Bill." It was time for the candidate to speak to the country. She saw Sam think about it, then turn his attention back to the wall screen.

The networks' anchors and their experts were discussing what had just happened. They all agreed that no one was going to believe that the President, or his administration, was behind the deaths of thousands of innocent people. What the voters were going to believe, and would take with them to the polls on election day, these politicos explained, was the image of their president under attack, along with his ineffectiveness on national security. And what if the President didn't bring to justice whoever was responsible? they asked. Would he keep his startling promise not to accept reelection? More important, who was going to vote for him if he didn't deliver? It was obvious, they all agreed, that Charles Foster Price had just jeopardized his presidency.

Sam stood and put on his suit jacket.

"Remember, Sam, America is looking for leadership right now," Jane coached him. "Leadership and humanity." She walked up to him and removed the jacket. She flipped it on the couch and told him to roll up his shirt sleeves and loosen his tie. "Image."

They left his office and walked to the front reception area. Outside the glass doors of the suite dozens of reporters and photographers swarmed and strained against the cordoned-off entranceway. Thankfully, security, the Capitol police, and the Secret Service agents assigned to Senator Howard had been able to stop them from barging in.

The senator pulled the glass door open, and the TC lights lit up the hallway. He walked out onto one of the many walkways surrounding the atrium of the Hart Building and held up his hands for silence. "Please! I will make this brief. I have a lot of work as you can imagine." There was quiet, except for the clicking of cameras and scuffling of shoes. "I'm sorry you had to wait so long for my comments. Out of respect to the office of the President, I felt it was only proper for our Commander-in-Chief to address the country first. Now that he has, I must say that the events of the last few hours have personally devastated me. I created the HOPE Cities to bring people together, not to tear them apart. Why is that such a difficult concept to accept? Where is all this hatred and rage coming from? And, worse, where is it all leading?"

Sam was silent for a few seconds so the questions could sink in. Jane, although pained by the words she had written for him, took pleasure in his delivery.

"Please, my friends, ask yourselves: If this continues, what will become of our democratic society? Of our once civilized world?" Sam paused to change tone, which gave the men and women before him the opportunity to try to get his attention. He refused to acknowledge their questions and continued to stare into the cameras, his face filled with emotion. "Now - in response to President's Price's speech, all I can say is that he has given us his promise. I am positive he will do all he can to bring this catastrophe to an end. That's all I have to say right now, I'm sorry. Thank you for coming." Sam turned, and a guard opened the glass door for him.

"Sam, do you think the President's comments will affect the election?"

"Senator, what about the HOPE Cities? Can they be rebuilt?"

He walked back into the suite without answering.

Jane interceded. "Please, Senator Howard has been emotionally tried today. He will answer all your questions at a later time."

"Jane, will all this change your campaign? Will President …"

The press hurled question after question at Jane Weisser. She remained there for the next ten minutes, spinning everything thrown at her.

Congressman Lawson and Chairman Ekart took over for Jane, and she returned to Sam's office. He was standing in the middle of his office, hands on hips, watching the six panels of the wall screen. Jane's eyes followed his. The violence was rapidly spreading from the HOPE Cities throughout the country like a contagious disease. Africans were killing whites, Latinos were killing whites, and the lower economic classes were taking out their vengeance on the upper classes. Jane didn't know what to think. She cleared her throat to say something, but she got dizzy and had to sit down.

"Jane? Are you okay?"

She tried to tell him she was all right, but no words came out.

Sam took some ice from the bucket on the coffee table. He sat down next to her and rubbed it on her forehead. She missed his warmth. He bent her over and rubbed it on the back of her neck. She missed his touch. She couldn't wait for this election to be over so she and Sam could again ...

She missed them!

Jane ate some chocolate cake and her blood pressure returned to normal. Emotionally, however, she felt as tightly wound as piano wire. "Sam, I have to go home."

"Do you think that's a wise idea? I mean, this is Washington. How safe will you be? "

"Call an escort car for me. If I run into a problem, I'll call you on my videophone."

After a moment of hesitation, Sam said. "I want to hear from you as soon as you get home. Understand? Now, please ... be careful!

Jane grabbed her coat and purse from her office and left the suite. Two escorts met her at the elevator and walked her to her white Mercedes in the Hart Senate Office Building garage. They then got in their cars She looked in her rearview mirror and realized it was the first time she had seen her reflection since returning from Baltimore. She had on no lipstick, her smudged make-up made her face look like she had two black eyes, and her hair … "Dear God!" she cried in vain, "and I was just on national telecomp."

As she drove out into the nighttime streets of Washington, D.C. Jane remembered the scenes on the TC in Sam's office: Looting and rioting had already begun in different parts of the city. She looked to her left, and to her right, then in her rear-view mirror. She took a deep breath. "Be brave, Janie, be brave."

Inside the gray cement basement of his modest, two-bedroom Maryland home, Garrison Miller, the grand marshal of the People for a White America, celebrated with his four most trusted henchmen. They toasted the events of the day and spewed out venomous racial slurs with equal exuberance. Miller sat back and smiled at the thought of all that had happened today. "Soon, Daddy, your dream of a white America will come true. I promise you." His late father, 'Daddy' Garland Miller, had been grand marshal of the Louisiana KKK. Ten years ago, the FBI arrested 'Daddy' for the deaths of three African boys in New Orleans. His father was innocent. Garrison was sure of it, but the FBI had framed him and had made it stick. For nine years, Garland Miller remained on death row, until his execution three months ago.

Garrison Miller's mood was dampened by the memory of the day Moses McBride publicly pressured Louisiana's governor not to grant the 'professed racist' another stay. The government had killed his father because of that man. Miller drank his beer to wash down the bitter memories. He thought about his nemesis in life, Moses McBride. He thought about America, or what had become of it.

He hated both.

Soon, it would be payback. The thought of what could be, of what was going to be, gave him an erection. He fantasized about it some more until it was time to begin the meeting. "Quiet down, y'all," he yelled when he awoke from his thoughts. "It's time to start." He took another gulp of beer, remembering his goal in life.

When all was quiet, the five men sat around the wooden table and looked at each other. A lone bulb dangled above them. The six-foot, two-inch tall Garrison Miller, with black marble eyes, greasy blond hair, and a blond beard neatly trimmed but now specked with crumbs of food and driblets of beer, stood. His look was gruff and unkempt now, but, when he needed to, he could appear well-groomed and appealing - All-American. "It's time to contact our state leaders and hit the nigger churches. With the country in such chaos, they'll run weeping to their God."

His followers mumbled in agreement.

"Hah!" he laughed out loud. "No God can save them now."

The ruling board of the People for a White America joined in the laughter and celebration. They drank their beers, spat out more racist slander, and toasted the future.

"TO A WHITE AMERICA!" Garrison Miller shouted and raised his bottle.

"TO A WHITE AMERICA!"

CHAPTER TWO

Wednesday, November 2nd
Six days before Election Day

Jane awoke at five o'clock. Unable to fall back asleep, she got out of bed and sat at the bay window inside her Georgetown home. Foxhall Road was deserted. She lit a cigarette. The taste of the smoke revolted her and she put it out after the second drag. Instead, she sat there in her white cotton nightgown, with her feet tucked underneath her, and thought about yesterday. She shuddered as a cold shiver traveled up and down her spine.

Jane got up from the bay window. Having had a restive sleep after drinking too much, she was still a little dizzy and had to steady herself. She walked around the writing table and sat down on her bed. She reached over to the keyboard on her night table and turned on the telecomp. CNN was showing the massive unrest that had already spread to many parts of middle America. Jane heard her good friend, news anchorman David

Elliot, intone in a grave voice, "Not in one hundred and fifty years, not since America's Civil War, has something this divisive …" She saw an explosion of a high school in St. Louis. The newscaster couldn't continue. As she watched scene after scene of screaming people running through America's inner-city streets, fleeing or attacking each other, Jane's nerves overloaded and her mind went blank. She couldn't look at it anymore. She reached for the keyboard on her night stand and turned it off. She noticed her hands were shaking. Her whole body was shaking. All she could do was crawl back in bed and hide.

As she lay there with the blanket up to her neck, Jane thought about all the poor people who had lost everything. She remembered her childhood, growing up in Brookline, Massachusetts. A liberal home, where they passionately argued politics and world affairs, her parents had taught her compassion for those less fortunate and how to live in a humanistic way. They spent their Thanksgivings in soup kitchens helping feed the poor and hungry of Boston. Christmas was spent every year in shelters, where the Weisser family would bring with them new toys, which they'd purchased throughout the year, so every child would have something of their own come that happy morning.

Jane smiled at the fond memories. It was the same moral philosophy she had tried to instill in Taryn. But, recently, their relationship had become strained. Mother and daughter had been at odds with each other the past year. The Georgetown freshman felt the need for the greater independence afforded by dormitory life, even though the university was less than two miles away. Last evening, Jane called Taryn before going to sleep. They agreed she would stay at school until things calmed down. Then she would return home. Now, more than anything, Jane wanted to talk to Taryn again to reassure herself of her safety.

She reached over to the telecomp keyboard and pressed the number 3, for Taryn's dorm room. A recorded message, 'Due to excessive calling ...' Jane pushed auto redial on the keyboard, lay back down and closed her eyes, and waited. She reminisced about her baby, now a young woman. The last eighteen years had gone by so fast. Too fast. Oh, how she'd love to relive them all over again. Not that the present was at all bad. On the contrary; with Taryn, and Sam, and TWO, she had everything she ever wanted in life.

The ringing of Taryn's phone a couple of minutes later disrupted her thoughts.

"Hello," the sleepy voice said.

"Taryn, it's Mom. Are you okay?"

"Jeez, what time is it?"

Jane looked at her clock. "Five-thirty."

"I'm fine. (Yawn) Why are you calling so early? Is something wrong?"

"I have to talk to you, Taryn. I have to see you're all right. Indulge me and switch on the video."

Taryn Weisser appeared on the wall screen a second later, a bearded man asleep by her side. Jane felt a momentary blush of embarrassment; not for herself, but for her daughter. "I'm sorry. I didn't know you had someone over." She took a few deep breaths to get over the shock. "Turn off the video so we can talk privately." Jane waited a second or two, then asked, "How are you, sweetheart? Any problems on campus?"

"It's pretty quiet now, but of course it's the middle of the night. Most everyone, I assume, is still asleep. Like I should be."

"I'm not sorry I woke you."

"No, I didn't think you were."

"You'll understand when you're a mother."

"*If* I become a mother."

"From what I just saw, you're a prime candidate."

Taryn didn't respond.

Sensing her daughter's anger, Jane changed the subject. "Tell me, what's happening on campus?"

"Once in a while I wake up to sirens or gunshots, but that's about all."

"I'm happy you're staying put. We'll talk later about sending a car to pick you up."

"Don't bother, I'll get a ride."

"Taryn, I said I'll send a car and that's final!"

"No, Mom. I can ..."

"Let me repeat myself: You'll understand when you're a mother."

There was an uncomfortable pause.

"Are you using protection, sweetheart?"

"Mother!"

"Let me rephrase that. The psychologist in me knew better, but the mother didn't. Make sure you both use protection. Is that better?"

"You know, Mom, sometimes you prove the theory that half of analysis is anal. Aren't you the least bit upset at what you just saw?"

"Why? Are you *trying* to upset me?"

"Mother, sometimes *you* can be trying. I'm not trying anything."

"Then I'm not upset. I know who I am; ergo, I know who you are."

"Psycho babble."

"Reality. You are me!"

"Is that a compliment or an insult?"

Jane laughed at the question. She had to break the tension, somehow. "I sometimes wonder that same thing myself." She waited for Taryn to react. Say something! There was no more conversation. It had been that way for the last year. Just some small talk - then nothing. Taryn had turned independent, almost defiant, and Jane didn't know why. Was it the time the election had taken away from them? They were always so close. Best friends. Now, they were just mother and daughter. Jane felt a pang of loss and regret. She couldn't bear the thought of losing her only child. From the way things had been going this past year, they seemed headed toward an estrangement. "I love you, you know."

"I know, Mom. I'll talk to you later."

After exchanging one-sided kisses, Jane curled up in bed, relieved of her worst fears. Taryn was safe. That was all that mattered right now. She derided herself for not knowing what to do about their problem. Here she was a psychologist, trained in every theory of human behavior, and she was unable to treat their relationship. Maybe it was better that way; after all, 'a doctor who has herself for a patient is a fool.' Jane made a decision: After the election they'd get counseling and work it out.

Jane closed her eyes and thought about Sam. Her unshakeable trust in him always made her forget her problems and worries. He was the one constant in her life besides Taryn. With Sam, *she* felt safe.

They had met when they were juniors at Yale. He was playing the title role in MACBETH at the University Theater, and after the opening night performance she had gone backstage to introduce herself to him. The tall, handsome actor was the talk of the school, 'a rising star,' not to mention the heir to Howard Oil. He was still in make-up when Jane walked into his crowded dressing room. As soon as she looked into his hypnotic, gray eyes, her heart leaped.

He offered her his hand. The touch of his warm skin against

hers sent messages throughout her body. "I just wanted to tell you how much I enjoyed your performance. It was Macbeth up there on stage, not Sam Howard."

"It's just acting."

"Yes, I'm sure it is, but it was so real."

Sam interrupted the compliment with one of his own. "Would you care to join me for a cup of coffee?"

That first date was magical. Their coffee lasted into the early morning hours as they talked and laughed together. A moonlit walk across the Commons, hand in hand, and a gentle kiss on the lips at her dorm door ended the beautiful evening. As Jane laid in bed that night, she mentally replayed everything he had said to her. She relived every word and every touch one more time, then again, until her hands found the spot that made the memory of their time together even more wonderful.

Sam persuaded Jane to run his campaign for senior class president. Over the next few months, she turned the campaign into a public relations frenzy, a media event throughout New Haven. She made Sam Howard an icon, a *wunderkind*, adored and revered by all, not just by those on the Yale campus. He easily won the senior class presidency, and they began sleeping together that very night. It was the next natural course of events in their relationship, and neither could, nor wanted to, resist it.

He was amorous and passionate, relentless as the sea, and never before was she so swept away. His tongue tasted every part of her body, from head to toe and then back up again. Where am I? In Heaven? Jane Weisser had lost her mind, her body, and her heart to Sam Howard.

They made love and they talked and they laughed, then they made love again and talked and laughed some more. It was a wondrous feeling to communicate every fiber of your being, to open up completely and share and accept and give and take.

Making love was different from having sex, Jane had realized for the first time. It was physical, spiritual, emotional, and ... exceptional! That first night seemed timeless - an eternity that was over in a fleeting moment.

"I love you, Sam!" Jane startled herself by yelling it out loud in her Georgetown bedroom. She caught her breath and shook the memories from her mind.

Jane got out of bed and again sat in the bay window. Sirens wailed: police, fire, ambulance - an endless profusion of emergencies. After a while, it was too much for her. She turned away and knew what she had to do. People, everywhere, were depending on Sam Howard. She would book him on a tour of the twelve HOPE Cities.

Early in the morning, CNN received a letter claiming responsibility for the destruction of the twelve HOPE Cities. It was signed Garrison Miller, Grand Marshal, People for a White America. It provided specific details which verified its authenticity. One hundred and forty-four bombs, strategically placed underneath the buildings' gas lines and at various support positions, had leveled the dozen residential hi-rises in each HOPE City. The other three-hundred and fifty plus bombs, just as well placed, and just as well hidden during the last month, had blown away stores, businesses, and entertainment facilities.

With the President briefed, fourteen FBI cars converged on a quiet, tree-lined street of modest homes in New Carrollton, Maryland, a short distance from the nation's capital. Miller lived there and worked nearby as a part-time security guard at Warwick Industrials, using the alias Gary Walters. The suspect was home in bed, the stake-out informed the Baltimore bureau chief. It was time to take Garrison Miller. The chief announced it to the others, and fifty men equipped with bullet proof vests and semi-automatic machine guns raced their cars toward the house and surrounded it.

Gary Walters awoke to a voice blaring his real name. "Miller, this is the FBI."

He jolted up in bed. He didn't hear the rest of the announcement; his mind and heart were racing with panic. He looked out the window next to his bed and began sweating. There were guns pointed at him. And there were more at the other window. "Shit!" Miller tried to clear his mind and figure out what to do.

There was nothing he could do. He put his hands behind his head. He didn't want to give them any reason to shoot him.

The agents kicked in the kitchen door at the back of the house and pulled Garrison Miller out of bed. They forced him to dress while the others ran through the four-room home in search of evidence.

"Hey, what gives?"

No one answered him.

"What'r'ya looking for?" The agent standing next to him slammed the butt of his machine gun into the suspect's stomach. Miller felt his insides cave in from the blow. He fell to his knees, gasping for air.

"We got it!" he heard one of the men in his crowded bedroom announce.

Miller saw an agent emerge from his closet carrying an old typewriter under one arm and blueprints of some sort in his other hand.

"Garrison Miller, you're under arrest for the destruction of the HOPE cities. You have the right to remain silent."

The grand marshal of the People for a White America trembled in fear and pain.

"Anything you say can and will be held against you."

"I'm not Garrison Miller. I'm Gary Walters!" he managed to gasp, while struggling to breathe.

An agent continued to read him his Miranda Rights while another cuffed his hands behind his back. They then dragged him kicking and screaming outside to the padded truck.

"I'm innocent, I tell you!" He felt his body shaking in fear. "INNOCENT!"

Inside Jessie McBride's fourth floor Harlem Hospital room, there was a quiet peace, a different feeling from the insanity of the outside world. She lay there in a coma, wrapped in white gauze. Moses's heart ached as he watched her every breath. He blamed himself for what had happened to his family. The doctors had told him they didn't know whether the girls would make it or not. He had tried to pray, but the agonizing vision of his people being slaughtered disrupted his thoughts. He had to make it better. But how? Somehow he had to do something. But what? Everything was crazy and out of control. Everything that had once been in balance was now unbalanced. The world's order was now in disorder. He felt useless. Scared.

"Moses." She said it softly, but it was unmistakably her. Jessie was back!

There was still hope. He stood and leaned over the bed so she could see him. "Yes, my sweet, I'm here."

"Where's DaNell?"

She was so weak. Frail. He couldn't tell her yet. "How you feeling, Jess?"

There was a long pause. "What happened?"

She was asking questions that Moses didn't know how to answer. He wished he had spoken to the psychologist like the doctors had suggested before talking to his wife. "Here, Jessie, take a drink." Moses held the cup of water between his bandaged hands. She took a sip from the straw and winced with pain. "There, that's better, isn't it?"

"Thank you."

"The doctors said you'll be out of here real soon. In the meantime, I'll be by your side until you regain your strength. I promise, Jessie, I won't leave you again." If he had stayed home like she had asked him, instead of going to church, than none of this would have happened. "I'm so sorry. Please forgive me."

"Don't blame yourself, preacher man." She had called him that since the day he was ordained, and every time she said it, she said it with loyalty, admiration, and affection. A few minutes later, she again asked, "How's DaNell?"

"Fine. She's going to be just fine." Moses held in his grief. He felt the lump in his throat and the pain in his heart. His daughter was in another room of the burn unit, unconscious and in critical condition. He had just come from visiting her.

"I want to see my baby."

"Soon, Jessie."

"How long have I been here?"

"Please, Jess, no more talking, you need to regain your strength. Just close your eyes and rest. I won't leave you."

"You're a good husband, Moses. A good man. But, you should be with our people right now. They need you."

He wasn't going to argue with her.

Jessie McBride fell back asleep. Moses sat by her side, holding her hand and holding in his tears. He thought about what he should do. Yes, his people needed him, but so did Jessie. Yes, he could wait there, but Jessie was right; he was a 'preacher man,' and he had a responsibility to his followers. Even in her half-conscious state she was amazing in her selflessness and compassion. Dear, sweet Jessie. For twenty-four years, she had been his reason for living. What would he do without her?

He sat by her side and held her bandaged hand in his own.

Jane met with her staff around the conference table inside her office, then individually with each component of the campaign: press, research, scheduling, communications, treasury, field, outreach, legal, advance, and issues. When she was done, and they had all left, she stretched and glanced at her watch.

Jane exited her office and walked toward Sam's, looking at the pictures that lined the hallway walls. The photo of him and Patty Howard waving, taken when Sam had won his first term in the Senate, caught her eye. Jane vividly remembered that first campaign. It was twelve years since they had last spoken. He had invited her up to his Greenwich, Connecticut home to ask her to be his campaign director. Although he was married with one child, and another was on the way, she had to see him. After all, it *had* been twelve years. If she had said no, she didn't know whether she would ever have the opportunity again. She *had* to see the man she knew she would always love.

"I'm a Democrat, Sam," she told him when they sat down to discuss it in his study, "you know that. All my clients on the Hill are Democrats because I believe in their platform, their philosophy. Directing a Republican campaign would go against everything I've worked for. I'm sorry, Sam, but I'm afraid I have to decline your very tempting offer. I hope you understand."

Sam stared into her eyes. "Ideology and philosophy have replaced our bipartisan system, Jane. It's no longer Republican versus Democrat; it's conservative versus liberal."

"Nevertheless," Jane said, "the Republicans have done a good job in associating 'liberal' with 'communist', 'socialist', and everything else un-American."

"True," Sam continued, "but even so, the Republicans have been losing all these years because of their conservative platform.

I'm convinced that a social Democrat running on the Republican ticket would assure a victory. And if I have to run on their ticket to get elected, then that's what I have to do."

Jane's emotions inclined her to accept Sam's rationale. How could she not? It had been twelve years! How in the world could she resist the opportunity to be by his side for the next year?

Despite the media-created uproar generated by the defection of a prominent Democratic strategist to the opposition, Jane had run a brilliant and successful campaign.

Jane put that fond memory at the back of her heart and opened the door to Sam's office. If she had let party loyalty prevail that day, where would she be now? Not with Sam, that was for sure. It was the best decision she had ever made.

Sam was speaking on the telecomp when Jane walked into his office. She sat down on the beige sofa. When he disconnected, he asked, "What are the overnights?"

"Nationals have it 46-42 in Price's favor. Nothing's really changed. Statewide - California and Florida have moved closer to us, but we've lost ground in Illinois, Pennsylvania, and Ohio."

The phone rang, and Sam answered it. With the TC on, and with their staff drifting in and out, Jane sat down on the sofa and returned to the speech she was working on. Once in a while, she looked up at Sam and fantasized about them making love. She wondered if it entered his mind as often as it did hers. She also wondered if they would ever make love again. Fourteen months ago, when the campaign began, was the last time. Stop it, Jane! she commanded herself. There's more to a relationship than that.

What relationship?

A short while later, Jane took a break from her work and flopped against the back of the sofa. It was time to talk to him about touring the HOPE Cities. Those poor people needed Sam

Howard, now more than ever. When they were again alone, she said to him, "We're going to have to put the campaign on hold, Sam, so you can visit the HOPE Cities and help organize relief programs. Also, out of respect, we should cut back on commercials and other promos for a few days. If we don't, it might look insensitive and opportunistic."

Sam reacted as if he'd been struck. "Insensitive? I built the HOPE Cities. How can my campaign possibly look insensitive?"

"By making it seem like the election is foremost, not the needs of the people."

"What America needs right now, Jane, is a leader who will react in a time of crisis. And no greater crisis has ever beset our country. No, I think we should continue our campaign steadfast and strong and start promoting a hard stand on crime and terrorism. That's what the people of this country need right now."

"Your image would be better served if you put the campaign aside for awhile. Your image is the most important …"

"I know, I've thought about that. Believe me I have. But, doing what is right for the country is what's important, Jane. And the right thing right now is to get on with this campaign. If we don't, our democratic system will come to a halt and our enemy, whoever it is, will win."

Jane approached his desk. They couldn't very well continue campaigning, not with everything that had happened. But, a humanitarian tour would accomplish the same. It was what they had to do. "Is winning the presidency all that matters, Sam?'

He was stunned. "I can't believe you think that."

"I'm sorry, but there are people depending on you to help them."

"Yes, there are. But, there are even more people depending on me to win this election and turn the country around so something like this never happens again. The election, right now, is what's most important. If Price wins, the fighting will escalate and the country will fall apart."

Jane shook her head from side to side. "Planning for the future is all fine and good, but you can't forget about what is happening now! You will be doing yourself, and everyone else, a disservice if you ignore the present in favor of the future. Showing your leadership is the right thing to do. For the people *and* for your campaign. You've proven your record and your qualifications. Don't forget your character is just as important."

He sat behind his desk and remained quiet for a moment.

"What I'm saying, Sam, is that America wants a president with a heart. You have that heart. Show it to them."

Sam looked at her standing before his desk. "You're right, Jane. As always."

"Not always."

He smiled in resignation and punched the button on his telecomp keyboard. "I think Bill should come with us."

"Good idea."

"Jackie, get me Congressman Lawson, please."

Relieved that she had gotten him back on track, Jane left his office and returned to her own at the front of the suite. She thought about this humanitarian tour of the lost HOPE Cities. Ethically and politically, it was the right thing to do. They would begin tomorrow.

Jane walked into her office and saw Paco Ramirez seated at her desk, disconnecting the telecomp. His eyes were wide open in fear. "What?" she asked.

"That was my contact at the Bureau. They've arrested Garrison Miller and charged him with the HOPE bombings."

"Garrison Miller? The PWA guy?"

"None other."

Jane tapped in 'TC' and 'CNN' on the keyboard. Melinda

Murphy's image filled the wall screen. The reporter was already broadcasting the report from outside Garrison Miller's home.

"A short while ago, the FBI arrested Garrison Miller, alias Gary Walters, grand marshal of the People for a White America. Members of this organization are suspected of being responsible for much of the racial unrest in America's inner cities, as well as for many of our most heinous racial murders. The FBI has never been able to implicate Miller in any of those crimes, but they believe him to be the force behind them. The evidence - blueprints of the Hope Cities, along with an old Smith-Corona typewriter, which typed the letter CNN received - were found inside Miller's home here in New Carrollton, Maryland." The broadcaster paused for a second and listened to her earpiece. "President Price is now making a statement inside the White House Press Room."

The scene switched to the sixty-two-year old leader. "We *refuse* to accept or tolerate the promotion of prejudice in our country. We *refuse* to be held hostage by people of hate. I hope, my fellow Americans, that you will see it is the terrorist we should be punishing, not our neighbors. It is time we all live in peace again, with each one helping each other, unafraid to walk our beautiful streets. As I promised you a quick end, I now ask for your promise for a quick beginning, a beginning of a new America where we can all live together as one family. Thank you, my friends, for your faith and trust in me."

The press shouted a multitude of questions at President Price, which he confidently answered. Once again, he seemed like a leader.

Jane lit a cigarette and mulled over the political ramifications for Sam.

"I just hope this is the guy who did it, and the Democrats aren't framing this white elitist to save the President's ass."

It was a perceptive thing for Paco to say. Who would know if it were true? Before she could respond, the next scene CNN broadcast showed FBI agents earlier leading the suspect away from his Maryland home.

"I'm not Garrison Miller, I tell you!"

Jane stared at the man's bearded face. He seemed familiar, only she couldn't place it. Where have I seen him? she asked herself. Unable to come up with an answer, she tried to shake it off. But, then, the vision of Taryn's boyfriend in bed with her early this morning popped into her mind. Oh, my God, the blond beard! Was it the same man? After all, she had only gotten a side view of his sleeping face, but they did look similar. Taryn had told her, when they first began dating the month before, that his name was Gary. Jane had wanted to meet him, but, because of the campaign, she had yet to have the opportunity. She berated herself for that. It was her neglect that was causing the rift in their relationship. Gary, she repeated to herself. Garrison!

Jane was full of emotions. Rage and worry were juxtaposed with fear and panic. Before she could confront any of them, she had to warn Taryn. Nothing else mattered at this point. Not Sam, not the election.

While FBI Director Coyles answered questions from the multitude of reporters at the news conference, Jane punched in the number of her daughter's dorm room on the keyboard. She had questions of her own.

It took a few minutes to get through, but soon Taryn's face was on the wall screen, replacing Director Coyles to a small box on the bottom. "Taryn, your boyfriend Gary …"

"Stop, Mom! He's not this Garrison Miller. It's all a mistake."

"And how do you know that? How long have you known this boy?"

"Man! I met him last month. He's in one of my classes."

"Listen, Taryn, they wouldn't have arrested your friend ..."

"Lover!"

Jane cringed at that thought. "Then why did they arrest him. Why him?"

"I don't know. Who's this Garrison Miller anyway?"

"Jeez, girl, where have you been? Didn't you read People Magazine last month? There was a full-page story on him."

"I never read People."

"How true!" Jane said, driving home the point of just how much her daughter had changed this past year. Biting her tongue, Jane knew she had to be careful and not appear threatening. The last thing she wanted was to push Taryn farther away from her; maybe forever into the arms of this alleged mass murderer. "Listen to me, Taryn. People Magazine called him, 'The Most Hateful Man in America.' Granted, there were no pictures of 'Miller the Killer,' but that's just what he is. A vicious killer. He's grand marshal of the PWA. You do read newspapers, don't you?"

"Why should I? My poli-sci professor said, 'The man who reads nothing at all is better educated than the man who reads nothing but newspapers.' Anyway, it's all propaganda, one-sided. You can never believe the press. You taught me that yourself."

Jane rolled her eyes. "First, it wasn't your professor who said that, Taryn, it was Thomas Jefferson."

"Well, it's manipulated by those in power. You do it every day. Right?"

Taryn was goading her, like she had been doing of late, and Jane ignored it. She had to get through that eighteen-year old heart. "The PWA are modern-day Nazis committed to annihilating the African race. Please, Taryn, you have to stop seeing him. You have to get away from him immediately! I can't stress it strongly enough."

"But, as you said, there's never been a published picture of him. So, how can they be sure Gary Walters is this Garrison Miller?"

Jane didn't have an answer. Her stomach tightened. She reached into her desk and took out the Tums bottle and popped a few into her mouth. She had always trusted Taryn's insight. Why not now? "I'll send a car for you."

Taryn disconnected before she could say anymore.

Jane sat behind her desk, worrying about the situation. "Why did the FBI arrest Gary Walters? Why him? Why Taryn's ..." She could hardly form the word in her mind. " ... lover?" She looked up at Paco who had witnessed the conversation. "You know I would never ask you to use your contacts unless it was an emergency, Paco, but this involves Taryn."

"Jane, Taryn's like a sister to me. You know I'd do anything for her."

"We have to find out everything we can about this Gary Walters."

Paco turned to leave. "I'll call you as soon as I have something."

Jane went to the wet bar, opened the Johnny Walker bottle, and poured herself a drink. God forbid if Taryn was dating Garrison Miller, sleeping with the man responsible for the deaths of ... how many? The numbers, reports indicated, were rising every hour. What a frightening thought! Only, it was worse, she realized at that moment. She had to go on this humanitarian tour with Sam. How could she leave Taryn in such a dangerous situation?

After a moment to quell her rampaging emotions, Jane, as she had done so many times in her life, reached into a deep reserve of will and determination. There were decisions to make.

Things to do. There were answers to everything that was happening. If you look at things logically, she reminded herself, there is a logical explanation for everything. She would find the answers to those questions.

She swallowed the double Scotch whole.

Questioned and vocally harassed by the FBI for almost seven hours, by Director Coyles himself at one point, Garrison Miller felt exhaustion consume his body and mind. He cried out, "I didn't do it!" many times throughout the ordeal. He was beginning to feel nauseous from the claustrophobic feel of the small room, with its table and few metal chairs. A large mirror was on one wall. Obviously two-way. The rest of the room was bare. Cold. The government knew how to torture its citizens, knew how to break them. But, he wouldn't break. No, there was nothing they could do to make him admit to anything.

"C'mon, Garrison," a muscular detective, with short-cropped hair, said. He pulled down his knotted tie and opened his shirt collar. After so many hours, he was sweating badly. "Why are you doing this to yourself? Cooperate with us and it'll go a lot easier for you." The detective's name was Connelly and he was the FBI's most successful interrogator. Yet, after all these hours, he still hadn't gotten anywhere with the man who insisted he wasn't Garrison Miller. The prisoner still refused to tell him what he wanted to hear.

"C'mon, Garrison," one of the other three agents harassing him added. "We're all tired, aren't you?"

"I don't know nothing."

"But, the typewriter and the letter, and the maps of HOPE found in your closet."

"I DIDN'T DO IT, GODDAMNIT!"

Connelly was now behind him, in his ear. He grabbed

Miller's hair and jerked his head back. Their faces met. "Yes, you did, you racist scum. And we're gonna stay here all night, no matter how long it takes, until you admit it. You hear me?" Some spittle sprayed into the accused man's face, and he flinched. "Now, again, tell us how you did it and who else was involved."

Miller sat there on the hard chair and thought about what to say.

"You're Garrison Miller, grand marshal of the People for a White America. You must have loved what happened yesterday, didn't you?"

Again, he didn't answer.

"DIDN'T YOU?"

"I'm not Garrison Miller, and I didn't do it!"

"BULLSHIT! NOW TELL US!" Connelly screamed, and he pushed the suspect's head away from his.

Garrison Miller, hate monger, leader of the most rabidly pro-white extremist group in American history, sat there feeling numb. He felt the urine, held in for those last seven hours, fill his seat and run down his leg. The realization of what was happening to him, and what was going to happen to him, made him even more nauseous. It took all of his willpower to hold in the bile that had filled his throat.

The agents, with their hands on their hips, or crossed in front of them, their guns prominently displayed, went through the routine yet again. 'Miller the Killer' was wearing down. It was just a matter of time now.

Garrison Miller was exhausted. His body sagged, and the puddle they were making him wallow in was now cold and beginning to irritate his thighs. It was humiliating. Inhuman. He needed a cigarette more than anything, but every time he'd asked for one, they just laughed at him. Instead, they tantalized him by blowing their smoke in his face.

"When you're ready to tell us the truth," Agent Connelly repeated for the umpteenth time, "you can have a smoke. That's a pretty fair trade, I'd say?" The other agents in the interrogation room murmured their assent. Those who smoked, collectively lit up again, filling the room with the toxic fix. "Ahh," they said after each drag.

Anger finally overtook the fear. "Damn it, I told you before, someone must've broken into my house and planted that shit after forging that letter and claiming responsibility as me." Miller looked up at their disgusted stares. "Go on, check the security sensor in my house. If it shows someone entering sometime between midnight and eight this morning, I can account for my whereabouts. It will prove I was framed." They didn't react, and Miller yelled in exasperation, "I'm innocent, you assholes! If you would do your job, instead of harassing law-abiding citizens, maybe this country would be a safer place to live in."

The FBI men continued staring down at him, then at each other, all puzzling over the same question, 'Do we have the wrong man?' 'Is this guy just a dupe?' 'A setup?'

"ASSHOLES!"

Jane and Sam finished an onion and bacon pizza for dinner. The rest of the evening they would devote to planning for tomorrow, the first stop on the tour. Jane could see Sam was distracted. Worried. She knew what it was. The President's promise to arrest the person responsible before accepting reelection had him thinking of a sure victory. He had probably never entertained the possibility that the President could actually do it.

Suddenly, Sam bolted forward and reached for the keyboard on the coffee table between them. He turned up the volume and tapped in CNN. There, on the screen, was a thin, dowdy woman in front of Gary Walters' house facing a throng of reporters.

"My name is Maddy Olcott and this is my home," she said, pointing to the small house behind her to her right. "I've lived here for the last year with my ten-year old son. For the past six months, Gary Walters has been my next door neighbor and friend. He's not the person responsible for the horrendous things the FBI has you believing about him. Whatever he may have done in the past, this is not his work. It's the work of the United States government."

"What?" Jane gasped in disbelief.

The noise in front of the small homes got louder as the reporters shouted their questions at Maddy Olcott.

The sound level subsided, and she continued. "Late last night the phone woke me up, only it was a wrong number. It rang again, but it was the same wrong number. I couldn't fall back asleep, so I went into the kitchen for a drink. Of water." She took a deep breath. "Standing there in the dark, I saw a man in a black fedora hat, overcoat, and gloves. I couldn't really see his face because it was night, 3:30, and his hat was pulled down over his forehead. Anyway, I saw this man - at least he walked like a man - he was quite short, I remembered thinking, about five-five. He was carrying an old-fashioned typewriter and some large folded papers right there between our homes." She pointed behind her. "You can see how close my kitchen is to Gary's. I kept out of sight and watched him open Gary's back door and enter. He came out a few seconds later, empty-handed, and walked back up this driveway to the street. He then got in the back seat of a black limousine which drove away.

"Today, when the FBI came here and arrested Gary, I saw them carry out an old typewriter and a pile of papers, like the ones the man carried in the night before. I also saw that same limousine parked down the street in front of that blue cape over there." She pointed to the house about two-hundred feet from them. "The car was facing this way and I saw the same person looking out the window at what was happening. The same black hat was covering his eyes. When the FBI cars left, his car made a U-turn and drove away." There was a mumble from the crowd gathered on Maddy Olcott's small front lawn. "Please, listen to me," she yelled above the rising clamor, "Gary Walters is being framed."

"Miss Olcott," a female journalist called out, "what makes you so sure the United States government is involved?"

A frightened Maddy Olcott looked down at the ground, as if contemplating whether or not to tell them. She took a deep breath, then spoke. "The car and the man who broke into Gary's house last night was the same car and man I saw today when they came and arrested him. The car and the man were all I saw last night. Today, I saw this same limousine drive away. And when it did, I saw the license plate. It ..." Maddy's lips trembled. " ... was government issued."

The noise increased to a new level, like the swirling wind in an enclosed area. Maddy covered her ears. "Did you get a look at the license plate?" "What could you see?" "What did it say, Miss Olcott?"

Maddy's eyes darted in all directions. "Considering what is happening in this country right now, I refuse to tell what I saw until I get protection for my son and myself."

"This is unbelievable!" Sam yelled after the shocking disclosure. "Miller was framed by someone in Price's government!"

Jane turned away from the scared face of Maddy Olcott to the concerned face of Sam Howard. She saw a genuine look of compassion for Charles Price. She knew why; this wasn't how a presidential election should be decided. It wasn't fair to the candidate, or to the voters. Jane watched him rub his forehead and turn his chair to the wall of windows that looked out to the Capitol and the busy streets of Washington, D.C. She needed to anticipate the possible fallout from this turn of events. "Sam, if someone connected with the President's administration is implicated, then either Price will be judged guilty of complicity or negligence. On the down side, I have to tell you, is with all the problems the President has faced these last few days will come suspicion."

"Suspicion?"

"I'm afraid so. Will the voters suspect Sam Howard's campaign staff of manipulation? Will they wonder whether we were behind the 'What evil foe?' plant in the Oval Office? And will they think we were behind the framing, and the unframing, of Gary Walters, resulting in the framing of someone in Price's administration?"

"But, that's ridiculous," Sam protested.

"Yes, but it will cross some voters' minds. And, yes, they will believe it because that's what they want to believe." Jane saw Sam mull over the questions. No, this was not good for the election. Not for the people, not for the incumbent, and not for the challenger. With all the President's misfortunes, doing nothing was Sam's best course. If he tried to take advantage of the situation he would appear opportunistic to the press and the people.

Jane looked at Sam with concern and compassion. His furrowed brow showed he was deep in thought. She tried to say something, but he shook his head that he'd heard enough and waved her away.

She left his office for her own. There was a lot of spinning to do. The present was racing toward a fatal crash with the future, and her job was to assure an anxious country that her candidate, like he'd done with America's largest cities, could bring this runaway problem to a safe halt.

Jane walked into her office and stopped in her tracks. She had lost sight of an even more disturbing problem. If someone framed Walters/Miller, then the FBI would have no choice but to free him. Which would mean he and Taryn would resume their relationship. If he's Gary Walters, this incident was merely unfortunate. But, if he's really Garrison Miller like the FBI suspects, then ...

Dear God!

She needed a drink.

CHAPTER THREE

Thursday, November 3rd
Five days before Election Day

Since the arrest of Garrison Miller, the fighting that had overtaken the United States had begun to diminish dramatically. There had been a reduction in sporadic bombings and a decrease in random killings. But, after Maddy Olcott alleged that the leader of the PWA was innocent, and that the government had framed him, the enraged masses now believed it was all an insidious plot by their president to save his reelection effort. It was the spark that fueled the flames. The rioting, the bombings, and the killings escalated.

The country was tense, ready for someone to lead them into battle.

"I want to know who is behind this as soon as the Attorney General and the Chief Justice finish with this woman," an angry

President Price told his staff. There were only five days until the election, and Sam Howard's numbers were beginning to close in on his.

The President sat behind the Buchanan desk in the Oval Office. He twirled around in his chair and looked out at the Rose Garden and Andrew Jackson's timeworn magnolia tree. The telecomp rang, and he turned back around to his staff and tapped the button to connect him to the caller. It was the A.G. The President listened on his private line, then hung up and dismissed everyone except his young press secretary, Paul Baker.

"It hasn't been a very good few days, Mr. President, but I have some ideas about how we can turn things around."

"Shut up!"

The White House press secretary sat quietly in the chair facing the President's desk, his mouth agape from the chief executive's outburst.

"What you did was illegal, Paul. ILLEGAL! I've kept a clean administration. Now, in one stupid move you've screwed yourself and my presidency."

"Please, Mr. President, I don't know what you're talking about."

"According to the FBI agent who questioned your driver after the woman gave them the license plate numbers, he said he drove you to New Carrollton that night and again the following afternoon. His story corroborates the woman's."

"Now, wait a minute, sir, I had nothing to do with any of this. I was home that entire night."

President Price rubbed his hands through his thick white hair. "Damn it, I'm still ahead in the polls, even with this HOPE Cities travesty. We can't lose on some conspiracy to disgrace this administration. Tell me, Paul, why would your chauffeur lie? Why would he purposely implicate you?"

"I wish I knew. Harry has been with me for the last three years, and he's been a trusted and loyal friend. I can't believe he'd deliberately lie like that." There was an awkward silence for a moment. "Mr. President, we can deny these charges and push it off until after the election. According to my sources, this Maddy Olcott has been a prostitute, a drug addict, and she even lost her kid for a few years."

"We can't! It will be worse for us when the Republicans find out. We have to protect this administration and the Democratic Party. We have to act first and show the people we won't tolerate any illegal activity in this campaign. I'm sorry, Paul, but until we find the person who planted that evidence you're under arrest."

After having spent the last two nights in Harlem Hospital, Moses McBride left his comatose wife and daughter to return to the First Abyssinian Baptist Church three blocks away. Friends had visited him last evening with fresh underwear, a purple shirt, black pants, socks, shoes, and a coat. They told him they had a prayer vigil planned for the following morning at ten. It was now 9:30.

With his head, neck, and hands bandaged in white gauze, Moses walked with four of his followers/bodyguards through the smoky rubble once known as Harlem. Fires were still burning, and people were still out looting and killing. Moses tried to ignore the tragedy of it all. He had to focus on the healing. "God is merciful. He will help us. Faith is the cure, and our faith will heal us."

"Amen," the four large men answered in unison.

Moses opened the doors to the old church and saw just how needed he was. More than two-hundred African men, women, and children filled the pews. All frightened. All praying.

They turned to their leader for guidance and assurance. For the first time since being ordained, the responsibility felt overwhelming.

Moses walked through the sacrosanct room and stared at the faces of the scared and innocent who had fled their homes for that safe haven. Tears filled his eyes and he swallowed to relieve the tightness in his throat. "My friends," he began from behind his pulpit, "we come to God for God promises us that in His home we will find peace and sanctification. Let us pray." After a moment of spiritual reflection, Moses continued. "Praise Jesus, let us not fall into the Devil's hands. Praise Jesus, let us not be tempted into retribution. Vengeance is the Devil's seduction and we, as the children of God, must say no. If God has turned us all into Jobs, then we must show Him we are worthy, that we will, no matter what, follow the divine path that He has chosen for us. Then and only then will He welcome us into His Kingdom." Moses had to make them believe him. Trust him. He had to give them hope. "I stand here before you today and ask you to …"

The two doors at the rear of the sanctuary flew open and the morning sun illuminated the large room. Everyone turned and looked. Moses stopped preaching and saw the darkened silhouettes of a half dozen men standing in the doorway. Silence filled the air, and the world stopped for the briefest of seconds. It took only that short time for everyone to understand the intrusion. Some began crying, and some yelled, 'Jesus take me now!' Before any of the bodyguards positioned in the back of the sanctuary could pull out their weapons, hundreds of bullets mowed down the crowd of worshipers. The sounds of automatic gunfire were deafening. The Lord's home became a slaughterhouse as human flesh, blood, and bone, sprayed a viscous crimson rain upon everything in sight. It created a cacophony of sight and sound almost hallucinatory to Moses McBride.

As quickly as it began it ended and the killers disappeared. All that remained behind were the dead and the wounded.

Some crazy someone was trying to wipe out America's African people.

Moses was paralyzed in shock. But, then he heard the cries of the children, and he dashed down from his pulpit to help the wounded survivors. Looking at this scene of almost incomprehensible horror, Moses found a new resolution. Was it time to react? He looked at the carnage all around him.

No! It was time to act.

Senator Sam Howard and his Vice Presidential running mate, Texas Congressman William S. Lawson, stepped from their limousine onto the rubble of the Capital HOPE City. It was the first stop in the twelve-city humanitarian tour that Jane had set up. HOPE comprised the area from 14th St. N.W. to 7th St. to Downtown. The political entourage passed by the charred ruins and concrete mounds of what was once a vibrant community. They walked through tent cities and makeshift triage units, stopping to listen to the victims' tales of woe. With so many dead and countless more injured, the area hospitals in and around Washington had been filled way beyond capacity. The Red Cross and the National Guard had set up medical relief centers. The candidates viewed this holocaust while a large following of stranded survivors, almost all African or Latino, followed them. The networks turned on their telecomp cameras when Sam reached the microphones in front of a hi-rise apartment that had crumbled to the ground at H and 7th Streets. A gas main had exploded, leveling the entire area.

The architect of HOPE faced his followers. A thousand

sets of eyes, desperate, pleading eyes, stared at him. Before he could open his mouth to speak, they all vanished into a blurry mass as Sam's mind flashed back to that horrible Graduation Day. The day his parents and his sister were shot dead! Then two more shots tore into his shoulder and hip …

Sam shook his head to clear the visions. Although it was a cool November, he was perspiring. He had to look presidential. He turned away to regain his composure and view the destruction one more time.

A moment later, he stood up straight and returned his attention back to the crowd. He saw Jane scratch her right eye, the sign to look into the camera more. He did as instructed, and America saw a tear run down his cheek. He stood there, as if in a trance, and remained silent for a few more seconds.

The crowd quieted down, and the candidate began to speak slowly and unsteadily. "I don't know what to say, I really don't. There are no words that can express how I feel right now." He took a couple of deep breaths, then continued with incredulousness and disbelief in his voice. "What has our society turned into, where brother beats brother, friends become enemies, and fear is our foremost emotion? What does one say? What explanation does one offer?" This was not the speech Sam was supposed to make, but he didn't care. The people wanted hope, he would give them hope. "America doesn't have a justice system. It only has a legal system, and we need justice!"

When the shouts subsided, Sam continued. "Not revenge - justice. And in order to get justice the people must take back control of America. We must change our government into a government of representation as it was intended to be."

The applause and shouts were thunderous.

"Next Tuesday you have a choice. A new America, your America, or this." He waved his arm at the devastation around them and everyone quieted down.

Riding his emotions, Sam went on with the impromptu speech. "The number one concern in America today is safety. Without it, we are prisoners of our own society. Safety and security are more important than any other issue, for, without it, we cease to live. We merely exist. We must first feel safe, and be safe, before we can think about curing our other ills. My friends, I promise you that when I am president I will immediately put before Congress the Howard Crime Bill. You may want stronger gun control laws, but I ask you to look at the bigger picture."

For a moment, there was silence as Sam's lure of anticipation drew everyone in. He had baited them, and they wanted an answer. Any answer.

"We must build more maximum security prisons. Enough so that everyone convicted of first degree homicide once, or of a felony three times, is sent there for the rest of their life, without any chance of parole."

There was another onrush of applause and screams. "Put 'em away!" "Get 'em off our streets!" "Lead us to the Promised Land, Sam!"

"Within a federal partnership with select American manufacturing companies, these prisoners would be paid by these companies for the work they would be required to do. The product they create would then be infused into mainstream American commerce. In return for these jobs, the prisoners would pay the government for their room and board, and any security, medical, and utility fees. If the prisoner has any dependents, their paycheck would reflect that deduction. Cut off from society, these prisons would be a society of their own. Away from us forever."

The people agreed with Sam Howard and they enthusiastically showed him. Placards waved from side to side, and up and down, and Sam forgot the past. He felt whole again. Wanted and needed. Loved.

"The Howard Crime Bill is a stricter and more effective deterrent than the failed alternatives. It would not just deter murder with guns, it would deter murder with *any* type of weapon, as well as rape, aggravated assault - ALL felonies."

The crowd roared at this bold plan, this plan that would finally make them safe. "MAKE IT HAPPEN, SAM!"

Jane was irate. This wasn't the speech they had prepared and rehearsed the night before. This wasn't supposed to be a campaign stop. This was a humanitarian tour. They had agreed there would be no politicking, no reference to Price or the election.

"The Howard Crime Bill would deter crime and get these criminals off America's streets once and for all, saving the American taxpayer substantially in law enforcement and exorbitant death penalty appeals. Money that will instead be used to build and staff these new prisons. The Howard Crime Bill will change American society for the better. Then, and only then, can we even begin to think about our future. Safety first. Isn't that what our parents taught us and what we have taught our children? Our safety is what we have to take care of - what we *must* take care of - before we do anything else. We owe it to our children."

The people loved it. They loved their Uncle Sam. "GOD BLESS YOU!"

Sam waited until all was quiet again. "Yes, my friends, believe me, I promise you I will make your lives safe and secure so that something like this never happens again, so that this catastrophe, this fear, is never even a thought or a worry in your minds."

The applause and the roars wouldn't stop until Sam raised his hands to let him continue. He smiled, then turned somber.

"I know you're scared right now, and, believe me, I understand. So was I when I lost my reason for living. I, too, was a victim of violent crime. It was ... is ... a horrible memory." Sam's suede gray eyes turned glossy. The pause added a mysterious quality to the proceedings. "What was supposed to be one of the happiest and proudest days of my life turned into the worst day of my life, a day that still haunts me." He paused again, then proceeded. "It was the day I graduated Yale... "

It was two hours before the start of graduation ceremonies. Sam, his parents, and younger sister were all smiles inside the Howard limousine as they drove away from the Yale campus toward Wooster Street.

On New Haven's famous street of restaurants, the long, black car slowed to a stop behind a line of traffic. Sam looked out the window, but saw nothing as he was deeply focused on his valedictory speech. For the first time, he would be performing in front of his father. Sam was confident about his message and his skill in delivering it. It was the paternal review that had him so worried. For the last four years, his father had refused to see him act in any of the plays he'd been in. Theater was for sissies, not men. The most heralded actor in Yale history was nervous, as if the critics were deliberately out to pan him.

"Roberts," James Howard called to the chauffeur after a few minutes of waiting in line, "I think we'll get out here and walk the rest of the way."

The family of four began the short walk to Delmonico's Restaurant.

"What can be more wonderful?" Sam's beaming father asked as he breathed in the life-affirming air. "A beautiful day, a beautiful family, and my son graduating summa cum laude, class valedictorian, from my alma mater. I ask you, what can be more wonderful than this moment?" The proud father strolled along, then stopped under a blossoming lilac tree. The purple-blue flowers filled Wooster Street with its perfume, and James Howard reached up and picked a few. He handed one to his wife, Grace, and one to his sixteen-year old daughter, Britney.

They inhaled their fragrance, and Sam smiled at the happiness on their faces. He loved his mother. He loved his little sister. The women in Sam Howard's life meant everything to him. He thought about Jane Weisser, the woman he loved most of all. She was with her parents. The families would be meeting for the first time after the ceremony for celebratory drinks at the Yale Club. Maybe that's what was making him nervous, he thought.

No - it was definitely his father.

As Sam fantasized some more about Jane, four members of New Haven's most violent gang, The Black Alliance, stepped from a dark alleyway and blocked their progress. One of the men had a small gun by his side. He raised his arm and pointed it at their heads. "Listen up, you rich mothafuckas. We can make this simple and quick, or we can kill y'all. It's your call." Sam looked at them, then at his parents' and sister's faces. Their fright made him dizzy and he felt his spine go weak. He didn't know what to do. He knew he should protect them, save them, but he was frozen in place. He was just too scared. Before he could think about it anymore, one man reached out and grabbed Britney's handbag off her shoulder. Another, taking his cue from the first, took his and his father's watches and wallets. At the same time, the third man went for his mother's purse. The fourth, the leader of the gang, the one shouting the orders and the threats, kept his weapon aimed.

Sam's mother refused to let go of her bag.

"FOR CHRIST'S SAKE, GRACE, LET HIM HAVE IT!" his father yelled.

Panicked and oblivious to her husband's pleas, she wrested it away and then swung it at his head. "STAY AWAY FROM ME!" she screamed, as the sequined purse scraped the side of his face.

"YOU BITCH!" The incensed thug swung a brutal blow to her face.

James Howard instinctively came to his wife's aid and wrestled the man off her with surprising strength. One of the gang members jumped in to help his friend, knocking Britney to the ground. The petite girl screamed in pain as her head hit the concrete pavement. The gunman whipped his pistol in her direction, then back at the father.

Sam jumped to his sister's side. On his knees, he held her in his arms to comfort her and shield her from the attack.

The leader of The Black Alliance began shooting his weapon at them. Sam saw his mother and father fall as bullets tore into their backs and their heads, spewing blood and tissue everywhere. A second later, a bullet whizzed by his head and imploded into Britney's face.

The beautiful sixteen-year old girl hung over her brother's outstretched arms. "BRITNEY! OH, GOD, PLEASE!" She was convulsing, dying, and all Sam could do was watch her life drain from her body …

"It was the last thing I saw before two bullets tore into my shoulder and my hip," Sam told the mesmerized crowd. He looked out at the sea of faces listening to him, but the only thing he saw was the faces of his dead family. He had done nothing to save them. His father was right: He was a sissy, a coward frozen like a deer in the headlights. A nausea all too familiar to him attacked Sam's senses and, as always happens whenever he relived that nightmare, he broke out into a cold sweat.

Jane wiped the tears from her eyes. Sam had never talked to her about it, although, like him, she too had to mourn the death of a sibling. She had tried to get him to open up to her shortly after the funerals, and then again after they reunited twelve years later, but he couldn't. He wouldn't. Now, he was reliving it for the entire world. This disaster had gotten to him more than she realized. She waited for him to continue, as did the now-almost fifteen-hundred people, many with tears in their eyes. They all knew about the famous man's history. To hear it directly from him was a powerful, emotional experience. Jane now knew what Sam was doing. Sam was making them, for the first time since they had descended into their own personal Hell, think and feel for someone other than themselves. Sharing tragedy would help alleviate their pain and suffering and, at the same time, make them his. Psychologically, it was ingenious. Politically, he had them in his hands, along with the millions of viewers watching on TC.

"I awoke three days later ... my parents and my sister gone, with no goodbyes." Sam couldn't continue. He took out his handkerchief and wiped his face.

His audience was having the same reaction. Many were hugging each other, their grievous crying turned to tears of empathy.

"I promise you, my friends, I will do everything in my power to make sure your hopes and your dreams will one day again be filled with possibility."

"We love you, Sam!"

"Temporary housing at this very minute is being readied for those of you who are still in need. For the last few days, I have been in conversation with many area hotels and motels, and with the managers of apartment buildings and condominiums with unoccupied units. Everyone will have a place to stay until we figure out what to do. Shelter is our number one concern right now. I have also been talking with area supermarkets and restaurants. No one will go hungry. I promise."

Jane sighed. Except for the 'Howard Crime Bill,' he was right on track. As she thought about it, she realized that the second part of his speech, the cathartic disclosure leading into the last part he was now delivering, had made the people embrace the first part, the Howard Crime Bill, that much more. Yes, Sam, we'll do anything you want, you poor man.

The speech ended, and the cameras followed Sam, Bill Lawson, and their entourage through the crowd to their limousine. Everyone, it seemed, wanted to touch their hero. They pushed in toward him, threatening to stampede in their eagerness to tell him their troubles and to thank him. The Secret Service agents had a difficult time protecting the candidate, but Sam, always accessible to the people, became one of them. Talking, consoling, and listening, he embraced them and assimilated them so that they became part of him.

Sam and Bill waved a final good-bye when they reached their car. They got in, followed by Jane.

Her anger at her loss of control returned. Sam was trying to win the election based on society's insecurities. The country needed answers, a formula, and there he was writing a prescription to cure America's ills. "What was that?" she asked as soon as they pulled away.

"Excuse me?"

No client had ever taken control of their campaign from her. She wasn't about to let it begin now. "There are five days to go, Sam. Don't start thinking you can run this campaign yourself."

Sam nodded in apology and said, "I know I can't, Jane, but let me tell you what I want to do from here on in, and I think Bill concurs with me."

Jane looked over to see Bill Lawson nodding in agreement.

"I want to offer the people programs, changes they can believe in, ideas that will work. My crime bill may be extreme - Hell, it is extreme - but it's what the people want, and this country needs, right now."

"The only problem, Sam, is that if you don't present it correctly, it will appear as if you're trying to capitalize on a tragic situation. And the people will recognize that. Also, a candidate gets into trouble when he tries to do too many things. You have to stick to a central point. Ours has been 'A New America.' We have to stay on that track or we'll lose all credibility." It was suicide to change course in the middle of an election. The people would think the candidate was panicking; talking one game one day, another the next. It was more important to stay on one winning theme which the people could identify and associate with the candidate. But Jane saw that Sam had made up his mind. He had a fierce look of determination.

The FBI freed Gary Walters earlier in the day. There were no fingerprints on the Smith-Corona typewriter or on the blueprints of the HOPE Cities. The security sensor showed a man in a black fedora hat entering his back door at 3:36 a.m. His alibi about being with Taryn Weisser checked out. They could no longer legally detain him. Not unless they wanted a lawsuit filed against them.

Now, Garrison Miller was sitting in the basement of his New Carrollton, Maryland home with the four most trusted men of the PWA. There was Carl Block, his best friend since early childhood. Tommy and Lonnie McKay, his cousins, harebrained and vicious, accompanied Jimmy Siefert, the old militia man who had organized the Montana PWA four years ago. All were dedicated to a white America like him. All were dedicated to the future. To the death of Moses McBride.

Miller turned to the dated color television set and watched the reports of the nationwide devastation. He opened a beer and drank it down whole. He belched and popped another. "Look at those niggers rioting. They're giving every white man in America a reason to kill them. How stupid can they be?" The wide-eyed man chugged back most of the brew and laughed along with his friends. He thought about his father and the promise he'd made to avenge his murder. Miller held up the rest of his beer in a quiet toast to his memories. His past had become his future. "I'm gonna get you, McBride! Jane Weisser doesn't know it, but she's gonna hand you to me on a silver platter."

He laughed again.

At 9:00 p.m. EST, the major networks and their affiliates broke away for a special report. The Reverend Dr. Moses McBride of the First Abyssinian Baptist Church in Harlem, New York, the elected leader of the National African Caucus, was about to address the country. It was Thursday evening and almost everyone was home watching TC. All eyes not engaged in rioting and fighting were glued to the image of the heavyset African leader. He had a look of angry resolution, as if the fires of Hell were burning in his eyes. He was not the same man the country had come to admire and respect throughout the years.

When all was quiet inside Harlem's Martin Luther King, Jr. Community College Moses stared into the eyes of every American watching and began his speech. The voice that came out was different from the soothing voice America had come to know. It was a voice now filled with brimstone. A voice now laying blame. "Back in 1865 America handed the Negro a false bill of goods. Freedom, they promised us: Freedom to learn, freedom to live. Freedom to be free! Only, what we got instead was the freedom to be poor and destitute, the freedom to work and live in substandard conditions, the freedom to die in America's streets. Yes, white, rich America has given us the freedom to starve, to be imprisoned and treated like caged animals. We are still slaves. We have yet to be freed!"

Although the words and feelings emanating from the man who had patterned his life after Dr. Martin Luther King, Jr. weren't anything like the words Moses had followed and preached his entire adult life, he didn't care. They had to be said. And heard. This subjugation had gone on far too long. It was time to stop it.

The crowd that had gathered to hear Dr. McBride thought nothing of the irony that he was speaking these volatile words inside MLK, Jr. Community College. They cheered and roared their anger. They, too, had had enough. How long can you stay beaten without fighting back?

Moses waited for them to calm down. "It has been too many years since our brothers took to the streets of Harlem, Detroit, Washington, and other fine cities of color majority: Cities and communities tired of the white rich pushing them even further back into the rat-ridden, disease festering ghettos; into the crumbling, aged schools and hospitals; into a life where there was no hope. Because of the squalor America forced them to live in, our ancestors stood up in defiance. They refused to be pawns in the grand scheme of black annihilation, legal apartheid, American ethnic cleansing. They stood up so many years ago in the streets of Harlem, in the streets of Detroit, Washington, and dozens of other cities to say, 'I will defend myself!' And now, all these years later, and still nothing has changed. Just look at Sam Howard's HOPE Cities. IT'S GENOCIDE, I TELL YOU. GENOCIDE!" Moses screamed out from behind the podium, his fist thrust in the air.

"The government is trying to drive us out. They believe it is time to destroy us once and for all. They've tried in the past. They've lynched, and evicted, threatened, and cheated, and deprived us, and imprisoned us, and poisoned us with drugs. But nothing has worked for these oppressors. Not since America gave us the equal rights on paper we have always deserved has America been able to destroy us."

The uproar inside the college gymnasium was thunderous. Jumping up and down, their feet pounding the hardwood floor, they reacted as if their team had just scored the winning basket. The reverend's words had succeeded in stirring up memories of years of injustice and indignation. It had also filled them with a crazed but optimistic joy.

"Brothers and sisters, hear me out! Our people have taken to the streets, to their communities, and they are killing and looting and blowing up *our* homes, *our* businesses, *our* families. We're falling right into their hands. This is what they want. They want us to destroy ourselves, so our blood won't taint their lily-white hands, so our blood won't incriminate them. The enemy is white, rich America, not our people. Don't destroy your ally, your own kind. Carry your protestations to where it belongs. Fight on *their* territory. Take up your inalienable right to bear arms, your constitutional right to defend yourself, AND DEFEND YOURSELF AGAINST THE RICH, AGAINST THE WHITE ..."

The networks simultaneously pulled the plug on Moses McBride. On conference call, the presidents of the news divisions had agreed to end the reverend's speech if it got to the point of inciting riot. The news anchors spent the rest of the evening analyzing the effect it might have. Would the African people, anyone poor and needing an excuse to cause wanton acts of violence, heed Dr. McBride's plea? They didn't have to talk about it for long before they all reached the same conclusion.

With the rallying cry, 'The only defense is a powerful offense!' all around the country, people of color, people of poverty, came out in force to, at last, right their terrible past and present. Enraged that the white networks, those rich money mongers who controlled America's minds and emotions every day, would cut off the African leader's speech, they embraced its message completely. Everything Moses McBride had said was true. They were the victims of a plot to wipe them out for good.

It was time to take up arms. Time to strike before being struck again.

After speeches at the HOPE Cities in Baltimore, Philadelphia, and New York City, the Howard campaign jetted back to Washington. Jane returned to her office to spin the events for the press, calm the electorate, and apprise the state chairs. She left the Hart Senate Office Building at nine o'clock and drove north on Pennsylvania Avenue, past the White House into Georgetown. The art galleries, bookstores, quaint shops, fine restaurants, jazz clubs, and boutiques fashionably dotting her route home had closed out of caution, although all was quiet now. Jane drove through the residential areas, past the many old mansions with secluded gardens behind tall brick walls. Would these usually serene, tree-lined streets remain this way for long?

When Jane walked into her home, she felt at peace. Clean again. Her house was the one place she felt secure. She hung up her overcoat and read the stack of mail on the side-bar inside the large, open foyer. Bills, invitations, requests, the usual junk. She crossed through the hallway, into the wood-paneled study, and dropped the mail on her desk. The picture of her and Taryn caught her eye. Taryn! Dear God, had she gotten home safely from her dorm room? It had been such a hectic day that she'd forgotten to send a car for her. Jane rushed out of her study and up the stairs. At the top landing, she saw her daughter in her room asleep in bed. It was only 9:30, but everyone, everywhere, was emotionally exhausted. What better than to sleep it away?

Jane let out her breath and walked into her own bedroom. After she undressed and got into her flannel nightgown, she decided not to turn on the telecomp. She was depressed enough. She didn't know what to do, so she curled up under the covers, left the lights on, and reviewed everything that had happened since the HOPE Cities explosions.

"Mom, are you okay?" the sleepy, eighteen-year-old girl asked from the doorway to her mother's room. Taryn Weisser looked just like her mother. People often mistook them for sisters, only Jane understood it to be more of a compliment than an observation. The only differences between the Weisser women were that Jane had long, wavy brown hair to below her shoulders, and Taryn's was longer, lighter in color, and straight. Both were of average height, maybe on the tall side, but Taryn, being a teenager, always made sure her weight stayed below the norm. 'Vanity, thy name is not woman - it is youth,' Jane would always declare whenever she tried to get her daughter to eat more. Taryn's legs were also thinner than Jane's because, unlike her mother, the teenager wasn't a runner. 'A waste of time,' she exclaimed whenever Jane asked her to join her. What they both shared were the same ice-blue eyes and the same dimpled smile. Effervescent, was how Sam Howard had once described the women's look.

Jane sat up against the green wrought-iron headboard and patted the comforter by her right side. Taryn stood there in her long, baggy Georgetown night shirt. She hesitated, but then joined her mother under the bed coverings. As they lay together for the first time in more than a year, with Jane's right arm around her daughter's shoulder, she assured her. "I'm fine now that you're here."

"You can't bullshit a bullshitter, Mom. You've told me that a thousand times."

Jane broke her confident, in-charge character and said, "I'm worried, Taryn."

"You, the great analyzer, who can work out any problem? Gimme a break."

Was it sarcasm or compliment? "I'm serious. Nothing makes sense anymore." If Taryn's father hadn't divorced Jane after she'd given birth, would there be this friction between them right now? If she and Peter Gold were still married, would she just be a mother and a businesswoman, with no mother/daughter problems? Probably not, Jane realized. Parent/child conflicts were from a lack of communication, not from the lack of one parent. Some conflict was a normal part of the relationship. "I wish I knew what to do."

"It's Sam, isn't it?" Taryn said more than asked.

Jane's heart skipped a beat. "What do you mean?"

"Look at you: You're running the campaign of the Republican candidate for president and your own campaign to win back his love."

"Am I?"

"Are you?"

"Good question."

"Your happiness depends on the answer."

"Jeez, are you sure you're only eighteen?"

"I know you because I'm your mirror image."

"Psycho babble," Jane mocked her, remembering the conversation of the other day.

"See, we speak the same language," Taryn answered with a bittersweet smile.

Sleep beckoned, and the college freshman returned to her bedroom after her mother kissed her and she unenthusiastically returned the obligatory gesture. Jane noticed. Taryn was still angry with her. But, what had just happened, the playful communication, gave Jane cause for hope. It was good to smile again. Everything was going to be okay.

Jane turned on the telecomp. There on the wall screen was the now all-too-familiar picture of the bearded man. A shiver of dread went up and down her spine. The report was that Gary Walters' alibi had checked out.

"Miller had been with Taryn Weisser, the daughter of Dr. Jane Weisser, Sam Howard's national campaign director, when someone entered his house and planted the evidence. According to the FBI, he'd been with her in her Georgetown University dorm room from midnight until eight that morning. Mr. Walters," the reporter said, "was released this afternoon."

Even if Gary Walters wasn't Garrison Miller, Taryn's reputation was publicly blemished. "My poor baby!" How did her daughter's life get so complicated? Just a year ago, she was 'the good girl next door.' Now, she was rebellious and argumentative, with dangerous views and dangerous friends. She had become sullen and uncommunicative. They talked, but they didn't.

Jane got out of bed and lit a cigarette. Although Taryn was intelligent beyond her years, she was still eighteen. And an eighteen-year old girl's emotions always dominate her reason. Taryn was approaching this Gary Walters problem from her heart.

The ringing from the telecomp interrupted Jane's train of thought. She reached over to the night table and pushed the button. Sam appeared in a small box in the upper right hand corner, above the scene of a burning downtown Memphis. A second later, his picture filled the screen.

"How could Taryn have taken up with that madman, Jane? Doesn't she realize she can ruin me?"

"Taryn has done nothing to hurt you, Sam. There's no proof Walters is who they say he is, and it was proven he was framed."

"Please, Jane, watch her. We've come too far to lose now on something I have no control over."

"We're not going to lose!" Jane saw the fear in his face. She tried to sound like a wife, not a psychologist. She knew that the psychological approach was partly to blame for her deteriorating relationship with Taryn.

"Being behind in the polls at this point scares me, Jane. I know that doesn't sound very presidential, very leader-like."

"I understand, Sam. You're going through conflicting emotions right now. The thrill of the campaign and the devastating feelings about HOPE must be playing havoc with you."

"I love you," he said with a grateful smile. "You know that?"

"I know, Sam. Only sometimes I wish you'd never run for president. I would give it all up to return to the way we were before this campaign began. It's been a tough fourteen months for us. Especially for Taryn and me."

"Yes, I know, and I'm sorry. I'm sure everything will work out: For the country, for us, and, most specially, for you and Taryn."

She didn't know what to say.

"Good night, Jane. I'll see you in the morning."

Jane turned off the TC and sat in the bay window. No

Scotch; her head and stomach were already spinning. She opened the Tums Bottle and swallowed a couple. What a diet, she thought: Scotch, cigarettes, and antacids. She looked out at the Georgetown sky and noticed a blue car parked down the street, with two men inside looking up at her.

Jane dismissed it and got in bed. She prayed for one thing: Taryn's safety. There was no proof Gary Walters was this Garrison Miller. The security sensor in his home had shown that a man in a black fedora hat had entered his back door with a typewriter and maps. Someone had tried to frame him. He was innocent.

"Then why don't I believe it? Why do I have Paco checking him out?"

It was seven o'clock in the morning Baghdad time (11:00 P.M. EST) and the twelve old men of Al-Qiyamah, the Rising of the Dead, had just finished morning prayers.

"My brothers, let us speak Bi'-smi'llahi'r-Rahmani'r-Rahim," Sayyid Kassim said, and they collectively recited the Lord's Prayer. "Praise be to Allah, Lord of the Worlds, the Beneficent, the Merciful. Owner of the Day of Judgment, Thee we worship; Thee we ask for help. Show us the straight path, the path of those whom Thou hast favoured; Not of those who earn Thine anger nor of those who go astray."

Seated together inside Sayyid Kassim's palatial home, the twelve old men stared at the many horrific scenes on the satellite-fed multi-panel screen that filled one of Sayyid's living room walls. Rioting had exploded throughout the United States. America was quickly crumbling. Dying.

They watched with curiosity and joy.

"Allah akbar!" Sayyid said. God is good.

"ALLAH AKBAR!"

CHAPTER FOUR

Friday, November 4th
Four days before Election Day

Moses McBride was proud of his accomplishments this past year as president of the NAC. The African people needed a leader. Now, with racial unrest raging throughout the United States, he also needed to organize his people. Moses felt guilty that he was adding to it. But, he knew that in the end everyone would be better off. Equal. He really had no choice; America had proven to be anything but the land of the free. Do nothing, and a whole class of human beings would cease to exist.

In Washington, D.C., it was worse than the riots of '68. The Capital HOPE City was flattened, and many other areas in Washington were now under attack: Columbia Road to Park Road, the N.E. shopping area, the Wheeler Road area. Looters rampaged the stores, and there was nothing anyone could do to stop them. The Third Infantry from Fort Myer in Arlington,

Virginia came in their tanks and jeeps from the West, and the 6th Armored Calvary out of Fort Meade, Maryland came in from the East.

At 4:00 a. m. Moses McBride's troops overtook the D.C. Armory and hauled its weapons back to NAC headquarters at Howard University. The military fought back as bullets and hand grenades came flying at them. There had to be five-thousand people battling throughout the city, which made it impossible for the government to fight those shooting at them. There were fifty here, one-or-two-hundred there, and five-hundred or more somewhere else. By the time it took the authorities to search out their enemy, they were dead themselves. After a while, they just began to indiscriminately shoot back, regardless. It was chaotic.

Shortly after dawn, congregants of the First Baptist Church in Houston, Texas, gathered for an early morning vigil. News reports told of African churches being raided throughout the country, but seventy-five members were present to offer their prayers for the dead. And the living. The Reverend Calvin Strong began the service by leading his congregation in a hymn. It was peaceful inside the old building; a refuge in the pain and the suffering of the outside world.

Like an army sneaking up on the enemy, a dozen white men with semi-automatic guns rushed the historic church. Their orders had been clear. Destroy the enemy in their houses of worship! Make the country white again! Free America from the scourge of African poverty, crime, and overpopulation! The twelve men, ironically in black face, pulled open the two outer doors of the one room church.

As if rehearsed, the seventy-five congregants fell to their knees. They had been expecting this attack sooner or later, and they were prepared. As the assailants lifted their weapons, more than two-dozen men who had fallen before their pews rose up with machine guns of their own in hand. They fired round after round at the unwelcome guests before any of them could get a shot off. The sound was deafening. When it ended, and the twelve intruders lay still, the seventy-five parishioners stood up. All was quiet for a moment, until the Reverend Calvin Strong said, "Let us sing." The congregants turned around and sang as one, "We Shall Overcome".

Moses McBride had trained them well.

Before she left for the airport and the trips to the Boston, Cleveland, and Detroit HOPE Cities, Jane stopped off at her office in Sam's senate suite. The first thing she saw when she walked in was Paco's tear-filled eyes. "What's wrong? Did something happen?"

Jane's number one assistant in The Weisser Organization stopped pacing the floor. He looked up at her and the tears fell down his cheeks. "The bastards killed my parents. They blew up their souvenir shop. DAMNIT, JANE, WHY?"

The news pained Jane and her eyes welled. "I don't know, Paco. I don't understand anything anymore."

"Oh, God, what am I going to do? I have to do something!"

Jane put her arms around the short, thin man. Paco Ramirez was like a younger brother. His parents had always sent her and Taryn cards at birthdays and holidays, grateful for everything she had done for their son throughout the years. They were good people, people who deserved a better fate. The tears rolled down her face as Jane thought about the hundreds of thousands of people in the country presently living with that same anguish. "I don't think there's anything anyone can do, Paco."

The other members of the campaign staff walked in for the meeting, and Jane opened her morning briefing book. With everyone gathered around the conference table, she began.

"What are the numbers, Larry?"

Larry Waldman, the respected pollster, looked up from his notes. His wire-rim glasses rested on the bump of his hawkish nose, and his wiry hair gave him a frizzled look, as if a bolt of lightning had electrically charged him. "Price is still in front by three; however, those battleground states we've been after seem to finally be moving our way." Larry had his people up every night getting half-samples, sometimes full ones. His numbers, in every election since joining The Weisser Organization, had always proved accurate.

They discussed the intelligence reports their field people had faxed in overnight, as well as what was going on in each state, where Price was traveling, and everything that had happened since yesterday's meeting. "What are the papers saying, Kerri?"

Kerri Robbins, number three in command at TWO, began her report. "It's really a mixed bag. Most of the dailies are calling on the President to do something, characterizing him as 'a weak example of the leadership this country needs,' according to this morning's Washington Post. The New York Times, on the other hand, is questioning Sam's humanity, labeling it 'an opportunistic response to an ineffable situation.'"

"I was afraid that might happen. Anything else?" Jane asked.

"Yes," the plumpish redhead said. "The Atlanta Constitution today says: 'We can no longer support the candidacy of President Charles Price. He has proven, during these last few days, to be an ineffectual leader. Sam Howard is the only person capable of turning this country around.'"

Jane heard from the other seven members of her team. When they finished, she gave them their orders for the day and they left to begin their work. Paco remained in her office gazing fixedly at a corner of the ceiling. Jane walked up to him and sat by his side. She took his head and rested it on her shoulder.

Paco grieved for a while, then regained his composure. He thanked Jane for her sympathy and apologized for not being able to contribute to the meeting. He then told her what he'd learned about the questionable man in Taryn's life. "I'm afraid I didn't find out very much. This Gary Walters is twenty-eight, single, and he's auditing Taryn's political science class. According to the professor, Walters asked his permission to sit in, saying that politics interested him. He's also worked since August as a part-time security guard at Warwick Industrials in New Carrollton. Prior to that I hit a dead end. There's no trace of him any earlier."

"That's suspicious," Jane said. "Why would a man's past end four months ago?"

"Maybe he changed his name."

"Why?"

"Maybe he's hiding something."

"Like he was at one time Garrison Miller?" Jane thought about it. "I think the reason they've never found Miller, and have never seen a picture of what he looks like, is because he's always changing his name and appearance. He has to keep his real identity a secret."

"Then the big question is, why is he auditing a poli sci course at Georgetown? Nothing came up in my search that showed him ever enrolled in any institution. Do you think he's sitting in on Taryn's class just to get close to her?"

There was a short pause to consider that possibility. "Or Sam."

"Madre de Dios!"

Jane lit a cigarette. She went to the bar and fixed herself a Bloody Mary. "Let's look at the facts, Paco. After months of tailing him and losing him, the Bureau believes that Gary Walters is

Garrison Miller and that he's the one who blew up the HOPE Cities."

"You're forgetting there's substantial proof that someone framed him."

"Do you really believe that? I think Miller set up his own framing to throw everyone off track."

"But if the FBI hasn't been able to prove it, how can we?"

Jane needed Paco working on the campaign, but with Taryn, and maybe Sam, involved, this was more important right now. "Since there's nothing in Gary Walters' past, start digging into Garrison Miller's. We have to know whether Miller is Gary Walters, so we can stop him before he does anything else."

"I'm sure the Bureau knows more than we do, Jane, but since they've yet to do anything, it can only mean one thing."

"I know. They have nothing that can stick." Jane's mind went into overdrive. "Besides investigating Garrison Miller's background, it's also time we checked out Michael Salaman, the man who humiliated the President on TC, and Harry Morton, who said he drove Paul Baker twice to New Carrollton. They're the only other inconsistencies since all this began. I can't help wonder whether any relationship exists between them."

"Can we afford to take the time away from the campaign?"

"Can we afford not to?" Jane and Paco walked out of her office into the reception area. Seated at the large desk, talking into headsets, were two receptionists. Members of the senator's staff dashed in and out past them. "Paco," she called to him as he walked to his small office, "I'm really sorry about your parents." He turned and smiled, but was too choked up to offer his thanks.

Jane returned to her office and her work on the campaign. She found it increasingly difficult to concentrate. Her mind kept focusing on Taryn, Sam, and Garrison Miller. She looked at the

Johnny Walker bottle. It was tempting, but she had to stay lucid. She had to stay in control of an out of control situation. To do that, she had to discover what plot was being perpetrated, and who were the plotters.

All the morning talk shows feasted on personal stories of death, destruction, pain, and fear, as well as stories about President Charles Price's inability to end it. However, the biggest topic of conversation was Sam Howard's speech in the Capital HOPE City and in the other cities he'd visited yesterday. The Howard Crime Bill was definitely radical, they all agreed, but it was already embraced by a seduced society who now believed the country had no other choice. There were also stories recounting Sam's past and the murders of his parents and sister. It added a personal dimension to a surreal situation, a reality to a nightmare growing worse by the minute. Whereas before the bombings and the nationwide rioting began President Price was ahead in the polls by as much as eleven points, his lead had since fallen to three.

There were only four days until the election. Would Senator Howard overtake the President, profiting from the president's inability to control the situation? Or would efforts to find the person or persons responsible for the HOPE Cities bombings and end the country's hostilities by election day prove successful and win reelection for Charles Price?

The Patriot HOPE City in the Roxbury section of Boston was bustling with people awaiting the presidential candidate. Most were homeless, displaced by the almost complete destruction of their community. However, there was an anticipation in the air, a hope. They spoke amongst themselves about what Sam Howard could do for them, and what President Price wasn't, and most everyone agreed that the Howard Crime Bill was a step in the right direction.

A loud roar near the gates of HOPE erupted as Sam Howard arrived. He walked through the crowd, shaking hands, hugging supporters, and stopping now and then to listen. He finally walked up to the microphones and looked at the rubble around him.

Jane stood at the front of the crowd, within view of Sam, ready to direct him. His sorrowful face made everyone feel as if he knew firsthand what they were going through. After all, HOPE was his child. And like them, he had lost that child, too.

"We love you, Sam." "Please help us." "Give us hope!" There were hundreds of homemade signs - 'Uncle Sam for President,' 'SOS - Sam Our Savior,' 'Sam Howard, the people's HOPE!' - besides all the official placards the campaign volunteers had distributed.

The crowd quieted as Sam Howard began speaking to the people who most identified with him. "Just a short distance from here is the famous Boston Freedom Trail. Freedom ..." He stared into the TC cameras and asked, " ... when will all of our people have it in this great land of ours? Look at what decades of incivility have done to us. Look around and ask: Will we ever be the country our forefathers meant us to be? I'm afraid we won't, my friends, if America continues its greedy attitude of 'I want it all.' We won't if we continue living only for ourselves. In a civilized society we *must* be our brother's keeper. We must be a people concerned about *all* people if we ourselves want to be free."

The crowd, which Jane estimated to be more than a thousand strong, applauded. They loved Sam Howard, yet he was still behind in the polls. Jane understood why. The middle and upper classes didn't want someone in the White House promising to even the distribution of wealth. Corporate America, grown rich on the seemingly endless supply of wealth generated by the bull market of the 90s, only to have lost most of it during George W. Bush's reign, was still trying to regain its wealth and power. America was anything but brotherly, and the American people were proving that beyond a doubt.

"The Howard Crime Bill will rid our streets of that element of society that has filled our lives with death and despair. However, I come here today to tell you that it is going to take more than a crime bill to change our society into a society of compassionate, understanding, and accepting people. A society where everyone, no matter how rich or how poor, how black or how white, can live together peacefully and progressively, with one goal in mind: To rebuild a country where every individual has the means and the freedom to develop his or her abilities to their full potential."

"Sam's the man! Sam's the man!"

"To change America for the better, to change *us* for the better, the first thing we have to change is our antiquated educational system. The three R's - reading, 'riting, and 'rithmetic - is how our children have been taught since the beginning of time. But, we're now in the third millennium, and we have a responsibility to our children, to America's future, to educate tomorrow's leaders and teach future generations the skills they need so they can survive in a world that is becoming increasingly more complicated. That is why, my friends, I put forth to you the Education Reinvention Bill.

"We must do away with the provision that allows our children to drop out of school at the age of sixteen. All children *must* stay in school until graduation and that will be law! The excuse that a child must go to work at sixteen to help support the family does irreparable damage to the future of the child being forced to be his family's provider. Staying in school until graduation is the only thing that will break the chain of poverty and relieve an overburdened welfare system, which will make America, and the family, stronger."

There was a murmur from the crowd of people, mostly uneducated. Education was a commodity for the rich. They needed that paycheck to survive. Jane noticed the uncertainty on everyone's faces. They couldn't see the forest through the trees.

"American schools must incorporate into their present curriculum new Life Studies courses. Within partnership with the fifty state universities, a Master's degree program, created by the country's top educators, psychologists, sociologists, and state education commissioners, would be offered in part scholarship to already certified teachers.

"On the elementary level, classes in confidence and self esteem, manners and etiquette, ecology and the environment, safety, study habits, and the new three R's (respect, responsibility, and reward) would become part of the curriculum. On the intermediate level, students would take yearly courses in money management, interpersonal communications, and social awareness (which includes a cooperative commitment in volunteerism). High schoolers would study one course in each of their eight semesters in career development, comparative cultures and religions, philosophy and logic, ethics and morality, analytical and deductive reasoning, persuasive speaking, colleges and college life, and parenthood. These new courses would ensure a future society in which all people would live together, peacefully, in a financially productive and socially responsible manner."

The crowd became attuned to Sam's message. To change people, people had to change. To change society, society had to change. And change could only begin with our schools and our young. The applause got louder with each new idea and it swept across Boston. As others saw the logic behind it, more and more people realized the future depended on it.

"With crime reduced per the crime bill, and mandatory student graduation, the cost of this new educational system - for a safer, richer, and happier society - would be recouped with the money saved on a consistently reduced welfare system. The Education Reinvention Bill will put more people in the work force paying taxes, buying homes, and generating money in the American marketplace."

Sam was a master at presenting his ideas. He got the crowd thinking and believing. Jane watched them react in amazement. Sam Howard gave everyone hope, not just with words, but with his conviction and delivery. He was the consummate actor.

"The Education Reinvention Bill *will* change America for the better. I ask you for your trust. We *must* change. *Now!* For a safer, richer, and happier society."

The people of Boston raised their signs and screamed as if at a national convention. "Sam's the man! Sam's the man!"

After he told them about his immediate plans for temporary shelter and food distribution, Sam ended the speech. "Thank you, my friends. I love this country. I love you. Now, let's do something about it. Together, as a family!"

The newspaper photographers' cameras flashed as Sam Howard and Bill Lawson smiled for them. They walked through the adoring crowd shaking hands, hugging the ladies and the children, promising to do everything in their power to help those who needed help.

Jane looked at the people's hopeful faces. She looked at the burned-out buildings. The future was daunting, but at least one leader had the power to make the people believe in themselves and in their country. As she walked back to their limo, admiring Sam's enormous talents, she wondered: Can the country survive without Sam Howard as president?

The fight for economic justice, for survival, had spread to lands of color throughout the world. Civil insurgence was destroying Cuba, Haiti, Rwanda, Somalia, Uganda and many other third world nations. Thousands of innocent people were already dead in each of these countries. The perennially downtrodden of the world were rising in anger as the flame of revolution raced from country to country

Violence erupted in Jerusalem as seven Muslim mosques exploded within minutes of each other. The death toll was 197, with over 400 injured seriously. Muslim extremists seized the opportunity to incite a *jihad* - a holy war - throughout the region. Although there was no official participation by the governments or armies of the surrounding Moslem countries, borders were violated as Moslems streamed into Israel to avenge their people and their God. Jewish and Moslem civilians grappled hand to hand while the Israeli military was stymied by the chaos and confusion much as their American counterparts had been in the HOPE Cities rioting. The birthplace of three of the world's major religions was once more embroiled in fighting fueled by bitter hatreds and age old animosities. The Jewish state was under siege by a crazed population of true believers with a clear sense of their divine mission to destroy it.

The Howard campaign visited Cleveland and Detroit, then returned to Washington. By 8:00 p. m. Jane was on the phone in her office, telling each state campaign director what to do next, and each network what spots to run nationally and when. She was also briefing the press about Sam's Education Reinvention Bill. The candidate had gotten the optimistic juices of the people flowing once again. Like ravenous animals scavenging for anything edible, America hungered for a sense of hope and something to believe in.

With Jane Weisser dangling the bait, America was hooked.

The enormous success of The Weisser Organization throughout the years was due to Jane's belief that politicians had to be performers if they wanted to win over their audience. Sam Howard was proof of that. Each candidate she represented was aware of this philosophy, and each one willingly put their careers in her capable hands. Like a master sculptor, she molded them and their candidacies. She was in charge. She was the one who called the shots.

And her clients always won.

TWO included researchers, poll takers, scriptwriters, and image consultants, along with vocal coaches, interpersonal communications experts, and acting teachers. A school for politicians, performance boiled down to passion. If you couldn't convey your beliefs, how could you expect everyone else to feel passionate about them? It was Jane's credo with all her political clients: Let your passion show!

The Weisser Organization was large, and almost half of its sixty people were at work on this campaign, ten in Sam's office alone. The rest were at TWO's headquarters on Massachusetts Avenue, overlooking Lincoln Park on Capitol Hill. They were in constant contact with Paco Ramirez and Kerri Robbins who shuttled between the offices at least a dozen times a day. Those not fortunate enough to be in the Howard camp were busy on other campaigns, or on other public relations business for a variety of nationally and internationally known corporations.

At nine o'clock, Jane looked at her watch. It had been a long day, and she needed a break. She pressed the 'on' button on her keyboard and the telecomp wall screen lit up. CNN was broadcasting from Israel. The report was about the seven mosques blown up in Jerusalem, and the civilian rioting it had ignited. "Dear God," she said to the empty room, "this insanity is everywhere." She then thought: Bombs! Like HOPE.

Jane tapped the mute button and pressed the one for Paco's office. A minute later, he was standing before her desk. "I want you to get in touch with Senator Rawlings' contact at the Mossad and find out what type of explosives destroyed those mosques. Then find out what kind of bombs leveled HOPE."

"You think there's a connection?"

"Probably not, but we have to check every angle."

"No, we don't. The FBI and Homeland Security have to check every angle. We're campaigners, Jane, not investigators. Walters is one thing; Taryn's life comes first. But, don't go trying to solve the crime of the century."

There was silence for a second. Jane could have reiterated her request, made it a direct order, but she knew her silence would net the same results. After Paco refused to flinch (he'd seen it many times throughout the years), she took another approach. "If Miller and his PWA blew up HOPE, and the same type of bombs were used in Israel, then my daughter, my Jewish daughter, is with the man who may be trying to start a third world war. Considering Taryn and what just happened in Israel, and considering our candidate, don't you agree we need some fast answers?"

"Yes."

"I want you to stay in Washington tomorrow. Call me as soon as you have something." Paco left her office, and Jane sat there with an empty Scotch glass in one hand and a cigarette in the other. She couldn't believe the FBI would free someone like Garrison Miller. She couldn't believe that Taryn might be dating 'the most hateful man in America.'

A few minutes later, Jane got up to fix herself another drink.

As she did, she saw Sam standing in the doorway. He walked in and sat in the chair next to her desk. Jane sat back down - empty-handed.

"It's been a rough week, Jane: For the country, us, the campaign."

"I know, Sam."

"How's Taryn dealing with it?"

Jane's stomach constricted. "You know Taryn. She's bullheaded, like her mother. She insists there's no connection between Gary Walters and Garrison Miller." Jane pondered her and Taryn's deteriorating relationship. "She was at odds with me before. This problem, I'm afraid, has made a bad situation even worse."

"I'm sorry."

"I can't believe I've turned into such a terrible mother."

"No, you haven't! Listen to me, Jane. I know you have Paco checking out Miller. Only a loving, concerned mother would do that." Sam leaned in and took her hand in his. "I'm worried about Taryn, too. As soon as I heard about her involvement with this Gary Walters, I asked Director Coyles to check into Miller's background. For her safety, and ours, it's imperative we know whether he and Walters are one and the same, as the Bureau suspects." Sam released her hand, sat back and crossed his legs, and told her what he had learned about the man. "Garrison Miller's late father was 'Daddy' Garland Miller, grand marshal of the Louisiana KKK. Ten years ago they arrested 'Daddy' for the killings of three young African boys in New Orleans. He remained on death row until they executed him earlier this year. Miller was eighteen at the time of his father's arrest, and for the next five years he drifted aimlessly, until he disappeared. A few months later the People for a White America was born. Miller had changed his name and the FBI tried to stay on his trail, but he always disappeared and reappeared under a new identity. Never having been arrested, there is no record of his fingerprints anywhere, nor is there a picture of the man. They believe that along with his new name he got a new face.

"Now, the reason there's been no trace of Miller these last few years, and why Gary Walters suddenly appeared in Maryland four months ago, is because Gary Walters is really Garrison Miller. He and his PWA are the masterminds behind the HOPE bombings. The man is dangerous, Jane. And smart. Framing himself and using Taryn as an alibi to stay one step ahead of suspicion shows just how smart he is."

"You know, Sam, at first I thought so, too. But, I can't help asking myself: Why would Miller frame himself and bring attention to his existence if he's been trying to keep his identity a secret all this time? It doesn't make any sense. No, I think someone else set him up."

"Maybe. But, he's a slick bastard. You have to keep Taryn away from him."

"DAMNIT! A madman's been let loose and my daughter could be his next victim. What's wrong with the FBI? Why did Coyles release him?"

"Because there was no proof he was involved in the bombings. And Taryn was his alibi. I'm sorry, Jane. Is there anything I can do?"

"No, Sam, I'll figure something out." She desperately wanted to run to him, wrap her arms safely in his, and cry. However, fourteen months ago they had agreed to suppress their emotional as well as carnal urges, so as not to give the press any opportunities to open any propriety issues. "Thank you for checking him out and telling me."

He stood to leave. "Are you going to be all right?"
She nodded.

He bent down and kissed the top of her head. "I'll see you tomorrow."

Sam left, and Jane poured herself a double at the bar. She drank the calming drink, grabbed her coat and purse, and left the senate suite. There was only one thing to do: She had to meet her daughter's boyfriend.

Jane arrived home at close to ten o'clock, read her mail, and went upstairs to her bedroom and changed clothes. More comfortable in jeans and a white Ocean City sweatshirt, she was ready to confront Taryn. She pressed the button for her room. The teenager answered, and Jane asked her to come to her bedroom. A moment later she appeared in the doorway. Jane noticed they were wearing the same sweatshirts they had bought the summer before last on their yearly trip to the Jersey shore. The silence between them foreshadowed the argument still to come. "We have to talk about Gary Walters, Taryn."

"Jesus, Mom, not this again!"

"Gary Walters and Garrison Miller are the same man."

"I refuse to believe it. Or listen to this crap!" She turned to leave.

"Well, you'd better. You're not safe around him."

Taryn stopped and turned back with a look of scorn on her face. "That's where you're wrong, mother. I feel safest when I *am* around him. Safer than anywhere I've ever known. Gary is always there for me. He listens, he loves, he treats me like I'm part of his life. I *am* part of his life!"

Jane took each comment as a personal rebuke. Each one stung painfully. She didn't make her daughter feel safe anymore; she wasn't always there for her; she didn't listen; she didn't love? If Taryn really believed that then she had failed miserably as a mother. If she didn't feel loved then nothing could ever pain Jane more. For God's sake, her child was the most important part of her life. Didn't Taryn feel secure in that knowledge?

"You know, this is the first time in a long time that a man has been interested in me for me, not for being the daughter of the powerful and influential Jane Weisser. Gary could care less about politics. He doesn't even know who you are. That's why I haven't introduced him to you. I don't want him to know. Now you're trying to break us up, all because of how the publicity might affect you and Sam and this goddamn election. Well, that's not going to happen, mother. I love Gary, and he loves me."

Rather than argue that she was dealing with a very clever man who, of course, wouldn't show his hand until he had to, Jane, nevertheless, knew she had to persist in the matter. Her words had to break through to that eighteen-year old heart. She hoped she wouldn't break it, but, soon, this man would, so it was better that she be the one. "Sam found out that ten years ago, when Garrison Miller was eighteen, his father killed three African boys. He remained on death row until they executed him eight months ago. For the last five years there has been no trace of Garrison Miller. And Gary Walters can't be traced back before this past summer."

"This is all about Sam, mother. Don't make it out to be something else. Like I said, he's afraid that the daughter of his national campaign director having an affair with a man *unjustly* accused of a heinous crime could hurt his chance of getting elected." There was a long pause. Like her mother, Taryn, too, knew when to be non-verbal. She had learned from the master. "And you're going along with the man you love because his becoming president, his success and yours, is more important than your own daughter's happiness."

Jane had heard enough drivel. "Listen to me, Taryn!"

"It's all just coincidence. Even the FBI agrees. They released him because there was no proof. They released him because Gary

Walters is who he says he is. Now, until you can prove differently, mother, like you, I have to trust my man." The teenager spun on her heels to leave the room.

"Wait!" Jane called out. Taryn stopped and turned back. "Fair enough, but I want to meet this man of yours."

"Fair enough." She turned around and walked out.

Jane was distraught. Her daughter didn't trust her anymore. She couldn't make her daughter see reality. She was failing as a mother and as a psychologist.

Feeling like the commander-in-chief in a major war, a contemplative Garrison Miller paced the gray cement basement of his Maryland home. In every urban city in America the Africans were killing his soldiers and his losses were mounting. He had not counted on such an organized and well-armed resistance. McBride was smarter than he gave him credit for. Miller sat down to think about his strategy. For the last four months he'd been planning it.

The news was on the old television set. Miller turned and listened to Sam Howard tell the HOPE Cities refugees how education reform would reduce the welfare roll and make our country a more congenial place to live in. "You stupid fuck, let 'em all die. They've ruined America, can't you see that?" The son of 'Daddy' Garland Miller was angry at the world. Didn't people understand? Didn't they realize it was the Africans and the Latinos who bred poverty and crime along with their many unwanted children? With the death of them the American Dream would again be within every good American's reach. Didn't anyone understand? "The only way to change America is to rid it of its scum. People like Moses McBride and Sam Howard. Niggers and nigger lovers."

Granted, the African people were fighting back like

cornered rats and many of his followers were dying for the cause, but Garrison Miller knew one thing for sure: With every death of one of his came many more deaths of theirs. And with the death of every one of his, more and more people were going to join his cause. It was inevitable. He was going to win this fight. America was going to be all white or it would cease to exist.

The grand marshal of the PWA opened a beer and imagined it. Never before had he been this close. He wasn't about to let the opportunity slip away from him. Moses McBride was going to die a painful death. And then ...

He loved to fantasize about what would then happen.

The ringing of the telephone awoke him from his daydream. He picked it up, adjusted the erection inside his denim jeans, and heard Taryn Weisser's voice.

"Gary, remember when I asked you if you knew who my mother was and you told me you didn't? Well, it's about time you knew. She's Sam Howard's national campaign director. I'm sorry I didn't tell you sooner."

"I told you, Taryn, the only reason I'm taking Poli Sci 101 is because it's required. I've heard your mother's name before, but, for the life of me, I couldn't tell you why."

"She believes you're this Garrison Miller."

He said nothing. If he was going to get to Moses McBride through this political menagerie, he had to find out all they knew.

"Sam Howard told my mother that he had you checked out and that you are Miller. Of course they have no proof."

"They have no proof because it's not true. Until all this happened, I'd never even heard of this Garrison Miller."

"It's probably just their way of trying to stop me from seeing you. The election comes first in their eyes, and I guess they're afraid of the negative publicity this has generated. I'm sorry."

"So, what's the problem?"

She hesitated. "My mother …"

"Taryn, I thought you believed in me. I thought you believed in us. Why would Garrison Miller date Taryn Weisser? I read up on this Miller, and the last thing he wants is for anyone to discover his identity. Dating the daughter of 'the most influential woman in Washington' would blow his cover. Miller would be crazy to be in this relationship. But, I'm still here."

"Gary, you don't have to prove anything to me. I believe you. But, I'm afraid you're going to have to prove it to my mother. She wants to meet you."

Miller considered this new complication. If he refused to meet her, everyone's suspicions would heighten. And that would be dangerous. He thought about it while Taryn waited for his response. Jane Weisser wanted to meet him. Did that mean there was a window of opportunity open regarding her belief in his innocence? The leader of the PWA smiled. However slight that opening, he knew he had to convince her he was Gary Walters. Originally, his plan was to kill Moses McBride, as her daughter's guest, at the inaugural ball. The notoriety associated with his arrest now ruled that out. Even if her mother did believe him, after what had happened, there'd be no way she would allow Taryn to invite him. He felt it was still important to stay in Jane Weisser's life. Somehow, he knew, she could lead him to Moses McBride. "Sure," he told Taryn, "I have nothing to hide. I'd love to meet your mom."

Jane sat at the large rococo desk in her study. Her desk was her pride and joy, her favorite piece of furniture in the house. Sam had bought it for her as a 'thank you' gift after she steered his campaign to victory in his senate reelection bid six years ago. The priceless piece was built in France in the early 18th century and was marked with elaborate ornamentation: exquisite scrolls, foliage, and animal forms. Jane marveled at the ornate craftsmanship every time she sat down behind it.

The front doorbell rang. Jane was busy adding the next few days of the campaign schedule to her telefiles. She couldn't afford an interruption now.

"I'll get it," Taryn yelled.

She heard her daughter gallop down the stairs and open the front door. She looked at her watch. Eleven o'clock? Who would be calling at her house at such a late hour? As soon as Jane asked herself the question, her mind returned to the telecomp and she forgot about it. There was too much work to do.

Taryn walked into the study a moment later. "Mom, this is Gary."

Jane's head snapped up from the screen. There he was, blond beard and all, in person. Her stomach tightened. She didn't know what to say. Do. She'd wanted to meet him; however, she was totally unprepared for this surprise visit.

"A pleasure to make your acquaintance," he said from the opposite side of the desk. He reached across and smiled.

Jane accepted the man's hand. "Why don't we go into the living room," she offered. As the two turned to leave the study, her eyes met Taryn's. There was a smirk, a smug 'I'll show you' look on her daughter's face. Jane took a deep breath to control a sudden flash of anger. It was time to unmask this creep and show Taryn who he really was.

The couple sat together on the white floral print sofa, and Jane sat in one of the two matching swivel chairs opposite them. A rectangular glass coffee table, with a silk flower display in the center, separated them. The fireplace was to Jane's right, and two ceiling spots illuminated the pictures of her and Taryn above it. Jane noticed him looking up at them. She sat there and waited.

He turned his attention back to Jane and spoke first. "I don't know why Taryn took so long to introduce us, but I'm glad we finally have the opportunity to meet."

Jane dug her toes into the thick white carpeting and studied the man before her. He had on new black jeans, a plaid shirt, and black alligator boots. He wore his blond hair combed back, and his beard and mustache were evenly trimmed. "Taryn tells me you're in her poli sci class."

"I never told you that."

There was an uncomfortable pause. Her eyes remained transfixed on his, and the psychologist in her took over.

"Obviously, you had me checked out, ma'am. Can't say as I blame you. Any good mother would've done the same after what happened to me."

So cool, so confident. "Thank you for understanding, Mr. Walters."

"Please - Gary."

"Tell me, Gary, why are you so interested in poli sci?"

"Without sounding disrespectful, Mrs. Weisser ..."

"Doctor."

"Excuse me?"

"It's Dr. Weisser."

"As I was saying, Dr. Weisser, without sounding disrespectful, I would've expected your first question to be, 'Why are you so interested in my daughter?'"

"Second question. First, why poli sci?"

"Well, I've always been interested in the way our government runs."

He was lying. Why couldn't Taryn see that? If politics interested him so much, then how come he told her he didn't know who her mother was? Damnit, Taryn was a psych major. Hadn't she learned yet that a psychologist has to be a detective in search of inconsistencies. Behaviors, patterns, and reactions - they're all clues.

"To answer your second question, I'm interested in Taryn for the same reason any man would be: She's beautiful, intelligent, fun to be with. I've never met anyone like her. Do you want me to go on?"

"Spare me, I know my daughter." Yes, Taryn was wonderful, but she was a child. Inexperienced with life. If he had never met anyone like her, then he hadn't been looking very hard. "Third question: Why is Taryn so interested in you?"

"I'm afraid you'll have to ask her that yourself."

Taryn answered without being questioned. "Gary is thoughtful, kind ..."

"But, you're ten years her senior. What could you two possibly have in common?"

"Everything. We're two kindred souls, if I can be so corny." He took Taryn's hand in his to make his point.

It was too obvious, calculated to create an effect. The man read like a book.

"And I want to spend every minute with her."

Jane saw her daughter totally captivated by this cheap and obvious act. This bastard was going to break her little girl's heart. She had to stop him. "Tell me - why the suspicion on the FBI's part? And I'm not sorry for being blunt."

"Apologies aren't necessary, doctor. It's a perfectly legitimate question."

"I wasn't apologizing." She was getting angrier by the second. How much more she could take, she didn't know.

"Mother!"

"Why did they arrest you?" She watched his body language. His shoulders stiffened slightly, his eyes turned away from hers for a split second, and his hands clasped each other for support.

"I suppose I look like this Garrison Miller. Other than that, I'm at a loss myself."

There was another awkward silence. Jane looked deep into the man. His black eyes, like glossy marbles, refused to retreat again. Anyone else might be taken in by his sincerity, his false charm, but not Jane. With what had happened to him, he was too calm, too sure of himself.

Taryn broke the tension. "Why don't I go fix us some coffee. Gary?"

"That would be lovely, thank you."

Lovely? Too affected. What apparently lower-middle class man used that word? Taryn left the room, and Jane stared him down.

"Any more questions?"

"Lots."

"The third degree, heh? You still don't believe who I am?"

"Oh, I know who you are, all right." This son-of-a-bitch couldn't fool her.

"You say that as if I'm hiding something."

"Aren't you? Never mind, I know your answer. You see, I had you checked out, as you've already deduced, and there is no trace of Gary Walters prior to four months ago. I find that pretty odd, don't you?"

He just smiled at her.

Jane edged forward on the couch. She had to intercede and get her daughter far away from this madman. She pointed her finger and said, "Yes, I know who you are. I also know what you've done, and what you're planning, so don't bullshit me. You don't know who you're dealing with."

Garrison Miller edged forward to meet her look. "I tried to be polite. I tried to be social. Obviously, you're not willing to meet me halfway, doctor." He stared at her without blinking.

"Now that Taryn is out of the room, let's get one thing straight. Your daughter loves me, and that's all that matters. There's nothing you can say or do to stop us."

The tactic worked. She'd inflamed his ire, and he showed his true colors. "Then you really don't know who I am." She stared into his cavernous eyes. "Watch out, Mr. Miller. If anyone can stop you, I can."

"Miller?" he laughed, then stood. "I thought you were smarter than that, doc."

Jane stood up to face him. "Heed this warning, Mr. Miller: If you continue seeing my daughter, you're digging your own grave. And trust me, I will be the one shoveling the dirt back into it in the end."

"Hah! You don't know how wrong you are."

"Get out! And don't ever set foot back in my house again. Understand?"

Garrison Miller walked to the front door. As he opened it to leave, he turned back and said, "The question is do *you* understand?"

Jane closed the door and felt the adrenalin racing through her veins. She walked to the bar and poured some Scotch into a glass. She downed half the drink, wondering whether he would take her warning seriously.

Taryn walked back in a moment later with a tray of coffee and donuts, a smile on her face. The smile left when she saw Jane alone, an almost empty glass in her trembling hand. "Where's Gary?"

"Mr. Miller left, Taryn. And he won't be coming back."

"YOU OLD BITCH! HOW COULD YOU DO THAT TO ME?"

"I did what any mother would do, Taryn. Can't you see that? Can't you see he's not who he says he is?"

She trembled in rage. "Can't you see who *you* are? You're jealous of my happiness. Just because you can't have a real relationship with Sam, you're trying to ..."

"Shut up and sit down!" Jane ordered. She had to make her daughter think logically. "God, sometimes you're so thickheaded."

The teenager refused. She stood there in defiance, her arms crossed in a stubborn manner and her weight shifted onto one foot, waiting.

"For the last time, listen to me. Gary Walters is really Garrison Miller."

Taryn ran to the front hallway. "I don't believe it. I love him. And you can't keep us apart. I'd rather be with him than with you." She grabbed her jacket from the closet and reached for the door.

"Taryn!"

"Goodbye mother. Thanks for nothing!"

"STOP RIGHT THERE!" Jane couldn't believe she was going to say it, but she did. "As of this moment you're under house arrest."

"WHAT?" the teenager screamed, turning on her heels, a look of disbelief on her tear-streaked face. "YOU CAN'T GROUND ME LIKE A TWELVE-YEAR OLD!"

"I'm sorry, I really am, but I have no other choice. I love you too much to let you go out that door and get yourself killed."

"And if I do? I have the legal right to make my own decisions, you know. I'm over eighteen. Or have you forgotten that?"

Jane had never wanted to issue the threat, but her daughter's life was at stake. Her head was spinning from the confrontation and the Scotch. "If you leave, then I have no recourse but to stop paying for your college education. Believe me, Taryn, it's a promise I intend to keep forever if you walk out that door."

"I'll take you to court."

"And I'll win!"

"Then, I'll go to my father."

"Get real, Taryn. You've never even met Peter Gold. I'm sorry, but I assure you he doesn't want to meet you now, let alone pay for your college education." Having said those hurtful words to her child, Jane had to hold back her tears.

Taryn burst out crying and ran up the stairs to her bedroom.

Jane felt relieved, although it hurt to have to remind Taryn of her father's lack of interest in her. At the landing at the top of the stairs, she saw her daughter whip her body around. She had a look of rage in her eyes.

"I really hate you," she seethed. "Each and every day I've come to hate you more and more." She turned and stormed into her room, slamming the door behind her.

Jane felt flush. She felt faint. It was finally out. Her child hated her, perhaps justifiably. Where had she been the last year and a half, during Taryn's senior year of high school and the beginning of college? At a time of excitement and uncertainty, she was distant, out of reach. She had put motherhood on hold. No - she had put their relationship on hold. No - ignored it. No - abused it. How could she have messed up so badly? All she had wanted to do was prove to Taryn that Gary Walters was really Garrison Miller. Instead, she ended up driving her daughter farther away from her, and, still possibly, into his arms and into his world.

What now?

CHAPTER FIVE

Saturday, November 5th
Three days before Election Day

President Charles Price arose after only a few hours of light, fitful sleep. All through the night his rest was besieged by critical problems of state. American troops were needed to assist Israel which was tottering under the internal disruption of Moslem insurgency. Iraq and its neighbors had already cut off the critical supplies of oil on which the United States was still heavily dependent. Consequently, oil prices had skyrocketed to its highest levels in history and many poor people were going to freeze to death this winter. The nation itself would strongly oppose sending anymore American troops abroad when they were still needed at home to quell what had become a widespread racial/class conflict. Each day brought a new crisis. Any misstep by the president would surely be punished by loss of the election.

President Price walked from his bedroom on the second

floor of the White House into the Oval Sitting Room and out onto the Truman Balcony. Although it was cold outside, the early morning air always helped him think more clearly.

After swimming his customary twenty minutes in the White House pool, the President dressed and walked back upstairs to the Oval Office. Rejuvenated, he paced back and forth along the eagle of the U.S. seal woven into the thick, blue presidential rug. He had to act as Commander-in-Chief until all this ended, not presidential candidate. It was Saturday, and there was still another debate scheduled for the following evening. Fearing only questions on all the killing, and more humiliation, the President walked behind the Buchanan desk. He looked out at the Rose Garden and decided that the only thing he could do was cancel the last debate. He was sure Sam Howard would understand. And if he didn't, it didn't matter; the people would understand.

President Price sat down and turned on his telecomp. He asked his secretary to get Senator Howard on the line. With what he was about to do, Charles Price accepted his fate: He was going to be a one-term president.

Sam received the call (via his office) at his Fairfax, Virginia home. He was alone in his bedroom readying himself for today's trips. "Yes, Mr. President, what can I do for you?"

"This is a very grave situation we're in, senator."

"Yes, sir, I agree."

"A very grave situation. I have done all I can legally do to protect our citizens. I'm sure you understand that as president I have to represent the people first before I can represent myself to them. In all good consciousness, I cannot work on my campaign right now. My staff will continue, but I cannot personally participate."

"I'm sorry to hear that, Mr. President."

"Yes, I'm sure you are." A second of uncomfortable silence was followed by, "I'm sorry, senator, that was wrong of me. Please accept my apologies."

"I want you to know, sir, that I feel for you at this time. May I suggest we cancel our debate tomorrow night. It might look insensitive, for lack of a better description, if we were to prioritize that now. I know you have more urgent matters on your hands."

"Thank you, Sam."

"And I will instruct my staff to let the press know that we agreed on this together."

"I do appreciate that, sir," the president told his opponent. "Good day, and, I mean this, good luck."

"Thank you, Mr. President. Good luck to you, too." Sam disconnected the call. He stretched out on his king-size bed, thinking about the country's unrest and the election, just a few days away. Although he was still behind in the polls, it was obvious the tide was shifting. There was a real possibility he was going to become president. The feeling was daunting, and at the same time exhilarating. He held out his hand in front of him and stared at it. It remained steady.

The fighting was non-stop and vicious. Only a few African churches remained standing throughout rural America. There was no place to pray, no place to mourn their dead, no place to seek solace with their Lord. The white man had struck at the core of their being. He was ruthless and cruel and relentless.

People were starving and had no choice but to take to the streets in search of food and medical assistance. Money was useless. Most stores and banks remained closed. Whites were fleeing the cities, and the minorities were fleeing the white suburbs. Nothing could turn it around. Like the cancer it was, it kept growing. Everyone who had a reason to hate was out searching for the cause of their hatred. Anyone with a grudge knew they could kill their adversary with impunity. With their constitutional right to bear arms, they felt invincible, free to commit offenses in the guise of defense.

Revenge was sweet!

God bless America!

The National Guard, the Army, and the Marines, as well as the FBI and state and local police forces, were on twenty-four-hour a day duty. As the numbers of civilian casualties rose faster than anyone could count, the number of the country's peace keepers, the men and women in uniform, rose just as quickly. Nothing, not even those trained to tide such unrest, could stop this tidal wave of resentment. The poor and underprivileged wanted their dreams realized immediately and at any cost. The American class system had to end once and for all. Only there was a class of people refusing to give up what was theirs: A class and race willing to fight to keep their exclusive access to the American Dream from being shared.

America was drowning in its own selfishness and greed.

In Miami, Florida, seven young African men captured the Hallmark store across the street from Temple Emmanuel, the city's newest and largest Jewish house of worship, quietly killing the shop owner and the three customers inside. With almost all of rural and suburban America's African churches in ruins, it was time for payback.

An eye for an eye ...

Like with the Muslim people in Israel, the word of the Lord drove them. They locked the door, turned out the lights and put up the 'Closed' sign, and prepared for their moment of glory and their subsequent escape.

At 11:30, after Saturday morning services and 'kiddush' ended, the congregants began making their way outside. It was sunny and warm, a perfect God-given day. The seven African men, crouched by the front window of the card shop, looked at each other with nervous anticipation on their faces. "Ready to make history?" one of them asked, excited, yet scared at what they were about to commit.

"Make it happen, Jamal. Kill those fuckin' Jews!" another one said.

The young man shook with the knowledge that hundreds of people's lives were now in his hands. It was his destiny, he reasoned. What he was about to do was destined to happen, they had told him when they gave him this assignment. These 'Hymies' had devised the master plan to destroy their people. It was time to make them pay with their own blood.

"Now, Jamal, go, go, go!" the leader yelled when he saw the worshipers leaving the modern synagogue.

The man with the sonic detonator in his shaking hands was the newest member of the 'The Angry Africans' gang. It was his initiation. And it was justifiable. Without another thought or hesitation, he pushed the red button.

Congress Avenue lit up like the Fourth of July: Fire, concrete, blood, and bone sky-rocketed into the infinite blue above. Everything that had been there a moment earlier was gone, as God's home, along with the souls of two-hundred and twenty-six men, women, and children, soared up to Heaven by way of Hell.

Like in every major city in America, there was a large Jewish population in Miami. Within hours, a backlash of hatred exploded throughout south Florida. The Africans would rue the day they came after God's children.

... and a tooth for a tooth!

* * * * *

Moses stood by the side of her bed crying. He kissed her on her lips, then took one more look at her before leaving the room. He remembered the day she was born, and how kissing her for the first time had made him feel. She was all he ever wanted in life. Now, he had kissed her for the last time, and it was the worst possible feeling. All he wanted from life was to join her in death.

As he walked back to his wife's room, he asked himself and his God, "WHY ME?" He looked around in the other rooms and felt guilty for forgetting that he was not the only person grieving right now. Tens of thousands of others around the country were experiencing the same loss, the same pain. He had to focus on what to do. The fighting around the country was out of control, and the reports were that white fatalities were fewer than half of his people's. The Africans, the Latinos, and the poor whites who had joined his cause were being slaughtered. White males were running wild, killing any enemy they could find, anyone who was recognizably different. Although his people had made their point, the white point had been shoved down their throats. "How could things have gotten so out of hand, gone so wrong?" He had to do something.

Moses decided to go to church. He walked up to the four men who accompanied him everywhere and told them. He put on his overcoat as a doctor stepped out of Jessie's room. "Dr. McBride, your wife just awoke from her coma."

He hurried into the room. Jessie McBride, still covered in white gauze, lay there with her eyes half open. Moses felt more vulnerable than ever before. Tears filled his eyes, and a tightness gripped his heart. "Hello there, my sweet," he whispered on bended knee, staring into her eyes. It took everything in his power not to cry. He had to stay strong for Jessie.

"Hi preacher man."

It was a raspy voice, a voice hardly recognizable to him. "Don't try to be a hero, Jessie. If you're hurting, tell me, and I'll tell them to give you something."

"They won't let me see DaNell."

Hearing his daughter's name flooded Moses's mind with unbearable pain and guilt. "DaNell's been hurt, Jess. It's too soon to move either of you."

A hushed stillness preceded her whisper. "Telecomp. Lemme see her on telecomp."

Moses closed his eyes. She was too delicate to know. He said nothing, and that, along with the look on his face, spoke the truth more surely than words.

"Oh, Moses, NO-O-O! NO-O-OO!" Jessie McBride cried. She thrashed her body, but each move proved too painful. Her body lay still, except for the racking throbs she couldn't hold back. The nurse took her bandaged hand to console her, and the doctor administered a sedative to her IV. "Our baby. They killed our baby!"

Moses joined in her mourning.

"Lord," she tried to scream, but it came out sounding glottal, "take me now, take me to DaNell! AAAHHHH!"

"Jessie, please!" he begged her.

She cried some more, and Moses cried for her, for DaNell, for everyone.

"She was so beautiful, Moses, so talented and smart. She could have done so much, accomplished so much. Oh, Moses, why?"

"I don't know, Jessie, I have no answers. Maybe some day all this will make sense. Until then, I promise you, I won't let her death go unpunished. No matter what it takes, no matter how long it takes, they will pay!"

She was drifting back into sleep. "Please, Moses ... do

the right thing."

The right thing? He stood there and wondered, What did Jessie mean by 'the right thing'? Revenge for DaNell? Or ending the fighting and the suffering? "Jessie, what do I do?"

She was asleep again.

The doctor spoke to Moses about his wife's condition, the treatments, and the prognosis. There wasn't much hope.

Unable to do anything there, Moses left Harlem Hospital. 123rd Street was literally wiped off the map, as were all the surrounding streets. What had made it worse was that the African people were taking out their vengeance on each other and robbing the shops that were the lifeblood of their existence. But they saw no other choice. They needed food, clothing, whatever it took to survive. All that the people of Harlem had left was their religion. Every day they made their way to the First Abyssinian Baptist Church on 123rd Street, praying for their Lord to lead them to salvation. Most were homeless. Many of the children were orphaned. They had nothing, except their prayers for a miracle.

Miracles? There were no such things as miracles. Moses McBride had lost his belief in his Lord. As a man of the cloth, this had been unimaginable in the past. But, now, how could he believe any longer? He walked toward his church, with four of his followers who had the honor of protecting him, and looked around at the deathly scene. Chaos and destruction were everywhere to be seen. Moses knew he should try to stop it before it got any worse. It was time to cut their losses. But, surrendering, showing submission, would bring on even greater racism, more economic despair, resulting in bondage to rich, white America. Unless the African people won this civil action, the white man's uncivil action against them would continue unabated. Normally, Moses would talk to his Lord; it always made him think more clearly and more logically. But, now, he no longer believed in a savior. It was now up to the African people to save themselves. There was nothing he could do for them.

All of a sudden, an explosion lit up the sky. The sound was deafening as the First Abyssinian Baptist Church blew up before his eyes. Moses McBride felt the shock wave, first physical, then emotional. He fell to his knees and froze in horror and disbelief as he stared at what had been one of the last few buildings standing on 123rd Street. He watched as a blinding fireball of orange-red light burst up toward Heaven. Moses followed it with his eyes. They began tearing, as if he'd just looked directly into the sun.

Moses looked back down and saw God's home fall into the bowels of Hell. Rage consumed him, replacing any feelings left inside. His Lord had abandoned not only him, but his people as well.

The crowds got bigger at each HOPE City Jane, Sam, and Bill visited. The candidate had become a whirlwind, a take charge leader in this time of confusion and anarchy. The beleaguered and the oppressed believed their savior had come in the form of Sam Howard, and that he would ultimately win and save them. He left Chicago after lunch feeling confident about Tuesday.

There were more than two-thousand followers waiting for him at what was once the St. Louis HOPE City. Only a few buildings remained standing. It looked like the aftermath of a nuclear attack. The smell of charred wood and burnt gasoline was still in the air. And on the ground, everywhere, was blackened - everything.

"Sam, we love you!" "God bless you, Sam."

"Thank you." He waved and tried to smile.

It took another five minutes before the Central High

Marching Band stopped playing the rallying songs of victory and making a surreal scenario even more surreal with its joviality and celebration. Framed between the Corinthian columns at the entranceway to the St. Louis HOPE City, Sam stood tall and upright behind the mass of microphones. The sun shone behind him, and its rays seemed to emanate outward from his body. He appeared Herculean to the crowd. No, Jane thought - Godlike. She looked around at everyone's hopeful faces. It was amazing. Everyone was transfixed, as if Sam had come there to give them new lives. The TC cameras were still, the photographers ceased jostling for position, and, for a moment, there was peace and quiet. After a few seconds of silence, a silence that was almost religious in its anticipation, Jane pointed to her nose, the sign for Sam to start. Their eyes met, and he began his speech on cue.

Ten minutes into his speech, Sam had the crowd mesmerized. After telling these suffering people what he was going to do for them now, he reiterated his plans for changing America. He spoke about the Howard Crime Bill and his Education Reinvention Bill, and everyone listening was in an enthusiastic frenzy. Anything Sam Howard proposed, they would try.

"But, there is more that has to be done. Just a few ideas cannot bring about change. We have to change everything if anything is to work. I've told you how I will address crime and education. Now, I would like you to hear my plans regarding unemployment and job creation."

There was a thunderous applause. Jobs! It was what everyone needed. Yes, take care of our security and plan for our children's future, but then help us earn enough money to be a family again.

"We must all work. We must all accept responsibility as

contributing members of society. Without a collective contribution, society collapses. Therefore, I propose the Federal Jobs Program.

"Every American should have a job, and if that means America has to create them, then that is America's responsibility. The money saved in the long term will more than pay off the cost in the short term. Logically, if more people are working, more taxes will be paid to the government to run efficiently and profitably. The less government has to pay in entitlements and benefits to take care of its people, the more money it will have to pay off its debt to the world, making America more self-reliant and stronger."

Sam spent the next fifteen minutes outlining his plans for retraining the unemployed. When he was done, he summarized his feelings and plans with his new mantra: "Yes, my friends, working together, we *will* have a safer, richer, and happier society." Sam conveyed his commitment to accomplish these goals by always using the word 'will' rather than 'can'. Because of that, Sam's enthusiasm was contagious. They believed in him. Sam Howard - for a safer, richer, and happier society.

The crowd of joyous converts to the Howard optimism chanted his name, raised their placards, and danced among the ruins of the past. The present and the future were all that mattered. Sam Hopward wanted them, and they wanted him. As did Jane, who cheered along with equal fervor.

On the return trip to Washington, Jane sat alone at the back of Sam's jet, working. Her videophone rang. She flipped it open and Paco appeared on the screen in her hand. "From Senator Rawlings' contacts with the Mossad, Jane, the same type of bombs was used in Jerusalem as in the HOPE Cities: C-4 and cordite. Also, my friend at Immigration told me that Michael Salaman, the cameraman who accused the President on TC of being behind the HOPE Cities explosions, is actually Mustafa Al-Salaam from Baghdad. He entered the country six years ago."

Same explosive in HOPE as in Israel. Verbal assault on the President by an Arab. What's the connection? Jane asked herself. Is there one?

"The Secret Service arrested him, but, after some lengthy questioning, they concluded he wasn't a threat to the President. He was bailed a few hours later and released for a future court date."

"And Harry Morton, Paul Baker's chauffeur?"

"Hassad Muhammed."

"Another Arab?"

"Uh-huh. He also emigrated six years ago from Baghdad."

"That makes two Arab connections in America along with the bombings of those mosques in Jerusalem."

"If they had been synagogues I could understand it," Paco said. "There'd be a connection: Arab terrorism against America and Israel. But mosques?"

They had no answers, just more questions. After some talk about it, Jane thanked him and closed the videophone. She played it out in her mind. All twelve HOPE Cities blow up, two Iraqis try to damage the President's reelection bid, mass rioting erupts, and the same type of bombs destroy the mosques in Jerusalem. A full circle, one might say. But, how does that circle connect? How does it all tie in? Could Iraq have blown up those mosques to make it look like Israel was behind the HOPE bombings? Jane asked herself. Are Garrison Miller and the PWA part of it? The possibilities seemed endless. And they were getting more and more frightening. She had to talk to Sam about it.

Jane got up and walked to the front of the jet and sat across from him. Before they left Houston, Sam had returned Moses

McBride's call. They had scheduled a meeting for the following afternoon at the Martiń Luther King, Jr. Community College in Harlem.

"Have Paco invite the press and the media on the q.t. Any publicity beforehand could put the meeting in jeopardy," he told her as she sat down. "I don't want anyone, especially Miller and the PWA, knowing about it until it's broadcast."

The mention of Garrison Miller was an unwelcome reminder of Jane's personal problems. She forced her mind to concentrate on what Sam was telling her.

"Have him stress the importance of secrecy to them. If America is to come out of this conflict on its two feet, we can't have our enemies knowing our plans and disrupting them. Whoever that enemy is."

Jane looked out the window at the clouds the plane was nestling on and thought about who that enemy might be.

"Something's on your mind," Sam said.

It was too crazy a scenario. Nevertheless, she had to get it out of her hands and into his. "I've been doing some investigating, Sam, and I found out that Michael Salaman, the man who disrupted Price's TC speech is really Mustafa Al-Saalam from Baghdad. And the press secretary's chauffeur, Harry Morton, entered this country as Hassad Muhammed."

Sam sat there for a few seconds and thought about it. "The possibility that Iraq is behind the HOPE bombings, as well as the mosque bombings in Israel, is far-fetched, Jane. Why would they risk worldwide sanctions again. What does that accomplish for them?"

"Didn't Iran do the same thing to Jimmy Carter in 1980? They kidnapped dozens of Americans, and that act swayed the election. Because of what they did, they forced out Carter, and Reagan won the White House. Just what Iran wanted: A president promising to give the country everything it wanted and remove all restraints on business. Iran knew it couldn't last. Sooner or later, the American people would have to pay for this rich man's Utopia, and the masses would rebel."

"So, what you're saying is Iran took those hostages just to put Reagan in office, knowing his ideas would eventually drive America into social and financial chaos."

And it almost succeeded. The country was sinking in a morass of debt and recession before the Clinton administration applied corrective action. "Iraq has obviously learned well from the past. Maybe that's what they're trying to do now. Make Price the sacrificial lamb."

"And put me in office so I can ruin the country like Reagan did, as you say? I sure hope that's not what they're thinking." Sam's voice was serious, but it had a mocking undertone to it.

Maybe she was wrong. With Carter and Reagan it made sense. It was the perfect revenge. But, with Sam in office, it wouldn't be revenge. Sam wouldn't ruin society. He'd improve it. "Maybe the opposite is true. Maybe they finally realize that the way America goes, so goes the rest of the world. Maybe this is their way of making sure the right man gets into office this time."

"That's a lot of maybes." He stared at her, as if trying to read her mind. "I'll look into it. Now, lets forget about all that and talk about us."

Jane felt a rush of pleasure and surprise. Us? The word made her forget. And remember.

"In a few days this whole affair will be over. Let's sneak out to the cabin one last time. Just us. No bodyguards, no agents."

Jane's psychological antennae rose. "Sam, believe me, I would love nothing more. But, we stopped going out there when you announced your candidacy for president. You said that an affair or whatever wouldn't look proper, that a conservative America would construe it as cheap and tawdry, and I accepted that. I can't believe you want to do this now and jeopardize everything. That means we've wasted fourteen months. How do you think that makes me feel?"

He smiled. "Just think how I'm going to make you feel tonight." Before she could rebuff him, he said, "Meet me at the cabin at nine o'clock." He picked up some papers and returned his attention to his work.

Jane walked back to her seat at the rear of the jet. With all the nervous anticipation of a first date, she was distracted from that moment on. It was all she could think about. That, and why, after fourteen long and frustrating months, and with just three days to go, Sam was willing to risk it all.

Although he was still ahead in the polls, due to so many people's fear of Sam Howard helping the Africans move up in class, President Charles Price's lead was beginning to look tenuous. He had done all he could, all that was possible and legal, and the fighting was still raging on in more than a hundred American Cities. Besides that, Sam Howard's wild ideas were the talk of the country. Everyone was jumping on the bandwagon, with everyone asking the same question: 'Can it work?'

They all had the same answer: 'It has to work!'

President Price sat in the situation room of the White House with his National Security Adviser, the director of the CIA, the Joint Chiefs of Staff, the Secretary of Defense, the Secretary of State, the director of the FBI, the secretary of Homeland Security, and the President's legal and political advisers. It was their daily meeting since the HOPE bombings and the civil unrest that had besieged the country. They still didn't know who was behind the bombings, or how to stop the anarchy. Well-armed, well-organized followers of Moses McBride contended for control of every major city in the United States. In opposition, the fifty state leaders of the People for a White America, under the guidance and rule of their grand marshal, Garrison Miller, were still successfully recruiting angry mobs into their ranks. The suburbs and the rural areas belonged to them and the many other white supremacist groups scouring the country. Like a warm front hitting a cold front, the two had clashed and a hurricane of hatred had flooded the country.

"Tell me, Jack, anything new on the Iraqi connection?" President Price asked CIA director Jackson Stiles.

"Only that we believe the two have returned to Baghdad. As far as we know, no one else seems to be involved." The heavy middle-aged director was smoking a cigar that befitted his presence.

"And your conclusions are?"

"Coincidence."

"I don't believe in coincidence!" the President said, emphasizing each word slowly. "Damnit, Jack, Intelligence should have had some answers by now."

"There is no evidence, no compelling reason to tie in the two Iraqis with the HOPE Cities bombings, although their timely presence and disappearance lead us to believe it is Iraqi sponsored. However, no known terrorist group has claimed responsibility, which means whoever is behind this is keeping things under wraps so they can strike again."

Charles Price was fuming. "The only way to end this conflict, and turn around my declining poll numbers by Election Day," he said, "is to arrest McBride."

The President's many advisers spoke out of turn and told him he should lay off America's African leader.

"Mr. President," General Leland Hollinger, the barrel-chested, gray-haired chairman of the joint chiefs, spoke up, "you can't arrest McBride. If he's taken prisoner, the fighting and the killing will escalate." Everyone reacted to the statement, and the elderly general continued. "He's not advocating murder, just organization and defense of his people's own neighborhoods."

"It's the same thing!" the President yelled, banging his fist on the table. "If he can organize them, he can unorganize them. He has the power to stop this insanity."

There was silence again as they contemplated the power of the presidency and how Price might use it.

White House legal counsel James Karp, a Dartmouth classmate of the President's, and best friends since their boyhood days in Nashua, New Hampshire, raised his left hand. The president nodded to him to speak. "If you arrest McBride, you must also arrest Miller. Fair is fair, if I may be simplistic."

"No can do," Director Harvey Coyles of the FBI, a lanky man, with a red bulbous nose, said. "We can't take in Miller after what happened last time. He has an air-tight alibi, and nothing ties him in with the HOPE bombings."

"But, everything ties him in with everything else. The PWA is his organization."

"Again, Mr. President," Director Coyles said as he filled his pipe, "what proof do we have? If we had any, we would have arrested Miller long ago." The fire on the match flared as he puffed away on his Chesterfield. Smoke filled the air above the men's heads, joining the CIA director's cigar smoke from the opposite end of the conference table.

"And as long as he's dating Jane Weisser's daughter," Counselor Karp added, "any harassment of Gary Walters can be, and will most likely be, interpreted politically."

President Price rubbed his tired eyes. He was between the proverbial rock and hard place. Legally, everyone knew, he couldn't arrest either of these leaders. But he had to do something. The Commander-in-Chief put his eyeglasses back on and looked at his staff. "For the last few days I have been trying to meet with Moses McBride, only he has ignored my requests, and then my demands, that we sit down and talk. There must be something, Jim, something in the Constitution, in the wording of our laws, that will legally find him in contempt. My God, if I don't stop this, more and more innocent people are going to die. And if I don't stop it, I will definitely lose the presidency, which means all of you will lose your jobs!" He leaned his head against the cold leather of the Executive chair. Reviewing the conflicting advice, he contemplated the possibilities and their probable outcomes. No one dared utter a sound. A moment later, he looked at William Davis, his secretary of Homeland Security. "Well, Bill, what have you got to say?"

The former Senator from Iowa cleared his throat. "We have all law enforcement personnel in every state on full-time duty. Their presence has quieted many of the most disruptive areas of the country. But there is only so much we can do. What we need are more men and women in uniform to fend off this madness. However, unless my department gets more funding to pay for this, I'm afraid the inmates have taken over the asylum."

It was not what the President wanted to hear. He closed his eyes to think about it all. A few moments later, he opened them and saw everyone waiting for a decision. "Jack, I want Intelligence on top of this Iraqi connection day and night until you're sure they are or aren't involved. Understand?"

Jackson Stiles nodded his assent.

"Now," the President finished. "There are just three days until this election, and I still don't know who's behind all this. I have to do something! Anything that will make me look like I haven't lost control." Out of desperation, the President of the

United States leaned forward and issued the directive. "Bring me McBride!"

Jane returned to her Georgetown home on Foxhall Road and noticed the blue Buick, with the two men inside, parked down the street. "Damnit! Who are they? And why are they watching me?" She turned away and unlocked the front door. Right now, she had to see Taryn. She had to make sure she was still home.

Jane hung up her coat and picked up the mail on the sideboard. She went upstairs and knocked on Taryn's door. "Taryn, are you in there?"

"What do you think?"

It hurt that she didn't trust her, but until that man was out of her life, how could she? She went downstairs to her study and called Paco to tell him about tomorrow's meeting in New York with Moses McBride. She then attempted to do some work, only it didn't help. First Taryn, then Sam occupied all her thoughts.

Jane turned off the telecomp and went into the living room to pour herself a Scotch. As she drank it, she weighed her dilemma. She knew she should stay home, to be there in case Taryn wanted to talk. From the tone of her voice a moment ago she knew that scenario was highly unlikely. She also wanted to go out to the cabin, not to find out his intentions, but because she needed his comfort. More than anything right now, she needed to feel loved.

After berating her selfish needs and vacillating whether or not to go, Jane told Taryn through her door that she would be back in the morning. "I'll be calling every few hours to make sure you're home. Don't ruin your future, Taryn. I meant what I said."

Jane left the house and looked at the blue Buick parked

down the street. She took a deep breath, pulled out of her driveway, and turned in their direction so she could drive past the car and get a better look at the men inside.

They were looking straight ahead, as if she wasn't the object of their interest.

Jane stared for the briefest of seconds. They didn't look sinister, or threatening, or even very interesting. But, what were they doing sitting in a parked car?

She thought about it until she arrived at Sam's secluded retreat at the end of a mile-long dirt road in Burtonsville, Maryland, just outside Laurel. There, snuggled in the middle of the woods, was their special place. They were the only two who knew of their life out there. Others who knew of the cabin's existence thought a loner by the name of Harrington lived there from time to time. No one ever saw them come or go. They never used Sam's hideaway underneath the Capitol building, the private rooms used by senators for reflection and contemplation and other things. That would have been obvious. Cheap. They were a couple, quietly committed to each other. The cabin made them feel that way.

Jane saw Sam's car parked out front. He was already there. That was unusual, she thought to herself. In the past, she had always been the first to arrive and the last to leave. It was probably just anxiousness on his part. Jane walked in, feeling just as anxious.

With her mother away for the evening, Taryn had called Gary Walters to ask him to spend the night. He told her about the warning to never step foot into her house again, and Taryn guaranteed him that 'the bitch lady' wouldn't be home till morning. If her mother could go out and have 'fun,' then she could stay home and have hers.

For the last half hour or so they had been drinking and making love around the living room: On the sofa, the coffee table, every chair, in every imaginable position. Taryn's sexual gymnastics in her mother's house expressed her growing contempt for her mother as much as any sexual desire for her partner. Now, they were doing it on the carpet in front of the fireplace.

The phone rang, and Taryn got up from the floor to answer it. "Oh, hi Cass. Sorry, she's out for the evening. She said she'd be back in the morning. Can I take a message?" Taryn listened. "Okay. See ya." She returned to her position beneath Gary.

"Who was that?"

"My mother's AA."

"You're mother's in Alcoholics Anonymous?"

"No, silly. That was my mother's administrative assistant. Although from the way my mother puts it away, she probably should be in AA." She grabbed her drink from the coffee table and drank the rest of it.

"From the way you put it away, I'd say 'like mother, like daughter'."

Taryn looked at him, then at her glass. Her mother had expressed the same thought to her. Was she like her mother? "Never mind that. Let's get back to what we were doing." She put the glass back on the table, and they resumed their lovemaking.

He took control and brought her back to a world of pleasure where there were no worries. To the point of no return. She didn't want to return. Reality was just too painful.

"Oh, God, Gary!" Taryn cried out. He was forceful, dominant, and he made her moan again. And again. God, she loved it. She loved how turned on he was by her and how much he wanted her. It felt so good to feel wanted. To be the center of someone's life. To be needed.

Taryn lay there exhausted, staring up at him. His eyes were closed and he was still plunging himself into her. Faster and harder. It hurt, yet it felt so good. It felt so good to feel so alive.

She wondered if he knew she loved him.

She was obviously in love with him. She had said she believed in his innocence, and that made him feel good. In control. The last person to love him was his father, then 'those niggers' killed him. They killed his father's love for him and took away his ability to ever love again.

His power over her excited him and he ejaculated, only he had no orgasm. No, that would have made him feel complete. He wouldn't be whole again until he killed Moses McBride. Anyway, he wasn't there to fuck Taryn. He was there to fuck Reverend McBride.

Taryn passed out underneath him from the pain and the pleasure, and all the liquor, and Garrison Miller had free reign of the Weisser house. Everything was coming to a climax. He laughed at his pun and got up.

Naked, he walked into Jane Weisser's study and thought: If I was Sam Howard, the only way to turn this election around would be to meet with Moses McBride and end this war. If Howard is planning to meet with McBride, that information might be in this room. Excited about what he might find in there, he saw he still had an erection. He smiled and followed it in.

It was the second time he'd been in there in the last two days. Last night, he'd only gotten a quick look-see before she'd ushered him and Taryn out. Now, he was free to see what he wanted. Free to take what he wanted.

The room was wood-paneled, with dark, ornate furniture.

In the middle of it was Jane Weisser's enormous desk. "Rich bitch! Damnit, why is it the Jews have all the money? Why is it they're so damn smart?" he asked himself, his hatred for the Jewish people rivaled only by his revulsion of the Africans. Miller quickly erased the emotion from his mind and sat in her big chair. He loathed everything she represented. He looked at her papers on top of the blotter. There was nothing that referred to any planned meeting in the next few days with McBride. He looked at her calendar - nothing. Her appointment book - nothing. Her desk drawers - nothing. "Shit! Now what?" Taryn could easily wake up, see he wasn't by her side, and go looking for him. He had to hurry or else she would catch him. If that happened, he would have to come up with some excuse why he was in there and risk proving her mother and Howard right.

Miller thought about it as he stared at the black screen of the Macintosh telecomp. It had to be in there. He got up, walked to the door, and closed it so Taryn wouldn't hear the 'ding' when he turned on the machine. He pushed the button marked 'Mac' and the wall screen lit up. 'Ding.'

'Enter your password' was the instruction on the screen. Miller thought about it. He typed in 'Jane.' 'Invalid password,' the message on the screen mocked him. He typed in 'Weisser,' and again the same message. "Fuck!" How many more wrong passwords would the telecomp allow him to type in before it shut down? He had to stop rushing and think clearly. Logically. If he were her, what would be the perfect password? He thought about her company, The Weisser Organization, but there were too many letters in the name to fit in the password box. Hmm, The Weisser Organization, T-W-O. He typed in TWO, hoping that would be the secret code that would gain him access to her files. Again, the screen flashed 'Invalid password.' "Shit! How much time do I have?" Miller stood up and walked back into the living room. Taryn was still asleep. She had really exhausted herself. She was going to be out for a while. He returned to the office to try again.

Because of his confrontation with her mother last night, there was no way in Hell she was going to allow Taryn to invite him to the inaugural ball. As president of the National African Caucus, Moses McBride would be there, he'd reasoned from the start. Now, he had to get to McBride some other way. Blowing up his apartment building hadn't done the trick, although the enormous pain he must have suffered losing his only child was intensely gratifying. Blowing up his church had only rid this world of a few more 'stinkin' niggers,' but not of Moses McBride. There had to be something in Jane Weisser's computer about Sam Howard meeting with him to end this war. There had to be. All logic pointed to it.

Inside the study, he sat back down behind the antique desk. "If not her damn company, how about her precious daughter?" he whispered to himself. He typed in 'TARYN'. To his relief, the telecomp accepted the password and the screen opened, displaying dozens of folder icons. He had to find out which folder held that information. He read the titles below each one, opening a few to no avail, until he came to the folder marked 'Campaign.' He clicked the icon, and it opened to show the documents inside. There were hundreds. Jesus Christ! It would take him all night to go through every one. Frustration was beginning to tighten his back and shoulder muscles, but he had to go on. Moses McBride's death was paramount to the PWA. It was the key to his meaning in life and to his vision for the future of America.

Miller noticed a document titled 'Schedule,' and he clicked it open. There were pages and pages, dating back more than a year. He clasped his hands together, and rested his mouth on his knuckles to think. He couldn't think of anything. He pointed the mouse to the menu bar and studied each heading for something that would give him an idea. Under, 'Edit,' he saw a command called 'Find/Change.' "Find, that's it!"

He typed in Moses McBride's name and the screen told him, 'Moses McBride not found.' How true, he thought. But, I will! He pushed the 'Okay' button and tried again. This time he typed in MM, in case she had used a shorthand code. It worked. On the screen in front of him was 'SH and MM. NY - Sun. 11/ 6 w/ press. QT.' He had found it. Sam Howard and Moses McBride were meeting tomorrow in New York, most likely to discuss ways to end the war. Garrison Miller leaned back in Jane Weisser's chair and smiled at his cleverness. It was up to him to make sure McBride and Howard made no progress. His war had to continue.

Without MM as their leader.

With MM dead!

"Gary? Where are you?" It was Taryn's voice, and it was getting closer. He had to think fast. As he reached down to the keyboard to shut off the machine, he remembered the 'ding' telecomps make when they're turned on or off. To cover up the sound, he pushed the 'off' button and yelled out at the same time, "I'm in here, Taryn." His voice masked the sound. The screen went blank, and he stood and turned around to face the wall of books behind the desk.

Taryn's heart ached nearly as much as her sexually beaten body. Gary's voice was coming from her mother's study. Why was he in there? What was he doing?

Why was she being so suspicious?

She knew why. Her mother's suspicions had naturally bred some in her own mind. Goddamn you, Mom! Couldn't you have at least gotten to know him? Taryn walked toward his voice, feeling the pain between her unsteady legs. The rough sex Gary liked to partake in was exciting, but it had its consequences. Usually for days. She pushed open the door and entered the room. "What are you doing in here?"

"I couldn't sleep, so I came in here to find something to read. Nothing's caught my eye yet." He turned away from her and put back the heavy tome he had taken down.

Taryn's heart returned to her chest. She walked up behind him and wrapped herself around his waist, resting her face on his muscular back. The feel of his skin against hers once again shot shivers of excitement throughout her body. "Come back to the living room, Gary. I'll put you to sleep."

Miller heard the seductiveness in her voice and felt her hand slide down between his legs. She gently took hold of his flaccid penis and stroked it. Jesus, not again, he thought. The girl just couldn't get enough. She had told him, when they first began making love, that she wasn't a virgin, but that she had considered herself one. The only other times she'd experienced sex were the year before when her boyfriend slipped it into her for a few seconds before 'shootin' his load,' and, then, a couple of months later, when a female friend of hers suggested they try it. She wasn't bisexual, she'd told him, but she had to try it like so many of the girls she knew were doing. That was her initiation into the world of sex, and it had been rather disappointing to say the least. No wonder she was so voracious, Miller thought. Sex was a new experience for her. Child! he berated her under his breath. Found a new toy and can't stop playing with it.

He turned around, and she led him back to the living room by pulling on his member, almost like a teacher leading a new student by the hand. It was embarrassing, immature.

Nauseating.

He would make her pay for it.

After rekindling the fire in the fireplace, they were at it again. Having gotten what he wanted, Garrison Miller pounded into the eighteen-year old girl with a vengeance, a hatred for all she and Jane Weisser and Sam Howard represented. Between moans and groans, she screamed from the forceful thrusts. He was hurting her and that made him feel good. Excited. His erection got harder as he thought about Moses McBride's assassination. The meeting with Sam Howard was the following day, and he still had to find out where in New York. It was to be a private meeting, open only to the press. That made sense. If word of it got out, there were people who would try to stop it from taking place. People like him. He laughed and shoved himself even harder into the girl.

Garrison Miller screamed in pleasure like he had never before done. Life sucked, but every once in a while when things went your way, it was truly ... orgasmic!

The twelve old men of Al-Qiyamah sat inside Sayyid Kassim's palatial home in Baghdad. After having viewed the rioting and destruction all around Israel, they were now watching the report about America's civil unrest on the satellite-fed multi-panel screen. Seventeen-thousand were already dead in the twelve HOPE Cities, and almost twenty-thousand were seriously injured. At least four-thousand others, they heard, had been murdered in the streets or in their homes, with tens of thousands more wounded.

Sayyid Kassim smiled at the ikwan, the brotherhood. Along with their western attire of slacks and sport shirts, the twelve old men of Al-Qiyamah wore their kaffiyah, the head cloth that had again become fashionable with the resurgence of Islamic pride. They spoke amongst themselves as they drank their gawha, a strong and bitter coffee. They reminisced about their sons, twelve boys murdered by America's trained killers. Multi-billionaires all - oil producers, date marketers, and tobacco manufacturers - they had one common goal.

They would make their sons' killers pay. In sha' Allah. God willing.

Sayyid Kassim, the leader of the group, stood, and the eleven other men followed. "My brothers, let us speak Bi'-smi'llahi'r-Rahmani'r-Rahim," and they collectively began reciting the Lord's Prayer. "Praise be to Allah, Lord of the Worlds, the Beneficent, the Merciful. Owner of the Day of Judgment, Thee we worship; Thee we ask for help. Show us the straight path, the path of those whom Thou hast favoured; Not of those who earn Thine anger nor of those who go astray."

They sat down, and Sayyid continued. "My brothers, I will now read from the glorious Quran. Surah VII. 'How many a township have we destroyed! As a raid by night, or while they slept at noon, our terror came unto them. And we rained a rain upon them. See now the nature of the consequence for evil-doers!'" He closed the holy book and said, "Praise be to Allah for our success. Allah akbar."

"Allah akbar!"

"Many years ago we took our oath of allegiance to Saddam Hussein and his brilliant plan to destroy the United States. Our operatives have eliminated the twelve HOPE Cities and their deaths are untraceable back to us. The lower classes are rioting and it has spread across the continent. Now the entire world will witness the death of America." The accomplices of Al-Qiyamah cheered the same sworn oath they had made when they began. "Death to America! Death to the infidels!" The billion dollars they had each invested in their clandestine revenge had been worth the long wait. Their children's lives would not be lost in vain. Al-Qiyamah - the Rising of the Dead!

The fathers stood and repeated their chant one more time for their great Allah to hear. "Death to America! Death to the infidels!"

A short while later, the eleven men left Sayyid's home for their own. Alone with his thoughts and memories, Sayyid walked to the wall safe and gently removed the Al-Qiyamah. He opened the delicate hand-written book. For what seemed like the thousandth time, he read the interactive blueprint for America's political death. Saddam Hussein had outlined every possible route to get them to where they now were. Everything was happening as he had told him it would. Sayyid Kassim thought about his closest friend and remembered back to the day when Saddam revealed his ingenious twenty-five year plot...

Inside the great dining hall of the presidential palace in Baghdad, President Saddam Hussein and Sayyid Kassim, his most trusted adviser and confidante, were eating muscouf: open fish cooked over fire, covered with sliced tomatoes and onions. A somber silence was in the air and it enveloped them like a shroud.

Saddam put his drink down and looked at Sayyid. America had left its mark on Saddam, and Sayyid could see it. Now all that the Iraqi leader wanted to do was strike back. To make America bleed.

"It is going to take a long time, my friend, and I probably will not be around to see its success, especially with George Bush and his sons determined to destroy me and my sons, all for the purpose of stealing our oil. However, a good president must prepare his country for the future. You are the one I have chosen to make our dream come true, Sayyid. You are going to turn the tables on them and covertly take political control of America."

Sayyid Kassim stroked his long, graying black beard. How?

he wondered. No one had ever been able to destroy the 'Great Satan' in the past. What made Saddam think he could in the future? He saw Saddam smile at him, then return to his plate of food. Sayyid knew not to ask questions. His friend would tell him everything in due time.

They finished their muscouf, and the President rose. He walked away from the table, and Sayyid followed him downstairs to his private 'war room.' There were no windows in the underground room. It was cold and impersonal. Dungeon-like. Saddam wiped a flake of fish from his black mustache and lit a cigar. He sat down and motioned Sayyid to do the same. He then opened the leather-bound book on the table. On the front page were the words 'AL-QIYAMAH.' The next page listed step one of the revenge, along with its many possible outcomes, followed by those outcomes' many possibilities, and so on. The interactive plot was in the President's handwriting, and no one but he, and now Sayyid Kassim, were privy to it.

"As you can see, I have planned for every possible coincidence, failure, or defeat. We can't afford to leave anything to chance." There were alternatives for every conceivable problem, all leading to the same result.

The Death of America!

Sayyid's mouth fell open, and Saddam laughed out loud. "Let me explain it to you from the beginning." The Iraqi president detailed each possible path they would have to take throughout the years. The massive plot was like a runaway train that couldn't be stopped. There were many tracks it could detour onto to keep it moving forward. Saddam spent the next two hours outlining and diagramming the intricate connections and bypasses. Nothing could derail Al-Qiyamah, he told him. And nothing would! "It can't fail, my brother. I promise you."

Sayyid Kassim had hoped to become president of Iraq one

day. With Al-Qiyamah, the rich oil man knew he would no longer be able to fulfill that dream. It didn't matter. This dream was bigger. This dream was more important.

"Any questions?"

Sayyid had only one. "Why have you chosen me? After all, this should be your glory, my President."

"The end result is what is important, not the glory. The political destruction of the United States is imperative to world peace. It is what is right, what we must do!"

"You haven't answered my question. Why me and not you?"

"We cannot involve my cabinet for security reasons. If it ever leads back to its political beginnings, it would put Iraq and all its people in extreme danger. Besides, Bush is going to make sure I'm dead long before our plot is concluded."

"But, you said it can't fail."

"It can't. Al-Qiyamah is foolproof. The only reason no country has ever attempted it before is because no one has ever had the vision, the courage, to do it. I have that vision! I have that courage!" Rolling the cigar in his mouth, President Hussein removed it and continued. "Because American Intelligence follows my every move, I cannot have anything to do with the plan from this moment on." He picked up the incriminating book and handed it to the new leader of Al-Qiyamah. "Sadly, it will be a private justice for you, my friend. But, the sentence of the criminal, I guarantee, will be very painful!"

Sayyid Kassim had no choice but to accept his fate.

The smile returned to the President's face. "We must begin step one immediately." He took out a list of names and biographies. "These are the eleven men who, along with you, will make up the Al-Qiyamah. Everyone else you use, and you will use many, must die after their part is done, so American Intelligence cannot trace it back to the twelve of you. Lead them, my brother. It is up to you to carry out our revenge. It is up to you to create the future. Allah akbar!"

"Allah akbar!"

The two friends looked deep into each other's eyes with a silent sworn promise.

To raise the dead!

Sayyid Kassim sat alone on the sofa in his living room and finished reminiscing. The Al-Qiyamah, open to the last few steps, lay on his lap. There were just two days until the American election. He laughed and held out his morning gawha in a toast to the past. "To you, Saddam Hussein," he said, wishing his friend and mentor could be there with him, enjoying their victory. "To your vision and your genius."

CHAPTER SIX

Jane awoke a little after midnight. The first thing she noticed was that she was still smiling. Although it had been fourteen frustrating months since they had last been intimate, it had definitely been worth the wait. She and Sam were still wild, hungry, voracious, ravenous, insatiable (she couldn't think of any more adjectives) animals in bed. More important, they were still in love with each other. The smile just wouldn't go away. She was happy she had come to the cabin; it had taken her mind off Taryn. She turned to her right to look at Sam, but he wasn't in bed. She listened and heard his voice coming from the combination living room, dining room, and kitchen.

Jane picked up Sam's large, white shirt, slipped it on, and got out of bed to join him, in case it had something to do with the campaign. As she walked into the great room, she thought she heard him say 'no one suspects' to whomever was on the phone. It stopped her cold, like an Arctic blast hitting her face. Sam looked at her from his seat behind his desk. There was no emotional change in his face, no expression of shock at being overheard. Just calmness. And a smile, like the smile he had on his face after they finished making love. Did she hear him right? She wasn't sure. 'No one suspects?'

Jane sat down on the sofa as Sam finished his conversation. When he hung up, he walked over and gave her a kiss on top of her head. "Who were you talking to?" she asked. Her mouth, she noticed, was dry. She picked up the almost empty glass of Johnny Walker she'd left on the coffee table and finished it.

"My son," he said as he sat down next to her.

"What did you mean by 'no one suspects?'" Jane took a cigarette from her pack of Merits, lit it, and blew out the lungful of courage. She had just broken the lines of trust between them, asking and accusing at the same time.

"Adam asked me whether there were any leads into who may have bombed the HOPE Cities. I said, 'Because of the enormity of the attack, everyone believes it's a group conspiracy. Therefore, there's no one suspect.'"

She looked at him and saw his expression change.

"Jesus, Jane, I thought you loved me. I can't believe ... Why on Earth ..." He couldn't finish the question.

"You've changed this past week, Sam. I no longer know you, and that scares me. The welfare of the people has always been your main concern. Now all you seem to care about is being president."

"THERE ARE ONLY A FEW DAYS LEFT, JANE! WHAT THE HELL DO YOU EXPECT ME TO CARE ABOUT RIGHT NOW?"

"No yelling, Sam. We've never raised our voices to each

other. Let's not start now. What I'm saying is you've developed this 'win at all costs' attitude."

Sam stared at her. "You say you love me, yet you don't trust me."

Jane didn't answer him. She didn't know what to think anymore. Just being there with Sam made her suspicious. Of what, she didn't know.

"I'm sorry you feel that way."

"So am I, Sam." He looked hurt, and she felt guilty about that.

"So, how do I go about regaining your trust?"

He was so sincere, his look so sweet. "Oh, Sam, I'm sorry. I don't know what to feel. This situation with Taryn and the campaign and the bombings has me questioning everything."

Sam kissed her and took her hand in his. "Let's go back to bed? We'll talk about it in the morning."

They made love again, at first tender and giving, then wild and frenzied, as if it were both the first and last time they would share their passion for each other.

When they finished, Sam closed his eyes and Jane lay in his arms.

"You do know, Jane, that if I become president, we can no longer use this cabin. No president can leave the White House without the Service in tow."

Was this their last time together? Jane felt a pain shoot through her. She thought about all the presidents who'd had their private liaisons, and it gave her cause for hope.

"I know I've asked you this many times, Jane, but I can't go on without you as my wife any longer. Being president without you in my life would be crippling to me. Please, Jane, marry me after I'm sworn in. I love you, I love Taryn, and you love the boys. What a family we'd have."

It sounded wonderful, but Jane felt that she couldn't be the First Lady. 'The Most Influential Woman in Washington,' as Time Magazine had labeled her, would generate unfair pressure, comparison, and criticism to Sam's presidency. Just look at the political history of the country: Rosalynn Carter, Nancy Reagan, Hillary Clinton. America has never been able to accept a strong first lady. And she was not one to be compliant. "You know the reasons why I can't accept, Sam. We'll just have to put our heads, and our bodies, together and figure out a way of sneaking me into the White House." She smiled at him seductively.

With just the light of the full moon shining in the room, Jane Weisser fell asleep on Sam Howard's chest. However, this time, she didn't fall asleep smiling. No - there was too much on her mind. There were the problems of the present …

… and as Sam had just reminded her, there were the problems of the future.

Standing before the dying embers still smoldering in the fireplace, a now-dressed Garrison Miller bent down and woke Taryn shortly after midnight. He told her it was late, that he had to leave. Who knew when her mother might return home? Like the child she was, she put up a stink. He kissed her full on the mouth and assured her they would continue this romantic evening soon.

He drove to Reagan National Airport, made a call, and, two hours later, exited New York's LaGuardia Airport. As he waited for a taxi, a professional-looking man in a black woolen overcoat and a hat pulled down over his eyes stood next to him. A moment later, the contact walked away, leaving behind a black leather overnight bag. Miller picked it up and got in the cab that had stopped for him.

When they crossed the East River into Manhattan, Miller

opened the bag between his feet. Inside were a name and an address, a Baretta handgun and silencer, and the essential clothes he would need to disguise himself.

At West End Avenue and W.71st Street, he told the cabbie to stop. He paid the Pakistani driver and walked three blocks to W.74th Street. Dressed in black jeans and boots, a gray turtleneck shirt, and a black leather jacket, the determined killer entered the old, brick building and rang the bell of apartment 3E.

"Yeah, who is it?" came the half-awake voice from the speaker a minute later.

"Miller, from editorial. I have some papers for you regarding the meeting."

"At three in the morning?"

Garrison Miller heard the disbelief in the man's tired voice. "Hey, you know our boss. He said it couldn't wait till morning. Something about a change in plans. Since it's confidential, it has to be signed for personally."

The buzzer shrieked, letting anyone within earshot know someone was entering the secure building. Miller looked around the lobby, saw no one, and took the stairs, rather than the elevator, up to the third floor. He couldn't afford any witnesses to his visit there. The fewer bodies he left behind, the safer.

At the third floor, the grand marshal of the PWA stood in front of the apartment of James Garafalo, the widely-read reporter covering the racial conflict for the New York Times. According to Miller's report, he lived alone. Miller knocked on the door. When it opened slightly, he slammed his way in and pointed the Baretta at the startled man's chest. "Listen carefully and you won't get hurt. Understand?" When the man didn't answer fast enough for him, Miller grabbed the man by the pajama lapels and pressed the gun to his throat. "Understand?"

His face turned as white as his nightclothes. "Y ... Y ... Yes."

"Good. I know Sam Howard's planning to meet with Moses McBride later today. It's your choice, Mr. Garafalo. Your life, or the place and time of that meeting."

The journalist was sweating …

"Don't play games, pal, and don't try to be a hero, or else your next byline will be in the obituaries."

… but he remained silent.

Miller kicked him in the groin, and he collapsed to the ground.

"So, it's going to be like this, is it?" He grabbed the man by his pajama shirt and forced him to stand back up. "Now, we'll try again. Where and what time is the meeting?"

James Garafalo kept the information, which was classified 'Top Secret,' to himself. Being the respected reporter he was, a Pulitzer Prize winner, it was all he could do.

There was silence for a moment, a stalemate, and Miller lowered his right arm. He pulled the trigger and watched the man collapse to the carpeted floor in a heap. "Keep your screams to yourself, my friend, or else."

James Garafalo bit his lower lip and fought against the intense pain of his shattered left kneecap. Blood was squirting upward and flowing over his leg, staining the hardwood floor around him a deep red. Fear and nausea overcame him and he vomited violently.

"Shall we try again? Or shall I shoot your other knee and make you a cripple?" He laughed as James Garafalo's eyes pleaded with him to do him no more harm. His tone then turned serious. "No more fucking around. Where are Sam Howard and Moses McBride meeting?"

"P … Please, a glass of water."

Miller looked down at the man. He walked into the small kitchenette and brought back a glassful from the tap. He also grabbed the salt shaker from the counter.

The reporter drank the water and placed the glass on the floor next to where he lay. Then his assailant opened the salt shaker and poured the contents onto his bloodied knee. He screamed out, but then stifled it and choked out, "Harlem's M ... Martin Luther King, Jr. Community College. T ... Two o'clock."

"Where are your press credentials?" Miller pointed the gun at his head.

"Top drawer."

Garrison Miller opened the top drawer of the wooden desk. Inside was everything he needed to assume the identity of James Garafalo. "Thank you, Jim. You've been very cooperative." He turned back and saw the look of relief on the man's face. The look lasted another second before a bullet left the chamber of the Baretta, traveled through the silencer, and imploded in the brain of the New York Times writer. Now, a different James Garafalo would be covering the conflict.

Miller drank in the bloody scene. Killing was exhilarating. He noticed he had an erection. He always had one whenever he thought how close he was to realizing his goal. He took out the press pass and ID from the man's desk and left the apartment.

At 3:40 a.m. there were only a few cars on W.74th Street. Miller stepped in front of an oncoming one and waved his hands. The driver of the mid-sized sedan screeched to a halt. The carjacker pointed the gun in the window and ordered him into the back seat. The frightened, young man did as he was told. Miller then shot him once in the head, pushed the body onto the floor, and drove uptown toward Harlem.

All the way there, Miller fantasized about a world without Moses McBride. It was going to be a glorious world: A world where the white man would no longer be afraid.

A world where the white man reigned supreme.

The skies above New York were jet black. A heavy layer of gray clouds had blanketed the stars and the moon. It gave Harlem the look of an urban ghost town. Like in a science fiction movie, it was ominous and forbidding. It suited Garrison Miller just fine.

He parked the late model Toyota Camry, covered the body in the back seat with a blanket he found on the floor, and walked two blocks to Martin Luther King, Jr. Community College. With his right hand in his jacket pocket caressing the Baretta, and the leather bag clenched in his left, he looked up at the top floor of the four-story apartment house that abutted the school. He glanced in every direction. There was no one in sight, and he entered the old building.

On the fourth floor, he removed the burglar tools from his pocket and was inside the rear apartment in seconds. All was quiet. If anyone was home, they were evidently asleep. Miller removed the Baretta from his pocket. His eyes adjusted to the darkness and he walked into the kitchen. It smelled like fried food. It reminded him of his mama back in Louisiana and the fried chicken she used to make for him and 'Daddy' every Sunday.

Miller checked the living room and the bathroom. All was still. He crept down the hallway. The floorboards creaked under his footsteps, but he didn't care. He had a purpose, a goal, and no one was going to stand in his way. The first door he opened was a bedroom. He was able to make out two small bodies in bunk beds against the far wall. They were sleeping, breathing heavily. A humidifier was on, filling the room with a warm dampness, which smelled like Vicks. It also reminded him of his childhood. Miller wiped the emotion from his mind. He lifted the gun, and two bullets spit out of the chamber and buried themselves in their soft targets. He listened and could no longer hear their sickly sounds.

Across the hall from the children's bedroom was another door, slightly ajar. He pushed it open and found himself face to face with the startled, young mother.

"MY BABIES!" She reached up to her mouth and screamed, but it was short-lived, as another bullet shot through the silencer and ripped into her hands and face. It thrust her body back onto her bed.

Miller turned on the light switch and saw she was alone. He looked at her black and red body splayed across the white sheets. The authorities, when they found them, would assume it was just another African family gunned down by - well, who cares. He loved it!

In the dark living room, he opened the overnight bag and removed the different parts of the weapon. It took less than a minute for him to put it together. He flung it over his shoulder and climbed out the back window of the fourth floor apartment.

Miller reached up to the gutter, which surrounded the rooftop, and pulled himself onto the flat roof of the building. He looked left and saw the abutting wall of Martin Luther King, Jr. Community College. It was six feet higher than the apartment rooftop, but he was able to climb onto it with minimal effort. Through the blackness of the Harlem sky, he saw another wall, except this one looked higher than the one he just climbed onto. Knowing that auditoriums were always the highest point of a school building, Miller deduced that the press conference would be in the largest space available to accommodate cameras, security, seating, and lighting. He had to get on top of this roof, on top of the auditorium. He went up to the wall, but he couldn't reach the top of it with his hands. "Shit!" He jumped to no avail. He ran and leaped, using his foot on the side of the wall to bolster him upwards, but he still couldn't reach the top of it. "Shit, shit, shit!"

Garrison Miller removed the flashlight, with the attached green gel, from his back pocket and looked around the blacktop. He let out his breath in relief; in a far corner were a couple of wooden crates. Again, luck was with him. Those few extra feet got him on top. Underneath him, now, was Moses McBride's Waterloo. He took out the flashlight again and surveyed the auditorium's rooftop. There it was: Not more than twenty feet from him was the trap door that entered into the lighting booth.

Only it was locked. It didn't matter. He only needed to exit from there, not enter. He had wanted to hide the gun inside the lighting booth, but unable to get in, he now had to find a new place. Miller turned around and saw a pipe of some sort, its opening shaped like the bell of a sousaphone. He would have to hide the gun in there. He couldn't carry it in with him tomorrow, not with all the Secret Service and police swarming the place. He hid the weapon and let out a macabre laugh. "In less than twelve hours, McBride, you're gonna be one dead nigger."

Back inside the dead family's apartment, Garrison Miller walked into the bathroom. He shaved off his blond beard and mustache and dyed his hair black, making sure to clean up every piece of hair. Not that it mattered; with all the killing taking place in Harlem, no one would investigate this scene. Miller stared at himself in the mirror above the sink. He now looked more like the picture on James Garafalo's press credentials. He opened the leather overnight bag his contact had given him at LaGuardia Airport, removed the brown suit, shirt, and tie, and hung them on the shower rod to loosen the wrinkles.

With everything ready for tomorrow, the grand marshal of the People for a White America paced the apartment and reviewed each step in his mind. Confident it was going to go off without a hitch, he sat down on the couch and waited. He couldn't fall asleep. He was too excited. Instead, he just sat there with an erection, fantasizing about the kill.

Like a flag leading into battle, it never once wavered.

At six a. m. Jane sat down with Sam at the dining table in the great room. It was unusual to have breakfast with him; in the past, he had always left before her. Jane wondered about it. As a psychologist, she knew something was awry when people behaved abnormally. Why was Sam there with her? Why the change in pattern and behavior?

Why that marriage proposal so soon after their confrontation last night?

They closed up the cabin and put their belongings in their cars. Jane sat behind the wheel of her white Mercedes 750 LS, and Sam walked up to the driver's door. "I forgot my key. Let me have yours so I can lock up."

Jane reached into her pocketbook and handed him the key. She watched him with curiosity, and disappointment, walk back to the cabin, lock the door, and then get in his black Lincoln. He blew her a kiss and drove down the mile-long dirt road that led out of the woods. Sam had driven off with her cabin key. He'd said he'd forgotten his. "Then, how did you get in last night before me?" she asked out loud. Sam had lied to her. As she drove down the road she realized she couldn't trust anyone anymore.

Jane thought about it and decided not to go to New York for the historic meeting. Instead, she would return to Georgetown. She had to talk to Paco. She had to find out if there was any connection between Garrison Miller, Mustafa Al-Salaam, and Hassad Muhammed. Her daughter's welfare came first, not Sam's.

* * * * *

Before leaving for New York, Sam stopped off at his office. Seated behind his desk, he drank his morning coffee and thought about Jane. Her suspicious behavior last night had him worried. Was her loyalty waning? Did she still believe in him? His mind turned to his two boys: Adam, fifteen; and Brad, thirteen. Oh, how he loved them. They were his life. And how they loved him. Thankfully, they were safe at home with their maternal grandparents in Fairfax.

Sam looked out the wall of windows to his left. It was a beautiful morning, with a cool breeze and clear blue skies. Although it was Sunday, the Hill was still bustling. Congressional aides were running from here to there, getting the offices ready for the dozens of representatives and senators who worked without a day's rest. Staff members were hurrying to or from meetings, some which had begun in the small hours of the morning. No, Washington never slept, and Sam loved it. He loved the feeling, the omniscient rush he got every morning as he drank his first cup of coffee and looked out at the world. He wondered what the view and the feeling would be like from the Oval Office. If only his father were alive to see what he'd accomplished. His father: The man who called him a sissy for wanting to be an actor. The man who told him he would never reach his ultimate potential. The man who questioned Sam's capacity for leadership and even manhood. Sam's mind wandered far away, envisioning once again his parents' horrific deaths. Britney in his arms, her face imploding before his eyes, and the two bullets tearing into his shoulder and hip. Sam shook off his reverie and stared at the Capitol dome. He was perspiring, but not gasping for air. He took out his handkerchief and wiped his face. It wasn't so bad this time.

* * * * *

Paco Ramirez, Kerri Robbins, Larry Waldman, and the other members of the campaign staff stuffed inside Jane's office were sitting at the conference table when Jane arrived. The one-by-one briefing from the different components of the team ended with Tim Parker, the RNC liaison to the campaign. He took everyone through the country, state by state, and explained the party's strengths and weaknesses. "According to Larry's state polls and your media polls, Jane, we're going to win New Hampshire, Virginia, Florida, Maine, Connecticut, Indiana, Colorado, and Texas. We have no chance in Michigan, Montana, Pennsylvania, Illinois, New York, and Massachusetts. We can still win Ohio, California, Georgia, South Carolina, and West Virginia, so those are the states where we should be spending our money."

"Are we going to win?" Jane asked.

"Overall, the numbers are promising. They're slowly moving in Sam's direction."

"A properly evasive answer. Thank you, Tim." She turned to the others. "Sam will be in New York today with Moses McBride. The result of that meeting should have quite an effect on the overnights. Try to get some rest today, because the next forty-eight hours are going to be Hell."

Everyone left, leaving Jane to talk to Paco about more personal matters. "Have you found out anything about the Iraqis?"

"Not much. After Mustafa's arrest, he was questioned and bailed, as I explained to you yesterday. Hassad, on the other hand, disappeared after they questioned him. Intelligence thought they'd returned to Baghdad, until they found Mustafa's body in Rock Creek Park last night, with a bullet in his head."

"What about the mosque bombings? Anything on that?" Paco Ramirez was a vital cog in the machine known as TWO. During the last eight years, he had comprised an incomparable network of informants. From the CIA to the FBI, to the Hill, and even the White House, everyone talked to him, and many owed him favors. "From what I hear, the president's convinced some fanatical Islamic group blew them up to make it look like the Israelis were behind it. As long as they believe that, Jane, I think we should forget the Iraqi connection and concentrate on Garrison Miller again."

Jane thought about all the coincidences and all the inconsistencies, as well as Sam's disturbing behavioral changes of late. She hated to do what she had recently decided, but she knew she had to. There were just two days left. "No, Paco. I think it's time to pursue another avenue of thought." Jane looked at her trusted assistant. "Sam Howard."

"Sam? What do you mean?"

Jane thought once more about what she had overheard Sam say on the phone. Was he talking to his son when he told him, 'No one suspect'? Or did she really hear him say, 'No one suspects'? Jane didn't know what to think. She loved Sam. Now she was questioning his role in all this. Why?

Role - that was the key. The great actor Sam Howard had stepped out of character of late. And stepping out of character was not the sign of statesmanship …

… it was a sign of acting.

"Why are you suspicious of him?"

"A lot of things have happened since HOPE blew up: A lot of things that, when added together, sum up to more questions instead of answers." Jane recounted all of the suspicious events: Going out to the cabin after fourteen months, overhearing him on the phone (or mishearing him), his accidentally taking her key, all the coincidences and benefits to him in between, his psychological change of late, and her being watched by the two men in the blue Buick. "So, what do you think we should do?"

she asked when she finished.

"There's nothing we *can* do. It's all conjecture."

Jane was silent for a moment. She tried to come up with the least harmful way of broaching this possibility with someone who could look into it. "Maybe I should talk to Bill Lawson. That way, if I'm wrong, I can't hurt Sam's chance at winning the presidency. Bill's a good man. I know I can talk to him."

"I think that's a good idea."

Jane sat across from Paco at the oval conference table and thought about Garrison Miller and the PWA. "Something still doesn't make sense."

"What?"

"If Garrison Miller is involved in the HOPE bombings and the nationwide rioting, or if he's working in conjunction with Iraq, then why is he seeing Taryn? Where does she fit in? And why has he hung around since his arrest?"

"Like you said, maybe he's trying to get to Sam through Taryn and you. After all, his philosophy is the antithesis of Sam's."

Jane nodded in agreement.

"Which, if you believe, blows your theory that Sam may be behind it."

Paco was right, but Jane still felt uncomfortable. She had to dig deeper. "I'm sorry, Paco, but too much has happened this week, and too much of it indirectly involves Sam. In good conscience, I can't go into Tuesday without some answers."

"I think it's a waste of time, but if that's what you have to do, then go ahead."

"I know everything about Sam except for that year he disappeared after his family's murders. I tried to get him to talk about it, but he refused; he said he wanted to forget the past. But I have a gut feeling it may have something to do with the present situation."

"Is there anything I can do?"

"Since we're looking into coincidences, Paco, I'd have to label Patty Howard's death right before Sam won reelection to the senate six years ago as suspicious, too. I may be wrong, I sincerely hope so, but I think we should check and make sure. Why don't you find out all you can about the person who crashed into her car. If I uncover anything on my end, or if I find myself getting into too deep waters, I promise I'll call you."

Jane worked a few more hours before leaving for Georgetown. All the way home, she thought about the key. Why did Sam lie and take it from her? Why doesn't he want her having access to the cabin any longer?

Jane checked her messages on the answering machine in her study, then went into the kitchen and made some coffee. She checked on Taryn, who was still asleep in her bed. It was Sunday. With all her daughter had gone through lately she had every right to sleep away the morning. She walked into her own bedroom with a steaming mug of coffee, a couple of shots of whiskey thrown in for good measure, and began analyzing Sam's past.

After his parents and sister were killed on graduation day she had driven back to Boston to spend the summer with her family. She and Sam had spoken a few times a week for a few weeks, but, by July, all communications had stopped. Jane sat at the writing table between her bed and the bay window and remembered how crushed she was back then. In late August, she had tried to visit him at the Howard's Greenwich, Connecticut mansion on her way to Columbia University in New York City. The housekeeper, Mrs. Stanton, had told her Sam wasn't home, but Jane knew differently. While pulling into the long, circular driveway, she had seen him peering out from behind the curtains of his upstairs bedroom window. Come

Thanksgiving, when she had called to see how he was doing, Mrs. Stanton said: "I'm sorry, Ms. Weisser, but Sam left at the beginning of the month. He said he wouldn't be back for a while."

Jane thought about that as she walked circles around her bedroom. She decided to call the dean of the Drama department at Yale and ask some questions. The beginning was the best place to start.

She told the switchboard operator who she was, and David Campbell immediately returned her call from his Guilford, Connecticut home. Jane stared at the image of the Tony Award winning director on the wall screen. He had thick, wavy brown hair. His lined face made him look as if he was in his forties, or maybe early fifties. How come teachers were never this good looking when I was a student? she asked herself.

"Dr. Weisser?"

Jane apologized for the awkward silence. She returned her mind to the task at hand and asked him if he could give her some insight on the senator as a student. "We're doing a documentary for election night, Dean Campbell, and your comments would be helpful."

"Although I wasn't here when Sam was an undergraduate, I heard, throughout the years, that everyone - faculty, students, and the people of New Haven alike - thought Sam Howard would one day be considered America's greatest actor. He was that versatile. You see, Dr. Weisser, a good actor is a good illusionist. Through skill in his art, he can change into someone else and make his audience believe they are witnessing reality. Sam Howard was a master illusionist. The Drama School had invited him to return for his MFA, but his family was killed on graduation day and they never saw him again."

The man wasn't telling her anything she didn't already

know. As she fumbled for what to ask next, Dean Campbell asked her to hold on; he would make a phone call. A minute later, Professor Robert Richardson, the great Shakespearean actor, his white beard and long white hair flowing around his cherubic face, appeared next to David Campbell on the split screen in her bedroom wall.

"Bob, meet Jane Weisser, Sam Howard's national campaign director."

"No introductions are necessary, David. I'd know that beautiful smile anywhere. You've accomplished a great deal since you were at Yale, Dr. Weisser, and all of us are proud of you. You were the talk of campus when Time voted you 'The Most Influential Woman in Washington.' It is an honor to finally meet you."

"Thank you. It's an honor to meet you, too."

"Bob was one of Sam's teachers. He may be able to shed a different light."

Robert Richardson repeated everything Dean Campbell told her. He finished his remembrance by saying, "After graduation, I wrote to him, I even tried calling him at his home, only I was told he had left and wouldn't be back for a while. After a few months of waiting for him to return my correspondences, I gave up. Obviously, Sam wanted his privacy, and I wasn't going to deny him that. The death of his family was traumatic, and if he needed some time and seclusion, then I wasn't going to disturb him. I heard that after a year he returned to the States and entered Harvard Business School. I couldn't believe it. Business? Why wasn't he pursuing his acting career?"

Jane remembered Sam's dream. 'I'm going to be the most famous man in the world one day,' he had told her many times.

The professor continued: "I had guessed the reason was because of his relationship with his father. James Howard was not at all happy that his son was studying to be an actor. He was adamant that Sam follow in his footsteps and run Howard Oil. Sam told me many times that, no matter what it took, he would prove to his father that he could be great on his own terms. It was sad, but it was that motivation that made him so successful."

After some more talk, Jane thanked the men and disconnected the conference call. She considered one of Professor Richardson's statements. 'I heard that after a year he returned to the States and entered Harvard Business School.' Hmm, so Sam had left the country for a year.

Jane sat at the writing table and called the four international airports that served the Greenwich, Connecticut area: Bradley, JFK, LaGuardia, and Newark. When each of the airports were on line with her, she asked them to check their computer banks. She gave them the six months after graduation along with the year in question. The campaign needed to know the itinerary for Sam Howard during that time. Although that was privileged information, they all deferred to the credentials of the candidate's campaign director. Each airport promised to call her back as soon as they had an answer. Jane had always relished anonymity, but celebrity had its advantages.

Less than thirty minutes later, Jane received a call from JFK Airport. Sam Howard had flown on American Airlines to London, England on November 4th. "That makes sense. Sam had always wanted to see London's theater district." Jane thought about it. "If all he did was go to England that year, then why didn't he ever talk about it?"

She decided to call Heathrow and Gatwick Airports in London. When she had each one on line, she requested information on whether Sam Howard had flown out of England during the months of November or December.

Twenty minutes later, she received the first call. There was no record of Sam Howard having flown out of Gatwick during those months, or in the following three. A little later, Heathrow rang her with the information she needed: Sam Howard had departed London on a November 22nd flight. Destination: Baghdad, Iraq.

The color drained out of Jane's face as she mechanically thanked the airport agent and disconnected. Although the Irish coffee was now cold, she drank the rest of it. She noticed her hand was shaking. Why did Sam go to Iraq? Was it as innocent as conducting business for Howard Oil? She thought about it. If Sam had gone there to sell the company, there would be a record of it.

She called Connecticut information and received the number for the Connecticut State Hall of Records in Hartford. Was travel to, and business with, Iraq illegal back then? Jane dialed the number and got a recorded message that the Hall of Records' hours were Monday through Friday, 9:00 a. m. to 4:30 p. m. "Damnit!" It was Sunday. She would have to wait until tomorrow. That meant she would lose twenty-four precious hours. And there were only forty-eight hours to go until Election Day. Jane realized there was still one more thing she had to do: She had to search the cabin. After taking her key, Jane suspected Sam was hiding something. "What's in there that he doesn't want me to see? And how do I get in without him knowing about it?"

She pondered the future with trepidation, as she fixed herself a double scotch. Everything now depended on her ability to discover the truth and to choose the right course of action.

Sam and Moses sat knee to knee in the school's music room. For more than two hours they discussed ways to end the bloodshed that was tearing apart the country.

"Moses, I'm not president, yet, and anything I promise will

not materialize if I'm not elected. You understand that?"

"Of course I do, Sam, but we have to give these people something, so they don't feel their fight has been in vain. Something to make them hope again."

"I know, my friend. But, all I can give them are promises."

"That's all we're asking. The African people believe in you, Sam. Your promises are their hope."

The men negotiated, and Moses felt the frightening responsibility of having a say in the future of America's African people. Like the great Frederick Douglass, who had sat down with President Lincoln during the civil war, he, too, had the future of the black man in his hands. He had to make wise choices and decisions. And the most important was not to give any ground on his demands. They had lost too much already. He was confident Sam would agree to all he asked. After all, Sam needed him right now as much as he needed Sam. By ending this conflict, Sam Howard would surely be elected president. Moses seized the moment.

At 3:20, their meeting ended and the two leaders shook hands. They readied themselves to meet the media, helped straighten each other's neckties, and walked side by side to the auditorium. Moses felt his heart racing. The building was cold, and he was perspiring. What if they couldn't persuade the people to lay down their arms? How do you convince a people in fear for their lives? He took a deep breath, opened the stage door, and walked onto the stage.

After several tense minutes during a Secret Service check of his invitation, his credentials, and his person, a relieved James Garafalo, nee Garrison Miller, was allowed into the school's auditorium. In his brown suit and tie, brown shoes, black hair (sans beard), and horn-rimmed glasses, he looked like a typically fashioned-challenged journalist. Seated in seats and crouched in front of the stage were a dense cluster of other journalists, reporters, and cameramen. TC cameras mounted on platforms were scattered all around the room. The houselights and stage lights shone blindingly. Miller scrutinized the men and women standing at the exits and entrances and around the perimeter of the room. The place was crawling with Secret Service agents. Miller turned around to look at the lighting booth. SHIT! He had never considered there might be a balcony in the auditorium. The darkened lighting booth was high above the last row of the upper level of seats. His original plan was unworkable. He took stock of the situation and considered what to do. He was too close to stop now.

Miller exited the double doors at the back of the auditorium and stood in the lobby. He ignored the many reporters filing past him and looked at the staircase that led to the balcony. Security had roped it off. It didn't matter. Even if he could get up there, he wouldn't be able to climb the ladder that went from the last row of balcony seats up the wall to the booth without being seen by the security around the brilliantly-lighted thousand-seat room.

In the crowded lobby, Miller saw a door at the back of the brick auditorium wall with the words CONTROL ROOM written in bold letters. Yes, he was still in control, in control of Moses McBride's life and death. Miller removed the burglar's tool kit he always carried with him. Taking advantage of the crush of people moving around the lobby he was able to slip through the metal door without anyone noticing anything out of the ordinary. He relocked it from the inside, squirted some fast drying epoxy glue into the tumblers, and climbed the dark staircase to the lighting booth that overlooked the auditorium. Some light was filtering in, but it was still dark enough to do it unseen. If someone did see him, it didn't matter; he had his escape well planned.

Miller entered the booth and noticed the metal stairs that led to the rooftop. He crawled over to them and climbed to the top. The trap door was locked, but the wood around it was old and dry. With the sounds of hundreds of curious correspondents drowning out the noise he was making, he easily broke the wooden frame. He pushed the door open and climbed out onto the roof to retrieve the hidden rifle.

The White House had found out about the secret meeting planned for two o'clock at Martin Luther King, Jr. Community College in Harlem, New York. On the president's orders, forty-eight FBI agents converged on the college a few minutes before the scheduled time. They scattered themselves throughout the auditorium and waited for the wanted man's entrance on stage with Sam Howard. They had had no time for their usually thorough precautions.

Inside the White House, President Price waited for the newsbreak of the arrest. He loved the scenario Director Coyles had briefed him on earlier. "It's about time Sam Howard had events work against him," the President said to his staff members seated around the Oval Office. "With McBride's televised arrest for treason, the voters will associate Howard with McBride and sedition"

Jane sat down behind the rococo desk in her downstairs study. She turned on the telecomp and pressed the CNN button. The wall screen next to the door to her office lit up, but, as of yet, there was no report on Sam's meeting with Moses McBride. Jane nervously tapped her red fingernails on the desk blotter. White backlash to the African militants was keeping Sam behind

President Price in the latest polls. The result of this meeting would determine the outcome of the election. More important, the result of this meeting would determine whether or not the country survived. She decided to do some work to get her mind off her worries. She pushed the 'Mac' button on the keyboard and the wall screen changed to its computer mode, leaving CNN as a small box on the bottom of the wall screen. 'Ding.' There on the screen were the words, 'Secure files not closed before shutdown. Automatic closure invoked 2016:11:06:01:49:10'. Jane's eyes blurred. She had never shut it down improperly. "What the Hell?" She hurried out of the study to the bottom of the stairwell. "Taryn! Get down to my office, now!"

A minute later, the sullen teenager walked in.

"Have you used this telecomp recently?"

"I've never used it. You told me it's off limits." Her voice was still full of attitude.

Jane stood at her desk and tried to make sense of it. "Someone's been in this room, Taryn, and someone entered my system early Sunday when I was away." She looked back at the teenager for an answer. "Was anyone in this house in the last twenty-four hours?"

"No … no one's been here."

Jane heard the lie. It didn't take a psychologist to hear it. Any mother could hear the change of pitch and timber. "Who was it?"

Taryn stood there shaking. "G … Gary."

"YOU FOOLISH LITTLE GIRL! I have been trying, for eighteen years, to juggle my career and motherhood. Now, I'm facing the biggest challenge of my professional life, and you're working against me. How selfish can you get?"

Taryn stared at the blue carpet by her bare feet. Suddenly, her eyes opened wide and she cried, "Oh, my God, Mom, you were right! Gary Walters *is* Garrison Miller. He convinced me he wasn't. He said: 'Why would Garrison Miller date Taryn Weisser where he would be seen in the spotlight?' Until now, it made perfect sense to me."

Jane saw the color drain from Taryn's face. Her world was crumbling all around her. "What changed your mind?"

Taryn spoke in a soft, quivering voice. "It just hit me. He said if he were this Garrison Miller, then dating the daughter of 'the most influential woman in Washington' would blow his cover. He lied to me about never having heard of you. How did he know the press called you that? Then I found him in your study last night. Oh, Mom, I'm so sorry, please forgive me. I would never do anything to hurt you." Her voice grew softer and trailed off as she sank into the leather couch, rocking back and forth, and sobbing gently.

Tears ran down Jane's face. She rose from her chair and sat next to her daughter. She held her as close to her as she could to comfort her. The pain of losing the man you love was bad enough, but to realize he never loved you, and was just using you, was unbearable. Humiliating.

"I loved him so much. How could he do this to me?" Taryn wailed.

Jane spoke in a loving, motherly way. No psychology, no games. Just mother and daughter again.

With Taryn calmed down, and with no report about the meeting on the TC yet, Jane attempted to find out why Miller was in her files. She pressed the button that returned the screen to the last opened file. It took only a couple of seconds before she realized what Miller had in his possession. "Dear God! We have a problem, Taryn. Miller knows about the meeting Sam is having with Moses McBride."

Taryn got up from the couch and walked behind the desk.

Standing next to where her mother was sitting, she read the wall screen. "It doesn't say where the meeting is, Mom."

"Miller's a smart man. Believe me, he's there right now."

"But, why?"

Jane felt her blood boiling in her veins. That burning sensation raced to her eyes, and she had to close them for a few seconds, for fear of fainting. She took a deep breath and looked at her daughter. "Why? To kill Sam. Garrison Miller blew up the twelve HOPE Cities, and now he's going after the man who built them. The two men represent opposite ideologies. If my fears are correct, Iraq is the supporting force behind the PWA and everything that's happened this week. I have to do something, Taryn!"

Senator Sam Howard and the Reverend Dr. Moses McBride entered the stage from the left wing adjacent to the music room. The noise in the auditorium rose to a crescendo, then diminished. They walked to the mountain of microphones at center stage. Sam began to speak. "I called this press conference today ..."

Director Herbert Knox of the New York FBI, along with his agents, ascended the stairs at both sides of the stage and approached them. Sam stopped talking and watched as the men stepped up to McBride. "Moses McBride, by order of the President of the United States, you're under arrest." Director Knox showed him his identification and the signed arrest warrant.

"This is ridiculous! What are the charges?" Sam asked, indignant at Price's ploy.

"Treason."

"Treason?" Sam couldn't believe Price would be this foolish. Didn't the President know that by arresting the African leader the fighting would escalate, not end? "Please, before you arrest Dr. McBride, he has something to say to the country. Something that will save lives. Surely, you won't deny him that opportunity."

Director Knox nodded to the preacher. He and his men stepped back.

Sam knew the President couldn't very well arrest Moses McBride after the reverend went on national TC and called for his people to put down their weapons. That would be political suicide. And if Price didn't follow through, it would be a severe blow to his credibility with the electorate. Sam laughed under his breath. By ending the fighting, his fight with Charles Price was over, too. Nice try, Chuck!

"Like all human beings," Moses McBride said to the many cameras before him, "I deplore the senseless deaths and the senseless suffering that people of all color and class have had to endure this past week. It is abominable, and it pains me deeply." The heavyset man pulled a handkerchief from his pocket and wiped his brow. "Senator Howard and I have spent the last few hours together discussing ways to end this conflict, and I believe - no, I know we have come up with solutions: Solutions that will help everyone, without taking away from anyone. Solutions that will work." Moses turned to the man who was going to be the next president and smiled. "Sam has promised that, if elected, equality will be more than a promise. Justice will be more than a wish. He has also promised a proposal for long term, interest free loans for poor Americans, guaranteed yearly cost of living raises for minimum wage earners, and a national public school system that includes day care until age five. We must *never* forget the past, but we must also keep our eyes open to the future. Sam Howard *is* that future! In unity, Sam and I ask everyone to put down their weapons."

Sam stepped forward and stood by the shorter man's right side. He looked into the cameras, smiled, and waved. How could he lose now?

* * * * *

Miller crawled back to the trap door on the auditorium roof. With the sniper scope equipped rifle by his side, he reopened the door and climbed down the stairs into the dark lighting booth.

Jane called information for the FBI. While she waited, she listened to Dr. McBride's pleading request. Unbearable tension riveted her in position as she watched the screen, dreading the crackle of gunfire, and hoping Miller's plans had fallen through.

Moses continued his speech. "With what Sam Howard and I have put together, the African people, all minorities, all the disadvantaged ..." He stopped in mid-sentence when he saw a flash of light in the lighting booth at the back of the balcony. " ... will have new opportunities, new programs, and new futures once again. With Sam Howard, we will have peace and HOPE. This is not an act of surrender for there are no losers and no winners. We have all lost in this terrible episode in our country's history. It's time we all win. With Sam Howard's ideas, we all *will* win. This unilateral cease fire will be the end of ..."

The end of you, McBride. Bye-bye, blackbird! Crouched inside the booth, Miller lifted the rifle, rested it on the control board, and focused on his target. McBride's fat, black heart was centered in the cross hairs of the scope.

" ... this nightmare. We all want peace!" Moses, his attention caught by the brief light in the booth, felt something was wrong. He looked up to the rear of the balcony again and saw a rifle barrel emerge from its darkness. "GUN!" he screamed. As he turned to his right, he heard the explosion and felt the back of his left shoulder tear open. The force was so powerful that it catapulted him into Sam, knocking the senator down to the floor.

Jane screamed, and her heart palpitated. It looked as if Dr. McBride had been shot, but Sam was down, too. "Oh, my God, SAM!" She disconnected the call before the Bureau answered. Until she could make sense of her and Taryn's danger, it was best not to say what she knew. Mother and daughter sat on the couch, holding onto each other for support and comfort. Waiting to hear what had happened …

      … and who lived or died.

Miller knew he would only have one shot, but McBride saw him and moved. He was probably still alive. Like the trained killer he was, Garrison Miller erased the emotion from his mind and began to execute his escape plan.

      Miller, feeling his heart pounding, and the sweat dripping down the small of his back, dashed up the stairs to the hatch and pushed it open. He climbed out onto the roof. He ran across the black tarmac, jumped down to the school's lower roof, then jumped onto the flat roof of the adjoining apartment house. He lowered himself into the top floor window at the back of the building. As far as he could tell, no one had seen his escape. All eyes were on the community college.

      But, just in case, he knew what he had to do next.

Director Knox stayed on stage after ordering his men up to the lighting booth. Dozens of FBI and Secret Service agents ran out to the lobby and the balcony stairs. A few stopped to try to gain access through the control room door in the lobby. It was locked. The agent in charge summoned the janitor to assist them, but it was futile; the key wouldn't go in. It was the same with the door at the top of the balcony wall, which led into the booth. The would-be-assassin had frozen the tumblers.

Inside the apartment, the first thing Miller did was take apart the weapon and tape it to his legs. He then put on the nun's outfit and habit his New York contact had left for him in the leather overnight bag. He looked in the mirror. Perfect! Miller had been inside the apartment less than five minutes when he opened the front door and walked outside. He looked, to anyone interested, like so many of the other 'New Traditional' Catholic nuns in their 'retro' habits, going in and out of apartment buildings, tending to the sick and the hurt. He viewed his surroundings. There were police cars prowling up and down the street, their sirens and lights activated. The presence of so many police officers, however, brought out angry mobs of Africans deeply resentful of white man's law. Bullets flew, as the hundreds of Africans present launched hand-held explosives at the dozens of men and women in blue. The scene quickly filled with anarchy, panic, and blood. Moses McBride may have called for an end to the fighting, but not everyone had heard it. It was a perfect diversion for Garrison Miller. He watched the rebellion and thought: Red blood on white officers in blue. How American! The Sister, with the Baretta in her right hand tucked inside her left sleeve, made her way up the street, away from the killing field. S/He turned the corner and entered the car that belonged to the dead man covered on the back seat floor.

Livid that he blew his chance, Miller drove away, pounding the armrest by his side. His dream of killing Moses McBride, his father's executor, thwarted once again!

President Price paced the Oval Office. He was fuming. There was no way he could arrest Moses McBride now. Not after the

African leader had just announced the conflict was over and had saved Senator Howard's life? "HOW COULD McBRIDE GO TO HOWARD TO BROKER A DEAL? I'M THE COMMANDER-IN-CHIEF!" he screamed at his campaign director, his chief of staff, and his legal counselor. "DAMNIT, THIS WHOLE THING HAS BACKFIRED IN MY FACE!

The president sat down in his Executive chair and closed his eyes in resignation. His face fell into his hands. He'd been politically humiliated again. A succession of disastrous events plagued his presidency just days before the election. It was an incredible run of bad luck.

If it was luck.

The news reports throughout the afternoon were all calling Moses McBride a hero for saving Sam Howard's life. Jane felt a personal debt to the man, not just because he had saved Sam's life, but because she felt responsible for his being shot.

Seated behind her desk, Jane also thought about the political ramifications of what had happened. When added together, there was only one: Sam's poll numbers were going to surge just two days before the election. Was Sam's luck just his good fortune, or was it a carefully plotted scheme?

The networks were reporting that there were no clues as to who had tried to assassinate Senator Sam Howard. They had, however, the make and model of the gun from the ballistic report on the bullet taken from Moses McBride's shoulder. Jane knew who, but she still had not conveyed the information to the authorities.

Without any thought, Jane walked into the living room and poured herself a drink. Would telling them it was Garrison Miller, that he had broken into her telefiles, be the wise thing to do now? Would Miller, or his people, come after them if she said anything? Jane finished the drink and poured another. She decided that her daughter's safety overrode all other considerations.

She thought about Adam and Bradley, Sam's teenaged sons. Since Patricia Howard's untimely death six years ago, she had been supportive and affectionate to them. A reassuring word, a hug, a kiss, she freely gave because she loved them like her own. Adam was a sensitive boy: intelligent, thoughtful, and kind. Jane had a special place in her heart for him. Bradley was the boisterous, well-meaning rabble rouser. She considered how traumatized they must be by the assassination attempt and longed to give them her comfort and assurance.

Twenty minutes later, Jane and Taryn left Georgetown and drove across the bridge into Virginia. There was little traffic leading into Fairfax, and they arrived at Sam's estate without any problem. Maybe Moses McBride's words had gotten through, Jane hoped.

Whether seeing the mansion for the first time or for the hundredth, Jane was reminded of Jefferson's Monticello. Along both sides of the long, circular drive were rolling lawns, bordered with flower beds. The house was white, with a two-story portico and tall columns in the front. A large stone wall, with black gates at both ends of the driveway, surrounded the estate. Jane announced herself, and the gates swung open. She drove up the slight incline, the white gravel crunching beneath the tires, and parked at the front door.

Martha Kelleher, the boy's maternal grandmother welcomed them in. They had all been close friends since she and her husband moved down to care for the boys after their daughter's death. In the large foyer, Jane fondly remembered the times they had all spent there those last six years. Taryn was three years older than Adam, who was two years older than

Bradley, but the three of them played like any family of one sister and two younger brothers. They laughed and fought and grew up together to be good friends.

"It's been such a long time," the grandmother said, offering them hugs and kisses.

"Well, Martha, with this campaign, there's been so little time. I didn't even see my parents when we were in Boston the other day."

"Shush, there's no reason to apologize. I'm just glad you're here."

Sam's father-in-law walked into the foyer.

"Tom, you handsome devil!" Jane exclaimed, and they embraced warmly. Adam and Bradley came downstairs from their rooms. Jane couldn't suppress a broad smile. They were tall and handsome like their father, with sparkling gray eyes to mesmerize any woman. Adam walked up to her and kissed her, followed by Bradley, and Jane wrapped her arms and her heart around them.

They walked into the elegant living room. Two chairs book ended a roaring fireplace. In front of it was a rectangular glass and brass coffee table, flanked on each side by beige sofas, all which rested on a large Oriental rug. An ebony grand piano stood near the rear wall of windows. Throughout the enormous room were reminders of Patricia Howard. It didn't make Jane jealous. How could she expect anything else? As she looked at the pictures, she thought about the terrible car accident two weeks before Sam's reelection. Was it an accident? she asked herself. Or, was Patty Howard murdered? And, if so, by whom? The questions made her queasy. She forced it out of her mind, but, before she did, she made a mental note to call Paco when she got home.

Everyone spoke about the assassination attempt, about

Moses McBride's heroic action, and about the election. Jane then excused herself to go to the bathroom.

On the way back, she stopped in the kitchen. Jane remembered that Sam kept a set of spare keys in the drawer next to the refrigerator. She had considered going out to Maryland and breaking a window to gain entrance, but had thought better of it; all the windows were wired with alarms. She went to the drawer and pulled it open. There it was! Sooner or later, he was going to notice it missing. With a little luck, she'd find nothing and return the key before he knew. If she found something, she realized, it wouldn't matter.

Jane walked back into the living room and apologized for having to leave. Everyone understood. She hugged the boys at the front door and said to Sam's oldest son, "I'm happy your father and you are keeping in touch during this time, Adam. It's important to him that he speak with you and Bradley as often as possible."

"Thanks, Jane, but I haven't spoken to Dad in days. I can't wait till Tuesday."

"You mean you didn't talk with him last night?"

"No."

So, Sam had lied to her last night. Why? What was he hiding?

Behind the wheel of her Mercedes, crossing back into D.C., Jane asked herself many questions. The one she repeatedly came back to made her realize that her investigation into Senator Sam Howard was warranted.

"What is it that 'no one suspects?'"

Sam flew home to Fairfax, Virginia after he visited Moses McBride in Harlem Hospital's emergency room. His late wife's parents were already in bed, but Adam and Bradley were still awake. When Sam saw them, his eyes lit up and his smile widened. He hugged and kissed the boys at the front door, and was relieved that, at fifteen and thirteen, they still allowed him that immeasurable pleasure.

Sam walked into the living room with an arm around each one. They sat down, and he told them what had happened. "Dr. McBride saved my life by throwing himself in front of me. He's a real American hero, boys. I'm happy to say the fighting around the country, in respect to his wishes, has diminished the last few hours. We've succeeded so far. By tomorrow, we'll know for sure."

The teenagers were proud of their father, their American hero. Sam could see that from their smiles. Could any man be as lucky as him? Not even the presidency came before Adam and Bradley. The three best friends 'shot the bull,' spoke a little about sports, specifically the effect the civil unrest was having on the NFL, and they all laughed at some ribald jokes Sam had heard on the campaign trail.

"Oh, I forgot!" Adam said. "Jane and Taryn came by to visit a little while ago. I haven't seen them since - jeez, I can't remember how long it's been. I gotta tell you, Dad, Taryn is looking real good."

Sam was bewildered. Two days before the election and Jane was making social calls? Granted, she loved the boys like her own, but why visit now?

Bradley cut off his older brother. "Y'know, Dad, being old and alone isn't all it's cracked up to be, I hear. I wish you and Jane ..."

Sam wasn't listening. He was thinking about Jane. Trying to think like her. She had taught him all he knew, and one of those things was that when someone breaks a pattern something is amiss. What was amiss with Jane? Sam stayed deep in thought, but he could only come up with one possible reason for her visit today: Maybe she came here to comfort the boys after the attempted assassination. That was Jane: motherly, compassionate, concerned for the boy's emotional state of mind. He rebuked himself for being so suspicious of the woman he loved and who loved him. He had to keep reminding himself of that.

Sam kidded with his sons a while longer, then went into the kitchen for a snack. After eating some crackers and Muenster cheese, he took out a cigar from the box next to the refrigerator. He felt his pockets for his lighter, but it was in his suit jacket in the living room. He went to get them, but then remembered the box of stick matches in the drawer in front of him. He took them out and lit the cigar. As the plumes of smoke formed a cloud above his head, Sam dropped the box back in the drawer and closed it.

He immediately pulled it back open. "Shit!" He'd been too obvious, too sure of himself. He had broken the pattern, and Jane, being the behavioral expert she was, had noticed. He'd been too careless, too trusting, too much in love.

Damnit! He was so close.

There were just thirty-six hours to go and Sam Howard had a problem. Never once during the last fourteen months did he ever imagine the problem would be Jane Weisser.

It wasn't yet ten o'clock, and Jane had gone from the numbness of Johnny Walker Black to the anesthesia of sleep. Nothing could bother her anymore. She was finally at peace.

The ringing of the front door shattered that euphoria, and Jane jumped out of bed. She tied the belt of her robe around her waist and rushed downstairs to quell the incessant noise. Maybe it was Paco. She had been trying to reach him since returning from Fairfax. She opened the door. Staring at her with an angry look on his face was Sam.

"I've been trying to ring you, but your line's been busy."

"I disconnected it. After seeing how close you came to being killed today, I was frightened out of my wits. I had to escape that feeling. I chose Scotch and sleep."

Sam walked in past her, his hands in his gray cashmere overcoat. He shot her a severe look of reproval. "Why did you take the cabin key from my kitchen drawer?"

A pain shot through her head, which forced Jane to close her eyes and wince. It made her look guilty, she was sure. "After that attempted assassination, I had to see the boys and make sure they were all right. I took your spare because you forgot to give me back mine when you locked up this morning."

Sam stared at her. "Let me have it."

Jane didn't know how to react. To look innocent she had to question him. "Why?"

Sam hesitated answering. "We can't go out there after I become president, I told you, so you don't need it anymore."

For some reason, it felt like he was breaking up with her, although she knew better. Nonetheless, she felt like a teenager again, like the time Bobby Gordon asked her for his ring back. Jane went to the foyer closet and took the key from her coat pocket. The impasse was cold and impersonal.

"We leave for California tomorrow morning at seven." Sam walked out of Jane's Georgetown home. He turned back and said, "I love you, Jane. Be careful."

Jane watched him leave. Be careful?

There *was* something! Hopefully, Paco found out what it was during his search into Patty Howard's car crash. If he did, she would have the answer and know what to do.

The campaign was over. With Sam and Moses ending the conflict, and with the assassination attempt, one more day on the campaign trail wasn't going to change anything. Expecting it to be a close race, Jane had pre-arranged for Sam to visit the state with the largest electorate the day before the election. Now, it wasn't going to be close. Tomorrow's numbers would show him with a big lead. Because the people of California were expecting the candidate, the worst thing Sam could do would be to disappoint them. He had to go. But she didn't. Jane knew this decision would sever her relationship with Sam forever. Thankfully, the media hounds had yet to pick up on their differences. What was happening around the country had overshadowed any interest in the internal workings of the campaigns. Now, there was only one thing left to do, and with only one day to do it in.

Jane removed the duplicate key from her coat pocket. Earlier, on her way home from Fairfax, she had found a Home Depot open and had a copy made. In case Sam found out she had removed his spare and asked for it back, she'd still be able to get into the cabin. It was something she always taught her clients: Anticipation and preparation is the key to winning. No matter what it took, she was going to win whatever she was in the middle of.

Jane walked into her study and reconnected the telecomp's phone line to call Paco. As she did, it rang. She pushed the 'on' button and Kerri Robbins appeared on the wall screen in front of her. She was crying. "What's wrong, Kerri?"

"It's Paco. He's dead!"

"WHAT?" Jane collapsed into her chair. "HOW?"

"I don't know. I just got the call. Oh, God, I can't believe it!"

Jane felt sick to her stomach. She spoke with Kerri for a few minutes, until she felt her friend was emotionally stable. After a good cry of her own, she made some calls.

She found out the facts about Paco's death. Someone had planted a bomb in his car. "Dear God, Paco wasn't just another victim of this rioting. Someone deliberately murdered him!"

Jane understood all-too-well. Paco had gotten too close. Too close to the truth behind Patricia Howard's death. Waves of guilt and dread overcame her. She was responsible for Paco's murder. She had killed him. It made her remember her little brother, Michael, whom she hadn't seen in thirty-five years. Since the day she lost him. She fought the memory back with what was left of her will. But the memory could not be denied.

A long fit of remorseful weeping, and another double Scotch, numbed her emotions as she relived her life with Paco Ramirez. "God, he can't be dead!" she said out loud, trying to convince herself he wasn't. She thought about what she'd been doing these last few days, and knew it was right, what had to be done.

Nonetheless, she cried until she passed out.

CHAPTER SEVEN

Monday, November 7th
One day before Election Day

It was 7:30 in the morning, with a light rain falling over the mid- Atlantic states. Senator Sam Howard sat aboard his private jet at Dulles International Airport, with members of his campaign and the press, waiting impatiently for Jane Weisser. With Bill Lawson scheduled to be in the South later today, and with Paco Ramirez dead, he needed her with him. She wasn't at home, and she wasn't answering the videophone in her car. Where was she? Sam dialed the pilot. "We can take off now, Dave." The Concorde would be in Los Angeles in two and a half hours, at 7:00 PST. After breakfast with the mayor, he was scheduled to speak at a rally at LA HOPE, the fire ravaged South-Central area, where more than two-thousand people had been killed. A quick jump north to San Francisco for a noontime lunch and speech at Stanford University, and he'd be back East before eight o'clock. He was going to be on the Pacific coast all day, and Jane was going to be in Washington. He hoped she would be in Washington. The alternatives worried him.

Alone at the front of the plane, Sam picked up the phone and called the car. "Dan, where are you?"

"I'm following the subject on Massachusetts Avenue, sir. She left home five minutes ago. Looks like she's heading to work."

"Good. Don't lose her. No matter what it takes, stick to her. If she heads toward Maryland, call me!" He hung up, and the aircraft jettisoned up through the clouds. The thought of Jane discovering the secrets at the cabin made him queasy. The thought that she might already know made him feel even worse.

After the morning briefing with her staff, Jane called Congressman William S. Lawson's office and made an appointment to see him. An hour later, she sat down before the Vice Presidential candidate inside his office in the Dirksen Office Building.

After a few pleasantries over coffee, Jane got to the point of her visit. "Bill, I've always respected you, you know that, don't you?"

The tall Texan laughed and spoke in his southern drawl. "Not always, Miss Jane. Don't you remember when we first met six years ago at the senate inauguration ball?"

Jane remembered attending the ball with Sam after the people of Connecticut reelected him to his second term. Only, she didn't remember meeting the congressman.

"You overheard me talking to some of my colleagues in the House about my proposal to cut taxes, and I caught your disbelieving eye. I remember coming up to you and asking what a diehard Democrat like yourself thought of my ideas? You proceeded to tell me a story about our twenty-seventh president,

William Howard Taft, another Republican."

Jane shook her head. "I'm sorry, I don't remember."

"It went something like this: At the end of a campaign speech, Taft asked everyone to vote for him. One dissenter stood up and declared, 'Not me.' 'Why not?' Taft asked him. 'Because my father and grandfather were both Democrats. And I'm a Democrat, too.' 'That's not a good reason,' Taft pointed out. 'What if you were all horse thieves?' 'Well,' the man said, 'then I guess we'd all be Republicans.'"

Jane laughed. She remembered the story.

"At the time, I didn't think your questionin' my honesty was all that amusing, and again I asked you, 'What does a Democrat think of my ideas?' You matter-of-factly replied, 'The world is populated with bullshitters, congressman. And you can't bullshit a bullshitter.' Do you remember that?"

Jane apologized. "Sometimes my mouth gets me in trouble, Bill."

"You walked away from me and I countered with, 'But, isn't that what you do in your work, Dr. Weisser? Bullshit the public?' You turned back to me and said, 'Sir, my profession calls for it. Your's shouldn't!' That statement, that challenge, changed my life, Miss Jane, and I'll always be grateful. Y'see, from that day on, I tried to be a congressman who spoke nothing but the truth. So, the truth is, you didn't always respect me. I do believe, however, you've come to respect me these last few years. I hope I'm right."

"I stand corrected." Jane smiled, but she couldn't keep it on her face.

"Now, what's on that brilliant mind of yours?" The congressman folded his hands, and, out of respect for her, as always, waited for her to explain.

"I've been up most of the night, most of this past week,

thinking about this, and you're the only one I can talk to about it. I can't go to the president. If I'm wrong, I'll have altered American history for no reason and ruined Sam's chance at leading this nation. I can't go to anyone else for that same reason. Only you, because your future is also at stake. And because of that, you'll keep it to yourself if my fears prove unfounded."

"Miss Jane, I have no idea what you're talking about. Please, take it slowly and start at the beginning."

She hesitated and lit a cigarette. "I have some ideas about who's behind the HOPE bombings and the riots."

"You do?" the Congressman asked, startled.

"Yes." For the next twenty minutes, Jane related all the coincidences, as well as all the inconsistencies. For some reason, she couldn't look directly at the congressman. It was almost as if she felt guilty, or maybe foolish, for bringing something this absurd to his attention. Finally, she came to the end of her surmise. She looked him in the eyes and said, "Everything that has happened this past week benefits above all others one person." She hesitated. "Sam." Jane stopped and looked at the congressman's open mouth.

"I can't believe you think Sam is involved."

"That's why I came to you with this and no one else. As Sam's partner, you'll keep this under your hat if I'm wrong."

"From what you've told me, I'm going to need more proof that Sam is involved before I can do anything."

"Bill, Sam spent the year between Yale and Harvard in Iraq. Why? With everything pointing to Baghdad, it's just too much of a coincidence."

"Maybe he went there to sell Howard Oil."

"Fine, I can accept that. But, to whom did he sell it?"

"What does it matter?"

"It could be the key to all the strange coincidences. It could either absolve Sam or convict him."

The congressman punched in the number of the Securities Exchange Commission on his keyboard and asked them to fax Dr. Weisser the information on the sale. After some more discussion, Bill Lawson looked at his watch, then apologized. "I'm sorry, Miss Jane, but I'm afraid I have to leave. After all, it was you who scheduled me on this last southern two-punch." The always gracious Texan walked to the closet next to the door and put on his overcoat. "I wouldn't worry any longer if I were you. Sooner or later, as the good book says, the truth will emerge, and whoever is behind all this will be dealt with swiftly and harshly. Remember, you can't bullshit a bullshitter. If our Sam is hidin' somethin', believe me, it will surface."

Jane stood, and he took her hands in his and kissed her cheek.

As they walked to the bank of elevators, Congressman Lawson said, "Since I'm from Houston and you're from Boston, mind if I zing you back for that Taft dig?"

"Yes." Jane looked up at the tall man. "But go ahead anyway."

"President Kennedy had a wonderful story about Texas pride. Seems a man from Boston was visitin' the Alamo. A native Texan was braggin' about the bravery of the men who'd fought there. After listening for a while, the man from Boston couldn't take it anymore and decided to brag about his own city's favorite son. He interrupted him and asked, 'Did you ever hear of Paul Revere?' 'Oh, yes,' the Texan answered. 'He's the guy who ran for help.'"

Jane laughed. After wishing him good luck in Atlanta and Miami, she left the Dirksen Office Building. Bill was a real *mensch,* a genuinely good person. One of the few in Congress. It was raining heavier than before, which made it feel colder, and she opened her umbrella.

Jane walked north from Independence Avenue along 1st Street, between the U.S. Capitol and the Supreme Court, toward the Hart Senate Office Building on Constitution Avenue. As she passed the Capitol, she stared at the dome and its cast-iron statue of Freedom. She turned her gaze to her right and looked at the impressive white steps and columns of the Supreme Court. The power and glory represented by that maze of buildings around her always filled her with awe and humility. Could it be corrupted and weakened by the grand plot of a self-serving individual?

At 12:30, Jane received the fax from the SEC in her office. Central Texas Oil and Petroleum had purchased Howard Oil for 12.3 billion dollars shortly after Sam's parents and sister were murdered. She remembered the disclosure of Sam's records last year to the elections committee of the senate. It had shown him to have a net worth of $350 million after investing $12 billion as the general partner for a fifty-one percent ownership in HOPE. No improprieties there. She had to dig deeper. If Sam had sold Howard Oil to an American company as these records indicated, then he wasn't in Iraq for business reasons.

Jane called the Texas State Hall of Records. It took no time to find out the particulars of Central Texas O&P. It was a subsidiary of Intercontinental Oil in Houston. The CEO then, and now, she read on the fax coming into her telecomp printer, was Clarence Donleavy. The next item she read drained the color from her face. Donleavy was born of an American father and an Iraqi mother.

Jane went to the bar in her office and poured herself a liquid lunch as she tried to make sense of all the possible connections. The Scotch had become a daily ritual. She knew why she'd been drinking so much. It was not so much an attempt to feel good as it was an attempt to feel nothing. The best way to cope was not to cope. Jane drank half the drink and thought some more about the past. After graduating Harvard Business School, Sam had built his first HOPE City in Bridgeport, Connecticut, then in New York and Boston, using a good deal of his own wealth and his persuasive skills to garner local support. Everything about that was above board. Jane relived their reunion, their campaign for the U.S. Senate, and the passage of the landmark legislation which funded the building of the other nine HOPE Cities, Sam being awarded the Nobel Peace Prize, and his decision to run for reelection. Then, two weeks before he was reelected to another six-year term in the senate, his wife died in a freak hit and run accident a mile from their home in Fairfax, Virginia.

Jane turned on her telecomp and searched the backdated news files. In seconds, she was reading the Washington Post's front page story about Patricia Howard's death. The name of the man whose car had hit her was Carlos Herrera. The following day's paper showed a picture of the man. Now what? Without Paco and his contacts at INS there was no way to find out if Carlos Herrera had entered the country as someone else. She was at a dead end.

Jane turned on the wall screen to catch the satellite transmission of Sam's speech at LA HOPE. Despite her warning not to take over his own campaign, he had done just that. She felt useless; he was winning without her. "It'll be interesting to hear what promises he makes this time," she said as she finished the Scotch and began to feel its effect. Sam was full of promises for everyone: For the African people, for American society, for her.

The speech had yet to begin, and Jane's mind turned to the cabin in the Maryland woods. Specifically, the best time to go there and search it. Being on the opposite coast, she knew Sam wouldn't be back until late. But, what about the men following her in the blue Buick? With rush hour traffic at its height at six, she could best elude them then. She then considered the safety of her daughter. If Paco was killed because he had gotten too close to the truth, then someone knew what Paco was doing. Someone must have bugged her office, or her house. Sam? Garrison Miller? The Iraqis? Whatever the answer, Jane no longer felt it was safe for Taryn and her to stay in Georgetown.

Jane took the elevator down to the lobby of the Hart Building and walked to a pay phone. She slid her credit card in and Taryn answered on the third ring. "Listen and don't ask questions. Go next door to Mrs. Ferguson and call me back at this number." Jane gave it to her and hung up. Three minutes later, the phone in the booth rang. Jane answered it and said, "Pack a suitcase for each of us and go to the Watergate Hotel. Just in case you're being followed, which you won't know, take a long time and go every roundabout way. Use cash and sign in under ... uh ... Aunt Rich's name."

"Mom, you're scaring me."

"Taryn, do exactly what I say and you won't have any reason to feel scared. This is just precautionary. We have to play it safe."

"You know something, don't you?"

"Taryn, do as I say! I'll call you at the Watergate in a few hours." Jane hung up and returned to her office. Anticipate and prepare! She closed her door and switched on the TC. There on her wall screen was Sam's beaming face. He appeared before a throng of avid supporters looking much like a Messiah surrounded by ecstatic worshipers.

Jane poured some more Scotch in her glass and thought about the last few years. She and Sam had meticulously worked on his platform before he announced his intention to run for president fourteen months ago. His acumen in business management and organization was well known and admired by the American people. The HOPE Cities were a living testament to his skills and ideas. Their proposal was to run the country in a fiscally sound manner, in which the government would answer to its people like a board of directors to its stockholders. This was the basis of their entire campaign approach. However, during the last week Sam was making bold, new promises. Promises he knew neither he nor anyone else could keep. It was the classic ploy of demagogues to gain power over a desperate people.

Feeling a little queasy, Jane plopped herself on the sofa and listened to the great actor work his audience.

" ... and because we sat down as people, people with a common cause, a common need, my hero and yours, Moses McBride, and I have come up with a comprehensive plan to help *all* people. The nationwide unrest has diminished greatly the last twenty-four hours. Everyone wants peace, and everyone is looking for a new beginning. A beginning with a purpose. A beginning with justifiable means to a safer, richer, and happier end."

It was what the thousands of desperate people gathered shoulder to shoulder at LA HOPE wanted to hear. They wanted to be safer, richer, and happier. They screamed and applauded and waved their signs for their savior to see. They loved him. The Messiah had come, at last, in the heart and soul of Sam Howard.

"Along with the Howard Crime Bill, the Education Reinvention Bill, and the new Federal Jobs Programs, I would like to put forth to my California friends an idea that is equitable, fair, and, most important, past due. It is something we must do if we are to be a progressive society, a society for everyone. We, the people of the United States of America, must take back control of our lives by taking back control of our government. And the only way we can do that is with the Election Reform Bill."

Jane stared at him and drank some more Scotch. Sam was brilliant. Throughout the entire campaign, he knew just what he was doing and what he had to do. Her very own Election Reform Bill was the perfect finale.

"My ideas on election reform are radical, yet logical. Within the first thirty days of my presidency, I will propose a constitutional amendment which will lower the voting age to sixteen. Teenage crime has risen over the last three decades because America's youth feel alienated. They fear their future, and, consequently, they enter adulthood with a defeatist attitude. They have no hope because they have no say in their own future. It is time to give them their say; it is time to give them the responsibility of helping shape their future. Our forefathers said that taxation without representation is tyranny. Again, like with capital punishment, America has to abide by its own laws. If an American sixteen or older earns a salary and pays taxes, then he or she must have a say in electing their representatives.

"In the first thirty days of my presidency, I will also put forth to the legislative branch a constitutional amendment to restructure Congress. All terms of office should be for four years. The U. S. Senate would go from six-year terms to four, and the House of Representatives would go from two-year terms to four. Six years is too long for senators to go without being accounted for by the people who put them in office. Two-year terms in the House are unfeasible in that representatives must spend most of their time raising funds for their next campaign. It is more efficient to have four-year terms for all the people's representatives, with no term limitations. And this includes the most important representative of the people, the President. It is the people's right to elect whoever they want for as long as they want. A government *by* the people. If you're for term limits, then vote for the opposing candidate. But, if an elected official is doing an exemplary job in public office, we should keep them there to continue that fine work. No one, not even our government, should be able to take away that inalienable right from us."

The people showed their approval with their thunderous applause and with their shouts of "SAM'S THE MAN! SAM'S THE MAN!" It made sense. When you looked at it logically, it was the smart thing to do. But, what did it have to do with them? With California?

Jane got up and poured herself a few more shots of Scotch. She knew what was coming next. How many times had she lectured him about it at Yale? She remembered it vividly, as if it were yesterday. Sam was passionate about those ideas because Jane was passionate about them.

"I advocate implementing a campaign tax in the amount of $20 for every person and dependent, which would be matched by the federal government. A family of four would pay $80 a year. Based on a population of 250 million taxable Americans, it would mean $40 billion every four years for the approximately 2,500 incumbents and challengers who run for president, U.S. Senate, U.S. House of Representatives, and governor. No candidate could spend any more than the amount they receive. Equal amounts for each office. The Presidential candidates would receive the most, then those running for U.S. Senate, and so forth down the line.

At the end of the election, their accountants would have to make public all monies spent. This would stop candidates from outspending their opponent, from spending one week of each month traveling to raise funds for their next campaign, from taking PACs, and from granting favors. Most of all, it would insure honest voting in Congress. In return for this free funding by the people and the government, our elected leaders would have to spend a minimum of four days every month in town meetings hearing their constituency's views on upcoming bills. To keep campaigns on a high level, I propose that any negative campaigning would reduce that funding by ten percent."

It was about time our politicians represented us instead of their own interests and pockets. It was about time America's voice returned to Washington. The country was also sick of negative campaigning. It had turned their society aggressive, hostile, angry, and cynical. Taking control of our politicians meant taking control of society, which meant taking control of our lives and our future. Although it meant money out of their own pockets, the people rallied behind it. The cheers and chants forced Sam to stop and smile. Jane saw it and finished the drink. She could no longer feel the numbing effect of the Scotch. All she could feel was betrayal.

When the crowd quieted down, he continued. "Regarding the electoral college, the president must be elected by the *people.* A constitutional amendment abolishing the electoral college and allowing the popular vote to elect our president is essential in order for the people to legally, and equally, have their say in government."

Again, the collective approval of the masses interrupted Sam. The applause became so loud that Sam had to yell the last line. "ALL VOTERS AND ALL VOTES WILL ELECT OUR OFFICIALS, AND THEY WILL RUN AN ABOVE BOARD CAMPAIGN AND SERVE THE PEOPLE THEY REPRESENT IN AN HONEST, COMMUNICATIVE, AND DUTIFUL WAY! THIS WILL BE OUR LEGACY TO OUR CHILDREN AND TO OUR FUTURE."

"YES!" "We love you, Sam!" "God bless you!" Each and every day the love and admiration of the people grew for Sam

Howard, 'Uncle Sam', the future President of the United States of America.

Jane couldn't watch anymore and she turned off the telecomp. Sam had employed all of her tactics with astonishing effect. Not once during the campaign had he belittled President Price or Vice President Fuller. It was Jane's rule. By never mentioning the competition, you don't publicize the competition. You render them non-existent. Publicity was psychological. By not acknowledging Charles Price, the president, himself, was forced to stop his negative campaigning, which proved positive for Sam and made Price look defeatable. Psychological warfare was the best way to run a campaign. Mass manipulation of society's emotions was more effective than appeals to reason. She had done all that for Sam. Now, Sam Howard had taken that lesson one step further. Acting the greatest role of his life, he was seducing, hypnotizing, and controlling that society. Jane felt like an accomplice, yet she didn't know why. There was still no proof of wrongdoing. Wasn't he innocent until proven guilty?

The cabin held the answer to it all.

Jane's tension was finally submerged in an alcohol induced lassitude. She locked her office door, with the 'Do Not Disturb' sign on the outside, turned off her telecomp and its incoming phone line, and lay down.

She was asleep within minutes.

By 3 p. m. Jane was awake alone in her office, thinking and trying to tie the pieces together. She returned to the Washington Post news files on her telecomp and typed in Carlos Herrera under 'Find.' The first find brought her to the accident report. The next three finds were follow-up stories, then - nothing. She returned to the first and studied the man's picture. He looked Latino. Maybe Patty Howard's death was innocent. Jane thought about it and refused to accept it. Paco was murdered by a car bomb. Someone had stopped him from finding out the truth. She looked at the photo again. Carlos Herrera was dark-skinned. Maybe he was Arab, not Latino. Paco had told her that Mustafa Al-Salaam had been found dead in Rock Creek Park soon after his arrest for disrupting the President's speech. If the Iraqis were behind everything, and they killed their people to erase the trail leading back to them, then maybe they killed Carlos Herrera, too. Jane typed in the word 'murder' under 'Find,' to be sorted by date for three months following the car crash. Every murder in Washington, D.C. flashed on the screen, one by one, in order of their dates.

It took more than an hour to scan them, but at 4:30 Jane came to one that raised the hairs on her neck. A body had been pulled from the Potomac River on December 11th. A close-up of the bloated face was on the front page of the Post. It didn't look like Carlos Herrera, but a distinctive scar, shaped almost like a question mark, ran from his left eye to the bottom of his nose. Jane printed the picture of the dead man, then returned the microfilm to the story of Patty Howard's accident. She printed the photo of Carlos Herrera and compared the two.

They both had the same scar.

The man, the article said, had been identified through his fingerprints as Faad Aziz. From Baghdad, Iraq!

Sayyid Kassim sat in his living room in Baghdad with his eleven old friends, the men of Al-Qiyamah, watching the telecomp. The news continued with the coverage of the cease of hostilities in the U.S. It had been slow at first, but it had progressively spread, and peace was on the American horizon at last. The Iraqi news report continued with the latest numbers in the U. S. election: Senator Sam Howard was now leading President

Charles Price 51-47 percent. Helping end the racial conflict had not only showed America how much of a leader Sam Howard was, it had also showed the world how much of a leader Charles Price wasn't.

Sayyid Kassim thought about the past, about his son and all the sons murdered at the hands of America. The hatred still burned inside him. He may have quenched his thirst for vengeance, but that hatred would always be there. Tomorrow was the culmination with the American president being asked to leave office. Part one of the Saddam's plot was a success. Part two would be, also.

Unless …

Sayyid Kassim stood to think. There was only one problem: Dr. Jane Weisser. However, he knew how to eliminate that problem. The leader of Al-Qiyamah continued his celebration. He lifted his glass and announced for everyone to hear and rejoice in, "Our great Allah has struck down the evil-doers. Allah akbar!"

"Allah akbar!"

Sam boarded his Concorde jet at 2:00 p. m. and left Palo Alto, California for Washington, D.C. He would be back in two and a half hours, 7:30 EST. He would deal with Jane then. Not showing up for this final campaign stop was the last straw. A confrontation was now unavoidable. It was now obvious she knew more than she should. She was now part of it. He loved her, but he could not allow her to destroy his life's ambition.

Standing in the middle of her office, Jane couldn't catch her breath. An Arab, an Iraqi, had killed Patty Howard. All the evidence indicated Sam's complicity in an astounding variety of ruthless actions, including his own wife's death.

And who knew what else.

At 6:30, she took the elevator down to the garage and entered her white Mercedes sedan. She pulled out into the heavy downtown traffic and decided to go home to Georgetown first, pack some clothes, then go out to the cabin before joining Taryn, incognito, at the Watergate Hotel.

Jane drove north along Massachusetts Avenue and noticed each time she looked in her rearview mirror that a car was following her, a black Lincoln. Frightened, she recalled her last conversation with Paco.

'Jane, I don't mean to worry you, but I think I'm being followed,' he had told her when they last spoke. 'Two foreign looking men in a black Lincoln.'

Jane looked in her rearview mirror again. A black Lincoln, with two men inside, was still following her. She accelerated the car and wove in and out of traffic around the many circular intersections of Washington and Georgetown. Ten minutes later, after repeated anxious glimpses in her mirror, the car was nowhere in sight. Relieved, but still shaken, she drove through Georgetown to her home on Foxhall Road, constantly checking her rearview mirror.

Jane was in the house for less than ten minutes packing papers and money, everything she would need for the next few days. She locked the front door and took off for the cabin in Burtonsville, Maryland.

On K Street, heading toward New York Avenue, she started looking in the mirror again. There was no black Lincoln, but a phalanx of three cars trailed her as she turned onto Route 50.

One of them was a blue Buick.

The Secret Service agent in the passenger seat of the blue Buick, sworn to secrecy and paid off by Sam Howard for his discretion, answered the ringing videophone. "Talbot here."

"Dan, I just landed at Dulles. What's the situation?"

"We just turned off 50 onto I-95. Dr. Weisser looks to be heading north toward Maryland, senator."

Sam told him to back off. He would take it from there.

Sam stepped off his private jet, and the press quickly surrounded him. "I'm sorry, but I have to rush. I'll talk to all of you first thing in the morning." Inside the limousine, he told his driver, "Take me to my office." His private car was in the senate garage. He had to get out to the cabin, alone and unseen, which meant dismissing his Secret Service agents. He'd done that the night he went to the cabin to meet Jane, now he'd have to again. They weren't supposed to leave his side, but a future assignment to President Howard might depend on their taking candidate Howard's orders.

Seated in the back of the limousine, Sam closed his eyes and thought about Jane. With a 51-47 lead going into the election tomorrow, he wasn't a sure winner yet. He couldn't let love interfere with that.

Jane was puzzled and relieved when she saw the blue Buick pull off at the next exit. She wondered where the black Lincoln was.

Thirty minutes later, Jane turned off the highway and drove west along Sandy Spring Road into Burtonsville. She turned right a short distance later and drove along the dark streets until she came to the dirt road and the one mile trail that led to the cabin. She didn't see the black Lincoln parked amongst the foliage on the side of the road.

Jane reached the end of the narrow and secluded road that winded through the woods. It was quiet and dark, with only the light of the full moon, and the sound of crunching leaves underneath her shoes echoing in her ears. She took out the key and entered the cabin. It was always exciting walking into that dream world. Only now, the dream had become a nightmare. She looked around with fearful anticipation. There was nothing in the great room, nothing in the bedroom. Her mouth was dry and it was hard to swallow. She went into the bathroom and took a drink from the tap, then gazed about the room, alert to previously unnoticed details.

When she saw it, her heart started pounding. Taped to the back of the toilet was a handgun in a holster. Her senses heightened by the discovery, she returned to the combination living room/dining room/kitchen and looked at everything with increased awareness. There was a closet next to the couch. She went to it and tried to open it, but it was locked.

Shrouded by darkness, the two Arab men sitting in the black Lincoln watched the narrow opening to the dirt road. The one called Abdullah Nasir, thin and dark-skinned, and committed to Sayyid Kassim, said to the burley, and equally committed, Mahmoud Halam, "In the name of our great Allah, it is time to take vengeance on the Yehoudi."

The driver's eyes widened and his fingers twitched in anticipation and excitement. Killing was a pleasure. Killing Jews was ecstasy.

It was easy to snap away the wooden molding of the door frame with the tire iron from her car trunk, and Jane had it open in a few seconds. The coat closet had only one thing inside: a black metal, five-drawer file cabinet, with a push-in lock in the upper right corner. It was a little more difficult than the door was, but Jane finally broke the lock with the tire iron and gained access to the drawers. There must have been hundreds of folders inside. Exactly how much time she had she didn't know, and she began leafing through the papers, reading, skimming, sometimes only visually registering the words on the pages. It frightened her that she was doing something illegal, but the need to know the truth spurred her on. Jane looked at her watch. Sam would be back soon. When, she didn't know, but she was determined not to leave the cabin until she found whatever secret was hidden there.

Twenty minutes later, her whole body and soul were shaken by the dreadful knowledge of what she found. The cabin's phone bills showed calls had been made to the same number in Baghdad, Iraq on the first of every month, until last month's bill. "SAM!" she moaned before breaking down into a fit of agonized sobbing. It was just too horrific to believe.

As Mahmoud started the car and shifted into gear, Abdullah grabbed his arm. "Wait!" Another car had pulled in from the deserted street and was heading toward the end of the private dirt road where they were parked. "Turn off the engine." Seated in the darkness, the two Arabs stared at the passing car, a twin of theirs, except for the tinted windows, which blocked any views of the occupants. The tension left their bodies. They would have to wait until the visitor left.

Sam hurried out of his car when he saw Jane's white Mercedes parked outside the cabin. He quickly opened the door and stepped inside. Jane was standing before the open closet, reading and crying. Their eyes locked.

"You've been prying into my affairs, Jane, and I'm afraid that hasn't been wise. Now …" It was difficult to issue the threat to the most important woman in his life. " … if you don't want to get hurt, you will stop at once and forget everything you've learned!"

"WHAT I'VE LEARNED? How about a plot to …"

"Don't tell me what it is, I already know."

"How could you, Sam?"

"History has proved that the African race ..."

"NOT THAT, DAMNIT! US!"

Us? He didn't understand. What did this have to do with them?

"HOW COULD YOU HAVE LIED TO ME LIKE THIS? YOU DECEIVED ME! Our entire relationship these last thirteen years ... these last six ... has been a joke. YOU USED ME!"

Sam watched Jane's eyes dart toward the door. Did she feel trapped? Did she think he wouldn't let her leave knowing his secret? He sat on the edge of the couch and beckoned for her to join him. "Please, Jane." She refused and turned away from his stare, hurt and frightened. Sam knew he had to make her understand. Now that it was out in the open, he owed her an explanation. He took a deep breath and began the story. "After my family was murdered, I went insane for awhile. When I recovered, I replayed the events of that horrible day in my mind, over and over. It wasn't fair, it wasn't right. They shot my parents and my sister in cold blood, and they died a horrible death, in absolute terror." Sam paused and visualized it all once more. "I live with that nightmare every day."

There was no response.

"They took away not only my family's lives, they also took away any joy I could feel in my own life. Becoming an actor meant nothing to me anymore. It was no longer important. Everything was just an act."

Jane turned to him with a cold look in her ice-blue eyes. Her milky-white face was flushed red. "Cut the theatrics, Sam. Jesus, I can't distinguish between you and the actor anymore. The frightening thing is neither can you."

Her comments cut through him like knives. Didn't she understand the pain he had gone through, the pain he was still going through? Didn't she love him anymore? Sam swallowed hard. He prayed not for her pity, but for her understanding. "Do you know what it feels like to be left all alone, Jane?"

She wouldn't answer him. She just stared into his eyes with a look of revulsion, sadly distorting her beautiful face.

Sam had to turn away from that look; it hurt too much to see. He got up and paced the floor of the great room. "Do you know what it feels like to suddenly lose everything that ever meant anything to you? Can you imagine what I felt, Jane?" He paused, hoping she would answer him this time, but, again, she didn't. Either she was using a psychological ploy, or she truly hated him now. He tried to keep the pleading tone out of his voice, but, as he spoke, he found he couldn't. "I knew I could never again be whole unless I avenged their murders. An old friend of my father's from the oil business, Sayyid Kassim, got in touch with me and brought me to Baghdad. There, we found a common bond. He had to avenge the death of his only son when America attacked Iraq, and I had to avenge the death of my family. We spoke for weeks, commiserating with each other, until one day he offered to buy Howard Oil. I had no interest in running the company any longer, and he wrote me a check, right there, for twelve-billion dollars."

Still pacing, Sam told Jane about meeting the eleven other men who had lost their sons, and about how they had become a family, united in their mourning, over the months. He stopped his discourse and turned to her, hoping she finally understood. She was staring down at the floor, a smoking cigarette in her hand. A look of anguish was on her face, as if she were in another world, reliving a grief of her own. Was she thinking about her brother Michael? Jesus, how could he expect her to accept what he had done when she, herself, had gone through the same pain?

"JANE!" he yelled. Her head jerked up to look at him. "I'm not strong like you. I couldn't just forgive and forget. I couldn't even live with myself."

She looked at him in disbelief.

"The men of Al-Qiyamah had a plan that would compensate for all our suffering. It was that plan that turned despair into HOPE. And HOPE made me a U.S. senator. Now, if the polls are correct, tomorrow it will make me President of the United States. Don't you see, Jane? I'm whole again. I'm where I belong. On top of the world, with you, like we were at Yale. My God, Jane, we're back where we started, where we left off. It's time to continue, as it was meant to be."

She spoke, forcing the words through a throat clogged and constricted with emotion. "Then you built HOPE specifically for its sacrifice and the effect it would have on the country and the election."

His silence was all the answer she needed.

When it finally registered, Jane's eyes filled with fire. "Paco! YOU BASTARD, YOU KILLED PACO!" She swung her arm to hit him, but Sam grabbed her, and the blow fell short. He sat her on the couch as she fought him in an impotent rage. "You murderer! All those people, all those innocent children. How could you?"

"Don't you understand, Jane? Society will flourish if we cut out the cancer that consumes it. Without the Africans and Latinos, and everyone exploiting the system, poverty and crime will be almost non-existent in the United States. Government assistance will be eradicated. Everyone left will live better and be safer and happier. It's the only answer, Jane, only no one has had the guts to do it. Well, I did it!"

"You're insane! Certifiably insane! You're a modern-day

Hitler bent on genocide. You're worse than Garrison Miller. Oh, my God, I can't believe I've spent a lifetime loving you. I can't believe I didn't see through to your rotten core."

Sam sat down by her side and said what was in his heart. "I don't expect you to understand all this, Jane. Sometimes even I don't. But, as Sayyid said, future generations will thank us for making it a world where everyone can live separately and peacefully, like all species were meant to live. Please Jane, it's politics, that's all. It doesn't change a thing between us. I love you. With all my heart. Without you I can't live." He looked at her and realized she was thinking, analyzing, trying to come up with a way to stop him. "There's nothing you can do about this, Jane, so don't try. Sayyid knows all about you. If you try to do something, or if word of this gets out, you and Taryn will be …" He stopped in mid-sentence, horrified that he had to even formulate this thought. His voice got softer, and he said it more as a plea than a threat. "No matter where you go, they will find you and kill you. I'm sorry, but I can't promise your safety."

Jane stood up and looked down at him. "What you're talking about is the covert overthrow of the United States government, Sam! Don't you see you're just a pawn in Sayyid's plot?"

He didn't respond with words. Instead, he looked up at her like a wounded animal, survival being its only instinct.

"A brainwashed puppet!"

Sam's voice hardened. "Be careful. As I said, I can't promise your safety."

"YOU SONOVABITCH!"

"It's up to you to decide, Jane. Is your patriotism more important than your and your daughter's lives?"

With a look of contempt on her face, Jane walked to the front door of the cabin.

"Stay in Washington where I can reach you at all times. I

also expect you to be by my side at the Park Place Hotel tomorrow night as if nothing happened."

She opened the door ...

"Do you understand?"

... and walked out to her car.

Sam felt the tears fall down his cheeks. He had lost his mother, Britney, and, now, the only woman he'd ever passionately loved. Patty had been part of the plan, expendable. But Jane was his sole reason for living. Now he had lost her as suddenly as he had lost his family. The only thing he had left, the only thing that would ease his pain, was revenge.

And tomorrow he would have it. Tomorrow at noon he would be the most celebrated man in the world. Wanted and needed and loved by everyone.

Even Jane could not change that.

Jane raced out of the mile-long dirt road, through the private streets, and left toward Laurel and I-95. She was angry. And scared. And confused. Tears streamed down her face. She didn't know what she hated more: Politics? Being a psychologist? Sam? She didn't know what to do. She was afraid of the Arab threat, and, now, of Sam, and there was still the danger that Garrison Miller posed. Although her assumption that Miller was behind the HOPE bombings had proved wrong, he was still one of the forces behind the nationwide rioting, not to forget his attempted assassination of the Republican presidential candidate. How safe was she and Taryn with that knowledge? With everyone out to silence her, there was only one thing she could do: She would have to remain by Sam Howard's side for the time being. But, she was damned if she was going to allow Taryn to remain there as a target. No, Taryn had to go. And she had to do it secretly.

She drove farther away from the cabin and thought about

Sam and all he had done. "The man never had the chance to prove himself to his father. Being president will do that." Jane understood Sam's mind. She tried to understand his heart, but it was a heart she now despised. It was a hateful heart, and she would do everything in her power to stop it.

She created him. She had to destroy him.

Jane drove south to College Park because she didn't want to call and leave a name. A trail. She had to send Taryn away without anyone knowing she was leaving. She knew there were Liberty Travel Agencies in most malls from coast to coast. At just before nine o'clock, she hoped there was one in the College Park Mall, and it was still open when she got there. She pressed down on the accelerator.

Jane arrived and took the escalator to the main level. Michael! her heart screamed at her. She hadn't been in a mall since he disappeared back when she was twelve years old. The memory was haunting. Debilitating. She tried to shake the nightmare from her mind by concentrating on the nightmare she was now living.

On the mall directory, she saw it: Liberty Travel. She ran down the sparsely populated walkway and read every neon sign. There it was! A woman was locking the glass door. "NO! WAIT! Please, I need a ticket for one on any flight tomorrow to Boston. Paid with cash. Can you take just a minute to help me?"

The travel agent recognized the celebrity and told Jane it would be an honor to help her. She reopened the door and let her in.

Less than fifteen minutes later, the teenager was ticketed under an assumed name to go along with her fake identification. Taryn would go to Boston and stay with her grandparents until Jane could figure a way out of this mess. Somewhat relieved for the time being, she walked away from the travel agency, thinking about what she had to do next.

As she turned left out of Liberty Travel, she never noticed the two men, Abdullah Nasir and Mahmoud Halam, lurking inside the doorway of the Brooks Brothers clothing store across from the travel agency.

"So, Mahmoud, she plans on running." He pulled out his portable videophone from his coat pocket. It was time to call Sayyid.

CHAPTER EIGHT

Tuesday, November 8th
Election Day

It had been more than twelve hours since he received the call and Sayyid Kassim was still angry. Sam had been nothing short of perfection up until now. Now, at the last moment, he was weakening. Jane Weisser had him - what was that American expression? - by the balls. It never failed with American men. Their women plied them with sex, addicted them, and then had a stranglehold on them forever. Sayyid laughed at that thought. It was just reward for the evils the Americans inflict on the rest of the world. He should have realized long ago what that combination could do to their plan. Sam had been susceptible like all the rest. His whore was a typical American woman.

But not for long.

Sayyid removed the white kaffiyah from his head and looked

at his watch. Eight o'clock. That meant it was noon in Virginia. He punched in the number on the telecomp keyboard and sat down to face the wall screen.

"You have not taken care of the problem, Sam, and I am not at all happy about it," Sayyid said a few minutes after their untraceable conversation began. "You have let me down. You have let Al-Qiyamah down and that is not good." The image of Sam Howard filled the wall of Sayyid Kassim's living room, and Sayyid stared at him. Ever since Saddam Hussein had his family killed the day he graduated Yale, he had used the American. He had taken a brilliant actor with a natural politician's talent and ambition and redirected it to a vengeance fueled by racial hatred. But, now Sam was wavering just as total victory seemed imminent. "You created this problem, Sam, I expect you to take care of it."

"Sayyid … "

"No, Sam, no excuses. There is no other way. You deceived us by not telling us about your feelings for the woman. It must now end! We've waited for this day for a long time and I won't have her take it away from us." Sayyid paused a moment for affect, although he didn't need to. His word was law. And no one, not even the eleven men of Al-Qiyamah, questioned it. "Now that she knows everything, there is no alternative."

"I understand, Sayyid."

"Good. Now this is how … "

Later in the afternoon, Jane and Taryn left the Watergate Hotel in their rental car. The agent had taken the elevator up to their room, according to Taryn's instructions, where she paid him in cash for one week plus the security deposit. Jane had stayed out of sight when the man arrived because she didn't want to be recognized. She had all the cash she could find in her Georgetown home, as well as the three-hundred dollars she withdrew from the ATM in the mall the night before, plus another three-hundred she withdrew this morning from the machine in the hotel lobby.

They took the small service elevator to the underground garage and drove into the heart of the city's biggest day. Jane looked up and down Virginia Avenue. To her surprise, and relief, no one was following them today. She let out her breath and headed toward Dulles Airport.

"So far, so good," Taryn said from the passenger seat of the Ford Focus.

"It won't be good until I see your plane take off."

After a long silence, Taryn said, "Mom, I'm scared. From what little you've told me, I can tell you're not safe. Please, come with me. It makes no sense to stay."

Jane thought about it. She had to play by Sam's rules until she knew what to do. If she wasn't by his side tonight, she didn't know what Sayyid Kassim would do. She had to play the role of the loyal advisor and confidant. It was her safest course of action.

"Mom?"

"I'm sorry, Taryn. And I'm sorry I got you in this mess. Please forgive me."

The teenager took her mother's hand in hers. "The apple doesn't fall far from the tree. Remember? I made the same mistake with Gary."

Jane let out a sigh, only it came out more as a cry. "Please, don't remind me. That's another problem yet to be solved."

They remained quiet for a few minutes. "But why stay?" Taryn insisted.

"I wish I could tell you. Really. Until I can, I have to ask you to trust me."

They drove south on 23rd Street, their hands clasped, afraid they might never see each other again. At least Taryn will be safe, Jane said to herself for what had to be the millionth time.

The plan was to drive across the Theodore Roosevelt Bridge into Virginia and take the George Washington Parkway to 123. Dulles was twenty-five miles away, a forty-five minute ride at the most. If all went well, they'd get there with about thirty minutes to spare.

As they left Georgetown, their car approached a four-way intersection. The light was green, and Jane drove into it. At the same time, a small truck came careening through the red light from their right. Jane saw it from the corner of her eye, but it was too late to stop or accelerate. The truck smashed into the passenger-side front tire of their rental car. Taryn screamed, and Jane did all she could do to keep the car from spinning out of control. The rear of the car fishtailed into the side of the white truck - the sound of metal against metal screeched in Jane's ears - and both vehicles came to an abrupt stop after bouncing off each other

"ARE YOU OKAY, TARYN, ARE YOU OKAY?"

Taryn was shaking and wincing. Her right side had taken the brunt of the impact when her door hit the side of the truck. "Yeah, I guess. How about you?"

"I'm all right, I think." A small crowd had formed around the site of the accident. Jane opened her door and tried to step out, but her left knee buckled; she had jammed it on the steering column. She regained her balance and was able to stand although the injured knee sent stabbing pains up her leg. "Slide over and get out from my side."

The eighteen-year old girl winced as she slowly got out of the car.

"We better get you to a hospital for x-rays."

"No, I'm sure I'm fine. If anything was broken, I'd know it."

Jane heard the growing crowd whispering around the two smashed vehicles. She ignored them and limped to the upholstery truck. The sign on the side read: Feller's Fine Fabrics.

"Are you all right?" she asked the stunned man seated behind the steering wheel. He was holding his forehead.

"Just a bad bump, that's all. And you?"

"We're fine. Do you need a doctor?"

"No, uh, I don't think so."

She helped him out, and the three of them waited on the side of the road for the police to arrive. Most of the crowd had dispersed when they saw the accident was minor, but a few curious ones remained and watched. After all, it was Jane Weisser.

"You're her, aren't you?" the man who introduced himself as Daniel Feller said, looking apologetic and impressed at the same time.

Jane acknowledged the recognition. Oh, to be anonymous, she thought. She looked at her watch and realized Taryn wasn't going to make her flight. Damnit!

"I just voted for Sam. I hope he wins."

"Thank you."

Mr. Feller returned to his truck and made a call on his videophone. Five minutes later, he walked back to them. "I'm sorry for ruining what should be the happiest day of your life, Dr. Weisser."

Jane nodded and turned to her daughter. Taryn looked dazed and a little confused. My poor baby, she thought. As she waited for the Georgetown police to show up, Jane realized what happiness really was. It wasn't what she was doing. It was better to enjoy the world, not control it. It was better to be Taryn Weisser's mother than Sam Howard's campaign director.

She exchanged information with the patrolman who arrived on the scene, and he called a taxi for her and her daughter.

Suddenly, they heard an explosion in the distance. Although it was a cool November day, and she was wearing her blue woolen coat, Jane began to shiver. Her insides shook from the reverberations of the explosion. Or, was it her nerves? Jane listened for another one, but there were none. What it was, she didn't know, but something had definitely happened nearby. Had the conflict not fully ended? Was this nightmare continuing? Everyone looked at her for an answer.

Thankfully, the taxi arrived a few minutes later. The young policeman on the scene assured them that their car would be returned to the rental agency, and Jane and Taryn were driven back to the Watergate Hotel.

Inside their room, Taryn went into the bathroom. Jane turned on CNN to listen to the latest news of the election. What she heard, instead, was the voice of Susan Teitel reporting live from Dulles Airport.

"Less than an hour ago, Flight 475 from Dulles to Boston's Logan International Airport exploded shortly after takeoff. Rescue workers are now on the scene, only it appears to be a futile effort. According to reports, two-hundred and forty-five people were aboard the American Airlines Airship. From the size of the explosion and fire that has consumed the plane, any chance of survivors appears to be minimal. But, this is unofficial speculation. Just last year …"

Jane ran into the bathroom and was sick.

Taryn was at the sink, yelling, "Mom, what's wrong?"

There was no answer, just Jane waving her out of the room. A few minutes later, after cleaning herself, she returned to the bedroom looking pale and weak.

"Are you okay, Mom? What happened?"

Jane sat down on the bed and told her everything. Whereas before, Jane had told her only certain things, so she wouldn't worry, it was now imperative that Taryn know it all. Ignorance, at this point, could be deadly.

They talked about it for close to an hour, then Jane returned to the bathroom, this time to be alone. She sat on top of the toilet, thinking about those unfortunate two-hundred and forty-five people. She noticed the ash fall from her cigarette onto the white tile floor at her feet. Her hand was shaking. Her whole body was shaking.

Sam Howard had just tried to kill her daughter.

Sam sat on one of the beige sofas inside the oversized living room of his Virginia mansion. Seated across from him on the other sofa were his former in-laws, the Kellehers. By his side were his two sons, Adam and Bradley. They were watching the election results on the four-panel wall screen on the wall opposite the fireplace. It was only ten o'clock, yet there was already an air of excitement in the room as each station relayed what was happening nationwide. TC cameras were there to record for the American public the candidate's reaction to the result. It was a homey scene, and the country was able to view this family portrait many times throughout the evening. What everyone saw was a widower who kept his former in-laws not only in his children's lives but in his as well. In his home. What a magnanimous man! What a loving man! Here was the living embodiment of family values. What an example for the rest of the country!

At 10:45, Sam heard what he'd been waiting all these years to hear when Eric Canfield announced, "NBC is projecting Senator Howard the winner. With …"

The red lights on top of the cameras turned on again, and the country viewed the victor hugging his two teenage boys, whose arms were wrapped around their father, congratulating him. Happiness was everywhere in the Howard home, and the people of this divided nation finally saw their hope of unification. A safer, richer, and happier society was soon to be theirs. 'Uncle Sam' had offered them peace and prosperity, and in return for that promise they had presented him the presidency.

In the upper right quarter of the split screen, Sam heard Melinda Murphy of CNN reporting the same. He turned up the volume for that quadrant. " … Sam Howard will be the next President of the United States. It is all but certain …"

The other networks had the same results. It *was* certain. He'd done it!

Sam closed his eyes and rejoiced. It had taken him a lifetime, but he'd finally achieved everything he was promised and he'd promised himself. At the same time, he had wrecked vengeance on America's African people for murdering his family. Sayyid was right. You can have it all. He couldn't imagine being any happier.

His emotional upswing was dampened by the image of Jane. He tried in vain to suppress the rising panic which accompanied it.

In New Carrollton, Maryland, Garrison Miller paced the cold, unswept floor of his cement basement. Things didn't look so good for white America. Carl Block, Lonnie and Tommy McKay, and Jimmy Siefert were equally upset as they sat around the small table, watching the old portable television next to the washing machine and dryer.

" … and CBS projects the winner to be Sam Howard …" Carl Block leaned forward and turned the channel. " … with two-hundred and eighty-three Electoral College votes, ABC News projects Sam Howard as the next President of the United States."

Miller pushed back the chair he'd been sitting in and stood. He slapped the bare light bulb above the table. It swung up and crashed on impact with the ceiling. The shattered pieces of glass and filament showered down on the men, but they didn't move, except to hunch over to avoid being cut. "SHIT! Everything's gone wrong. The niggers have their man in office, and not only is this war over, but I didn't kill McBride. And now the nigger's a fuckin' hero for supposedly saving the president-elect's life. SHIT!" Miller paced the floor. There had to be something he could do to get Moses McBride. He knew he wouldn't rest until he did. And what about Jane and Taryn Weisser? he asked himself. Do they suspect I broke into their computer? And do they know I was the one who shot Moses McBride? The questions, and the possible answers, wracked his mind. Miller ran his hands through his hair. For the first time in his life, 'the most hateful man in America' felt a feeling he had never before felt. Fear!

Kicking at anything and nothing, Garrison Miller dismissed it. Fear was for losers. He wasn't going to lose. It was only a matter of time before he won.

The leader of the People for a White America turned his blazing eyes on his men. "Bring me Jane Weisser's daughter."

Jane and Taryn Weisser sat at the foot of the king-size bed inside Jane's Watergate Hotel bedroom. Tears ran down the teenager's face. Her mother tried as best as she could to present a brave front. They had just heard the results.

"Well, I guess that's that," Taryn whispered.

Jane closed her eyes. Is it? Or is it just beginning?

Moses McBride stirred uneasily in his Harlem Hospital bed. The physical pain from his massive shoulder wound was kept in check by the strong painkilling drugs steadily dripping into him from his intravenous catheter. The mental anguish caused by his wife's critical condition, and the recent attacks on America's African communities, should have been relieved by the election of Sam Howard. Sam Howard, his good friend and friend to all the dispossessed minorities of the country, offered hope for the future. Yet, a vague feeling of uneasiness undermined any sense of satisfaction he could derive from Sam's victory. Moses turned his head and gazed at his comatose wife who occupied the adjacent bed. "There's hope for us now, Jessie." He paused and thought for a moment. "I hope."

The Park Place Hotel in Washington, D.C. was filled with revelers celebrating. It was the beginning of a new world and a new life for everyone. There was joy and peace and hope in the air, and the festive mood was intoxicating.

Jane Weisser stood at the back of the red, white, and blue decorated ballroom in a simple but elegant white dress, with pearls and heels to match. Tall and statuesque, her long, dark hair, sparkling blue eyes, and illuminating smile always kept her in the spotlight. Yet, Jane hated being in the spotlight. Her beauty, in tandem with her confident and assertive personality, didn't mesh with the public's expectation of her. They couldn't accept the combination of beauty and authoritative competence. Trying to remain unobtrusive, she engaged in some small talk, accepted congratulations, and thanked all those she needed to thank.

For Jane Weisser, the mood this evening was anything but intoxicating. For that, the necessary Scotch was already in her hand. Taryn was still at the Watergate. It was safer for them to stay separate so that Sayyid and his henchmen could not capture them both at once. Jane's own celebrity was also temporarily protective. What she had to do next was send Taryn away. Far away, until there was some resolution to this maddening situation.

Jane took a drink and closed her eyes to tide her anger. Begging forgiveness from the representative and two senators she was listening to, she walked away where she could be alone with her thoughts. She agonized over her recent decisions and course of action, but she had done what she had done because there was no other option. Now, she was doing what she was doing for the same reason.

Jane only had a few seconds to compose herself before she was again surrounded. But, then she heard, "Ladies and gentlemen, the President-elect of the United States of America." The music began, and a bright spotlight followed Sam Howard and his family to the dais in front of the Park Place ballroom. There was a thunderous ovation from the invited guests. In the pool zone between the stage and the crowd, Secret Service agents and members of the press moved in. Jane stared at Sam. He was milking it. She had the urge to pull on her right earlobe - Let's move on! The drink in her hand was empty, and Jane went to the bar for another.

"Thank you. Thank you. (Wave) Hi, thanks for coming. (The Great Smile) Please! Thank you. (Laugh) I appreciate it." Sam waved his arms for them to stop. They wouldn't, and the applause got louder.

Jane finished another drink and the rage inside her got louder.

"Today, America begins a new era. Into a safer, richer, and happier society."

Everyone shouted and hugged and danced where they were standing.

"With Housing, Opportunity, Prosperity, and Equality for every American!"

Yeah? What about America's people of color, Sam? Jane thought.

"Today, we forget the past and look toward the future. We forget the sins and focus instead on the dreams. Today, we leave behind acrimony and division and begin our journey to Utopia. Together as one great people!"

The people cheered, and the orchestra played 'Happy Days Are Here Again.'

Give me a break!

Sam held up his arms in an all-embracing gesture and his countenance told the country they were now his own. Sam Howard had taken them in. He soaked up their love and gazed up toward Heaven. You see, Dad, I told you. I TOLD YOU!

He let out a raucous laugh and looked down at his adoring followers. "Yes, my dear friends, you can believe. You can believe our dreams will come true."

There was more screaming and cheering, more singing and dancing and celebrating, more renditions of 'Happy Days Are Here Again,' and more and more Jane wanted to show Sam Howard for the fraud he was. She couldn't listen to the rest of his speech.   After Sam finished, and the crowds that had surrounded him had thinned, Jane decided that she'd had enough of Johnny Walker and enough of Sam Howard.

Although each time she approached, someone was in discussion with him, their eyes nevertheless met. He knew she wanted to speak to him alone. He continued the conversation with the House majority leader and made Jane wait. He was playing her game of control. The student had surpassed the teacher.

Jane put her drink down and walked through the crowd

surrounding the President-elect. She took him by the elbow, and graciously apologized to everyone. "Excuse me, gentlemen, but the senator is needed. I'm sure you understand." A good teacher knows how to regain control.

Jane escorted Sam past congratulating admirers to the far wall of the ballroom and a private room where they could talk. Walking in, she saw it was the bride's waiting room, an ironic coincidence given the white dress she wore and Sam's recent proposal. She looked at Sam standing a few feet away. "So, what was it? If I married you, they couldn't force me to testify against you at your trial for murder and treason? Was that it?" She let out a sarcastic laugh under her breath. "Thank God I didn't!" Her mind returned to Taryn and the jet that had crashed. "You tried to kill Taryn by blowing up her plane, you bastard, and, to use your own words, that wasn't very wise. I promise you that if anything happens to her I will make it my crusade to see you're hanged as a traitor."

"Heed that warning, Jane. Forever! Guard this secret. Your daughter's life depends on it."

"Or, I could put this in the hands of the law and get protection for Taryn and me!"

"I'm afraid you won't do that, Jane. You see, the five-hundred bombs that blew up the HOPE Cities were just half of the bombs planted throughout the country. During the last three months, Sayyid's men also planted bombs in America's worst hi-rise ghettos."

"WHAT?" Jane cringed, imagining the worst.

Sam remained silent.

"He'll be stopped before ..."

"No! He won't! No one will try to stop him because the consequences would be the deaths of tens-of-thousands of Africans. Sayyid has someone here whose instructions are to detonate the bombs if anything happens to him. His safety guarantees their safety. As well as yours and Taryn's."

"You're holding the country hostage!"

"I'm doing what is right!"

The sincerity in Sam's voice revolted Jane even more than the horror of the ideas he expressed. She could only shake her head in stunned disbelief.

Sam's portable videophone beeped, and the president-elect turned and walked into the adjoining attendants' room, leaving Jane by herself. Broken and scared.

Sam was by himself for the first time since early morning. He removed the videophone from inside his tuxedo jacket, opened it, and saw Sayyid Kassim's beaming face. Behind him he could see the eleven old men of Al-Qiyamah sitting in Sayyid's palatial living room. Happier faces he could remember only once: His parents and sister on graduation day as they walked along Wooster Street in New Haven. Sam recollected his family's beaming smiles, their happiness, the fear, the gunshots. He shook his head and cleared the terrible memories from it. He watched the old men celebrating. Having finally avenged their sons' deaths, their lives were now worthwhile. Sam had that same victorious feeling.

"Mr. President, *mabrouk. Salaam alaykum.*" Congratulations. Peace be upon you.

"And upon you be peace," Sam responded, as was expected, although he said it in English rather than in Arabic.

"Our plan has succeeded. Praise be to Allah!"

Sam heard the men swear their allegiance to their Lord.

"Maybe now America will understand that for democracy to work, they must take a separatist attitude. The species and the classes must remain apart for peace and security, because only with peace and security in the West will we have peace and security in the East. Everyone in their rightful place. Now, speaking of rightful places, Mr. President-elect, I understand Jane Weisser was in an accident and missed her flight. How lucky for her."

Sam heard the suspicious voice.

"But, not so lucky next time. Right, Sam?"

"Don't worry, Sayyid. I know what to do. Our secret remains safe."

A few close friends tracked Sam down and insisted he return to the celebration. He begged off from Sayyid's call and walked back into the Park Place ballroom from another door, having never told Jane that the minor car accident that had stopped Taryn from being on Flight 475 had been staged by him.

Alone in the bridal waiting room, Jane felt as alone as she had ever been. While the rest of her campaign staff, invited dignitaries, and supporters partied the night away, she felt helpless. Hopeless! If she didn't do something, Iraq would have an invisible stranglehold on America. If she went to the CIA, or the Mossad, doing anything to Sayyid Kassim meant certain death for so many more. DEAR GOD! she screamed to herself. And if she turned in Sam, poor Adam and Bradley would suffer for the rest of their lives. They had already experienced death, and had handled it well. But, a father who had slaughtered tens-of-thousands of innocent people while trying to destroy an entire race of people would be devastating. Who could live, who would want to live, with that legacy on their conscience every day?

Tears fell down Jane's face and her stomach knotted. She let it all out because she couldn't keep it inside any longer. She loved the boys too much to put them through that lifelong Hell. Even worse, she realized, was that turning in Sam also meant certain death for Taryn and her, as well as for countless African men, women, and children.

Jane shuddered. After a moment, she took control of her emotions and straightened herself out. She washed her face, fixed her make-up and hair, and walked back out to the celebration. "What do I do?" she asked from behind her plastic smile as she reentered the festive ballroom. Each option was worse than the other, and the only choice she had ...

... was to choose one.

BOOK TWO

... AND BEWARE THE
FRIEND WHO BECOMES
YOUR ENEMY!

CHAPTER NINE

Seven weeks until Inauguration Day

Mother and daughter remained secluded from the world inside their Watergate Hotel suite. It had been almost a month since the election. Desperate to do something, she concluded there was only one thing she could do. Only one way out with the least damage.

Jane Weisser had to, without anyone knowing she was behind it, assassinate the President-elect of the United States.

For days, Jane paced her hotel bedroom and living room, wondering how she could do it without getting caught. She had to make plans for the sale of TWO, find a new place for her and her family to live, and get new identities. She also had to set up a believable scapegoat - a person or agent to take the blame. But, first, and foremost, she had to get Taryn to a safe place, out of the line of fire.

Jane was overwhelmed with fear and uncertainty. There

were so many decisions to make - so many life and death decisions. Did she have the strength? Time magazine may have called her 'the most influential woman in Washington,' but what she was planning to do would end up influencing the course of American history. World history.

Jane pulled back the living room curtain. She looked over the carpeted balcony and saw a few small boats lazily meandering the Potomac. She looked at the Kennedy Center. As she turned away, she saw the blue Buick still parked across the street. Sam's men knew she was hiding at the Watergate, but it was still safer than staying at her Georgetown home. Was Sam having her followed as a warning? Would they try to stop Taryn from leaving, or follow her wherever she went? Jane let the gossamer white panel fall back. She went to the wet bar for a drink. There were so many things to think about. If Taryn was to get on a plane, they would know where she was going. How could she do it without them knowing? She swallowed the Scotch and realized she had to think with the hunted cunning of a fugitive.

By nightfall she had a plan.

When Moses McBride arrived for his meeting with Sam Howard more than a month had passed since the HOPE Cities explosions. It was time to talk to Sam about rebuilding them. Sam had promised to deliver, and Moses was there to collect.

Sam's secretary escorted the reverend into the senator's office.

"Moses, it's good to see you again." Sam stood and extended his hand.

"Thank you, Sam. There's so much we have to discuss, and I know you're busy."

"Please, sit down." Moses sat in one of the two chairs facing the president-elect's desk. "Now, what's on your mind?"

"The HOPE Cities," Moses told him. "There's a lot of anger and resentment among the tens-of-thousands of people who lost everything. We have to talk about what we can do for these poor souls until their communities are rebuilt."

"I'm doing all I can, Moses. The temporary housing, job placement, and food relief are taking up most of my time. I can't do anymore than I'm doing until January 20th."

Moses was unsettled by the statement. HOPE Cities were already funded and had been for years. Why did Sam, who was still a powerful senator, need to wait until after the inauguration to begin reconstruction? "Like we did when we met in New York to end the fighting, we need to give these people hope for the future, and we must take action now."

"Rebuilding HOPE will cost billions of dollars of money our government doesn't have, Moses. I'm afraid Congress doesn't feel it's a priority right now. I'm sorry."

"But, HOPE was your life's work, Sam. You changed America because of it. Only, now, America has reverted back to the way it once was because of its destruction. We need to rebuild it as soon as possible or racial conflicts will rip this country apart. You can bring the races, all classes of people, back together again, Sam. You, as president, hold American solidarity in your hands."

"True. Therefore, I have to do what is best for the *entire* country, not just for a group of misplaced persons, or of one race or class of people."

"And beginning reconstruction on the twelve HOPE Cities is what's best for the country." Moses felt his heart racing. His hands were sweaty. He hadn't expected this confrontation. Still, he had to convince the president-elect that the cities and its people had to be his primary concern.

"I'm sorry, Moses," he said, with what sounded like a final authority. "After the inauguration, I'll see what I can do. Until then, my hands are tied."

"Your hands are tied?" Moses asked in disbelief. There was an awkward moment of silence. "I see. Once again our government is going to take the attitude of majority rule. Once again the minority loses out. Is that it?"

"A president must do what is right for America."

"For white, rich America, that is. Right, Sam?"

The president-elect did not respond.

"So, it's to be politics as usual, is it?" Moses shook his head in disgust. "I, along with the millions of Africans who voted for you, thought it would be different this time."

"I have always championed the downtrodden, and I always will, Moses." But, with the billions of dollars it will take to rebuild HOPE, I can have thousands more police patrolling America's streets, and enough money to build and staff the prisons I will need for the Howard Crime Bill."

Moses McBride had gone there to talk about housing for his people, but all he got in return was the promise that more of his people would be imprisoned for the rest of their lives. He wanted to argue this point with Sam. However, voicing that opinion would be akin to accusing the man of being a racist, which would ruin whatever chance he had left to turn the president-elect's mind around.

"I'm sure you understand, Moses."

Moses understood all-too-well. He held his tongue about how many more poor Africans would end up in those penal colonies if Congress implemented the Howard Crime Bill before rebuilding HOPE. "You say it will take billions of dollars to rebuild. Most of that money, I assume, has been returned to the investors from the multitude of insurance companies that underwrote HOPE. What you're really saying is, the money which you all invested, and again have, will not be used for the same purpose for which it was originally intended." Sam's gray eyes, he noticed, were avoiding his. Before Moses could say what he thought about that, Sam changed the subject.

"Moses, listen to me. HOPE isn't the only way to improve the plight of America's African people. Think about it rationally. We're only talking about a few hundred-thousand people. I want to take care of, or rather help, all the African people. And the best way to do that is with *you*. You're the perfect liaison to the cities and their people. They listen to you. They respect you. And because of that, I'm putting forth your name to Congress for Secretary of Housing and Urban Development."

The announcement stunned Moses. He didn't know what to think, or how to react. He saw Sam sitting back, smiling.

"I believe that together we can, and will, make a difference, Moses. We're a good team, you and I. We proved that in New York."

They talked about what he could do at HUD, then Sam stood until his secretary walked in. Before he knew it, Moses was standing dazed on the street outside the Hart Senate Office Building. It would be an honor being a member of the president's cabinet; he could do more for his people from that pulpit. But, without the HOPE Cities rebuilt, and with the Howard Crime Bill enacted, the racial unrest that had divided the country was bound to continue. And it was going to be spurred on from the White House Oval Office. How in the world could he be HUD secretary in Sam Howard's administration knowing that?

Sam Howard sat back and sipped his coffee. He had appeased Moses McBride with the promise of a cabinet post. Now, he had only to appease Jane and Sayyid. Then, he would be free to govern without any interference. He smiled at the thought.

His father only ran Howard Oil, the seventh largest oil

company in the world.

He, Sam Howard, would rule the world!

Jane received a padded manila envelope in the mail. A few days earlier she had called Rachel Porter, her best friend from college, and had told her she needed three passports ASAP. "Two of them have to be for an elderly couple, and one has to be for a teenaged girl about Taryn's age," she had told her.

"And where am I supposed to get that?" her college roommate asked.

"All you have to do is send me your parents' and your daughter's. Please, Rich, I wouldn't ask this of you if it wasn't important."

"But, it's illegal to use someone else's passport, Pain." Jane's roommate had nick-named her 'Pain' shortly after they began their freshman year at Yale. Neither one had very much liked the other those first few months. Jane had found Rachel to be a spoiled, rich kid from Palm Beach, a 'rich bitch,' and Rachel had thought Jane to be loud and pushy, a real 'pain in the ass,' Jane the Pain, as she had called her many times. The nicknames they gave each other stuck, and they cherished them as terms of endearment from then on. By their sophomore year, they were closer than sisters. They were each other's maid of honor and Godparent to each one's daughter. Calling themselves anything but 'Pain' and 'Rich,' they knew, would feel awkward and unnatural.

"Rich, please. I can't think of anyone else to ask but you." Jane knew that if Paco were alive, she'd have new passports with different names on them in no time. "Will you help me?"

"I've always trusted you, Pain. If you can't tell me why you need them, or what's happening, then I'll have to accept that. I'm sure one day you will."

Jane had told her to send them to the hotel under her own name, which Taryn had registered them in.

Jane opened the padded envelope and looked at the passports. Confident it was going to work, Jane affixed Taryn's picture to replace Shannon Porter's.

The following day, they left for Dulles Airport. Jane looked at Taryn as they drove away from the hotel. She had a duffel bag with the costume changes she would need on her lap, which she had purchased a few days before at the Watergate shops downstairs. She also had the bogus passports.

"Are we being followed?" Taryn asked, afraid to turn around.

Jane looked in her rearview mirror as she drove out of Foggy Bottom and crossed the Theodore Roosevelt Bridge into Rosslyn, Virginia. "Afraid so." It was the blue Buick again. Sam was worried what she would do. Jane drove and thought about what she was planning. What choice had she? Do nothing and let the country become a puppet of Iraq? She had to do something to stop it. She had chosen the latter, and there was no turning back now.

After a brief silence, Taryn spoke her feelings. "I can't believe this country of ours. Is every politician a crook, Mom?"

"Not everyone, Taryn, even though sometimes it appears that way. It's just that the media always accentuates the negative and eliminates the positive," Jane explained, paraphrasing the great Johnny Mercer lyric. 'Getting the scoop' is big business. The problem with that is, in the name of business they promote cynicism, pessimism, defeatism, and every other societal destructivism you can think of."

"Even so, it seems like politicians are in politics to see what they can get out of it."

"Yes, sometimes it seems that way, and sometimes it is that

way." Jane hated to see her daughter so cynical about government, the government she worked so hard to create. "If it bothers you so much, you should go into politics and do something about it. Anyone who wants change can promote change."

"Me? In politics? You gotta be kidding."

"Why not? Plato said: 'Those who are too smart to engage in politics are punished by being governed by those who are dumber.'"

Taryn laughed. "Cool saying."

"In other words, darling: Don't bitch. Run for office instead." Jane stared at Taryn and saw that the quick lesson in civic responsibility had registered.

At the airport, Jane parked the car, and she and Taryn walked into the bright red American Airlines terminal. The day before, she had received in the mail the one-way ticket to London in the name Shannon Porter. Rather than go to their boarding gate, mother and daughter, as planned, entered a women's bathroom. The evening before, they had rehearsed this part repeatedly inside their Watergate suite. Now, it was for real.

It took a few minutes for the change. When they finished, they exchanged hugs and kisses. "Be careful, Taryn. If anyone grabs you, kick and scream and run." She hugged her again. "You don't know how much I love you and how worried I am about you. Having to send you away breaks my heart."

Taryn exited, dressed as a pregnant woman, with short blond hair and sunglasses. She turned right toward her gate. A minute later, Jane walked out in the opposite direction. She stopped at a counter and asked the agent some questions about the flights to Paris, while Taryn entered another bathroom in the terminal. She also saw the two men, who'd been following them, enter the first bathroom to look for Taryn whom they'd yet to see exit. So far, so good, Jane thought to herself. While the men were in there, she heard: 'Flight 325 to London's Heathrow Airport is now boarding rows 15 through 36.' She saw Taryn exit the second bathroom. The teenager looked completely different again. No longer pregnant, she now resembled the picture on her passport. Her short platinum blond hair was spiked in different colors, and her unrecognizable face was painted in an equally radical manner.

The two men dashed out of the ladies' room as Taryn waited in line to board. They ran around the crowded terminal, frantically searching for Taryn at the different gates. Taryn boarded her plane, and Jane returned to the parking garage. Now, she could bring down Sam Howard without worrying about her child's safety.

Jane entered the enclosed parking garage. Soon after, she heard the sound of running feet behind her. As it got closer, she turned and saw Sam's men. Her stomach tightened. Dear God, please help me! She looked around, saw a security guard at the gate, and ran up to him. "Stop those men; they tried to rape me!"

The guard stepped out of his glass booth and pulled out his gun, forcing the men to stop. Jane wasted no time getting into her car and driving away. No one pursued her.

After the Weissers had left the Watergate Hotel, Abdullah Nasir and Mahmoud Halam followed them in their black Lincoln to Dulles International Airport. They had watched Sam's men fail to find the daughter inside the terminal, then fail to capture the Yehoudi, the Jew, in the almost empty parking garage. Now, seated inside their car in the American Airlines parking garage, Abdullah Nasir picked up the videophone and reported his observations to Sayyid Kassim.

* * * * *

"In honor of my father's memory, I will kill Moses McBride at the inauguration come Hell or high water," Garrison Miller promised the men seated around the old wooden table inside the cinderblock basement. "In my father's memory, the death of that nigger will restart the civil war, which will bring about the rebirth of a new America. A white America. Like America was intended to be!" He pounded his fist on the table, knocking over a few empty beer bottles. The grand marshal of the People for a White America had worked himself into a frenzy. Soon, everyone would feel the same as he. The same as 'Daddy.' He recalled what his father had told him when he was twelve years old. "The black man is inferior to us, my boy. Scientists have proven they have smaller brains. Comin' from the jungle, they also have the killer instinct. In this dog-eat-dog country of ours, where everyone takes what they want, it's up to the white man to make sure they don't take what is rightfully ours. And the only way to do that is to make damn sure they never try. Ya understand what I'm sayin', boy?"

"Garrison, be reasonable," Carl Block said, snapping Miller's mind back to the present. "Because of their suspicions about you and HOPE, you'll be followed if you go anywhere near Washington. Think about it, man. You're followed wherever you go *now*."

"Why do we have to kill him at the inauguration anyway? Wouldn't it be easier to do it away from all that security?" Tommy McKay asked.

"McBride is always on the move, and wherever he goes he's got bodyguards around him," Miller said. "Because of that, we haven't been able to kill him, even when we blew up his apartment and his church. At least we know where he'll be on January 20th."

"But, what good is killing McBride if we're gonna get caught doin' it? And we're sure as Hell gonna get caught at the inauguration. Every cop and Fibbie'll be out that day," Lonnie McKay added to the argument.

"WHAT GOOD? WHAT GOOD?" Miller leaned forward, with both fists, clenched white, on the table. Some spittle dripped from the right side of his mouth to his chin. His black eyes were glossier than ever, and his normally pale face was red around his neck and ears. "I'll tell you what good. If I have to die for what is right, then so be it. I'm ready. I expect all of you to be. If you aren't willing to give up your own life for the cause, for freeing America, then get the fuck outta here!" The spittle on his lips flew in all directions. "DAMNIT!" He pounded his fist on the table again. "DON'T YOU UNDERSTAND? I want to kill Moses McBride in front of a worldwide audience because the world needs to see that white America won't tolerate this shit any longer."

"But, Garrison, why put yourself in jeopardy? They're gunning for you. Let me or one of the others do it," Carl Block told his best friend.

"I SAID I WILL KILL MOSES McBRIDE AND THAT'S FINAL!" The screams echoed off the walls of the concrete basement. When it was quiet again, he softly asked, "Now, how do I do it?" Miller knew he could get by the men who would be watching him outside his Maryland home. The tunnel underneath the house, from the dungeon to its hidden exit three streets away, would, as usual, provide him with his escape.

Jimmy Siefert broke the silence. "The only problem is you won't, no matter who you are or aren't, be able to get near the invited guests with a gun on your possession."

"Why don't we just do it from the parade route?" Lonnie McKay asked. "We can get a shot off much easier as he passes by."

"Yeah, but what if he's riding in an enclosed limo?" his brother retorted. "We'll have lost our only chance."

"Still, the parade gives us a better ..."

"NO! I will kill him before, or at, the ceremony," Garrison Miller said with finality. "I want to see McBride die up close. And before he takes his last breath, I want him to see my smiling face!" Miller drank his beer and fantasized about it. About another world. A far better world.

Jane Weisser moved out of her hotel suite the day Taryn flew off to England and moved into a different room a few doors down. Because Taryn had originally rented the room, Jane felt it was safest if she moved into another one, under a different name.

As prearranged, Jane took the elevator down to the lobby of the Watergate wearing a wig, sunglasses, and clothes that made her look old and frumpy. It was almost twenty-four hours since Taryn's plane had taken off. She walked through the lobby to the bank of videophones, took a seat, and opened a magazine. She covered her face and waited. At the prescribed time, one of the lobby's videophones rang once. No one seemed to take notice. Jane smiled and returned to her room upstairs. Taryn was safe in London.

In his bed, Garrison Miller was again filled with gleeful anticipation. "When everyone sees McBride dead, they'll realize the bullet that had hit him inside Martin Luther King, Jr. Community College had indeed hit its intended mark." Miller laughed, but then got serious. There was still a problem - two problems really.

Jane and Taryn Weisser.

Although they hadn't reported their information to the authorities, his men had yet to find the teenager. After McBride's assassination, will the Weissers go to the FBI and tell them what they know? The grand marshal of the People for a White America thought about it. He couldn't take any chances. He had to find Taryn Weisser. With the girl in his hands, the mother will keep quiet.

Miller lay there in his bed, trying to remember everything she had ever said to him. It took him only a short while to remember her mentioning grandparents in Boston ... and a great aunt and great uncle in London.

He laughed again and felt his loins rise.

CHAPTER TEN

Six weeks until Inauguration Day

Jane Weisser's commitment grew as her plan formed. Sam Howard, murderer and traitor, was not going to get away with what he had done. Baghdad was not going to control the Oval Office. America's African people were not going to be victims of genocide.

Jane paced the Watergate living room in her blue Rockport, Massachusetts sweatshirt, beige corduroy slacks, and bare feet. The plush carpeting was soft and soothing underneath her. She wore only red lipstick, and her long, wavy hair was tied back. She thought about Moses McBride, the next step in her plan. She had to enlist the help of the man who had taken a bullet for the senator when they met the press in New York. The man whose people Sam Howard had betrayed would gladly agree to the plan that would stop him from annihilating any more of them. Jane drank her Scotch and pondered. "How do I get to the reverend? Sam is still having me followed." She noticed the time. She had yet to eat breakfast or lunch. The fifteen pounds she had put on the last year was now almost gone. She hadn't been dieting. The pressure of the last few months was what had caused the weight loss. She took another drink and once again forgot about eating.

Jane knew Manhattan from her days at Columbia University, especially the theater district, where she often went as a doctoral student. It was also the place she and Sam had frequented when Sam was a second-term senator. Jane played out the escape scenario in her mind. If anyone followed her to New York, she knew how to lose them.

It was time to enlist Moses McBride.

Jane left the Watergate in her Mercedes shortly after noon, with the blue Buick following her. This time Jane was prepared to elude the tail.

She led them around Washington's many circular traffic routes: Washington Circle, DuPont Circle, Scott Circle, Thomas Circle, and Logan Circle, until she lost sight of them, and then continued her erratic drive north, out of the city and onto I-95.

For hours, she drove, daydreaming, wondering where Maryland had gone, as she passed through Delaware into Pennsylvania. She thought about Moses McBride. Would he accept her outrageous story, and also accept the responsibility of taking an active role in a presidential assassination? She thought about Taryn and how she was safe in London. She thought about Sam, and Sayyid Kassim and the men of Al-Qiyamah, and ... a blue Buick appeared in her rearview mirror. Dear God! How could they have found me? she asked herself. The answer was obvious. She'd never lost them. Obviously, they had planted a tracer on her car. Jane's mind accelerated. There was no hope of losing them on I-95. And even if she could, her car would certainly broadcast her position. They would know, even in

Manhattan, how to find her. She had to stop and be around people, for safety's sake. She needed time to think about what to do.

Jane looked to her right and saw the sign for a rest area a half mile ahead. She pulled into it and ran into the McDonald's.

Sam was in his office when his private videophone rang. He opened it and saw the picture of the man riding shotgun in the blue Buick.

"Dr. Weisser just pulled into a rest area on I-95 near Philadelphia, sir. She knows we're following her. What do you want us to do?"

The president-elect thought about where she might be heading. He had to know what she was planning, if anything. "I don't want her out of your sight. Keep me posted." Sam disconnected and leaned his head back in his chair. It hurt him that he didn't trust her, that she might not be loyal. He reminisced about them for a while, but the vision of Sayyid Kassim and the men of Al-Qiyamah disrupted his memories.

Jane raced her car north into New Jersey, confident she was no longer being followed. She had dashed into the McDonald's, behind the counter, and through the preparation areas. Without breaking stride, she had run out the rear door of the restaurant into the parking lot. Out of breath, she had raced around to her car and jumped back in. It was enough of a lead to get away and rent a car in Trenton, New Jersey. Now, behind the wheel, Jane felt confident she had lost them for good. It was time to concentrate on persuading Moses McBride to join her. However, could she convince a man of God to take a human life?

Abdullah Nasir drove the car, and Mahmoud Halam was on

the videophone with Sayyid Kassim in Baghdad. With the tracer planted on the car carrying Sam's men, they knew they would lead them to her. They had followed her from the McDonald's restaurant when she had left, without Sam's men in pursuit. She may have duped those amateurs, but not Sayyid Kassim's men.

"Where is she now?" Sayyid asked.

"She rented a car and is proceeding north toward the George Washington Bridge. Maybe New York."

"Or maybe her hometown of Boston," Sayyid said. He remained silent for a moment in thought. Sam's attachment to this Yehoudi threatened to destroy Saddam's brilliant plan. He couldn't allow an opportunity to dispense with this danger slip away so easily again. He had to fix the leak. "Kill her!"

Near Newark Airport, Jane saw the car behind her pull right up on her rear fender. She could see their faces in her rearview mirror. A shock of recognition and fear shook her. Arabs! Her clenched fists, tightly gripping the steering wheel, lost all feeling. She accelerated the Taurus, but the menacing car stayed close behind, close enough for her to see the look in the eyes of the occupants. The car made contact with hers, and she felt a jolt.

Jane pressed the pedal down even harder, not daring to take her eyes off the road to look at the speedometer. She had enough to do to keep the car under control, weave in and out of traffic, and watch for her pursuers.

The car got closer. It hit again just south of the GW toll gate. Jane accelerated, changed lanes, then quickly braked. As she abruptly slowed to fifty miles per hour, the speeding car to her left flew by. She was now behind them, and the other car entered the toll booth a half dozen cars before her.

Jane paid the toll and told the collector, "That black Lincoln up ahead rammed into me. Please call someone."

"Yes, ma'am."

Jane pulled out of the gate and let out her breath. Her hands were shaking. She drove even slower so they wouldn't get behind her again. She had to stay in control in order to stay alive.

Although they had lost valuable time at the rest area, Sam's men, after following the tracer to a Trenton, New Jersey Avis dealer, found Jane's Mercedes parked in their lot. They coerced the manager, by showing him their government identification, to tell them the make and color of the car the woman in question had rented. Delayed by their interrogation, they raced along I-95, in search of the white Taurus. The siren and the red flasher on their hood helped them recoup the time lost.

They didn't see what they were looking for until they reached the toll booths of the George Washington Bridge. Luck was with them. Up ahead at one of the many gates was the white Taurus.

On the upper span of the GW, the black car slowed, until it was alongside the Taurus. If they continued straight, they would head to New England. At the cut off to the Westside Highway, Jane veered sharply right from the middle lane into the exit. The Lincoln did the same from the left, causing the other cars to swerve, brake, and blare their horns.

With the sun setting over the New Jersey skyline, Jane drove at great speed along the highway that followed the Hudson River on her right, south into Manhattan. Her eyes anxiously darted between the road ahead and the rearview mirror. They were following her and closing in again. Traveling in the center lane, Jane forced herself to look at the speedometer. Seventy. Seventy-five. Eighty. Could she go faster and still keep control of the car?

She pressed down her right foot, and the heavy car lurched forward.

At 96th Street, the black car touched her rear fender, then accelerated. Jane felt her car being pushed. If her steering wheel gave an inch, the car would roll and flip into a spectacular crash. "Dear God, please get me through this." Jane floored the gas pedal and pulled ahead. The speedometer read eighty-five. "Why isn't there a cop ready to pull me over *now*?"

She darted from lane to lane, through the traffic driving at a considerably slower speed, all blaring their horns at her. No matter what she tried to do to escape, she couldn't shake Sayyid's men. She decided to stay in the middle lane. It was the safest, she reasoned; in the middle lane, they couldn't push her off the right side of the highway or into the Jersey barrier on her left.

Jane glanced at her rear-view mirror again and quickly returned her eyes to the road ahead of her. She ignored the pounding in her head and chest. Her full concentration was required to keep the speeding vehicle under control. Thankfully, the traffic heading south was sparse compared to the rush hour traffic leaving the city. She looked in the mirror again. Another pair of headlights was speeding up from behind, zigzagging between the cars. Jane gasped as the blue Buick emerged on the lane to her right and began closing the distance between them.

A moment later, Jane saw the black Lincoln speeding up in the left lane. Behind her was a lightweight pickup truck recklessly traveling at nearly the same speed. An explosion shattered her rear window and the rear seat window next to it. She looked in her door mirror. A gun was perched on the passenger door of the Lincoln, aimed at her. She pressed even harder on the accelerator.

Abruptly, the Buick swerved into the middle lane and forced the pickup into the passenger side of the Lincoln. The Buick veered back into the right lane as the Lincoln slammed into the median divider and rode up the Jersey barrier.

Jane's eyes opened wider as the Lincoln somersaulted over the highway at W.79th Street. It landed below the highway in a park that bordered the Hudson River and burst into flames, lighting up the darkened sky. The explosion was so deafening, the situation so maddening, that Jane screamed. She took a few deep breaths and realized she couldn't swallow. She needed a cigarette, but she couldn't let go of the wheel. Not at - she glanced at her speedometer - eighty-five miles per hour. The thought of a Scotch sliding down her throat, soothing the dryness and her nerves, assuaged her fear. The relief, however, was short-lived. Jane looked in her rear-view mirror and saw the blue Buick in pursuit.

She flew off the exit ramp at W.56th Street and raced through the lights, past the docks and piers to W.42nd Street. She turned left onto the wide thoroughfare, the tires of her rented car squealing.

The blue Buick followed her.

Jane sped to Tenth Avenue. Her stomach ached and she had to pee. She was frantic, which made her drive faster. In agony, she began to cry. It was all too much. Unable to control a full bladder, she found herself in a hot, wet seat which quickly chilled. Tears blurred her vision as her driving became more erratic and reckless.

Because it was rush hour, there was a lot of traffic on Tenth. Jane maneuvered the car into the right lane and turned onto W.44th Street. She approached the scene where her plan for escape would have to be executed. She fought to control her emotions and recall each detail. With Sam's men a few cars behind her on 44th, and the traffic stopping up ahead for the red light, Jane looked across Eighth Avenue. On her right was the lit-up St. James Theater marquee. On the other side of the street were the equally bright Majestic, Broadhurst, and Shubert Theaters' marquees.

The light turned green and Jane slowly moved forward with the rest of the traffic. She craned her neck to her right and, at the last second, swerved the car into the alleyway of a parking garage that connected to W.43rd Street. Leaning on her horn all the way through, she turned right onto 43rd and headed back north to Tenth Avenue. Luckily, the light was green. She turned right again. Sam's car, she could see from her mirror, was nowhere in sight. She let out her breath.

Jane drove up Tenth Avenue toward W.50th Street. Her stomach cramped and she was wet with urine. A wave of nausea swept over her. She wanted to grab a cigarette from her purse on the seat next to her, but her hands were stuck to the steering wheel. She looked in the mirror to get over to her right. "SHIT!" She couldn't believe it: The Buick was in pursuit again. The cramps worsened. "PLEASE GOD!"

Jane regained her composure and thought about what she could do to lose Sam's henchmen once and for all. She turned right onto 50th Street, passing through Eighth Avenue until traffic forced her to stop. Broadway was enjoying a boom of new musicals and revivals. Consequently, Jane had to wait in the line of traffic trying to cross Broadway. Sitting under the bright yellow marquee of the Gershwin Theater on her left, she rehearsed the move in her mind.

The cars continued to move at a slow pace toward New York's major thoroughfare. The light turned red again. Jane counted the number of cars before her. Seven. The light at Broadway turned green and Jane slowed her car to a crawl when she was next in line to pass through the intersection. The Buick, she saw from her side-view mirror, was four cars behind her.

Because parked automobiles lined both sides of the street, no one was able to pass anyone in the single row of cars trying to get through the light. The signal turned yellow, only Jane didn't move. Horns blared. The car behind her tapped her bumper. A second later, it turned red and Jane sped through it before the perpendicular traffic waiting to dart across 50th Street on Broadway swallowed up the intersection.

Jane drove across and looked in her mirror at the cars forced to remain behind. She lost them. She looked to her left to make sure the traffic on the one-way street didn't devour her. There was the Winter Garden Theater, all lit up. Jane remembered the night she and Sam had gone to the Winter Garden during their senior year at Yale to see CATS. What a night! 'Memory, all alone in the moonlight,' they sang on their way back to New Haven.

Jane dismissed the romantic memories of the past and grabbed her purse. Right now she felt more alone than ever before. Keeping her eyes focused on the street, she fumbled for a cigarette. She found one, lit it, and drove the rental car to a garage on W.57th Street, a few blocks from the Plaza Hotel. The cigarette had a wonderfully calming effect. Sometimes one's vices were so therapeutic.

With the cold December wind blowing in her face and through her wet clothes, Jane ran to the nearest phone booth and called the First Abyssinian Baptist Church of Harlem.

There was no more First Abyssinian Baptist Church of Harlem.

Through TWO's New York contacts, Jane was told that Moses McBride's office was now inside Harlem's Martin Luther King, Jr. Community College. When the connection was made with the switchboard, Jane asked to be connected to Dr. McBride's office.

"Sorry, ma'am, but the reverend's gone home for the evening."

"May I have his phone number, please."

"I'm sorry, but he requested that be privileged information."

"I understand." Jane had no recourse but to use her clout as a celebrity and aid to the president-elect. "This is Jane Weisser. Do you know who I am?"

"Yes, ma'am," the operator answered.

"Please believe me, this is a matter of life and death. I'm sure Dr. McBride would be pleased you assessed the situation and used good judgment. I can't begin to express how important this is."

The woman gave Jane the number where she could reach Moses McBride. She dialed it and again asked to speak to him.

"He's not here," the gruff voice on the other end said.

"Can you tell me when he'll be back. It's quite urgent that I speak with him." Jane explained who she was and was told the reverend was at dinner. He wouldn't be back until sometime after seven. She hung up, turned around, and viewed her busy environs. She crossed W.58th Street and walked in the direction of the Plaza Hotel. She passed many men who appeared to be Middle Eastern, many of whom were looking her way. Minutes later she entered the famous hotel.

Sam received the call shortly after the chase ended and he was livid. "You call every hotel in that city and ask them to connect you to Dr. Weisser's room. I don't care what you have to do, just find her!" Sam switched off his private videophone and flung it inside his desk. "Idiots!" He hoped she signed in under her own name. But, why would she? After deftly taking care of his men, she wouldn't make such a foolish mistake. He ran his hands through his hair. What was Jane doing in Manhattan? Was she still *in* Manhattan? He paced the floor of his senate office, then looked out the window at his city. He hoped it would remain his city no matter what Jane's intentions were.

Inside her Plaza Hotel suite, Jane took a long, hot shower. More relaxed, although the tension hadn't completely drained from her body yet, she dried her hair with the blow dryer and put on the white terrycloth robe the hotel supplied as a courtesy. She went to the honor bar at the other end of the suite and fixed herself a stiff drink.

At 7:15 p. m. she walked back into the sitting room, sat at the desk by the window, and called Moses McBride. Looking down on the light snow falling on Central Park, and the horse-drawn carriages parked by the entrance, she heard his well-known voice.

"Good evening, Dr. Weisser."

Jane turned away from the wintry scene and looked at his large frame on the wall screen. "Hello, Dr. McBride. You don't know me ..."

"Don't know you? Of course I know you."

"Yes, I guess you would, with your dealings with Sam Howard."

"Yes, and as an alumnus of Yale Divinity School. I was a few years ahead of you and Sam, but I remember your magnetic personality on campus. I also knew Sam through the student government. When he was elected senior class president, I realized, from all I'd read, that it was because of you."

Thank you, reverend."

"And you've proved many times since that a man is only as good as the woman by his side."

Jane laughed. "I'm afraid you may not think the woman by his side has been all that good when I tell you the truth about Sam Howard."

"And this, I gather, is the reason for this call?"

"Yes. Please - can you guarantee total privacy for this conversation."

Moses disappeared, only to return a moment later. "You have my word."

It was time to tell someone else what she knew. She swallowed her drink and said, "I need for you to meet with me at the Plaza Hotel right away. I'm in room 1205. Believe me, reverend, what I have to tell you is a matter of national security."

"You're going to have to give me a little more to go on than that, doctor. You see, I'm being followed. Certain people, I'm sure you understand, want me dead."

"I hate to imagine that, but I'm sure it's true. I was followed to New York, myself. Because of what I know, there are people who want to stop me. To be truthful, sir, involving you in this will make you an even more marked man."

"Please know that for my people's sake, I must be careful, Dr. Weisser. I can't put myself in any more danger than I'm already in. There are many agencies in the government you can talk to."

"I know who was responsible for the bombing of HOPE. It was a plot to destroy America's African people, Dr. McBride. And the plot, I'm sorry to have to tell you, is proceeding into its final stage." Jane saw that Moses McBride finally comprehended the severity of the call. His eyes were filled with rage. She waited for his response.

"I'll be there in a couple of hours, uh ... dressed as a delivery man with a package for you to sign. Let only me in and no one else."

"No one knows where I am."

"Don't be too sure, doctor; it could get you killed."

Jane swallowed the rest of her drink. "Thank you, Moses." She disconnected the telecomp and walked into the adjoining bedroom. She kept the lights off, flipped off her robe, and lay naked underneath the sheet on the king-size bed. Although she desperately needed to sleep for a while, Jane knew that sleep right now was impossible. Instead, she rehashed the conversation she'd just had with the famous man of God. Moses McBride sounded like a good and kind man. She was sure she was going to like him. She stared at the ceiling and prayed.

It felt good to finally share this problem with someone else, especially someone so personally involved. Sam Howard had lied to Moses McBride, as he had lied to her. Sam Howard had used both of them to further his odious ambitions.

Together, they would stop Sam and avenge the people he had betrayed.

An hour and a half later, Moses walked into the Plaza Hotel at 59th Street from the kitchen delivery entrance. Wearing a brown courier uniform and hat, the now-bearded reverend went directly to the elevators. If anyone stopped him, he would tell them he had a letter that had to be signed for in person. Seated near the elevators, and by the front desk, as well as on the 12th floor, were his armed bodyguards. One of the elevators opened and five people got off. He entered, unrecognized, followed by a couple and a man in a business suit. The couple pushed the button for the fourth floor. He waited for the other man. He pushed the one for the fourteenth. That meant that Moses would be alone with this man for eight floors. He couldn't take the chance. Moses pushed three.

He got off. When the doors closed, he pushed the up button again. A minute later, he was alone inside another elevator heading to the 12th floor. He exited and saw the hall was empty, except for his man at the other end. They made eye contact, and Moses walked to room 1205. He knocked, and heard, "Who is it?"

"Delivery, ma'am."

Jane unlocked the door, and Moses slipped in. She closed it, quickly relocked it, and walked back to the center of the room.

Moses noticed she was in disarray, not at all like the immaculately attired professional seen on TC. She had on blue chinos and a multicolored blouse that she had packed before leaving the Watergate. Her hair was tied back, there was no make-up on her face, except for lipstick, and she was barefoot.

"Thank you for coming. Can I offer you something?" She held up her glass.

"No, thanks. I don't drink."

Jane led him to the sofa and coffee table in the middle of the large sitting room. "I know I must have sounded like a crazy woman when we spoke earlier, but if you listen to what I have to say, you'll understand why."

Moses removed his hat and the beard and took a seat. "You said you know who was behind the HOPE bombings and the annihilation of the African people. You said it was a plot. And you said something about the truth behind Sam Howard. I'm here because of my own doubts about Sam. Now that he's won the presidency, he's not the same man he was before the election."

"Hah!" Jane laughed. "He's the same man all right, just not the one we all thought he was."

Moses looked at her. She had an expression of fear, and disgust, on her face.

"No, Moses, Sam is not our beloved 'Uncle Sam'. He's more like a modern day Hitler intent on exterminating the African people."

Moses felt his heart pounding and noticed he was clenching

his fists. He thought about Jessie and DaNell. He thought about what a fool he'd been to trust Sam Howard. The president-elect was responsible for everything that had gone so suddenly wrong.

"And as president, he will have the power to do it."

Moses looked into Jane's eyes, with his own look of fear and disgust on his face. "I think I'll have that drink now."

Jane got up and walked to the bar. She returned with a drink and handed it to the reverend. As he drank it, she told him everything: About Sam's family being murdered; about his obsessive dream of revenge against America's African people; about his trip to Baghdad and his relationship with Sayyid Kassim and the Al-Qiyamah; and, about the bombs still planted in five-hundred housing projects throughout the United States. She also told him about Patty Howard's death, about Iraq's involvement with HOPE, and how they had Sam build it just to destroy it and create a civil war. " ... knowing that when you and Sam ended it it would catapult him into the White House."

"Wait! Slow down!" Moses said, holding up his hands. "This is too much to comprehend. What does it all mean?"

"It means Iraq will covertly control America and the Middle East through the Oval Office." Jane saw the sick look on Moses McBride's face. She told him about the threats; about trying to send Taryn to Boston and the blown up flight; about sending her to London; and about the wild chase to New York. "The fate of the country is in my hands, Moses, but, more important ... my child's life is in danger." She saw tears fill his eyes.

"Because of Sam Howard, I no longer have a daughter," he whispered.

Jane watched him mourn for a moment. "Will you help me stop him, Moses? For our daughters?"

Moses drank the Scotch and winced. He didn't have to

think about it for very long. "You knew I wouldn't be able to say no."

"How can anyone with a heart and a conscience say no? Our destinies were thrown into our laps, and if we do nothing, we will lose. America will lose. And I don't want to think about where it will all lead if that happens."

"And the risks, if we do something, are just as bad."

"I'm afraid so, because there is only one thing we can do." She saw Moses look up at her, his elbows still resting on his knees, his expression quizzical and foreboding. "We have to assassinate Sam Howard."

"You're kidding? Why not just go to the authorities with what you know and with whatever proof you have?"

"I can't. If I do that, they'll kill Taryn and me, and Sam's sons will have to live with the legacy of what their father has done for the rest of their lives. That's if they'll be allowed to live. We can't allow the sins of the father ... well, you know. Besides, if I open my mouth, they'll blow up those five-hundred projects. Believe me, Moses, I've thought this all out. There's no other way."

There was silence for a while. "We'll never get away with it."

"Yes we will." Jane began detailing her plan to foil the Al-Qiyamah's plot. She explained how they could pin it on Garrison Miller, the grand marshal of the PWA. She ended the discourse by telling Moses that the man who had used Taryn was the same man who had shot him when he and Sam announced the end of the conflict.

"Then Sam wasn't the target after all."

"What do you mean?" Jane asked.

"Eight months ago, Miller's father, Garland, was executed for the murders of three African boys in New Orleans. I was the one who convinced the governor not to grant him another stay. At the time, I got some anonymous letters about how I was going to be killed for that. Garrison Miller didn't try to kill Sam. He was trying to kill me."

"All the more reason to use him as our fall guy. Since Sam Howard was the creator of HOPE, his assassination will tie Miller and the two acts together."

"You've really thought this out." He paused to ponder it some more. "I have to tell you, Jane, I'm impressed. It's a brilliant plan, and one that may actually keep us alive."

"From your mouth to God's ears." Moses didn't react to the saying. As a man of God, Jane thought she would at least get an 'Amen' from him. She thought that odd. She got up, poured them each another drink, and sat down on the sofa next to him. "Now, we have to decide: Do we do it before the inauguration and have the House of Representatives determine the next president, which could very well be Charles Price, or do we do it right after, so Bill Lawson can succeed him?"

"My people can't take another day of Charles Price."

"I agree. Sam's ideas, or I should say our ideas, are what's right for America today. I know Bill will continue to push them through Congress." Jane paused after the momentous decision, quaking with the enormous burden she was assuming. What she was doing was deciding the fate of the country. She was dictating history.

"Then it's settled," Moses said. "Come January 20th, there'll be two inaugurations."

They raised their glasses in a toast, sealing their commitment to this momentous undertaking and to each other. There was no turning back. It was what they had to do.

"Tell me, doctor," Moses asked her. "Why do I suddenly feel sick?"

* * * * *

Sam sat in the living room of his Fairfax, Virginia mansion with his teenaged sons, Adam and Bradley, watching the late news on the telecomp. Reports were about the pockets of rioting that had again ignited throughout the country. America's major cities were primed for war. Little had changed since the HOPE bombings. This lame duck administration was paralyzed, and the people wanted action.

Sam loved it. With the fighting resuming, his vendetta against America's African people was going to be realized. They would pay for what they did to his family: To his mother, his sister Britney, his father, who never got to see what a great and powerful leader he'd become. His father who had denied him the love and respect he deserved. Now everyone would love him. Sam returned his attention to the telecomp and the fires ravaging South-Central Los Angeles.

"Dad," Adam asked. "Isn't there anything you can do to stop this?"

"I wish I could, Adam, but until I'm sworn in there's nothing I can do."

"What about Moses McBride?" Bradley questioned his father. "Surely he can do something. Where is he?" It was the same question the papers and the broadcast media had been asking. America was on the brink of another national firestorm, and the one person who could extinguish the flames was nowhere to be found.

Sam thought about Bradley's question, then about Jane. Where is she? The ringing of his videophone disrupted his reflective mood. He excused himself and walked upstairs with the handheld instrument.

Inside the master bedroom, with the door closed, Sam sat on the love seat next to his bed. He flipped open the compact case and saw his man smiling.

"Senator Howard, we've found Dr. Weisser. She's at the Plaza. Room 1205."

It was good news. Were the Gods of Fate smiling down on him? Sam listened to Talbot tell him what he'd found out. Jane had signed in under her own name. The only problem was she was by herself. They still didn't know where Taryn was. "Keep a lookout in the lobby and follow her if she leaves," he told the agent.

Sam disconnected the videophone. Damn! As long as he wasn't a threat to Taryn, he was no threat to Jane. Taryn would talk if anything happened to her mother.

Before he could confront Jane, Sam had to get his ace back in the hole. He had to find Taryn. He stood and paced his bedroom as he thought about the life of Jane Weisser. He undressed for bed, thinking out loud, "Jane has already tried to send her daughter away to Boston. Most likely her parents' house." He thought about her relatives. From what he could recollect, the only other family she had was an aunt and an uncle on her mother's side in London. "Taryn was last seen at American Airlines International departures with Jane." Suddenly convinced that he would find Taryn in London he put on his red satin robe and returned to the love seat. It was time to call Sayyid.

The private videophone was registered in a fictitious name and post office box. He had learned his lesson well with Jane finding the old phone bills hidden at the cabin. Now, the link was encrypted and untraceable. Nothing could incriminate him, except Jane and Taryn. He dialed the number. Soon, the face of Sayyid Kassim was staring at him.

"Good morning, Sam, or rather good evening to you. I see you are ready for bed. We just finished our morning prayers and I am feeling quite well. Allah akbar."

Out of respect, Sam repeated the Islamic oath to their God. "Allah akbar." He then told Sayyid about the separation of the Weisser woman.

"You said she wouldn't talk. Will she, Sam? Even you can't be sure now." Pausing to register his displeasure, Sayyid said, "I will send my men to London to follow her. You promised me you would take care of this problem, Sam, and again you have gone back on your word. I sent my own men to do it, and you had them buried in New York's Hudson River. Thankfully, the police can't trace their identities to us. Now, either you take care of Jane Weisser, or the men I send to London will take care of her daughter. Do you understand? Have I made myself clear this time? Believe me, my brother, there will be no next time."

Sayyid's image disappeared from the small screen in his hand, and Sam sat there numb. He had thought by calling Sayyid, and having his men a threat to Taryn's life, it would be enough to placate Al-Qiyamah and keep Jane in line. He never thought he would have to decide between Jane and her daughter's lives.

Sam lay on his bed searching for some divine answer to this nightmare.

There was none.

And sleep wouldn't come.

Jane and Moses met every day until the project was failsafe. He arrived at the Plaza each day at a different entrance in a different disguise. By the fourth day they had every step of the plan laid out and every contingency covered.

"I'm sure you've heard Sam's nominated me for Secretary of Housing and Urban Development," Moses said, as they sat on the sofa and packed their papers away.

"How do you feel about that?"

Moses raised his eyebrows at her.

"Sorry. Force of habit," the psychologist apologized.

"I've decided to decline. I can't work for that man knowing what I know."

"Moses, think about what we've been doing these last few days. You may be HUD secretary in Sam Howard's administration, but you won't be secretary under him."

"Still …" The simmering hatred he had for Sam Howard boiled in his veins. He felt his neck muscles tense, and he reached back to massage them.

"I really think you should accept his offer. With Bill Lawson as president, you can rebuild HOPE," Jane counseled.

"*If* that's on his agenda."

"Call him and find out."

"What?" Moses asked, incredulous at the idea of calling up the Vice President-elect. "How do I do that and not tip our hand?"

"Simple. Tell him you want to accept Sam's offer, but you disagree on the issue of rebuilding HOPE. See what he says." Jane went to the keyboard on the desk and dialed the number for Representative Lawson's office.

A minute later, with Jane out of sight, U. S. Representative William S. Lawson was on the wall screen talking face to face with Moses McBride. The Vice President-elect had a calming, reassuring smile. It was warm, open, and perfect for a candidate. "Thank you for accepting my call, congressman."

"Nonsense, Dr. McBride," the gray-haired Texan bellowed, his voice filled with southern hospitality and charm. "Any friend of Sam's … well, you know what I mean."

Moses felt relaxed. There was something homey, warm about the man.

"And I'd be honored, sir, if you'd call me Bill."

Genuine, that was it. "Thank you. And it's Moses."

"Now, what can I do for you this fine day, Moses?"

Moses told him about his hesitancy in accepting Sam's HUD offer because of their opposite views on rebuilding the HOPE Cities. "I'm at a crossroads, and I was wondering about your feelings regarding this issue."

"I feel the same as you do, Moses. America needs to rebuild HOPE. However, as vice president, you must understand that even if I disagree with his policy, I must go along with the President."

"I understand, Bill. Your first duty is loyalty to the President."

"But, remember, my friend, you have an ally in me."

"Thank you, sir." Moses and the congressman spoke some more about what was happening around the country and what they could do about it. They bade each other farewell with words of encouragement and wishes for good luck. When the screen was blank, Moses turned to Jane. "With Sam dead and Bill president, HOPE will be rebuilt. I have to accept the nomination."

"I think that's a wise choice," Jane said with a smile.

Moses took a deep breath. There was a positive side to what they were doing. Not only were they going to save the African people, but as the new Secretary of Housing and Urban Development, he was going to make their lives better. Surely it was just to trade one life for millions. Their success would be proof of God's will.

And if they succeeded, then it had to have been ... preordained?

For some reason, Moses suddenly felt confident.

Jane left New York feeling just as confident. She drove back to the Avis dealer in Trenton and ruminated about Sam, his life, his death, life with him, and without him. She wondered whether she would soon be hearing from him. After all, she did elude his tail and escape surveillance. He would want to know everything. She glanced in her rearview mirror every now and then, but, as far as she could tell, no one was following her. But, then again, she thought, remembering Fats Waller's sly observation: 'One never knows, do one?'

Jane returned the Taurus and walked out to the parking lot to retrieve her Mercedes. As she reached her car, a man came out of nowhere and took hold of her elbow. Her heart dropped into her stomach with the weight of a medicine ball. Her knees turned gelatinous and she began to shake. Jane looked at his face and realized it was one of the two men she had seen inside the blue Buick.

"I'm sorry, Dr. Weisser, but Senator Howard wants to see you."

Jane said nothing. Her mouth was dry. Her abductor took her keys from her hand, opened the door, and closed it behind her. He then got in the passenger's side and handed the keys back to her.

"Just follow the car in front of you."

The man remained silent from that moment on. Once they entered I-95, Jane, for some reason, no longer felt afraid. Taryn was far away, and her newfound relationship with Moses McBride was known only to them. Another reason for this unexpected calm was that she was ready with an alibi for why she was in Manhattan. It was part of her contingency plan.

The two men escorted Jane into Sam's office, where they were left alone. The first emotion she felt was self-recrimination for helping get this madman elected to the nation's highest office. The second feeling was one of hatred. Sitting smugly behind his desk was the person responsible for ruining her and Taryn's lives, Moses McBride's, and the lives of so many innocent people.

"We have to talk about your trip to New York, Jane. If you remember, I told you to stay close by."

"Let's get one thing straight, Sam. I will not let Taryn get hurt. I will do everything in my power, everything humanly possible, to prevent that. As a parent, how can you expect anything less of me?"

He sat silent and glowering.

Jane was livid for being put through this ordeal, and her voice expressed it. "Now that the cards are on the table, Sam, understand that I've sent my daughter far away from here where she'll be safe from you and your slimy cohorts." She stared into his steel-gray eyes, but he still said nothing. "Jesus, is any of this registering with you?"

"Why did you go to New York?"

"MY GOD, YOU HAVEN'T HEARD ONE WORD I'VE SAID!"

"Answer the question," he said with a menacing deliberation.

Her throat constricted in pain and she reached for the glass on his desk. "So, your men found me. I thought they had waited the whole time in Trenton for me to return for my car." Thankfully, Moses had taken the precautions he had when he was at the Plaza, she thought. He was right when he said, 'Always assume you're being watched, no matter where you are.'

"Yes, they found you," Sam conceded. "It was a pretty good chase you took them on, but they finally tracked you down. You foolishly signed into the hotel under your own name. Now, again, Jane," he said, standing up behind his desk, "why did you go to New York and who did you see?"

Jane remained cool. Anything less would have been an

admission of guilt. "Now that the election is over, my clients in Washington and New York are demanding to see me. I've ignored them this past year and it's time I gave them my undivided attention again." She watched him mull it over. If you anticipate and prepare, you will always stay one step ahead of your opponent. Hadn't Sam learned that yet?

"You do know I could easily have that checked out?"

"If I was hiding something, do you think I would have signed into the Plaza under my own name?" Jane stared at him, but he didn't respond. "Just because I've lost my trust in you doesn't give you any reason to have lost your trust in me. I also find it insulting that I'm being followed. Is it really necessary, Sam? I've proven I'm reliable."

"For now I'm afraid it is."

After a moment of silence, Jane asked, "May I go?"

He nodded. As she turned to leave, he said, "Taryn is at your aunt and uncle's flat in London, and she's being watched around the clock. Please, Jane, for everyone's well-being, don't do anything foolish."

Jane felt the hairs on her neck rise. She turned back to look at Sam, but he pretended to be busy with some papers.

The one person at TWO besides Paco whom Jane could trust implicitly was Cassie Davenport, her administrative assistant. Cassie had come to work at The Weisser Organization thirteen years ago, during Sam Howard's first senatorial campaign, as a secretary. She had proved indispensable throughout the years: diligent, creative, and super-organized. She complemented Jane Weisser. Jane's intuitive but unfocused brilliance needed the steadying influence of a Cassie to keep her effective. If Jane was the director of the show, Cassie was her stage manager. At the beginning of Sam's second campaign, seven years ago, Jane had promoted her to her administrative assistant. No one knew the internal machinations of TWO better than Cassie Davenport.

Cassie was also Jane's confidant. They spent their Fridays after work at some out-of-the-way bar or restaurant, sharing their worries and feelings, their desires and dreams. Jane loved Cassie's unpretentiousness, her 'I am who I am, so you'd better accept me' attitude. With just a community college education, Cassie knew her lot in life and never made any bones about it. Just because her boss was a Ph.D. and a Washington powerhouse made no difference to her. They were friends, and that was what was important.

What Jane admired most about Cassie was her sexual confidence born of experience. She was one-hundred-percent woman through and through, although to look at her one saw a girl. Her sweet, innocent appearance belied her sophisticated femme fatale nature. Again, the opposite of Jane, who had only been with two men her entire adult life, but who, nevertheless, projected the image of a woman of experience. Cassie would always tell Jane about her conquests, and Jane would always listen with an envious ear. Cassie had tried it all, and she discussed it with her friend openly, without embarrassment. Some things she had tried just once, like group sex and s&m, just to see if she would like it. Fourteen years older than her, Jane always found herself imagining all she had missed whenever they got together for their Friday night tete a tetes.

Yet, Cassie Davenport's beliefs and principles were what made Cassie Davenport who she really was, not her organizational skills, not her sexual trysts. A die-hard liberal, she always stood up for the disadvantaged and the oppressed. Like Jane, she voiced her opinions and backed them with actions. She helped those less fortunate, and she shared her good fortunes. A proponent of the African cause, equal rights for all, she joined demonstrations and protested injustices. She even called in to work many times to tell Jane she wouldn't be in, for those reasons. Jane never balked at this time off. Cassie Davenport was a special person, with ideals and loyalties she had to respect. Because of that, Jane knew she now had to share *her* darkest secrets with Cassie. And get her involved. For the cause.

The Planetarium was their favorite place to meet. Located on Wisconsin Avenue in Georgetown, it was the most popular night spot for young and old alike. The building was oval in shape. The ground floor was a night club, with a continuous bar around the circumference of the room and a dance floor in the middle. There was also a balcony for dining around the entire room which overlooked the dance floor below. In good weather, the roof would open for dancing and dining under the stars. In inclement weather, stars and constellations lit up the ceiling. On Friday and Saturday, there was a midnight laser light show.

Jane and Cassie could dine without being noticed, get wasted without being seen, and get as personal as they wanted without being overheard at The Planetarium. It was the ideal place to wind down on Fridays after work.

Now, as Jane sat across from Cassie and drank her third Scotch, she wondered how to broach the subject of her friend's involvement. They had just finished talking about the date Cassie had lined up for later in the evening, and Jane felt a momentary twinge of envy between her legs.

Cassie put down her vodka and tonic. "Something's on your mind. I can tell."

Jane closed her eyes and took a deep breath. She began by first asking Cassie what she thought about the racial hostilities in America today.

"I think it's bullshit, that's what I think," Cassie said, her face filled with disgust. "Fuckin' bigots. It's a good thing our

Sam will be in office soon to do something about it."

Jane felt another twinge, only this time in her heart.

"It's unbelievable how this country and its people, after all these years, still treat its citizens of color. I've spent my life trying to change it, as you know. I've come to the conclusion that these are the deliberate policies of a hidden power structure, only how do you go about proving it? You can't."

"Maybe you can, and maybe you can do something about it." There was enough noise from the music that Jane didn't have to worry about being overheard. She spoke to Cassie for the next thirty minutes and explained everything that had happened since Sam's family was murdered, his involvement, Paco's murder, Sayyid Kassim and the Al-Qiyamah, and what was going to happen if it wasn't stopped.

"If I didn't know you as well as I do, Jane, I'd say you were nuts. A paranoid schizophrenic. Delusional."

"And you'd be right on all accounts. Sometimes I don't believe it myself, Cass, but it's all true. And I'm in the middle of it."

They ordered another round, forgoing dinner because they felt too ill to eat. They finished their drinks without any more words spoken between them. Finally, Cassie said, "What are you going to do?"

"Like I said, there's only one thing I can do. Moses McBride and I have to stop it. But, we need your help." Jane looked at everyone dancing below. How wonderful to have no worries, she thought. She wondered if her and Taryn's lives would ever be that carefree again. "I have to ask a big favor of you, Cass, and I know you'll say yes, which is why I feel confident in asking you." Jane told her what she needed, and the potential danger of her involvement, especially if she were caught.

"I've always admired Moses McBride. If we didn't live in

such a prejudicial society he'd be president, I've always thought."

"So, we can count on you?"

"Like you said, you knew I'd say yes."

"How could Cassie Davenport say no? I know of no one as ethical as you, although I feel guilty asking you to put your neck on the line."

They drank for the next hour, while Jane told her what they would have to do to eliminate Sam and Sayyid Kassim and pin it on Garrison Miller.

"No problem," Cassie said. "It'll be my pleasure." She held up her glass in a toast.

Jane finished her drink and turned to watch the people dancing under the illuminated planetarium ceiling, oblivious to the reality of their world. She hoped there would be no problem. She tried to share Cassie's optimism.

Moses McBride reiterated the story told to him by Jane Weisser at the Plaza Hotel. His six most loyal followers sat or stood around the NAC's temporary office inside Martin Luther King, Jr. Community College. Like Moses, they were astounded, angry, hate-filled. They, too, wanted revenge. The reverend told them what he and Jane were planning. It wasn't revenge. It was a matter of survival.

Busy preparing his cabinet, Sam dismissed his transition team when the buzzer sounded, only he didn't move to leave. He just sat alone in his office, staring at the clock on the wall. The clock, in every senator's office, indicated the progression of legislative events on the senate floor, as well as the time. Halfway between the numbers 2 and 3 was a red light that flashed when the senate was in session. It was presently flashing. Between the numbers 9 and 2 were six yellow lights. Three of them were lit. A buzzer was transmitting the same signal, calling for his presence on the floor. Sam ignored it. He was in the midst of another haunting flashback of Britney dying in his arms, her destroyed face, her blood splattering on him. The awful memories had gotten easier with time, but now, for some reason, they were worse than ever.

Sam awoke from the recurring nightmare and wiped away the perspiration from his brow with his handkerchief. He couldn't dispel the nausea consuming his body, nor the guilt eating away his mind. "IT WASN'T SUPPOSED TO BE THIS WAY!" he yelled.

One of the Secret Service agents dashed into his office from the reception area. "Is everything all right, sir?"

Sam didn't look at him. He waved him away and continued to stare out at his city. He felt sick. He knew why; by allowing Jane to leave his office alive, he had chosen who would die. He had played God. "I'm sorry, Jane." He continued to punish himself by remembering all the wonderful times he'd had with Taryn while she was growing up.

The president-elect looked out the window at the capital city, at the greediest nation on earth. He pressed his face against the cold glass and began to weep.

CHAPTER ELEVEN

Five weeks until Inauguration Day

The ruling board of the People for a White America sat, drinking, around the wooden table inside Garrison Miller's basement. "Our biggest problem, until today, has been what weapon to use to kill McBride. Well, here it is." Miller placed it on the table for them all to see.

"You're kidding, aren't you?" Lonnie McKay asked.

"I never kid. There's no way anyone will be able to get close to the Capitol inauguration morning. And anyone who does will be checked thoroughly. I can't carry a gun, a knife, or anything that appears out of the ordinary, let alone threatening."

"But, a pen?" Lonnie's twin Tommy asked.

Miller picked it up and stretched back in his chair. "Who's going to stop me when all I'm carrying is an innocent looking pen? But, this ain't no ordinary pen. Inside," and he unscrewed it, "is a hypodermic needle."

The men murmured in appreciation. Carl Block said, "A brilliant weapon, but it's the middle of the winter. With all the layers of clothing McBride will be wearing, the only place you can puncture him is in his face. Everyone will see you. *If* you can get close enough to him."

"Marc Geraldson in our Philly branch designed a pen that, when pressed open, will shoot out a needle filled with coral shake venom. Only a drop is needed, so if I can get within five feet of him, I can shoot it in his neck or face and get away before anyone knows what happened, or who did it."

Carl Block wasn't satisfied. "Again, I ask, how're you going to get close enough? Five feet or one foot, it's all the same. We gotta figure how to get you on the platform during the swearing in ceremonies."

"Or, on the other side of the Capitol beforehand," Miller said with a smile. "I figure it'll be a helluva lot easier to do it and get away when he first arrives."

"Still a tall task," Jimmy Siefert answered him. "The East Front Plaza, where the invited guests will be dropped off, will be filled with security. And those driving themselves will be parking under the congressional office buildings and taking the subway to the Capitol. I guarantee security will be just as heavy there. Beforehand or after the ceremonies begin, it will be just as hard to get near him."

Miller stared at their pessimism. Didn't they all know by now he wasn't going to take no for an answer? He wasn't going to give up. Not when he was this close. He finished the bottle of beer and opened another as they sat there waiting for his response. "We got five weeks to figure out how I can do it. I reckon we get busy."

Cassie Davenport was a petite woman of thirty-two who looked more like she was twenty. Her long, strawberry-blond hair, small breasts, dimples, and green eyes were the picture of winsome innocence. A staunch fighter of equal rights for any minority or cause, she had accepted her assignment with a relish after Jane and Moses filled her in on the duplicitous plot. "Sam Howard's death means America's survival," she had told them. "You can count on me."

They had gone over what she was to do, when and where she was to do it, and how, many times. She left Washington, excited. Her skin tingled as she drove her beat up old station wagon into New Carrollton, Maryland. Here she was, about to take a crucial role in history. No one would know her part, but she wasn't in this for the glory. She had to do it because her conscience and her beliefs dictated she do it. After years of meetings, rallies, conferences, and demonstrations, she had finally entered the battlefield. She realized she might not come out of it unscathed, but that didn't matter. As Jane had said to her: "It's what we have to do. We have no other choice."

If she came out of it wounded, or worse, at least she had stayed true to herself. For that, she felt proud. She'd led a noble life.

There it was - the house. White clandestine agents of Moses McBride had rented the small house next to Miller's, the one most recently occupied by Maddy Olcott and her son.

Cassie parked the car in front of the modest four-room cape. She carried some cardboard boxes filled with clothes to the front door and entered. The empty house was cold and uninviting. She put down the boxes, located the thermostat, and turned on the heat. She then looked out the window at Garrison Miller's home. She knowingly acknowledged the first twinges of sexual excitement. After all, she was bait for the killer. A whore for a righteous cause. There was something thrilling about that.

Her heartbeat quickened when she saw him dash outside to his mailbox.

In her pink turtleneck sweater and blue jeans, Cassie ran out the front door, down the steps, and fell to the ground. She yelped and grabbed her right ankle. "Owww!" Before she could attempt to rise, he was standing over her.

He bent down, his face inches to hers. "Here, let me help you." He lifted her by her arm. "Can you put any pressure on it?"

She tried. "No."

Miller took her right arm and put it around his neck and helped her walk back to the house. At the steps, he scooped her up in his arms and climbed the four wooden planks. "I guess I should introduce myself. I'm Gary Walters. I live next door there." He pointed to his right with his head and carried her inside.

"Glad to meet you." She winced in pain.

"That was a pretty nasty fall you took."

"Thanks for helping me. I hope I'm not too heavy."

"A little thing like you. Don't be silly. I could hold you all day."

"A tempting offer, I must say, but, really, we just met." She saw his eyes connect. It was flirtatious, teasing, an offering of possibilities. The seduction had begun. She smiled. "I'm Cassie Davenport."

He put her down on her bottom on the bare living room floor and looked around. "No furniture?"

"Not yet. I bought a few pieces, but I still have to buy some more. Until then, I'll be painting, fixing up, purchasing little things to get me going. I don't have much money, but as long as I have my sleeping bag, a refrigerator for some food and beer, and friends, I'll be all right." She smiled at him again and rubbed her ankle.

"Does it hurt much?"

She nodded. "I hope it's just a sprain and not broken."

"Here, let me see."

He gently touched her right ankle and looked up at her. Cassie felt his eyes penetrate hers in an act of visual intercourse. Who was seducing whom? "That feels nice. Thank you." She tried to stand. If she had learned one thing in her thirty-two years it was that men were predators. The pursuit made them hunger for the catch even more. Cassie stood and hobbled around the room.

"You really shouldn't walk on that foot. Let me run next door and get something for you to sit on."

Through the window that faced his house, Cassie watched him cross the side-by-side driveways. "All men are the same," she said as she saw him disappear. What was that great lyric Jane often quoted from the Broadway musical CHICAGO? 'Everybody you watch got their brains in their crotch.' Garrison Miller was classic.

A few minutes later, Miller was back, with a bean bag cushion for her to sit on and an ice pack and towel to wrap around her ankle. "Trust me," he told her.

His eyes had a compelling sincerity about them, but Cassie knew just how dangerous he was. She sat on the cushion, and he knelt by her feet. He removed her sneaker and sock and slid her jeans up to her calf. Cassie watched him react at the sight of her naked flesh. The pedicure she'd gotten the day before was proving worthwhile. He massaged her ankle - oh, he was definitely turned on - then put the ice pack on it and wrapped it in the towel.

He cleared his throat and said, "Keep this on as long as you can. It'll keep down the swelling."

She noticed he wasn't able to keep down his own swelling.

"This is sweet of you."

"Nah. Just neighborly."

"Well, neighbor, I appreciate the friendship. I hope I can return the favor one day. However, now I have a problem. I have to get this place cleaned, painted, and fixed up before my furniture arrives. Then, there's the matter of the yard. As you saw, the slate in the walkway needs replacing right away, otherwise I'll be needing your medical assistance again, which I really don't mind." She saw him blush. It was so easy flirting with an egotistical fool. "I don't know how I'm going to do everything with a sprained ankle."

"I happen to need some extra cash. If you like, I can do it."

"I don't have much money, I'm afraid."

"Whatever you can afford will be okay. After all, we're neighbors. Friends, I hope. How can I charge you more than a nominal fee under those conditions?"

He was being just as flirtatious in his own rudimentary way as she. The bait had been cast, and Garrison Miller had swallowed it whole.

"What do you say?" he asked.

Cassie Davenport looked at her soon-to-be lover and held out her right hand to him. "Here's to a new friendship, Gary. I'm sure it'll be a mutually rewarding one."

Five days after being confronted about her trip to New York, Jane flew into LaGuardia Airport. Now that Sam thought she was merely meeting with her other clients, there had been no problem getting to New York. As far as she could tell, no one had followed her to the Plaza. Of course, she could take no chances. She felt paranoid, but it was safest to always look over her shoulder.

During her first two days at the Plaza, Jane met with many

of her clients inside her suite overlooking Central Park: corporate CEOs, Wall Street executives, publishers, and leaders of the entertainment world. The third day she devoted to meetings with potential buyers of The Weisser Organization. After the last one left, Jane showered and changed into more informal clothes: new blue jeans, a red striped Oxford shirt, and blue Garimaldi loafers. She dried her hair, put on some make-up, and heard three knocks on the door leading into her suite.

Jane opened the door. Dressed as a restaurant delivery man in a green uniform, with a hat covering his dark glasses, and a false beard, Moses McBride walked in with her order. "Perfect timing," she said, "I'm famished."

Moses handed her the brown bag. He took off the hat, beard, and glasses, and sat down on the sofa beside her. As she devoured the corned beef on rye, he told her about Cassie's success at befriending Garrison Miller. They then discussed questions they each had regarding the assassination.

Hours went by, accompanied by numerous Scotches. Moses didn't partake this time, as he had at their first meeting. After her fourth one, he asked, "Do you really need that?"

"Why, does my drinking bother you?"

"Drinking doesn't. Having to drink does."

"Moses, I don't *have* to drink."

"You could have fooled me. Since I've met you, you've done nothing but. I'm concerned about it."

"Well, don't be. Now, where were we?"

"I'm sorry, Jane, but …"

"Moses, I said don't worry about it!"

"Don't worry about it? Listen, I've seen how that stuff destroys lives. It helped kill my daughter. I'm not going to put many people's lives in danger, mine included, only to have you screw it up because you're under the influence. I won't do it."

Jane saw he was serious. She knew she'd been drinking a lot lately, but she always drank more than usual. "Moses ..."

"Either you stop now, or I'm out of here forever. I'm sorry, Jane, but I have no choice in the matter. There's too much at stake."

Jane felt like a school girl who'd been sent to the principal's office. Like she'd been caught at something shameful. She brought the glass to the vanity sink and watched the Scotch disappear down the drain. A fear filled her body as she watched her hand shake. Can I do it?

Having to ask herself the question troubled her even more.

All the way back to Washington Jane obsessed about drinking, but this time her willpower proved victorious. She had two Diet Cokes on the plane.

As she drove toward Georgetown, Jane found she didn't need the alcohol to muster up her courage. Because Sam wasn't stopping her any longer, and Sayyid Kassim's men hadn't followed her to New York, she decided the time had come to check her Foxhall Road home. Why? she didn't know, but she had to make sure everything was okay.

Jane drove into the short driveway and unlocked the front door with the remote control from inside her Mercedes. She gathered the mail and went to her first floor office. The site before her drained all the courage right out of her. The study was in a total shambles. The desk drawers were emptied all over the place. She searched the office from top to bottom. Nothing was missing. She remembered when Garrison Miller broke into her telefiles, and she turned on the telecomp.

'Proper telecomp shutdown procedure not followed. Some files may be lost or altered.'

Miller had been in her house again. Jane needed a drink badly. She went to the bar in the living room and poured a double Scotch. She thought about Moses McBride's warning and put the drink down. She had to try. She owed it to him. She wondered whether it would be better if she stayed in her home as a deterrent to further intruders, but decided against it. The Watergate Hotel was still the safest place to be.

Jane relocked the house and drove away, the disturbing vision of her office fresh in her mind. She couldn't call the police; that would lead to questions, which would lead to an investigation, which would lead to ...

She could taste the Scotch she had left behind.

Sam's men had again followed Jane to New York. However, this time, they'd made sure their surveillance was undetected. They reported back to Sam, with pictures of all the guests who had knocked on her door. She hadn't left and hadn't made any calls on her hotel telecomp, except for food delivery and copy and messenger services. Of course, they weren't privy to any calls she had made on her personal videophone.

Convinced that Jane was finally telling the truth about meeting with clients in New York, Sam still had to wonder why she was doing it so secretly. "Why from her hotel room? And why hadn't she once, the entire time she was there, left her suite?" He sat behind his desk in his senate office questioning the odd behavior. It seemed too odd not to provoke suspicion.

Sam looked through the pictures again. The last one showed an African delivery man carrying a brown paper bag. Because his men had only gotten a side view shot, and it wasn't very close or clear because of the man's dark pigmentation, he couldn't make out the features. However, something bothered him about it. Alone with his thoughts, he switched on the telecomp and the wall screen came to life. He had fifteen minutes before his transition team was due to arrive. CNN was broadcasting, with live pictures from Houston. Rioting had closed the schools, fires lit up the urban landscapes, and seven people had been killed in the last forty-eight hours.

"With the Price administration essentially paralyzed, many fear the civil unrest won't end until after Sam Howard and his administration take office on January 20th," the reporter in Houston announced over devastating video shots of the city. "The White House is insisting that 'bringing the armed forces back to America's streets will only escalate the fighting and the distrust, and will tear apart the classes and the races even more.' Meanwhile, a nation casts about for leadership to end this vicious spiral of strife and distrust."

Sam watched footage of a policeman club a rioting African teen on the head. He thought about his absolute hatred, his reason for doing all he had done. He sat back, his hands clasped behind his head, and watched. This was real entertainment.

There was just a month to go and Cassie Davenport was warming up to her role. She never thought he would be so attracted to her girlish body. She never thought the attraction would be so mutual.

Seated on the old bean bag chair he had loaned her, Cassie drank from her mug of coffee and watched him paint the second coat onto the living room walls. His sneakers, jeans, and red and black flannel shirt were splattered with earth-tone, semi-gloss paint.

Miller stepped off the wooden ladder and wiped his face dry with the towel hanging from his back pocket. He picked up the can of Bud Cassie had put on the floor next to him and took a long drink. "I'm real hot."

"So am I."

Miller tilted his head to the side, like a dog trying to

understand a human asking it a question. He removed the flannel shirt. His wet v-neck undershirt clung to his tight body.

"I can only pay for the painting, not the performance," she told him.

He laughed. "You have a great sense of humor. I like that."

"Flatter me all you want, I'm still not paying a cent more."

Miller laughed again and climbed back on the ladder.

Hmm, Cassie thought as she stared at the taut muscles under his damp shirt. Now that's a body to swing from. She closed her eyes and tried to get into the fantasy of it. After a few minutes, she was sufficiently aroused to embrace her role as seductress. "I gotta tell you, Walters, you can make a fortune marketing that."

"What?" he said, turning to face her.

She saw she had his attention. It was time to build up his sexual ego. From what she'd been able to tell the last few days, it was going to be a piece of cake. "Studly hunk house painting and general contracting services. You know how many single women need their house painted? You know how many would pay someone like you for general services?" She saw him smile, and she took a sip of her coffee.

"General services?" His eyes lit up.

Got him! "Sure, as one of those single women in need, I can honestly say that most of them are looking for more than their house painted."

He stepped down from the ladder and wiped his hands with the towel. "And how could I tell if they were wanting to be serviced?"

"Well, uh, she might fall down and sprain her ankle."

"Is that what you've been doing?"

"No, but that's one way. Or, she might wait for you to make a suggestion."

He sat down on the beanbag with her. The crunching sound

echoed throughout the empty room.

"Anyway, it's a great business idea, I think."

"I think this is a great idea." He leaned over and kissed her.

His tongue slid into her mouth and he pushed his body close to hers. She felt his hardness purposely press against her left thigh. She pulled back from his lips, and asked, "Invitation? Or just bragging?"

Miller laughed again. "You know, I like you. I like the way you think."

She pushed into his erection. "Obviously." They embraced and worked themselves into a frenzy with their tongues and their hands. Then he stood and lifted her in his arms.

"God, you're so light." He looked around for where to lay her down, but the only place was on her open sleeping bag, or on the beanbag chair.

"A gymnast's body can bend in very interesting ways. Did you know that?"

Garrison Miller walked out of her house, into the cold winter air, and carried her into his home next door. He didn't stop until he placed her on his bed. Out of breath from the excitement, he stared at her and undressed.

Cassie did the same on the bed. His eyes refused to leave her body. He was ready. So was she. She lay back and waited.

Miller grabbed her hair and forced himself into her mouth, as far down her throat as she could take. "Jeez, you're good," he said, quivering. "I bet you like it hard and rough."

"I love it every which way." She saw him reach under his bed and remove some leather restraints from a box. Although she had tried it once, Cassie wasn't into bondage. To stay in control, she had to let him think he was in control. She had to excite him enough so he would want her again and again - at least until Inauguration Day.

He tied her wrists to the headboard and her feet to each of the legs of the old bed. Miller then pulled out a leather riding crop from the box. Oh, shit! Cassie thought. She felt her heart race; s&m. He snapped her nipples, and she screamed. There was a brief second of pain followed by the most intense sexual feeling. He continued to crop her body, until the pain overcame the pleasure. "STOP!" She saw the crazed expression in his eyes. "If you want to do this on a regular basis," she said, "you'll have to think about my recovery time." It was the right thing to say. Future sex, sexual security with someone into the same kinks as you, kept her in control for the time being.

Miller mounted her and pounded her insides. After a few seconds, he pulled out and ejaculated on her raw breasts, then dropped down next to her.

"Untie me, please."

"I can keep you tied up all night, you know," he whispered with chilling sincerity

Cassie was frightened by the gleam in his eyes. "You could, but tied I wouldn't be able to do those things to you never thought possible. Remember, I'm a gymnast."

He smiled, undid the knots, and fell asleep by her side.

Cassie looked at the welts on her breasts. Her body was on fire. She took a deep breath and looked at the clock. He would be out till morning.

She quietly slid off the bed an hour later. His snores were constant and deep. It hurt to put on her clothes, but with a little extra care, she was able to do so without wincing. She had to search his house. She needed certain things.

It took only a short while for Cassie to find what Moses had told her he needed. She removed one of many pairs of boots from his bedroom closet, his rifle from the hall closet, and a kitchen glass he had used that evening. The surgical gloves she had on would leave no fingerprints.

Cassie left the house and drove her car to a wilderness area about two miles away. There, in the middle of the night, she fired the hi-powered rifle into the wet ground. She pocketed the spent cartridge, made a call on her videophone, and returned to her house.

Moses McBride's men had shown her how to do it. She took out the fingerprint kit and expertly removed his from the glass. She affixed the thumb and forefinger prints to the cartridge, in the correct position, as if he had loaded it into the rifle himself. Satisfied with her work, she left it on the counter with the boots. Someone would pick them up later.

Cassie slipped back into Garrison Miller's house. She returned the gun to the closet and herself to his bed. Beneath the covers, Cassie looked at the man who was to be her lover for the next month. She thought about the next sado-sexual session and shuddered. The end justifies the means, she reassured herself.

She was making sure that Miller would come to a very mean end.

Jane added the final touches to her disguise: gray wig, glasses, long skirt, doubling her apparent age. Confident she could do no more to change her appearance. Jane stared in the mirror above the dresser. She looked just like her seventy-year old mother.

In the lobby of the Watergate Hotel, Jane searched the faces, and studied the behavior, of everyone nearby. No one took notice of her. She walked to the wall of phones and dialed the overseas operator. A minute later, she was talking with Taryn, minus the video.

They spoke about the weather and about what Taryn was doing every day. It was a real mother-daughter conversation.

Like the way it used to be. Jane was happy to be talking to her, but, at the same time, she felt sad. It had been three weeks since Taryn's departure. She wanted to hold her, hug her, kiss her. God, it hurt being separated from your child. She wondered how divorced parents dealt with being away from their children for long periods of time. It would be intolerable for her. Jane's thoughts returned to their problem. It pained her to have to frighten her child with the truth, but she had to, for her safety. "Listen to me, Taryn. Sam knows where you are, and I'm sure Sayyid Kassim does, too. You have to be extra careful. I don't think they would harm you because then I would talk, but they may try to kidnap you to assure I won't. Please, stay inside as much as possible. When you go out, make sure you're not alone."

"Don't worry, Mom, I'll be careful." There was a pause where neither one knew what to say to the other. "Mom - thanks for being honest with me."

"Why thank me? I'm the one who got you in this mess."

"As you've told me many times, 'Everything happens for a reason.'"

"Yes, I did, and I can't wait to find out the reason for all this." Jane turned her head to see whether anyone was watching her. No one was standing still in the area, just guests walking to and from.

"So, tell me, how would you like to live the rest of your life in Honolulu and go to school at the University of Hawaii?"

"Are you kidding? I'd love it!"

"That's good. Because that's where we're heading."

"Only I can't."

"What do you mean you can't?"

"I'm sorry, Mom, but I can't live with you any longer. Not as long as you continue drinking. Please understand."

Jane felt herself shaking from the embarrassing

confrontation. It was if she were the child and Taryn was her mother admonishing her. She tried to speak, to make an excuse, but something was caught in her throat.

"I've watched you my entire life get high on Scotch, and I've accepted it as you. But it's gotten out of hand this past year, and I don't like the person you've become. I'm sorry, Mom, but either you stop … or we'll have to go our separate ways." Her voice quivered, and she couldn't continue.

Jane thought about what Moses had said and the ultimatum he had issued. Now her daughter was giving her the same one. "It sounds as if you're calling me an alcoholic?"

"I'm not calling you anything, but since you've brought it up, why don't you ask yourself the same question."

"I've asked myself that question many times, Taryn. And the answer's always been 'no.' I'm not an alcoholic!"

"If you've had to ask yourself that question many times, then the answer is 'yes.' You are!"

"Taryn, please, you don't understand."

"I understand all too well. Like mother, like daughter, remember?" The teenager began crying. Through her tears, she said, "You don't know this about me, Mom, but I've been drinking since I was fourteen."

"What?" Jane's heart dropped. Her baby drinking? "But why? What reason in the world could you have to drink?"

"I don't know," she yelled, "I just do. You know how worried I am, how scared I am, that *I* may be an alcoholic? The truth is, I don't like the person *I've* turned into."

Oh, God, the sins of the parent. "What started this?"

Taryn paused to think about it. "Maybe it's because I grew up watching you doing it all the time. Maybe it's because I had a father who didn't care whether I existed or not. I don't know, it just started."

"I'm sorry, Taryn."

There was an uncomfortable silence. "Be honest with me, Mom, how old were you when you first began drinking?"

Jane thought back to her first drink. It was when she was twelve. Right after her seven-year old brother, Michael, disappeared at the mall and was never found. "I had a reason to drink. You don't!"

"I don't mean to sound like a shrink, but you just answered the question: If you have a reason to drink, you're an alcoholic."

Jane cried within. She had been trying to escape the memory, the responsibility of losing her little brother. Because of that, now she was losing her little girl. "So, is that what's been tearing us apart?"

"Yes."

"I thought it was all the time I was spending on this campaign. I know I haven't been around much, Taryn, especially with you graduating high school and going off to college. I've pretty much ignored you this past year. I'm sorry."

"C'mon, Mom, none of that bothered me. I mean it's your job. It would be hard being a spoiled brat if you didn't make enough money to spoil me."

Jane laughed. Taryn knew how to lighten the load at the right time.

"Anyway, the campaign is only temporary. Your drinking is a permanent part of our life. I'm afraid if you don't stop, then I won't stop, and it'll tear us apart for good."

Jane didn't say anything.

"You can't imagine how difficult it is for a kid to say all this to her parent. I mean it's really embarrassing."

"Just imagine how humiliating it is for the parent."

There was a long pause.

"I miss you, you know."

"I miss you, too, Mom."

"And I'm sorry, Taryn, I didn't realize how much my life affected yours."

Mother and daughter spoke some more, this time about their insecurities and their fears, their needs and their wants, and, in that short time, they grew closer than ever before. The honesty was sincere, and the sincerity was honest - the first time in more than a year - and each one accepted the other's promises without question or doubt.

"Thank you, Taryn. You've reminded me of an important rule of psychology and motherhood: Without honesty there is no communication."

"Touche."

Jane took a deep cleansing breath and changed the subject. "Now, what I need you to do is to arrange flights for you and your great aunt and uncle for Honolulu on Inauguration Day. Make reservations from a pay phone under the names on your passports, using the credit card I gave you. There can be no trace of you having left London. Book a flight for anytime before 7:00 p. m."

"Is the time important?"

"Very. Sam will begin walking the parade route after the senate luncheon, sometime between 7:30 and 8:30 London time. If you leave any later than seven, anyone following you will hear about the assassination and will try to kill you immediately." They spoke a few more minutes, assuring each other they would be all right, missing each other painfully.

Jane disconnected and dialed her parents' house in Boston. She looked at everyone in her proximity. When her mother answered, all she said was, "Go next door." Five minutes later, Jane called back.

"We've already sold the house, Janie, and Dad is in Honolulu looking for a new one," her mother told her. After reviewing the next four weeks, Jane was satisfied that all was well and on schedule.

"When will you be leaving to join him, Mom?"

"Tomorrow."

"Great, then I won't have to worry about you." Jane expressed her love and gratitude, and apologies, and told her mother how to reach her after she arrived in Hawaii. She walked back to the elevator in the deliberate pace of an elderly woman - Sam Howard wasn't the only great actor on this stage, she thought to herself - and returned to her suite, confident that everything was going to work out as planned.

It was the worst day of his life. A day he would never forget for as long as he lived. The day Moses McBride killed his 'Daddy.'

Garrison Miller had gone to the state penitentiary for his last visit. That damn nigger reverend had just met with the governor and had convinced him not to grant another stay of execution. The state had scheduled Garland Miller to die by lethal injection in four hours. Although 'Daddy' was all smiles for his boy's benefit, Garrison was livid. This would be the last time he would ever see his father, ever talk to him, ever touch him. "It's just not fair, Daddy, you didn't kill nobody."

"Listen, boy, I done my share of killin' in my day, believe you me. But I didn't kill them nigger kids. Now there's nothing we can do about it, so quit yer bellyachin'."

There was quiet for awhile, until their time together ended. Miller kissed his father one last time and promised him he would never forget.

The last thing 'Daddy' Garland whispered in his ear was, "Just don't forget what I always told ya, boy: It ain't over till the white king takes the black king. Y'understand?"

Garrison Miller understood all-too-well. It was war. It would always be war. From that moment on his dream had become his goal.

And his goal had become his life.

Miller stretched out on his bed and spoke to his deceased father. "Soon, Daddy, your killer will be dead. I promise you." Earlier, he had sent the McKay brothers, Lonnie and Tommy, to London to bring back Taryn Weisser. She would stay in the secret dungeon underneath the basement as long as he wanted or needed. He would have the inexperienced teenager by day and the compliant Cassie Davenport by night, or vice versa, or, better yet, together. He visualized a ménage a trois, raping two women at the same time, torturing them, pleasing himself, as in his most fevered daydreams. He continued fantasizing about the three of them in bed, almost hearing the delicious screams, until he was brought back to reality by the ringing phone. Miller cleared his head and answered it.

Lonnie McKay proceeded to tell him what he and Tommy had observed in London. "I don't think we're the only ones interested in the girl. Two foreign-looking guys, Arabs, I think, are watching her, too. She left the house a little while ago, and they rushed out of the flat across the street, but she got in somebody's car before they, or we, could get close. From what I saw, I don't think she was aware of them. Or us."

"Arabs?"

"Don't worry. They didn't see us."

"DON'T WORRY? I GOTTA WORRY. IT'S MY ASS!" Miller assessed the problem and told Lonnie what to do. "I want you to get rid of them and bring her home to me. Now!" He disconnected the old cell phone and lay back on his bed, thinking. Why in the world were two foreign-looking men, Arabs, following Taryn Weisser? Miller thought about the danger of the McKays being caught. About spending the rest of his life in prison. He thought about the two men again. Arabs? Shit, nothing made sense anymore.

What made sense was that he had to have the girl in his hands before her mother talked. "Maybe she doesn't know I broke into her computer," he said, staring up at his bedroom ceiling. "And maybe she doesn't know I was the one who fired the shot at Sam Howard." Garrison Miller speculated about it some more.

He wasn't going to take anymore chances.

CHAPTER TWELVE

Four weeks until Inauguration Day

Loaded with presents for Adam and Bradley, the Kellehers, and Sam that she had ordered from various catalogues, Jane arrived at their Fairfax, Virginia home late that snowy Christmas afternoon. She had spent the first part of the day working at the Washington Women's Center in preparation for the annual Christmas dinner they provided for the poor and homeless.

Seated around the brightly decorated tree in the living room, everyone began opening Jane's gifts. Jane watched and reveled in their delighted reactions. Tom Kelleher beamed at his new fly reel; he was an avid fisherman. Martha, his wife, unwrapped a gray cashmere sweater. Tears filled her eyes, and Jane responded in kind.

"My dear, you are the most loving and thoughtful person. Thank you for remembering us on our holiday."

"Please, you're my family," Jane answered, waving off the

unwarranted gratitude. "I just wish Taryn was here to share this moment with us."

"Where is Taryn?" Tom asked, as he played with his new reel.

Jane sneaked a peak at Sam and noticed his eyes were the same color as the sweater his former mother-in-law was trying on. "She's spending the holidays with friends. She asked me to send her love."

"It fits perfectly," Martha Kelleher said as she bent down to give Jane a kiss. "I don't know what's wrong with you, Sam Howard. If I were you, I'd marry this wonderful woman today. My goodness, you've been best friends for years. What are you, blind?"

Sam smiled at the comment and said, "I've been asking her for years, Martha, but she keeps turning me down."

"Can't say as I blame her."

Everyone laughed at the grandmother's playful jab, and Jane's mind wandered to a Christmas past. It was during their senior year at Yale, and Sam had wanted her to spend it with him and his family at their Greenwich, Connecticut mansion. She had declined the invitation. It was more important to spend the day helping feed the homeless at the local shelter. They had quarreled endlessly for a week, and they each felt they were right.

"This is what I've done every Christmas with my parents since I was a kid, Sam," she told him when he wouldn't relent. "This is my way of honoring your holiday."

"And for one year you can't? C'mon, Jane, my family wants you there. My father is counting on me to convince you."

Jane stood firm despite Sam's best effort to sway her. She had fed the homeless that year, and had done so every year since.

Sam's voice woke her from her memory. " … and someday soon I will convince this stubborn woman. She can't hold out forever." Jane saw him staring at her, a warm smile on his handsome, benevolent face. Oh, how she wished Sam Howard was really the man he appeared to be. She brushed away the conflicting feelings and smiled at the boys ripping apart the green and red wrapping paper on their gifts.

"WOW!" Bradley screamed. "A micro disc player and view goggles. Thanks Jane." The thirteen-year old leaned over and hugged her. "I love you."

Jane held in her tears. "I love you, too, Bradley. I remember you telling me about your collection of science fiction movies. Well, now you can watch them in the bathroom, in the car, in bed, anywhere."

Adam opened his heavy box and pulled out a large telescope. "You remembered me telling you how much I like astronomy. This is great! Thanks, Jane. You're the best!"

Jane felt overwhelming pangs of love intermingled with sorrow and was afraid she would cry, but then Sam unwrapped his gift and she felt in control again. "For the great actor, Sam Howard," she said, as he pulled it out of the box. "Never forget your past." Jane saw how uncomfortable she had made him and pressed her advantage. "When I saw this bust of Shakespeare, it practically spoke your name. I knew you would understand the meaning. Read the base. It's from the play you were in when we first met."

Sam read the engraving to himself.

"Read it out loud, Sam," Jane insisted.

He gave her a grudgingly guilty look. "'To thine own self be true.'"

"Oh, how beautiful," Martha Kelleher sighed.

"Yes, Jane, it is," Sam said in a soft voice. "Thank you. But, I starred in MACBETH. This quote's from HAMLET. Now," he said, as he turned to face the others, "Jane and I have some work to do." He rose from his seat, and Jane followed him as the others reiterated their heartfelt appreciation.

Behind the closed sliding doors of his study, they sat facing each other at his desk. "Thank you for making my family's Christmas so special. Martha was right. This was very loving and thoughtful of you."

"Like I said: They're my family, too, Sam."

"Yes, I know."

Sam felt as uncomfortable as he had ever before felt. Jane's message had been loud and clear. Confront her? Placate her? He knew he had to take command. "Please, Jane, tell me the truth. Why are you here?"

"I'm always here on Christmas Day, Sam. It's tradition."

"But ..."

"But nothing. The boys' emotional well-being is all I'm concerned about."

"Again, thank you."

"Don't thank me. I'm also your p. r. manager and we need to discuss the inauguration. There's a problem."

Sam felt pleased. She was still in his corner.

"No smirking, Sam. I'm not doing this for you. I'm doing it for the country. The image you portray on worldwide telecomp is either going to forge the world into a bright third millennium or drag it through years of anarchy and war. I'm responsible for that image. I want to make sure it's the right one."

Humbled, Sam asked, "What's the problem?"

"I'll lay it on the line for you, then give you my opinion. If what's been happening in our major cities these last few weeks continues to worsen and spread, there's no way the Service is going to allow you to walk the parade route on Inauguration Day. On the other hand, accessibility is key to the success of your presidency. The people need to feel close to you, almost as if they can touch you, be part of you, follow you to the promised land. They need to believe you're their savior. Riding in a bubbletop will not send the right message nor create the correct image for a country teetering on the brink of civil war."

Sam listened to, and thought about, every point Jane made. "And your opinion is?"

"You'll be risking your presidency if you ride, you'll be risking your life if you walk. But, it really doesn't matter what you or I think, Sam; you don't have a choice. The Secret Service is inflexible. They will insist on the bubbletop. I guess they have the authority in this matter."

"No, Jane, I'll be the President. I'll have the authority, the final say. If I choose to walk amongst my people, if that's what they want, if that's what will help heal them and unite the country, then that's what I have to do. I can't play it safe. I have to play it right. Anyway, with all the tension around the country, security will be so thick, no one will be able to get near me."

"But, Sam, think about it."

"I *have* thought about it," he insisted. "I will walk the parade route."

Of course he would, and Jane knew it all along. It was all a matter of how she expressed every sentence. Word structure, emphasis - what was said and how it was said - played a manipulative role in psychological persuasion.

She had taught Sam about presentation and persuasion. In the process she had learned a lot about performance. "There's more than one 'p' in politics," Jane often lectured. "There's presentation, performance, and persuasion. And if you use these three 'p's' effectively, you get the fourth one - power." Under Jane's coaching Sam had become a master of all the 'p's' of politics.

Yet, he was often strangely unaware when they were being employed on himself, as Jane was now doing.

Jane's mind returned to Sam's decision. He was going to walk the parade route. It was exactly what she needed him to do. His insecure ego and need to demonstrate physical courage would compel him into this act of bravado. Jane knew that an apparent attempt to protest the decision would only confirm it. "But, with everything that's been happening …

He cut her off before she could finish. "It is my constitutional right to decide for myself." He stood and led her out of his study. "The Secret Service can't take the right of free decision away from me."

Jane feigned reluctant acceptance as she walked through the living room. "Goodbye everyone. It was wonderful seeing you. Happy holiday."

They all rose, kissed her good-bye, and wished her a Happy Hannukah. When she and Sam were by themselves in the marbled foyer, she opened the front door to leave.

"Where in the world is Moses McBride?" he asked before she could get away.

Her heart skipped a beat, and her face felt flush. Did he suspect something? She answered with her back still to him. "How would I know?"

"I'm not asking you personally. It was a rhetorical question. His people need him. He can't abandon them now."

Jane turned to face him. "His wife is in a New York hospital clinging to life. I'm sure that's the only thing on his mind right now. Anyway, that's an interesting comment coming from you, Sam." She saw his eyes penetrate hers.

"I didn't abandon my people."

"No, you didn't. You abandoned your humanity!" Jane turned on her heels and walked to her car, angry, disgusted, but also pleased.

She held the power of the 'p's'.

Moses had spent the better part of Christmas Day at his wife's bedside. Earlier in the day, the doctor had called him. There wasn't much time left. Moses continued to stare at Jessie. For hours he had been holding her hand, but she was deep in her coma. Her blood pressure had fallen and her breathing was erratic.

At 9:47 in the evening Jessie McBride took her last breath. Moses knew Jesse was at peace with DaNell. He turned away and slowly walked out of the room with his head down, as tears rolled from his swollen eyes. Christmas Day, a day of magical birth, had become a day of death, a day he'd never be able to forget - a day he could never again celebrate.

Alone in his new apartment on W.118th Street, Moses succumbed to the temptation of bitterness, anger, and despair. God had abandoned him. God had never cared for Moses or his people. He was the white man's God who had cursed the sons of Ham, condemning them to centuries of suffering and servitude. Now, He had taken away Moses's reasons for living. He found the bottle of whiskey in the white metal cabinet above the sink. Furiously, he twisted off the metal jacket, deeply cutting the skin between his thumb and index finger, and gulped down nearly half a pint of the burning liquid. Retching from the potent drink, he choked out the names of his beloved "Jessie, DaNell".

By midnight he had consumed nearly a fifth of whiskey, but his rage and bitterness only intensified. He wept and moaned and cursed as he threw himself on his bed, punching the mattress with all his strength. He groveled on the floor, rolling and tearing at his clothing, rose to his knees and shook his fist at the sky, daring God to punish him some more. He found his leather-bound Bible given to him by his father-in-law as a wedding present and violently tore fistful of pages from the binding and flung them about the room. Finally, exhausted, and with the full force of the alcohol kicking in, he sagged into his armchair and spent his last reserve of energy in flinging the whiskey bottle against the wall. It shattered, adding sharp glass splinters to the rubble around him. Before the alcohol finally claimed his consciousness, he felt guilt and disgust at his own behavior.

He hoped tomorrow would never come.

The following day, Jane conducted TWO business on the telecomp in her Watergate suite. In constant communication with Kerri Robbins on Massachusetts Avenue, her company was still running, if not smoothly. Without Paco, and without her and Cassie there in person, Kerri was at her wit's end. Jane commiserated with her and tried to lift her spirits with words of praise and encouragement.

After Jane disconnected, she turned away from the wall screen, and continued her work. The ringing from her telecomp disrupted her thoughts a few minutes later. She pushed the phone button on the telecomp and Sam's face appeared on her hotel wall.

"I was thinking about our conversation yesterday, and I decided I want you by my side at the inaugural ceremonies. People will expect it."

Jane was dumbfounded. To sit by his side and have to listen to his lies while the world watched - well, that would take a masterful performance. She tried to think of an excuse, only she knew she had no choice. "Fine, Sam. I'll be there. Reluctantly."

"I also want you by my side during the parade route."

During the parade? Jane blanched at the implication. Her mind raced for a way out. Their relationship had turned into one of mutual mistrust.

"Jane? Do you hear me?"

"I'm sorry, Sam, but I can't. Yes, it's expected of me to be in the stands with you, but not the parade route. I'm not your wife. It would be inappropriate."

"Nevertheless, I want you there."

"Sam - the publicity, the second guesses, the innuendo, will be bad press for you. Especially now. The public will put two and two together."

"And what, come up with four as you've always said they may do?"

"Yes."

"Great. It's about time we came out of the closet."

"We? There's no more 'we' anymore, Sam. Can't you get that through your head? For God's sake, wake up!"

"Image, Jane. You're always talking about my image. Well, play the part and help me create that image. Not for God's sake, for the country's sake."

"And if I refuse?"

"Refuse?" He questioned her question with disbelief, and there was a frightening edge to it. When she didn't say anything, he said, "Ah, it's going to be a great day, Jane, a day we'll always remember. Just like we always dreamed. Remember how we dreamed back at Yale, Jane?" He sighed in remembrance. "Well, our dream is finally coming true."

Jane watched him revel in his delusion. It was as if he was in another world enjoying any scenario other than the one he was living. She walked to the bar - she couldn't take another minute of this - and poured herself a Scotch. Although she had remained dry since Moses and Taryn voiced their ultimatums, she instinctively reached for her pacifier. She turned back to continue protesting this turn of events with Sam, but the wall screen was dark. Still darker was her realization that a bullet meant for 'Uncle' Sam Howard might find her instead on January 20th.

The funeral service for Jessie McBride was small, yet public. The Reverend Dr. Moses McBride, President of the National African Caucus, leader of America's African people, was news. The press had stationed themselves nearby in the cemetery, with invited guests and dignitaries flanking the bereaved. The media was present because President-elect Sam Howard was there offering personal and official consolation. To all those in America watching, it looked as if there was finally unity among the races, with all mankind sad but encouraging, coming together as one in a time of sorrow and need. It was truly a heartfelt scene.

The short service ended, and they laid Jessie McBride to rest. Staring at her flower-covered coffin, Moses reminisced about the woman who made him who he was.

The oldest son of a single mother, and extremely bright according to his teachers, he was like everyone else in his community: Desperately poor, living day to day. His friends dealt with this problem by either pushing crack, running numbers, or pimping the neighborhood women. Moses, at seventeen, had yet to acquiesce to such temptation.

One evening, Moses came home and found his mother crying at the kitchen table. "What's wrong, mama?" he asked as he sat down next to her. She didn't answer him. All she did was force a smile on her tired face and wave him away, as if everything was okay. Moses saw the bills in her hands and the shame in her eyes.

Moses kissed his 'mama' and told her everything was going to be alright. He left their apartment and walked for miles, debating what he knew he had to do, until he came to a corner convenience store. Moses ambled inside and took a Coke from the refrigerated case. When he saw he was the only customer in the store, he approached the cash register and whipped out the pistol that society had forced him to carry for protection. His hand wouldn't stop shaking. "G … Gimme all the money. And fast, ya hear?" The frightened, questioning look on the beautiful girl's face made Moses' heart stop beating and his blood run cold. "Survival," Moses heard himself say. "People have to survive, don't they?"

The girl, whose name tag read JESSIE, stared into his eyes, into his soul. "Not this way!" her voice quivered. Moses paused for a second, feeling guilty for the sin he was committing. He saw the pin opposite her name tag - JESUS SAVES - and felt even guiltier. But, then he thought of his disconsolate mother and grabbed the wad of bills from the girl's trembling hand and ran home, her recriminating face and voice haunting him all the way. He wondered whether he would ever see her again. He wanted to, but how could he now? He had become just a common thief.

More than a year later, Moses and his friends attended a Christmas dance at the Boys and Girls Club of Harlem. It was time to 'line up some booty' for New Year's Eve, as one of his friend's had suggested a few days earlier. First, they would try the 'good girls,' to make their mamas proud of them. If that didn't work out, well, they knew where they could get it elsewhere.

Toward the end of the evening, the DJ played 'My Girl' by the Temptations. Inexperienced with women because of his great weight, Moses was alone envying his friends when a thin, lanky girl walked up to him and asked him if he would like to dance. Everything became a blur to Moses. His mouth went dry, and he began to perspire. He didn't care about 'booty;' he just wanted a nice girl who would love him.

A few minutes into the song, having yet to introduce themselves, the girl looked up at Moses and asked, "So, what did you do with the money?"

"Say what?" he responded, not knowing what she was talking about.

"Your *survival* money."

Moses looked into her eyes, saw the JESUS SAVES pin on her dress, and quickly made the connection. He felt his body go limp.

"So, what did you do with it? Spend it on drugs, liquor, women, what?"

Moses stared at her and said without thought, "I gave it to my mama for the electric bill and food. It got us through until she was able to find another job. I'm sorry."

Jessie Daniels pressed herself closer to Moses McBride. A few seconds later, she whispered, "No, I'm the one who's sorry. Let he who is without sin cast the first stone."

Jessie's influence worked wonders on Moses's character. She insisted he graduate high school; she insisted he apply to college; she even helped him study for his SATs, fill out his applications, and apply for financial aid. And because of Jessie Daniels, the once-unhappy Moses McBride gave his life to his Lord and Savior Jesus Christ, vowing to 'always do the right thing.'

The day Moses graduated Yale Divinity, he nervously asked Jessie to marry him. She turned him down. "But, why, Jess? Don't you love me."

"I do, Moses, but my father doesn't believe you're a righteous man, yet."

"You gotta be kidding? I'm a minister, for God's sake."

"Moses!"

"I'm sorry." Moses approached the Reverend Thomas Daniels and pleaded with him for his daughter's hand in marriage.

"Only when your soul is one with God's can I welcome you into my family, son."

Moses spent hours, then days, and weeks, in church praying for guidance, praying for a word or a sign from his Lord. He relived his life, asking for forgiveness, until he realized that one cannot ask for forgiveness, one must earn it. That very afternoon, he returned to the Daniels W.151st Street apartment after making two important stops first. With tears in his eyes, he approached his future (he hoped) father-in-law. "Eight years ago, I sinned, sir. I hurt innocent people and I realized I must make restitution in order to one day enter God's Kingdom. I have returned the $432.00 I stole from Jessie's former employer, along with eight years interest. I have also donated the same to the Boys and Girls Club of Harlem."

"And how do you feel?" Reverend Daniels asked.

Excited, Moses told them. "You should've seen it. Mr. Ramon's face lit up when I gave him his money and explained. When I was done apologizing, he offered me his hand. At that moment, I ..." Tears rolled down Moses's face. " ... felt God enter me."

"You are a good man, Moses McBride, a righteous man. Welcome, my son."

Jessie ran into his arms, crying, "Please, Moses, please ask me again."

Moses laughed a laugh as great as his girth. "I love you with all my heart, Jessie. Will you allow me the honor of marrying you and spending the rest of my life with you?"

Buried in his embrace, Jessie looked up to him and whispered, "The honor would be all mine, preacher man."

Moses awoke from his bittersweet memories and, in tears, said good-bye to his wife. He then turned to DaNell's grave and said a prayer for the product of his and Jessie's love. A moment later, he wiped his face with his handkerchief and walked away from the flower-covered coffin. The first one at his side was Sam Howard. The president-elect put a comforting arm around him while America watched this touching display of brotherly love first hand on their TCs and TVs.

"Oh, Sam, get real!" Jane said to the scene on her hotel wall screen. She had wanted to attend the funeral to support her new friend, but she knew Sam would be there, and she could find no explanation to give him as to why she would be present. Supposedly, she didn't know Moses McBride. If she'd attended, Sam would suspect a relationship. For everyone's safety, caution was warranted.

Jane turned off the telecomp inside her Plaza Hotel suite in Manhattan. She had the rest of the afternoon booked with prospective buyers of The Weisser Organization. She had the following morning booked with Moses McBride.

Moses arrived in disguise at the Plaza the next day. After exchanging hugs and tears and some comforting words, they discussed what they still had to do.

During a break, Moses admitted he had mixed feelings. "After burying Jessie and DaNell, a part of me just wants to forget all this and stop the killing. Yet, another part of me is so pissed off that if I don't do something about it I think my head will explode."

Seated next to him on the sofa, Jane put her hand on top of his. She remained silent for a few minutes while he reflected and came to terms with his life.

Moses returned to the present, and Jane changed the mood. She told him about her visit with Sam, about his reaction to the 'To thine own self be true' bust, and about how she had steered him into walking the parade route.

"I'm glad I'm not your enemy," Moses said with a forced laugh.

They resumed their discussion, building scenario after scenario, asking lots of 'what ifs' and 'how abouts,' and making sure everything they were planning was foolproof. Jane knew that the only stupid question was the one not asked. In that same regard, the right answer comes only after asking lots of questions. One of those 'what if' questions was now troubling Moses.

"What if it rains January 20th and he's forced to ride the parade in the bubbletop? We've yet to consider that possibility?"

Jane thought about it. "We need an alternate plan."

Moses stood up and paced the plush carpet. "The NAC still has four heat-seeking missiles we purchased from a Libyan arms smuggler right before the election." He sat back down and explained how they could do it. "However, the problem with blowing up the bubbletop is that we won't be able to pin it on Miller. But, at least Sam will be dead."

"Along with me."

"What?"

Jane's stomach churned. She took out the package of antacids from her purse and popped a few into her mouth. "Sam insists I walk with him in the parade."

"No way! It's too dangerous."

"What choice do I have? Anyway, Moses, we can't use missiles. Too many people could get hurt, killed, and we can't have that. Let's just pray it doesn't rain."

"But, if it does, we'll terminate the procedure and try again at a later time."

"I'm afraid not, Moses. On January 21st, I become someone else and forget this nightmare ever happened. For my daughter's safety, for our sanity, it's now or never."

"I understand."

Jane saw the tears fill his eyes and realized it was because he'd been unable to protect his own child. "Don't lose faith, Moses. Look at all the lives we'll be saving."

"Don't lose faith? With all my friends and family dead, and my people driven to the wall, how can I have faith? There is no God!"

"Moses McBride, you don't believe that!"

"Tell me, Jane, why should I believe in a God who lets even his own chosen people be persecuted and driven from place to place for over 4000 years and then be exterminated by the millions in horrible death camps? Why should I believe in a God who lets my people be enslaved and despised and oppressed - a God that lets innocent children be sexually abused and tortured and have their limbs hacked off in political vendettas? How can I believe in a God who allows evil people to prosper and triumph - a God who even robs the dignity of his most fervent followers in their old age by depriving them of their mental faculties and control of their own bodily functions - a God whose answer to my deepest prayers has always been "NO"? Why?"

"I don't have an answer, Moses, but one thing is for certain: Everything happens for a reason."

"That's fatalism, not faith. Anyway, my lack of faith isn't important here."

"On the contrary, it's very important. If you don't have faith in what we've set out to do, you're putting many people's lives in danger. Mine included." She saw him stare at her. It was what he had said to her about her drinking. "You have to go into this with your heart and soul, Moses. Only your belief in God will make you accept you're doing the right thing."

"That's what I always preached to DaNell."

Jane smiled reassuringly. "If you have faith in what we're doing, Moses, no one will be able to stop us."

The next morning, Jane drove home to Washington. Before

going to her temporary home inside the Watergate Hotel, she needed to stop off at her house on Foxhall Road in Georgetown. There were some papers she had to have regarding TWO for its sale. As she drove along the winding, uphill street, past the stately homes of her neighbors, Jane remembered her last visit there. Someone had ransacked the place and had entered her computer again. The most troubling thing about that was she didn't know who was behind it. Sayyid Kassim's men? Sam's men? Garrison Miller's?

Jane drove into the short driveway. She exited the Mercedes and pushed the remote control button on her key chain to unlock her front door.

An explosion, louder than any sound she'd ever heard, made her scream and cover her head. The front door of the house blew outward from the force of the blast and landed on the snow-dusted lawn.

Jane saw two men running toward her from a car down the street. Her heart pounded and she jumped back in behind the steering wheel. She threw the stick shift into reverse and almost hit them as she backed out of the drive. She raced down Foxhall Road toward her suite at the Watergate, the squeals of her tires proclaiming her fear and panic all the way.

She now knew: Sayyid Kassim wanted her dead.

Carl Block returned from Washington to New Carrollton. He entered the basement through the secret tunnel and dungeon. There, Garrison Miller and 'Cowboy' Jimmy Siefert were sitting at the round table under the lone, hanging bulb. Lonnie and Tommy McKay were in London observing the surveillance of Taryn Weisser. Block undid his overcoat and took off his gloves. "You should have no trouble killing McBride on the East Front before the ceremonies begin," he announced.

"What did you find out," Miller asked with a newfound excitement in his voice.

"I met with an aide in the Maryland senator's office under the guise of writing a novel about a presidential inauguration. I told him I needed to know about protocol, security, who sits where, time tables, etc. Well, this fresh-out-of-college assistant sent me over to an acquaintance of his at the Joint Committee on Printing."

"The what?" Jimmy Siefert asked.

"The Joint Committee on Printing."

Garrison Miller didn't understand what he was talking about, and he began to get antsy. "C'mon, man, get on with it. What the fuck did he tell you?"

"Every bit of security will be guarding Washington that day. There are only a few ways to gain access to the grounds surrounding the Capitol, let alone inside. Everyone who has to be there has an invitation. Ninety-five percent of those invitations are for the general public, and those seats won't get you within a hundred yards of McBride. The other five percent are color coded for those dignitaries who will be seated on the West Front. That's the invitation McBride has. He and the other guests will be entering through the East Front, which will be cordoned off, or from the subway station underneath the Capitol."

"So, how do I get within five feet?"

"With this," Carl Block answered with obvious pride. He held up the picture of the press badge. "The guy in the printing office let me take pictures of the invitations. When he showed me this badge, I knew it was the only way. If we can make a duplicate of it, you can get close enough to McBride to shoot the dart from the pen into his neck."

"A reporter, eh? Like I was when I shot him in New York."

"Yes, but this time you can get close to McBride, blend in

with the rest of the VIPs, and escape through all the hullabaloo and commotion afterward."

Garrison Miller thought about it and looked at his best friend. "It's ingenious!"

They celebrated with beer and pretzels, then some more beer and pizza. The leader of the PWA laughed at Carl and Jimmy's playfulness. He sat back on the wooden chair and dreamed about his promise to 'Daddy' Garland. He had been in contact with every state leader of the PWA everyday, assessing the damage to his people and their progress against the enemy. He knew 'Daddy' would be proud of how he masterminded this plot if he were alive today.

Soon it would be over.

Sam sat back in his senate office chair and felt good. He had just finished meeting with his transition team and everything was running smoothly. Jane was going to walk with him hand in hand in the parade, and the Senate Intelligence Committee was passing his nominees through one after another. The ringing of his private videophone disrupted his euphoric state of mind. Sam removed the phone from his desk and dismissed the remaining members of his staff. Sayyid Kassim's furious face, on the 4x4-inch screen in Sam's hand, bore into his eyes.

"This is your last chance to do something about the woman, Sam. The others and I have met to discuss it and it is what you must do. Do you understand what I'm saying?"

Sam's stomach knotted. The images of the past returned. "I can't. It would bring on questions. Innuendo. This whole thing could unravel."

"Make it look like an innocent accident. But, not like the one with your late wife. Kill her, Sam! Or we will kill the girl. Then, you will have to eliminate Jane Weisser to stop her from talking." The leader of Al-Qiyamah disappeared from the small screen.

The president-elect rose from his high back chair and paced the floor between the desk and sitting area. Just when all seemed so right, everything went wrong. He'd gotten what he'd wanted, but the price being asked to keep it was just too much. How could he kill the only woman, other than his mother and his sister, he had ever loved. He would die before he allowed anything to happen to her.

The world caved in on Sam Howard's shoulders. He had forced himself into playing God and Solomon at the same time.

Until the inauguration, Jane would be a willing prisoner inside her Watergate suite. There were no more trips to New York to see Moses McBride, to meet with clients, or to speak with prospective buyers of TWO. There were also no more trips to her Georgetown home, not after she had come so close to being blown to smithereens.

Yesterday, she had signed the papers with Stuart Holcomb of Holcomb, Meyers, and Smith, New York's largest public relations firm, for the sale of The Weisser Organization. Part of the agreement, for a sum too obscene for Jane to think about, was that she had to promise not to start another firm during the next five years. "Don't worry, Stu," she had told him, "as of January 20th, I am officially retired from public life."

The conflicting emotions from severing herself from the past - for that matter, from the present - left Jane with a hollow feeling inside. Her baby was in hiding, TWO as of January 20th was no longer hers, and, worse, she was all alone to deal with these feelings. There was no one with whom to talk. Share. Commiserate. Bitch.

Jane roamed the spacious rooms of the Diplomat Suite and

marveled at the beauty of where she was living. Underneath her bare feet was thick, gold carpeting. Brass-framed pictures blended into the gold and white silk wallpaper. Sofas in flowery patterns and highly polished furniture filled the suite, making it rich in luxury, yet warm and homey. Jane looked out over the balcony at the circular Watergate Towers apartment complex. She was thankful she had sold the company for all she had. What she was spending per day to live in such splendor was more than most families earned in a week. Jane added the weeks she'd been there, then multiplied it by seven. It was an astronomical total.

Bored, she noticed herself staring at the bar. She felt the withdrawal tearing at her nerves, her body being pulled toward the many bottles. She imagined the soothing taste of the Scotch, the burn in her throat as it slid down, the buzz, the escape. She fought off the temptation for as long as she could, but soon found herself holding a bottle and a glass. Before she could pour it, Jane turned away, hit the keys of the telecomp with her shaking hand, and called Moses at his New York apartment.

"Moses, it's Jane," she said when she heard his mellifluous 'Hello.' She tried to steady her voice as best as she could. "How are you doing?"

"Under the circumstances, I'm doing fine. How about you?"

She didn't answer him. Her throat wouldn't open.

"What's wrong, Jane?"

"I'm not doing so well, I'm afraid."

"Talk to me."

Jane knew he knew. She could sense it in his tone. "Please, Moses."

"Ask and ye shall receive."

"I need help, damnit!" Her body trembled along with her voice and she let it all out. "I'm an alcoholic and I need help! Okay?" For the first time, Jane admitted she had a problem.

Hearing the words, feeling the emotions, she realized she'd been in denial for a long time. Her admission, she noticed, also made her feel somewhat better, and the shaking lessened. "Is that it?"

"You had to say those words, Jane. Now, we can go on."

They spoke for more than an hour, and the desire, that addictive yearning, passed, returned, then passed again a few more times. But, at the end of the conversation, with the promise she could call him at any time, Jane said she still felt depressed.

"Of course you do, Jane, that's perfectly normal. It's all part of the cleansing process. You're fighting a terrible demon."

"Tell me about it. I feel like I'm in the middle of a tug-of-war."

"Addiction is a disease, and nothing to feel ashamed of. I guarantee your blues will disappear once your craving does."

"But, what do I do about the depression in the mean time?"

"Why don't you call Taryn?"

Jane smiled on hearing her daughter's name. The sound of her voice, she knew, would be the best high in the world. "I appreciate everything you're doing for me, Moses. You're a true friend."

"Think nothing of it. You're my number one concern right now."

Jane disconnected and Moses McBride's face disappeared from the wall screen. She quickly dressed in her matronly disguise, dashed down to the lobby, and called Taryn in London, never stopping to think it was the middle of the night there. Minutes later, the two were jabbering away like a couple of giggling, gossiping teenagers.

"Sam Howard insists that Jane walk by his side in the parade," Moses told his men inside his MLK, Jr. Community College office. "Sorry, Ray, but we have to scrap the laser idea. And Jane's not the only problem. If we want to frame Miller for the assassination of the president, we need to ensure that forensics finds the same type of bullet in Sam Howard's brain as is housed by a cartridge from Miller's rifle."

"But, Moses. Modern technology provides us with accuracy."

"The reason we agreed to do this in the first place was not only to rid this world of Sam Howard, but to finally rid it of Garrison Miller."

All was quiet until Ray Jackson again spoke. "I guess we can have the cameras rebuilt with a gun inside to match Miller's," he told him. The National African Caucus had an organization of followers nationwide, including scientists, engineers, craftsmen - the list was long and impressive.

"Only the safety factor, as you pointed out, is not as great as it would be with laser guns," Moses said. "Jane could be hit because there is now human error to consider."

The men mumbled and thought about it. The shooters had to be top marksmen. There was Jane to think about, as well as a background of innocent bodies.

"While the cameras are being rebuilt, you're all going to have to go to Washington. We have to know where to position each shooter. Timing is everything. I want angles, measurements, height versus distance. Take along the circumscope camera for a 360-degree virtual walk of the parade route. I want the physics of the whole layout. We have to be able, in a split second, to shoot, retreat, and leave the evidence behind."

"How much time we got, reverend?" Willie Taylor asked.

"Less than you think. We need to build a facsimile of the parade route and practice hitting a moving target. You have as much time as it will take to rebuild the video cameras with rifles in them instead of lasers. A week, maybe two at the most."

"And that's not enough time?" Willie asked.

"I can't send all of you together. Imagine a group of African men congregating along the parade route, taking measurements and pictures, searching out information about security and placement of stands. How long before some government agent uncovers our little plot? Each of you must collect bits of information separately. We'll put it together here on the computer when you all return."

"Okay," Ray said, "let's go over everything we need to find out. Then, we'll assign each man a set of tasks. Two weeks you say, Moses?"

"Try to get it done in less. And keep in mind that someone may be watching you. In Washington even the trees and buildings have eyes. Jane told me there's always a camera, somewhere, following everyone. There are eighty-five cameras alone scattered around the Capitol building. More, she said, are being installed for the inauguration. The cameras are monitored by the Capitol police, a force of 1300 who provide security for the 535 representatives and senators. There are, literally, eyes everywhere."

Moses listened to the men discuss it and make lists. The most important thing they had to do was pinpoint where Sam Howard would take his last step, and where they would be in relation to him at that precise moment. The height and distance and position of the cameras was the key factor here, and they talked about how they could find out that information.

Moses looked out the window of his temporary office. Everything looked dirty. It had snowed the day before, and, today, with the temperature rising into the 40s for the first time in a week, it had turned to brown slush. Nothing seemed beautiful anymore. Nothing was as it once was. And, now, to add worry to wrought, he had to plan for Jane's safety. Her life was in his hands.

* * * * *

At two o'clock in the morning in Chiswick, a middle-class neighborhood of London, the two men assigned to watch Taryn Weisser were approaching the end of their assignment. One of the two Iraqis was asleep on the bed. The other one was sitting in a wooden chair, drinking coffee, and looking out the window at the sleepy flat across the road. The family who owned the home they were occupying were dead, locked together in the parents' back bedroom. A few days earlier, they had broken in and shot them each - mother, father, and two preteen daughters - twice in the head. They had stationed themselves, since, in the older girl's bedroom, waiting to make their move on the Yehoudi's daughter. Their instructions until then had been to watch her. Now, Sayyid Kassim's orders were for them to kill the great aunt and great uncle and abduct the girl tonight. The Iraqi operative looked at his watch. In just one hour they would move.

Before the hour was up in Chiswick, London, two more men were inside the modest flat. They, too, were following higher orders. Garrison Miller wanted Taryn Weisser. They had been keeping a constant watch on the two Arabs who were keeping a constant watch on the teenaged girl. It was time to eliminate their competition.

It happened as quickly as it began. Lonnie and Tommy McKay, veterans in combat, tiptoed up the stairs to the front room of the three-story home where they had seen the man peering from behind the pink curtains. They dove through the open doorway, rolling to the floor and assessing the situation as they rose. Before the awake man at the window could pull out his weapon in defense, Lonnie put him to sleep with a silenced shot to his left eye. Startled by the noise of his friend falling backwards over his chair, the other Iraqi's eyes opened. Tommy made sure the prone man did not rise.

"Okay," Lonnie said to his twin, "now we can grab her

without any interference."

"I still think we should break in, kill the aunt and uncle, and take her. The faster we get back home, the happier I'll be," Tommy complained.

"No! I told you we can't do that. The old folks' deaths would lead back to Taryn, which could lead back to Garrison and us. We can't take a chance in possibly leaving anything behind in that house. When she comes out, we'll grab her."

Luck was with the McKay brothers. Just before sunrise, Taryn Weisser exited the flat, turned right, and ran one block to the corner store. Lonnie and Tommy smiled.

As she left the store with a container of milk and a loaf of fresh bread, Taryn felt a hand grab her elbow and twirl her around. She tried to scream, but a hand covered her mouth and held back her head before any sound could come out. She looked up at the man. He was thin, with an obviously once-broken nose and crooked, dirty teeth. "Don't make a sound, or I'll have to kill you."

Every nerve in Taryn's body jumped in fear. She looked around for help, but there wasn't a soul outside at 6:00 in the morning. No one to witness her kidnapping. The gross-looking man pushed her into the rear seat of the car, and the driver sped off. "Where are you taking me?" she asked her abductor, seated to her left.

"Back home, where you belong," Lonnie McKay answered.

Taryn wondered whether they were telling the truth. How could she leave England without her passport?

As if reading her mind, Lonnie McKay laughed. "These extradition papers, signed by a Maryland judge, for someone else in England, but since changed to your name, will get you home, no questions asked. And if you say anything, if you offer one hint that anything is wrong, there'll be a bloodbath with you in the middle of it. Understand?"

Taryn nodded. She stared at the driver, the apparent brother to the other, although he was heavier and his brown hair was straighter. She repeated his warning to herself and wondered how there could be a bloodbath. Security will never allow them past the metal detectors with their weapons. It was the first ray of hope. She would scream before boarding the plane and be rescued. Then, she'd have no trouble proving who she was.

As if reading her mind again, he said, "See this case?" He pointed to the floor by his feet. "Inside, is a vial of nitroglycerin. You and a lot of innocent people will die if the slightest thing goes wrong."

She didn't know whether to believe him, but she had no choice. He and his brother looked seriously fanatical.

They pulled up to Heathrow and disembarked. As they did, Lonnie McKay cuffed her hands and covered them with a sweater. "Have I made myself perfectly clear?" he whispered.

Only one thing was clear to Taryn. Someone wanted her badly enough to kidnap her.

In New Carrollton, Maryland, Garrison Miller's phone awoke him from a deep sleep. He had just given Cassie Davenport a good whipping until she was near tears. Then, he fucked the hell out of every hole in her body. He felt great. Miller went into the kitchen to answer the incessant ringing so Cassie wouldn't hear him. "Yeah?"

Lonnie McKay was calling from Heathrow. "We're about to take off."

"Any problems?"

"Not one. Thank God the PWA has members in the legal field."

"And Taryn?"

"She's been a good little girl."

"Good. Keep threatening her and bring her to the dungeon when you get back." Garrison Miller disconnected and returned to his bed. Cassie was asleep, or unconscious, he didn't know which. He dropped back down on the pillow, folded his hands behind his head, and laughed. "Jane Weisser was wrong," Miller whispered to the moon-made shadows dancing around the room. "Taryn is moving in!"

CHAPTER THIRTEEN

Three weeks until Inauguration Day

The controversy raged, fueled by media hype. The President-elect of the United States had announced he'd be walking the parade route rather than riding in a bubbletop limousine. He'd heard all sides on the issue. The Secret Service even ordered him not to walk in these troubled times. He told the country on the evening news: "I'm still my own man, with rights like every citizen. And one of those constitutional rights is the freedom to make my own decision. I will walk amongst the people and demonstrate that we all must overcome our fears." CNN ran a poll, as did many other networks and newspapers, whether Sam Howard, considering the tension and violence in the country, should ride in the enclosed limo or walk with the people whom he represents. It was the debate of the week. Whether on the political talk shows or in the streets, everyone had an opinion. Overwhelming numbers in favor of the new president walking the parade route flooded CNN's phone banks as well as the phone banks for ABC, CBS, NBC, and Fox, the New York Times, the Washington Post, the Atlanta Constitution, and other poll taking journals of national prominence. The results would have been a lot closer, but hundreds of National African Caucus members, through a network based in Moses McBride's office, rigged the counts by flooding the phone lines with computer-generated responses.

Not that it mattered. President-elect Sam Howard had made up his mind.

No one could tell this president what to do.

Sayyid Kassim had told Sam Howard what he had to do, but Sam wasn't listening to orders any longer. Taking matters into his own hands, Sayyid met with the eleven old men of Al-Qiyamah. Jane Weisser had survived the blast at her Georgetown home, they informed him, and the men following her daughter in London were found dead. "Rest assured," Amer Ibrahim said, "their identities can't be traced back to us."

"Sam is protecting them!" Sayyid told his accomplices. If Sam had his men killed to save the woman's daughter, then what might he be capable of after he's sworn in? "I want Taryn Weisser taken care of immediately! Sam must know we mean business."

"We can't," Osman Musuli, stroking his long gray beard, spoke up. "According to the men I sent to replace the two dead ones, the girl is missing now, or hiding."

Despite the anger that threatened to short circuit his reason, Sayyid forced himself to concentrate. "Then, we have to kill Jane Weisser. I can no longer trust Sam Howard."

Again, rather than use her personal videophone, Jane called London from the lobby to review the plan for January 20th and to let Taryn know what was happening on her end. When the transcontinental call went through, Jane heard her aunt crying. It was difficult to understand what the elderly Englishwoman was saying. She was frantic.

"I've been trying to reach you to let you know, but your phone hasn't been working, or it's been off the hook."

"Why, what happened?" Jane's heart began to race. She felt lightheaded. "Is Taryn okay?" Please say yes, please say yes.

"That's just it: Taryn's missing. I woke up yesterday morning and she wasn't in her bed. Whether she left, or was abducted, I don't know."

"DEAR GOD!" Jane was shaking.

"When we couldn't reach you, we didn't know what else to do. Scotland Yard has nothing to go on because Taryn and you have told us nothing. What is happening, Janie?"

Jane gathered her wits and told her what to do. "Go next door, Aunt Fran. What's your neighbor's number?"

Her aunt told her. Five minutes later, Jane called her back.

"Please, Janie, tell us what to do. We're frightened. I've never seen Uncle Neil this upset. He's had a migraine all morning."

"Get control of yourselves. I want you to meet me tomorrow morning at 9:00 at the Savoy Hotel. I'll be listed under the name Rachel Porter." Once she was in London, she could talk freely to them about the abduction. Then she would know how to proceed. "You'll have to leave for Honolulu immediately after our meeting. My parents are already there."

"What have you gotten yourself into?"

"You'll understand when we talk. Now, start packing. No one will know I'm in London. They'll think I'm in Boston. There's no reason for anyone to be following you." After some comforting words, Jane disconnected and broke down. Her body and mind went numb and she flashed back thirty-five years, to that terrible day in Boston when she was twelve years old. The day her brother,

Michael, disappeared and was never seen again.

Her mother had told her, after Jane had begged her to let her spend the afternoon at the mall, that she could go as long as she took her brother with her. "Remember, Janie, Michael's your responsibility. I'm trusting you not to let him out of your sight."

Jane Weisser loved her little brother. He was so cute and innocent. Her friends felt the same way about him, so it didn't matter that he was tagging along. She walked hand in hand with him into the mall, singing, 'I'VE BEEN WORKING ON THE RAILROAD,' and spent the afternoon going from store to store with her girlfriends.

"I have to go to the bathroom," the little boy said after they finished eating their burgers and shakes at the food court.

Jane saw the sign for the bathrooms. She watched her brother walk into it, then resumed her intimate conversation with the three girls. A short while later, one of her friends asked, "Where's Michael?"

Jane looked around, looked at the bathroom hallway thirty or so yards away, then looked back at the girls. She turned white and felt sick. Dear God! She jumped up from the table, and her friends followed her across the courtyard. She ran into the men's room, back out, and cried, "He's not in there. What do I do?" The four twelve-year olds ran through the mall, into every toy store, until Jane's crying attracted the attention of mall security.

An all-out search for the seven-year old boy began immediately. The mall manager called her parents, and they arrived fifteen minutes later. They grilled her, repeatedly asking the same questions over and over, hoping each time for a different answer than the one Jane had given them. Security called in the police, and they did the same.

Days went by without hearing anything, no ransom note, no body, nothing. Her parents ignored her; they were consumed by their own worry and grief. It made her feel worse than she had ever before felt. She had lost her little brother after promising not to let him out of her sight. He was probably in the hands of some crazy child molester.

Weeks went by, then months, and Jane couldn't bear the gut-wrenching guilt any longer. She blamed the police and the FBI for not finding her brother, then she blamed President Reagan. Why wasn't he doing anything about crime in America? She was twelve years old, and she had to blame someone.

One night when her parents were out putting up flyers of Michael's picture and description, Jane went to their liquor cabinet and removed the bottle with the prettiest color liquid. It tasted foul, then it got better, until she found the comfort she'd been looking for - then the comfort of temporary oblivion.

It was a debilitating memory, one that paralyzed Jane every time she allowed herself to dwell on it. She awoke from the nightmare and thought about Taryn in the hands of her abductors. Once again the nightmares of a loved one snatched away had become a reality. Only this time she wouldn't rest until her baby was safely back home.

Thirty minutes later, Jane entered the Hart Senate Office Building and rode the elevator up to Sam Howard's suite. She walked in on his meeting, and his eyes reacted on seeing her. "Can we talk?"

"Of course." Sam dismissed his transition team and they were left alone. "Is something wrong?" he asked from behind his desk.

Is something wrong? Jane held in her true feelings and began the fabricated story. "My mother is very sick and I have to go see her."

"I'm afraid that isn't a good idea, Jane."

She didn't respond.

"You know what you're up against. What we're up against. I can't allow it."

"Sam, we're talking about my mother."

"Yes, I know. We're also talking about your life. Listen, Jane, Sayyid's men are everywhere. You've been very lucky until now, but sooner or later …"

The thought obviously pained him and he couldn't finished the statement. Jane stared into his eyes. "If you were me, and it was your mother who was ill, what would you do?" Jane knew the mention of his mother would bring on emotions he couldn't handle. Sam Howard had loved his mother. He would've done anything for her. If he had a drop of humanity left in him, mentioning his family would tap into it. "You'd go to your mother no matter how dangerous it was."

"What have you told your parents?"

"Nothing. What they don't know won't get them hurt."

Sam hoped she was telling the truth. "You know I can easily call your father and ask him how your mother is feeling."

"If you must."

Sam stared at her a few more seconds. "So far you've been honest with me, Jane. I'll do what I can."

"Thank you."

"But, if I find out you're tricking me … forget about me, if Sayyid catches wind of this … well, as I said, I can't promise your safety." Her look of gratitude gave Sam cause for hope. He knew she'd one day love him again.

Forty minutes later, Marcel Gitaud, the make-up artist from the Kennedy Center, walked into Sam's office with Sonia Telgetter from wardrobe. Per the president-elect's request, they brought with them enough make-up and wardrobe for a cast of twenty.

When they finished, Jane looked in the mirror. "This is unbelievable!" With the latex mask covering her face, a gray wig, and frumpy clothes, she looked thirty years older. "I don't recognize myself."

Marcel and Sonia left, and Jane turned to Sam to thank him. "I'm really very grateful, Sam. You'll never know how much."

Sam smiled. He was sure he could win back Jane's love. This was the first step.

The New Year had started all wrong, with the fighting around the country growing worse by the day. Moses McBride knew he had to do something. If things returned to the way they were before the election, America's African people would be exterminated. To make matters worse, with the assassination of Sam Howard, the wrong message was going to be delivered. America's African people would believe that their savior had again been martyred, and would intensify their rebellion. As was proven just a few months back, the African people would lose. It was a scenario Moses played repeatedly in his mind. He was doing what he had to do, but it seemed to be a lose-lose situation.

Moses noticed he was perspiring. The other men of the National African Caucus had their coats on because the heat in the building was faulty at best. But, he was dripping wet. Usually, in times of stress, Moses would close his eyes and pray. He hadn't done that for a while now. Jane had promised him she would stay off the bottle, but he couldn't comply with her demand that he believe again. He had seen too much to believe a God existed. No merciful God would allow all that had happened.

Moses forced his mind back to the meeting. Earlier in the day, his men returned from Washington where they had reconnoitered the parade route and had taped it with the circumscope camera. They also had all the information they needed regarding security, the location of the stands, time tables, everything to ensure complete safety. They had gone as a team, albeit separately, and had put together a dossier on every inch and every minute of Inauguration Day. They also came back with a video of the last presidential parade because the inaugural committee had yet to set up the stands along Pennsylvania Avenue and they needed to know their exact placement. They walked from the NAC's makeshift office in the basement of Harlem's Martin Luther King, Jr. Community College to the Round Room.

The movie of Charles Price's inaugural parade four years ago wasn't filmed in circumscope, and they watched it first on the 36-inch monitor. The five men sat in folding chairs, their eyes taking in everything they were viewing. Ray Jackson narrated.

"The first problem we run into is we don't know where Sam Howard will begin his walk. He could start at the Capitol, or he could ride the limo a while and get out anywhere along the parade route. We need to set up two spots, in case of any problem, such as a spectator getting too close to him."

"That means using more gunmen," Moses countered. "And the more people involved, the bigger chance of a leak. I think, to be safe, we should stick to one spot."

"But, what if he doesn't get out of the car until further down the parade route, past the spot where we've set up?" Ray asked. "We'll have lost our only chance."

"So, set them up at the last vantage point in the route," Moses told him.

Ray considered it. "Now that we're not using four interconnecting lasers, we don't need four shooters. We'll put two at each spot. That way we're with the same four men."

Moses let out a sigh and nodded his head.

"We need two opportunities, in case the first one doesn't materialize." Ray Jackson forwarded the tape to the scene showing President Charles Price approaching 10th Street. "This is 10th Street, our first spot. If we place a man in the last row of stands in front of the Justice Building, and one in the last row of stands in front of the IRS building, both with six-foot tripods holding the cameras, we'll have two chances to get him. No one will see or hear anything." Ray turned to Johnny Williams and nodded for him to turn on the circumscope camera in the center of the Round Room. Johnny did, and the entire room lit up. Standing, they all looked around. It was as if they were walking down the middle of Pennsylvania Avenue, able to see all around them. "Approximately here where we're standing," he said, pushing a button on the camera to freeze the picture, "is where Sam Howard must step for a perfect shot."

"Sounds kind of risky. Won't the people standing around notice something?" Moses asked.

Clifton Reese, who was responsible for the fabrication of the special camera guns, spoke up. "My team has come up with a gun with a laser target designator built into the camera optics. The weapon looks like an ordinary TC video camera, and the user can put an infrared laser spot on the target. The laser spot can only be seen through the camera viewfinder. The gun has a super-efficient silencer and recoil damping system. The user can fire it from a tripod while still appearing to be only operating a video camera."

Isaac Mumford, at 300-plus pounds, a former NFL tackler, added, "And with all the noise the cheering crowd will be making, no one will see or hear anything."

Moses thought about Jane walking by Sam's side. He continued imagining the scenario, trying to come up with potential problems. "What if Sam walks over to the spectators to shake hands at both places," Moses asked. "Then what?"

"Well it won't be easy for him to do much veering," Ray

told the reverend. "The media truck will be in front of him, and all the official cars and Secret Service agents will be encircling him."

"Where's the second spot?"

"Around the corner from the White House and the presidential viewing stand." Ray fast forwarded the VCR to Charles Price turning right onto 15th Street. He forwarded the circumscope camera to the same spot and again they were there in the middle of the street. "As you can see, the street narrows somewhat on 15th, but the stands are situated exactly as we need them. With a man placed on the southern side, in the stands in front of Sherman Park, and the other one in the stands on the northern side, in front of the statue in General Pershing Park, we'll have as accurate a shot as we do at 10th."

"One more question," Moses said. "How are you going to get the two men seated in the exact spots you need them to be in?"

The usually quiet Isaac Mumford spoke up again. "Everyone who sits in the stands has to have a pass, which they will have purchased through various ticket agencies. We've ordered tickets for the four, plus four more to set up Miller. Soon as we get them, we'll make duplicates with the numbers of the sections on them that we need to be in. He pushed the telescopic button on the VCR/Printer, dividing the picture on the monitor into a tic-tac-toe parquet of nine boxes. The upper center square showed a section number. Isaac pushed 'Zoom-Box 2,' and a close-up of that box filled the monitor's screen. "You can see the number on the stands in front of General Pershing's statue reads 'Sec. 23.'" He fast forwarded the tape until it showed the stands on the other side, in front of Sherman Park. Isaac pushed 'Telescopic' again and the same sectional division appeared. He zoomed in. "And directly across from '23' is 'Sec. 28.' Using this, we'll also find the numbers of the sections by 10th Street and make duplicate passes for both places."

"Regarding security for the inauguration," Ray told everyone, "it's provided by a combination of state, city and federal police." He took out his notes and read them aloud. "The District of Columbia will put around 3,800 officers on the streets, the City of Washington another 1,500, in addition to 2,000 other officers and military personnel. The 1,300-member Capitol Police force will provide security at the Capitol while the 600 officers of the U.S. Park Police patrol the mall and the sidewalks along Pennsylvania Avenue. Other agencies involved include the FBI, the Secret Service, and the Army. From the tape of President Price's walk, you can see that besides all the security walking the route there are armed forces personnel standing in front of the stands on both sides of Pennsylvania Avenue approximately every five feet from beginning to end."

"Sounds impressive," Clifton Reese said in awe.

"Sounds impenetrable," Moses added."

"Exactly," Ray told them. He looked at Moses, "Still want to go through with it?" Before he could answer, he said, "Wait, there's more. An inspector I interviewed, under the ruse that I was a reporter, said that snipers will be lining the parade route, watching for windows opening and for people on roofs. We don't have to worry about that, but there will also be those on rooftops and in windows watching everyone in the stands."

Moses shook his head. What had he gotten himself into? He looked at his fellow conspirators. "Let me ask you. Do you think we can do it?"

They hesitated for only a second before collectively answering, "We have to."

Two men whom Jane had never seen before escorted her from

Sam's office to the garage underneath the Hart Senate Office Building. They weren't the two men in the blue Buick who'd been following her. She hadn't seen those men in days.

Seated in the back of a limousine, they drove her to Dulles Airport. There, the three rushed onto Sam's private jet. Jane thought they would leave her, but to her dismay, they remained on board. Whether or not Sam believed her story about her mother, he wasn't taking any chances. Just as she didn't trust him, he no longer trusted her.

At Logan International Airport in Boston, the two men rented a car. They drove toward Brookline, the birthplace of John F. Kennedy, while Jane removed the latex mask and wig. A little make-up here, a little make-up there, and she was Jane Weisser again.

Jane put the compact mirror back in her handbag and looked out at the streets of her childhood home. It was so peaceful and serene. Being a psychologist, she naturally questioned her emotions. Why did the past always seem better than the present? Was it human nature to want to return to the safety of the womb? For an instant, Jane felt the security a child feels in the bosom of her family. But, then she remembered Michael.

Jane caught her breath and focused on the familiar stores, this community of friends walking in the streets. She wished she could go to her family home, to see it one last time, but she feared Sayyid's men would be watching the house. Instead, she directed the driver to the address of family friends, a few streets away, whom she had earlier called and apprised of the scene. If she wasn't alone when she arrived, they were to play out the scenario. Jane opened the door and stepped out, but the men stopped her before she could walk away from the car.

"Just a minute, ma'am," the taller of the two men, the one who'd driven the limousine and the rental car, said. "Sam asked us to make sure your mother is okay. He wants us to personally offer her his well wishes."

"Fine." She walked to the front door, with them following close behind. The door opened before she reached it, and Jane called out, "Hi, Dad." She walked up to the elderly man and hugged him. "Dad, these men are friends of Sam's and want to extend his best wishes to Mom."

"Come in, gentlemen. And thank you for escorting Jane home." He turned and led the way into the living room.

Jane walked in and saw the old woman on the couch. An Afghan covered her legs. She went over and kissed her. "Hi, Mom, how are you feeling?"

"Better, now that you're home, Janie," the gray-haired woman said with a smile on her cracked lips.

"Senator Howard, ma'am, offers his kindest regards for a speedy recovery," the tall man said. "We'll leave you alone now." They turned and walked out of the house, nodding to Jane's father as they exited.

Jane walked to the window and watched them get back in the rental car. They sat there and didn't leave. She turned to her parents' friends and said, "Thank you, Will. Thank you, Sarah. Even though I can't tell you what this is all about - as my parents' oldest friends, I know you'll keep this a secret and forget about it."

"Of course, dear, we'll do whatever you tell us," the old woman answered, throwing the Afghan off her legs and sitting up.

"Okay, this is what we have to do next." Jane said, removing the Polaroid camera from her bag. "Do you have the clothes I asked for?"

Will picked up the bag and handed it to her.

Jane removed the blouse, slacks, and shoes. They discussed

the sequence and the timing of it, and what they would do in case any problems arose.

An hour later, Jane left the house in a gray jogging suit and sneakers. Everyone knew she was a runner, and it looked innocent enough. She ran down the steps, down the front walkway, and turned left at a slow pace. She didn't look, but she was sure the car was following her. At the corner, Jane turned right again and crossed the street. She noticed the car behind her turn right and follow. She was about fifty yards in front of them on the tree-lined streets of Brookline.

Ten minutes into the run, Jane picked up speed. She turned a corner, then another, and the car pursued. She jumped over some hedges and ran through a yard. Not yet winded, she ran to the prescribed corner where Will and Sarah Thompson were waiting. Alone.

Jane jumped into the back seat of their green Honda Accord, and Will accelerated toward Logan Airport.

"Here's the bag of clothes," Sarah said from the front and handed it to her. "I also packed a sandwich in case you're hungry."

"Thank you." Jane changed into the new outfit: A pastel blouse, purple slacks, an old pair of Sarah's Hush Puppies, and a black, woolen overcoat. She donned a medium-length wavy blond wig, sunglasses, and a large black hat they had packed for her. She then put on make-up to achieve a loud, trashy look, totally uncharacteristic of her own. From her pocketbook, she pulled out the first-class ticket to London's Heathrow Airport, which she had bought under the name Rachel Porter before she went to see Sam.

"And here's the passport." Sarah handed her Rachel Porter's passport with the new photo, which they had taken before Jane left to go jogging, affixed to it.

Thank God, Jane thought as they approached Logan, Rich

had sent hers along with Shannon's and her parents' passports. Jane remembered the attached note.

'You're a real Pain. But, I love you just the same. I don't know what you've gotten yourself into - your big mouth always gets you into trouble - but here's my passport in case you have to get away from some jealous wife in a hurry. (That's not it, I hope.) To use your words, I thought it was best to anticipate and prepare. I love you, Rich.'

They arrived at the busy airport, and her parents' lifelong friends dropped her off outside International Departures. They kissed and said farewell, and Jane ran to her gate. She'd outsmarted Sam Howard. It was time to find her daughter.

Taryn Weisser was more frightened than she had ever been in her entire life. Her abductors had warned her that their people would kill her and her mother if she did one wrong thing. Out of fear of asking the wrong question, Taryn kept quiet during the flight.

She never had to go through customs in Baltimore; the papers the men had shown the agents in charge were enough. They threw her into a car and drove onto the interstate. It was morning rush, and Taryn read the signs as they drove south on I-95 toward Washington, D.C. She didn't know where they were taking her. Or why. The men had said nothing and had offered no clues.

They blindfolded her, and the car exited the highway a short time later. In case of a problem, she assumed, they didn't want her to know where they were going. Parked on the side of a road, they led Taryn to a spot a few dozen steps away. They placed her feet on a ladder and ordered her to climb down. At the bottom of the hole in the ground, one of the brothers untied her hands while the other removed the blindfold. She was in a tunnel of some sort. A chill filled her body and she shivered, yet her face felt like it was on fire. They began a long walk, led only by the light from the two flashlights.

Garrison Miller noticed the stir in his loins. The bell had just rung, which meant they had entered the tunnel. In a couple of seconds …

The metal door to the underground dungeon flew open and Miller was face to face with Taryn Weisser. He noticed her shock, the pained look on her face, as their eyes met. He laughed his sadistic laugh. "Hello, baby. Come home to Gary?"

The eighteen-year old passed out and fell to the ground.

The 15x15-foot brick dungeon was cleared of the other men. Garrison Miller carried Taryn to the bed and tore off her clothes. Stomach down, he tied her arms and legs to the bed's metal posts. He undressed himself and fondled his favorite whip. The long, slithery strands of leather teased his sexuality and a thrill entered him. Miller looked down at the unconscious teenager. She was so beautiful, laying there naked and vulnerable. He laughed and felt himself get hard as the sinewy straps caressed his groin. He arched his back, brought his arm up behind him, and came around with all his might. The leather whirred through the air and resounded with a crack as it collided with its cushy target.

Taryn came awake with a blood-curdling scream and her body writhing in agony. The spasms of her muscles twitching beneath her creamy white skin, decorated in glowing red welts, excited Miller to the verge of orgasm.

It was almost more than he could take. His erection quivered, and he brought the whip around and flogged her buttocks again and again. Her screams thrilled him and spurred him on in his sexual frenzy. His orgasm coincided with Taryn's lapse into unconsciousness. He stood there panting, drenched in perspiration.

He dropped the whip at his feet. It was no fun anymore, now that she was out of it. Miller stood there, feeling wondrously alive.

"Anything to declare, Mrs. Porter," the elderly customs agent at Heathrow Airport asked Jane. She was finally in London, finally someplace where she could do something about Taryn, unfettered. "Ma'am?" he repeated.

Wearing the blond wig, dark sunglasses, and the wide-brim hat, almost like an international spy - God, was I stupid to think I wouldn't stand out - she snapped from her thoughts and said, "Excuse me?"

"I asked you if you had anything to declare, Mrs. Porter?"

"Uh, no." He was looking at her, studying her. Jane was able to read him. His body language screamed suspicion.

After a few seconds, he stamped her passport. "I hope you have a pleasant visit."

"Thank you." Jane took her bag and rushed away.

She didn't notice the customs agent pick up a phone.

Sam was alone in his home office in Fairfax, leaning back in his leather chair, smoking a cigar. It was the first moment he'd had to think about Jane and where she had gone. He should have known better than to think she would remain in Brookline. Her mother probably wasn't even sick. "How stupid could I have been?" he berated himself.

He dialed Jane's videophone number into his keyboard. A minute later, Jane appeared on his wall screen. She looked haggard. "Where are you? And why did you leave Boston?"

"My daughter is missing somewhere in London and I have

to find her. What else did you expect me to do, Sam?"

"I told you …"

"You would've done the same thing."

Sam had to think quickly. One wrong word from her mouth could ruin everything. "Don't go to the authorities, Jane. If you do, it's yours and Taryn's lives."

The screen went blank. Jane had obviously had enough of his threats. Taryn was all that mattered. There was nothing she wouldn't do to save her daughter. "Christ!" Here he was, across the ocean, unable to stop her from possibly divulging all she knows. He had to make some calls to his personal operatives.

As Sam picked up his videophone, it rang. Sayyid! What do I tell him? He's already abducted, and probably killed, Taryn. If he finds out Jane's alive in London, she'll never survive. He hesitated a moment to gain his bearings. He not only had to stop Jane from spilling her guts, he also had stop Sayyid from finding her. He put out his cigar and waited another second before opening the compact. The picture of the leader of Al-Qiyamah showed a face filled with indignation.

"I'm very disappointed in you, Sam. Al-Qiyamah is falling apart because of you. You have gone and made a foolish mistake, my friend, and that mistake is jeopardizing the lives of many people, mine and yours included. Do I make myself clear?"

"I think I'm clear on how to best handle this problem."

Sayyid knew he had to be conciliatory. He changed his tone of voice, yet remained firm in his insistence. "Where is she, Sam? We must not ruin what has taken us so long to accomplish. You have the power to change the world, to rule it. Don't destroy that dream." He hated Sam for his lack of discipline, for this American greed of having to have everything they desire. For having put him, Sayyid Kassim, into this position of submission.

"I have no idea where she's gone. She's just disappeared."

Sayyid slammed his fist into the keyboard and, with it, cleared Sam's image from his view. He filled the cup before him with gawha and felt the hot liquid slide down his throat. He closed his eyes and thought about this woman, this Yehoudi, who could ruin Saddam Hussein's Al-Qiyamah.

He finished the gawha and vowed to his great Allah not to let her. He had to find Jane Weisser. He'd had her Georgetown house tapped, as well as Sam's Virginia home, but they had stayed off those communication lines. Sayyid opened the file cabinet next to his desk and read the printout of Sam's videophone calls from the bill he received and paid every month in the name 'Harrington.' There it was. Jane Weisser's cell number. He worried she wouldn't answer the phone for fear of being located, but with her daughter missing she would probably answer it in case it was about Taryn. He punched the number onto the key pad in his office. A few seconds later, she was there. He wasn't broadcasting his image, but evidently her videophone was in position to. The sight of her unnerved him.

"Hello?" came the hesitant voice.

Her voice made his go icy. "Do anything and we will kill your daughter!" Although he didn't have the teenaged girl, she didn't know that. He disconnected and dialed the cellular operator, requesting the location of the number he'd just called.

Moments later, he heard: "We can't pinpoint an exact location, sir, but we can confirm the call was received somewhere in London, England."

"*Shukran.*" Thank you. Sayyid pushed the 'off' button and remained alone with his thoughts. So, she's in London to look for her daughter. He pushed another set of numbers onto the keyboard and spoke to his London operative again. "Keep watch on the aunt and uncle," he told the man. "Sooner of later, they will lead us to her."

After another gawha, Sayyid was optimistic. "The Yehoudi will never leave England alive. Al-Qiyamah is going to succeed, just as Saddam Hussein had said it would. Nothing can stand in its way!" He stood and looked out at his Iraq. "Not Jane Weisser, not Sam Howard. No one!"

CHAPTER FOURTEEN

Two weeks until Inauguration Day

It had been more than two months since the HOPE Cities bombings. Although the rioting had diminished to random incidents after Moses McBride and Sam Howard went on prime time telecomp just before the election, the fighting, these last few weeks, had spiraled to new heights. Crowded into dilapidated apartments, with little food, and no jobs, America's poor took to the streets in desperation. Throughout the United States, the inner cities were again the killing fields of democracy, as the storms of anarchy blew through the country. Looting, fires, anything to vent their frustration at a society that had forgotten them was fair. It was a nightmare gone bad.

And no one, not the president, nor the president-elect, was doing anything about it. The American people, not those in power, were the lame ducks in this political purgatory, this useless and uncertain time in American politics when administrations change.

"Not lame ducks, sitting ducks," Moses yelled at his TC. With the rioting mainly in America's urban areas, where his people and those of the lower classes lived, they were just that: Sitting ducks. It was too terrible to think about anymore. The only thing he could do was what he and Jane Weisser were planning to do. He had to kill the President to end this Hell.

Again, Moses was torn. Killing Sam Howard was going to send the wrong message to America's African people. They're going to think the PWA killed the president to crush any last African hopes, which is going to bring on even more fighting. Moses shook his head and paced the floor of his apartment. His people would be sure to flee the cities to attack the suburban and rural areas surrounding them. If that happened, just like in November, the African people would be outnumbered and outgunned. Which, like in November, meant the African people would be massacred. Killing Sam Howard might lead to the sudden, violent extermination of his people. Letting him live would lead to their systematic elimination.

He agonized and searched desperately for another option.

At nine o'clock in the morning in London, England, an elderly man and woman walked through the glass doors of the Savoy Hotel. They didn't see the two foreign men who had followed them seated across the Strand in their rented Land Rover.

After hugs and kisses, Jane sat them down in the sitting area of her suite and told them everything, as she had done with Taryn. The story, which had grown since then, took her a long time to tell. She then told her aunt and uncle what had to happen next.

The elderly couple expressed their understanding and their total trust in their niece.

"After you leave, I'm going to Scotland Yard to talk with

the Chief Inspector."

"But, won't that put you in danger, dear?"

"No. Yes. I mean I have to find out something. I don't know where else to start. I'm sorry, Aunt Fran."

"Shh. No apologies, dear."

"Now, you must leave. You were probably followed, and we have to get you to safety." Jane picked up their coats and helped them on with them. "There's a car waiting in the back of the hotel, next to the kitchen entrance. Sorry it's not more imaginative. I'm kind of new at this." Her laugh broke the tension. She kissed them and handed the keys to her uncle. "Be careful."

"You be careful, Janie. Please?"

Jane hugged her uncle again. "I'll see you in Honolulu right after the inauguration." They entered the elevator, and the last words Jane heard were, "We love you."

An hour later, Jane exited the Savoy Hotel. New Year's had come and gone, and most of the tourists had done the same. Jane put on her black woolen gloves and zipped up her burgundy parka around her neck to fight off the wintry cold air. She looked at her reflection in the glass doors. In her blond wig and oversized sunglasses, she looked ordinary. Nondescript. Good, that meant there'd be less of a chance of being recognized.

Jane stepped onto the pavement and turned left toward Trafalgar Square, where two men grabbed her from each side and tried to force her into their car. "Get away from me. Hel ... !" she tried to scream, but a hand covered her mouth, muffling her cry for help. Realizing what would certainly be fatal consequences of her capture, she furiously fought back.

Suddenly, four strangers joined the fray on her behalf. The two men who had tried to abduct her dropped her from their grip and ran toward the Square. Three of her four rescuers ran after them, while one, the oldest, stayed with her.

"Are you okay, Dr. Weisser?"

"Yes, thank you." Jane tried to stop her heart from pounding. Her mouth was dry. Thanks to these men, she was safe again. She looked up at the kind man reaching down to help her stand. He appeared to be in his mid-fifties, paunchy, yet strongly built.

"We can take you to hospital if you'd like."

"No, no, I'm okay. Just a little frightened." Jane was about to voice her gratitude when it hit her: How did he know her name?

The look on her face must have registered the same question. Before she could finish asking, "Who are you? he doffed his hat, gave a slight bow, and introduced himself. "Chief Inspector Perkins from Scotland Yard, ma'am. A pleasure to meet you."

Jane felt the tightness leave her body. "I was on my way just now to see you. But, how did you know I was in London. Or, that I was staying at the Savoy?"

"Customs agents recognized you at Heathrow, ma'am. Ever since your aunt and uncle informed us of your daughter's kidnapping, we have been trying to reach you in the States. We knew you would come over once you heard about it. I had hoped you would call first, though," the Chief Inspector said. "Any information you have, or anything you may have told us, we could have used that much sooner."

Jane heard the reproval in his voice. "I flew over as soon as I found out."

"Yes, I can understand that. But, tell me, Dr. Weisser, why in disguise? Is someone following you? Is there someone you're afraid of?"

Jane had to think quickly. She couldn't tell him about the Arab threat to Taryn and her. That would be a fatal mistake.

"Please, ma'am, whatever you tell us will help us find your daughter."

"I wish I knew something. All I can tell you is … there was this boyfriend of my daughter's …" She had to say exactly the right thing. " … who threatened her life a few months back."

The man thought about it for a moment. "Dr. Weisser, why would your daughter's boyfriend kidnap her and then try to abduct you? A scorned boyfriend may take the object of his desire, but her mother?"

Jane didn't know what to say.

"Why don't you tell me the truth, Dr. Weisser? Only then can we help save your daughter, and I protect you from harm."

Again, Jane didn't say anything. She looked down, as if she were deep in thought. Suddenly, a shot rang out from across the street. Before Jane could turn her head toward the sound, she felt a searing pain, as if a bolt of fire was traveling along her upper left arm. The pain spread through her body and built to an intensity she had never before experienced, until she could no longer breathe. She opened her mouth to cry out, but couldn't.

Jane hit the ground and blood splashed across her face. It was then that she realized she'd been shot, and her heart beat quicker, pumping out the blood even faster. The sky above her spun out of control, and she became nauseous, as she fought to retain consciousness. The Inspector was looking down at her with a frightened face. He was saying something, but it was coming out all garbled. She thought about Taryn just before a dark red haze claimed her.

Gangs of marauding young men and women, armed with guns, rifles, knives, hatchets, anything that would defend, and offend, made their way out of the cities into America's suburbs and heartlands. All law enforcement personnel throughout the country were on full-time duty, and they would remain so until they restored order.

Death and destruction had also made its way into New Carrollton, Maryland. Consequently, the FBI had to pull their watch on Gary Walters, aka Garrison Miller.

With all the fighting outside, Miller and the men of the People for a White America secreted themselves inside their underground dungeon. The McKay brothers, Lonnie and Tommy, stared at their prisoner on the old single bed, her hands and feet tied to the frame's legs. Garrison Miller sat on a lone chair next to her. A leather crop was in his hand. Every few seconds, he toyed with her like a mouse. Naked, she winced, but held in her screams as the two-inch wide piece of leather snapped against her nipples. Miller looked down at her and smiled. Little by little she was learning to take more and more.

Miller snapped her nipples again with the crop. They were now taut and red. Blood red. He liked that. He snapped her inner thighs, then in between her legs. From her cries, he could see that hurt. What a shame, he laughed to himself. What he had planned for her in the coming days and weeks would turn her into a willing slave. By the time she had mastered her lessons, she would be loyally submissive to him. Or, she would be dead, but he was prepared to deal with that.

"Please, Gary. I'll do anything you want. Anything. Just don't hurt me anymore. Please?"

"You'll do *everything* I want, and I *will* hurt you." Miller brought the crop down on Taryn's right nipple. The edge of the leather sliced her, and a trickle of blood dripped down her small breast. Miller's eyes lit up and his mouth lunged for it. He sucked it as hard as he could. When he finished, he picked his head up and saw she was crying. He smiled at her, showing off his bloody teeth.

* * * * *

Jane awoke and saw she was still in the hospital bed she had fallen asleep in. She looked around. Everything was white. Antiseptic. She closed her eyes and remembered last night. Her arm had been in such pain that the painkillers were useless. Sleep had been the only anesthesia. Now, worn out from all the drugs, her arm still throbbed. She noticed she had a headache, as if she had just woke up from a night of heavy drinking. Only this one came without the benefit of an intoxicating buzz. She longed for one right now.

In somewhat of a daze, Jane got out of bed, washed and dressed, and called for the nurse. Sister Mary Callahan walked into her room a few seconds later with a smile on her face. "I want to thank you and your staff for taking such good care of me last night. I appreciate all you've done."

"You're welcome, I'm sure, ma'am, but Dr. Crawford must authorize your release if you're planning on leaving."

"Fine. May I see him?"

The youngish-looking Sister checked her watch. "I'm afraid he won't be here for another three hours."

"Then I'm sure the doctor-in-charge can release me." Too weak and dizzy to stand any longer, Jane sat down on the edge of the bed.

"I'm sorry, ma'am, but, according to your chart, only Dr. Crawford can sign you out of hospital."

Jane didn't want to argue with the girl and she thanked her for all her help. Sister Mary left, and Jane mused out loud: "This is England. No one can hold me here without my consent. I'm free to go as I please." She got up and walked toward the door. It was probably not the best medical advice to leave, but if she wanted to she could. After all, she hadn't done anything wrong.

Outside her hospital door, a suited young man was sitting on a chair. Jane looked down at him and wondered why he was there. Was he guarding her, or waiting for her to leave? Obviously, her face showed signs of panic.

"Don't be afraid, Dr. Weisser." The unattractive man stood, hunchbacked, to meet her gaze. "I'm Detective Sergeant Geoffrey Hamilton. Chief Inspector Perkins put me on duty last night to watch over you. Said some unsavory elements were lurking about." He smiled to make her feel more comfortable, but the sergeant's manner of sheepish apology didn't make Jane feel any more comfortable.

"I was just on my way to see the Chief Inspector, Sergeant Hamilton. Thank you for your time." She walked past him toward the lift.

"Excuse me, Dr. Weisser," the demure detective said, hobbling down the hall after her, his Styrofoam cup of hot tea splashing onto his right hand and his pant leg. "The Chief Inspector gave me strict orders to escort you to him if you attempted to leave hospital." He stopped at the elevator, took out a handkerchief, and wiped his face, then his pant leg.

"Really? That was very kind of him, and I will tell him so myself, but I can manage alone, thank you." Jane pushed the 'down' button and turned away.

"Sorry, but I have me orders."

Jane had had enough. "Unless you plan on arresting me, Sergeant Hamilton, I will go see the Chief Inspector under my own free will."

He followed her down in the lift until she was standing outside the front entranceway of St. Thomas's Hospital. She didn't stop to sign out, or inquire about the bill. She would let Scotland Yard, or the English taxpayers, pay for the crimes committed in their streets. She was a victim here, and, according to her, victims shouldn't have to be victimized twice. She felt the pain in her arm, looked around, and heard the man say, "Feeling quite vulnerable, aren't you, Dr. Weisser?"

Jane didn't answer him.

"There are men who want to kidnap you, and there are men who want to kill you. Under those circumstances, may I offer you a ride to the Yard. I promise you, my intentions are quite innocent." He bowed to m'Lady in a mock gesture of deference.

A flock of reporters and paparazzi rushed toward them, shouting questions, snapping pictures, shoving, and yelling for her attention. Jane turned to the detective and nodded. She would be crazy, she now understood all-too-well, if she didn't accept his protective offer.

Fifteen minutes later, Jane sat across from Chief Inspector Clive Perkins inside Scotland Yard's tall glass and steel structure. His desk was cluttered, yet somewhat orderly, and she judged the Chief Inspector to be a man who could find whatever he wanted in this mess in seconds. She had to be careful with a man like that; it was the sure sign of a deductive mind. The last thing she needed was him deducing anything, which could end up hurting her and Taryn. She looked at him staring at her with a smirk. Whereas yesterday he appeared concerned for her well being, now he seemed suspicious.

"Dr. Weisser, I'm happy you're feeling well enough to have left hospital. That is indeed a good sign."

"Thank you for your concern, Inspector, but what concerns me is why there were orders to bring me in for questioning. Surely you don't think I had anything to do with my daughter's disappearance?"

"Please, Dr. Weisser, my only concern right now is in finding Taryn alive and safe. Then, I can busy myself with finding the culprits behind it. I had my sergeant bring you in because I didn't want you going off all cocksure that you could do the job yourself. You can't, and you will only end up getting yourself and your daughter killed if you try."

Jane remained quiet, analyzing his tone and demeanor. "I was on my way to see you yesterday, and again today, on my own volition, Inspector. I just want to do what's right so I can get Taryn back safe."

"Good, then let's start at the beginning, shall we? Tell me a little more about this former boyfriend, what's-his-name?"

"Garrison Miller." Jane waited to see if Scotland Yard knew of the man.

"Garrison Miller, the racist vigilante?"

"The one and only, I'm afraid."

"Why would you allow … ? I'm sorry, Dr. Weisser, as an Englishman and a gentleman, that's not a proper question for me to ask."

"I tried to make Taryn see the truth behind him. She was convinced he was this so-called Gary Walters, not Garrison Miller." Jane paused and took a cigarette from her purse. "Do you mind?"

"I'd rather you not."

Jane nodded that she understood. She put it back in her purse and asked, "Do you know what it's like trying to change the mind of a teenaged girl who thinks she's in love?"

Perkins laughed. "I have two of my own. Eighteen and sixteen. See all this gray hair on my head?"

Jane told the Chief Inspector for Scotland Yard how Garrison Miller had used her daughter so he could break into her telecomp to ascertain Sam Howard's schedule. She finished by incriminating the man for everything that had taken place since the HOPE Cities explosions. In case anything happened to Taryn or her, Moses would still go forward with the plot. Therefore, she had to make sure all fingers pointed to the PWA.

"Like I said yesterday, I don't think Mr. Miller would kidnap your daughter and kill you because of his love for her. But, he very well might if he was aware that you knew he invaded your telefiles, and that you were threatening to take it to the authorities."

"I haven't been in contact with him since I threw him out of our house, so there's no way of him knowing what I am or am not doing."

"Then why would he kidnap Taryn? And if you've posed no threat to him all this time, why would he come after you?"

Jane had no answer and she became more nervous. She felt as if she were digging herself in-to a hole. "I'm not saying Garrison Miller is behind this. You asked me if there was anyone I could think of who'd want to hurt us. He was the only one who came to mind."

Perkins rested his elbows on the arms of his chair and pressed his fingertips together. "You know what I think, Dr. Weisser? I think you're keeping something from me, and that doesn't make me very happy."

Jane fought to keep her composure.

"You see, the men who grabbed you didn't want to do you any harm, although they were quite rough in the way they handled you. After my agents captured them, they admitted they worked for President-elect Howard. He sent them to London to make sure you didn't get hurt after you told him you were coming here to look for your daughter."

"And I see they failed. If you hadn't interfered with them, Inspector, I wouldn't have been shot."

He stared at her and said nothing. But, what he next said chilled Jane to the core. "I was able to get a glimpse of the driver of the car when he shot you, and I noticed he looked foreign: Mexican, Spanish, Middle Eastern - yes, more Middle Eastern than not, I think. A lot of people seem to want you and your daughter, Dr. Weisser. I find that most interesting. Why don't you tell me why.

Jane was exasperated. "Let's stop playing games, Inspector. I don't care whether you believe me or not. I have no idea why any of this is happening. I just want to find my child. Now, how do we do that?" Jane sat back and stared at his pensive face.

"President-elect Howard personally asked me to put you on the next flight back to Washington."

"The last I heard, England is still a free country. Although, since my arrival, I have yet to witness that."

"Yes, your arrival," Chief Inspector Perkins said, leaning forward in his chair.

Jane felt her muscles tighten and her shoulder ache. "I plan to stay here and find my daughter with you or without you, Inspector."

"No, you won't. You see, you entered this country illegally, under a false passport. That is a crime punishable by law, and I can arrest you here and now if I so choose."

Jane's defenses broke down and her shoulders slumped. She grabbed her wound. "But, we're talking about my baby. Don't you understand?"

"Yes, I understand, Dr. Weisser, and the safest thing you can do is to let us handle the investigation. If you don't, you will end up dead, as will Taryn, and possibly some of my agents. We're the professionals. Let us do our job."

"I'm sorry, Inspector Perkins, but I can't go back without my child."

"Please, doctor. One call and I can have Rachel Porter arrested, too."

Jane's mind spun out of control. She felt dizzy. "You said you're a father. Surely you see why I must stay. Would *you* leave under such circumstances?"

"I'm sorry, ma'am, but I'm afraid I have no choice but to arrest you for entering Great Britain illegally."

An hour later, Chief Inspector Perkins escorted Jane to her Savoy Hotel suite, and then to the gate of her departing plane. She had no choice in the matter. With Sam's assassination so close, and Taryn's life or death the result of her actions, she couldn't afford the publicity of an arrest. Besides, she couldn't find her daughter if she was behind bars.

"The most important thing you can do right now is get on that plane and go home."

"The most important thing I can do right now, Inspector, is get my child to safety, which you and Sam Howard are stopping me from doing."

"No, ma'am, what we're trying to do is to get you to safety so we can safely save your child."

Jane nodded and walked through the door onto the plane. She didn't look back.

Two men stood across from her gate with the passengers of another departing flight. After the door closed behind her, and the Scotland Yard detective departed, one of them pulled out a videophone and made a call. Having earlier replaced the two Iraqi operatives murdered at the flat across from the aunt and uncle's home, their work for Sayyid was done.

They wouldn't live to remember it.

Seated on the plane, Jane hoped no one would recognize her. Dear God, what a mess! she said to herself. Not only did she screw up everything in London, but now she had to face Sam after lying to him about her mother.

Hour after hour she suffered the pain in her shoulder. The

liquor cart stopped a few rows ahead of her. She thought about how a drink would taste right now. God, she felt lousy. Having to fight demon alcohol at a time like this was maddening.

The cart passed without anything being removed for her. As it did, Jane caught the eye of a man sitting a few rows ahead of her who looked familiar. He stared for a second, then turned away. Too quickly, she thought.

Until the plane touched ground, the familiar looking man didn't turn her way again. Jane felt a little less worried. She passed him on the way off, and by the time she reached the carousel to retrieve her lone bag, he was nowhere in sight. All she now had to do was return to her suite at the Watergate to rest and regroup. Having boarded under the name Rachel Porter, and with the promise from Scotland Yard that no one would know she was on that flight, no media were there to greet her.

Jane walked toward the exit and showed the woman her claim slip. She exited the terminal into the unusually mild January sun and headed toward a row of taxi cabs. Suddenly, a hand grabbed her right elbow, and her body stiffened, then another one grabbed her left. She felt a weapon of some sort pressed into her back.

"Don't make me kill you. One word and you die immediately!"

The words were spoken in an Arabic accent. Her body shook, but Jane forced herself to stay calm. She didn't want anyone interfering, causing the man to shoot her and possibly kill innocent bystanders. She was ready to do whatever they wanted to get Taryn back.

Almost as quickly as they began their escort, Jane's arms were freed. Two men, one on each side, had attached themselves to Sayyid's men and were leading them away in opposite directions. Jane was dumbfounded. Relieved and grateful, she turned to see who her saviors were. They were almost out of sight, but she was able to see one of them as he turned back to her. It was the man from the plane.

She looked around her. She was standing alone and felt extremely vulnerable.

Jane returned to her Watergate suite and fell face down on her bed. She had gone to London to find Taryn and had returned home with nothing but a gunshot wound to show for it. She was back to square one. Not only did her arm ache, but her stomach was churning and her head was pounding. All she wanted to do was get drunk and escape this nightmare. She found herself staring at the wet bar. She had looked at it many times since her talks with Moses and Taryn, but she hadn't opened it.

With a new resolve, Jane opened the cabinet and removed the half dozen bottles of Scotch, vodka, and gin, intending to empty them down the sink. Wavering, she reconsidered, fighting the urge as the alcohol exerted the full force of its power.

Temptation and addiction won.

The pain was pacified.

"She's back at the Watergate?" Sam disconnected his videophone after speaking with the two men he had assigned to watch Jane. Sayyid had tried to grab her at the airport, however things were working in his favor. He felt invincible - a man of destiny. Alone in his office for the first time since he'd arrived hours earlier, the President-elect of the United States got up from his desk and sat on the sofa facing the wall screen. He turned on the telecomp, took a drink of coffee from his oversized mug, and listened to the news.

Eric Forsythe was reporting from Tel Aviv. After months of fighting in the region, Israeli Prime Minister Dov Avraham had disappeared. It was only a matter of time, the analysts concluded, before the government toppled. "With little help from the United States because of our own problems at home, Israel is unable to defend itself against so many countries, first civilian-wise and now militarily," the newscaster said. "Political leaders here are anxiously waiting to see what Sam Howard will do when he is sworn in as president next week. Until then, the situation seems likely to worsen."

"So, that's Sayyid's game," Sam whispered to himself. "Al-Qiyamah is one brilliant plot. Rioting in the U.S. distracts us from the situation in Israel. All of Saddam's enemies are punished."

Sam walked to the windows and thought about Sayyid's probable reaction to what he had done to save Jane. He was sure he would be hearing from him soon.

The headache was the worst Jane could ever remember having. It felt like her head was clamped in a vice-like grip. Despite a ravenous hunger, eating was out of the question, as her hangover clawed at her stomach and roiled its contents.

Jane got out of bed and showered. She dried off and still felt queasy. She thought about the fear Taryn must be going through and felt even worse. When she finished dressing, she knew what she wanted. She needed comfort. Support. A shoulder to lean on. She needed Moses McBride.

She dialed his number in New York and reached him as he was leaving for work. "I fell flat on my face, Moses. God help me, I wasn't strong enough, and I got stinking drunk last night." Jane told him about her trip to London, about being shot by Sayyid's men, about being thrown out of the country by way of threat, and about almost being abducted at the airport. "I'm sorry, I really am. I tried to fight off the urge, but it was staring me in the face and it just overpowered me."

"If you're looking for advice, Jane," Moses told her, "I will tell you what I've told everyone I've counseled: Just forget about it and start over. Every day is always day one. Today, tomorrow, forever."

"Moses, I can't go through this alone any longer. The stress of not knowing where Taryn is, or whether she's safe, of what we're planning, of Sayyid, Miller, and Sam all out to get me, has unraveled me." She started sobbing. A few months back, this emotional venting would have been unthinkable. What had made her 'the most influential woman in Washington' was her personal strength and conviction. She still had the conviction, but the strength was no longer there. "Please, Moses, I can't be alone any longer. There's an adjoining suite …"

"Say no more, I'll be there as soon as I can."

Jane roamed the suite in her bare feet. She made herself some toast and coffee and looked out the window at the Kennedy Center. She thought about having a drink, but dismissed it. As she sipped, and relived the last twenty-four hours, things began to add up. She didn't have to worry about Sam. Only Sayyid Kassim and Garrison Miller were the real threats. Sam's men in London weren't trying to abduct her. They were trying to save her from the gunman they had seen across the Strand. Also, in the airport, Sam's men had again saved her when they had snatched her from the grip of two assailants. Sam was risking his own life to save hers. "Damnit, Sam," she yelled, the words echoing off the walls of the suite, "how could you have done something this horrible? How can someone so hateful and cruel be so wonderful and loving? How can I still feel something for you?" The words made her feel ill again. She had to kill the man she loved most.

Jane went back to bed and looked at the clock on the night table before closing her eyes. In approximately six hours, Moses would arrive from New York. She hoped he would bring with him the sweet deliverance she so desperately needed.

CHAPTER FIFTEEN

One week until Inauguration Day

Moses McBride moved into the room next to Jane's, which she had rented a few hours earlier. Dressed as an electrician, he was heavier looking than usual when he arrived. Under his workman's clothes, he had on four additional layers of clothing. He couldn't carry in a suitcase. Good thing it was winter, he reasoned. Insulated like that, he had broken only a slight sweat.

As Moses undressed, he thought about Jane. He really liked her. No matter how frightened she was, or how weak she thought she was, Jane Weisser was gutsy, and he admired her. Not only was she planning to kill the President of the United States, but she was going to kill the man she loved more than anyone else in her life, except for Taryn. Yes, Jane Weisser was an extraordinary woman.

Moses showered, dressed in black slacks and a purple shirt, then lightly knocked on the door that joined their suites. A second later, Jane opened it from her side. She tried to smile, but her lower lip trembled and gave her away. She was scared. The withdrawal symptoms she was experiencing were wracking her body. Moses saw the pain in her eyes and embraced her. It was the therapy she needed most.

They drank coffee on the sofa in her suite, and he spoke to her about the power of stress and addiction, of self awareness and self esteem, and about optimism and hope. Jane expressed the disappointments in her life, and Moses imparted the same wisdom he always preached to his congregation: "Be more accepting and less expecting and you will be happier." What was it his professor had said during psych class at Yale Divinity? The psychologist is his own worst patient. Jane had known it was time to seek help. It was the first sign that she was going to get better.

"I never told anyone, Moses, but I've been living a lie for nineteen years." Moses was a clergyman. Maybe this confession would free her. She slid off the sofa and tucked her legs underneath the coffee table. This way she didn't have to look directly at him. "A few days before my wedding to Peter Gold, I realized I couldn't marry him unless I saw Sam first. HOPE City in Bridgeport had just opened, and he was in meetings in Boston regarding the next one he was planning to build. I tracked him down and visited him in his hotel. I had to know if he still loved me before I went ahead and married Peter. This is a long story," she said, turning to him. "I hope you don't mind."

He shook his head and smiled that he understood her catharsis.

"I told Sam I was getting married, but that I couldn't go ahead with the wedding if there was still something between us. I remember shaking, praying he wanted me as badly as I wanted him. I felt like a teenager. Anyway, he said he loved me with all his heart, but he also said he couldn't marry me.

"'It's just not in my plans right now, Jane. And I have no right to ask you to wait for me,' he said. 'I don't know when I'll be ready.'

"'But, what do I do?' I asked. 'How long do I wait?'

"Holding me in his arms, he quieted my questions with kisses, and we made love again and again. It was a night I'll never forget. But, when I awoke the following morning, Sam wasn't there. He had checked out of the hotel, with only a note for an answer and a goodbye. It broke my heart. 'Dearest Jane,' it said. 'I will always love you. Never forget that.' That was it. I took the rest of the week off and spent it at my parents' house in Brookline, drinking myself into a stupor and wallowing in self-pity. Peter and I got married in Boston that weekend, and after our honeymoon, we returned to New York. I dove into my work, progressing rapidly in the firm, until Taryn arrived nine months later." There was silence for a moment as Jane remembered back.

"Are you trying to tell me Sam Howard is Taryn's biological father?" Moses asked. He put a hand on her shoulder to comfort her disclosure.

"NO! I mean … I don't know," she confessed. "That's the problem. I was pregnant for nine months, wondering whether Sam or Peter was the father. After I gave birth, Peter could tell something was wrong. I couldn't make love to him anymore. I felt guilty for loving Sam. And I felt cheap not knowing who the father of my child was."

"I'm sorry. It must've been Hell."

Tears came to Jane's eyes. "Peter walked out on me shortly after Taryn was born. He said he wanted a paternity test taken because I was no longer being intimate with him. I couldn't do that. If Sam were the father, Taryn would have been my 'Scarlet

A,' and Peter - God, it would have humiliated him. A paternity test was out of the question. Peter accepted my refusal as an admittance of guilt. He left me and moved to California. Everyone assumed it was because he couldn't deal with my advancement in the firm; you know, your wife for a boss. I was relieved, but I was tortured not knowing who Taryn's real father was. I decided, then, that in case it was Sam, I didn't want to know. I couldn't bear being the mother of his child and not his wife."

"And to this day you don't know?"

"No." Jane thought about it and broke the silence. "If I have a test done, and I find out Sam is the father, I was thinking I could appeal to him to save his daughter's life."

Moses spoke to her with understanding and sympathy in his voice. "Jane, I think you know Sam isn't Taryn's father. I believe you've spent eighteen years hoping it may be true just to keep a familial fantasy alive."

"What do you mean?"

"Although Taryn looks like you, and not Sam, you'd know if Sam was her father. A mother can tell. Her child would have traits, mannerisms, telltale signs, all pointing to it. By admitting you don't know whether he is or isn't, you're really saying he isn't."

Jane thought about it. Moses was right. She'd been deluding herself all these years just to keep her and Sam bound together by the child of their love. How could she have not realized that? Maybe she had, but like her drinking, she'd been in denial. How foolish she'd been. Jane returned to her seat on the sofa next to him. "Thanks for listening, Moses. I feel a lot better having shared this with you. I guess I was scared with the thought that I may be killing Taryn's father."

"Only when you begin talking about your problems will your problems begin to disappear, Jane. Remember that.

Regarding Peter Gold, I think Taryn and you should start focusing on what you have, not on what you don't have."

Jane marveled at the wisdom of Moses McBride. He was right. It was time to smell the roses again. She couldn't wait for January 21st.

Jane continued to talk about Taryn, and Moses felt as if he knew the teen. And loved her, like her mother did. He, in turn, spoke about DaNell, about her addiction and her dreams, how he had failed as a parent, and Jane helped him cope. Theirs was a friendship, mutual and heartfelt. They were of like mind and soul, sharing the same grief.

By nightfall, they were joking and laughing. Jane's pain, Moses could tell, was waning. With a renewed commitment in her eyes, she looked almost like her driven self again. Good, Moses thought, as he watched her resolve reinflate. It was what they needed if they were to be successful in this perilous undertaking.

They planned their next few days and spoke about the day in question, the timing and the accuracy needed, and any other problems they might encounter before and after.

"Cassie has the drug that one of our men, a pharmacist, put together. Mixed in orange juice, it's undetectable," Moses told her.

"But, what if he doesn't want anything to drink? She can't force him or she'll give herself away."

"Oh, he'll need something to drink, all right. You see, before breakfast she'll slip another drug into his eggs, which will make him extremely dry-mouthed." He saw Jane smile at him, and they called it an evening. He left her suite through the adjoining door, confident they were going to pull it off.

"Yes," Moses said after he got in bed and smoothed the

covers over his ample belly, "like Saddam Hussein's Al-Qiyamah, every step has been well thought out."

At the circular Watergate Apartments building across from the hotel, a man with binoculars opened his cellular videophone and pressed in a long distance number. When the connection went through, he spoke about what he had just seen. "I can see them from my room. The reverend just left and has gone to bed in the room adjacent to hers."

Sayyid Kassim felt his head ache. "Why?" he wondered aloud. He disconnected the call after giving the operative orders to keep a close watch on the two. He looked at the old men of Al-Qiyamah seated around the conference table and told them about it. "What are they planning?" he asked, more rhetorically than in search of an answer. After some discussion about what they should do about it, he pounded his fist on the oval table. No, this wasn't part of Saddam Hussein's infallible plot.

Garrison Miller untied the ropes from the headboard of his bed and removed them from Cassie Davenport's wrists. They had just made love again, and Miller marveled at the welts he'd inflicted on her tight, little body with his whip and crop. She could take so much, and it was obvious she enjoyed it. She enjoyed everything about him. That was odd, Miller thought. He had never found someone so into it, so into everything he loved and believed in. Since she'd entered his life, she always agreed with whatever he said. That was definitely odd. She either loved him, or she wasn't being truthful with him. It was always safest to take the side of caution. What are you hiding from me, Cassie Davenport? And who are you really? Miller stared down at her, laying naked, and vulnerable, on the bed.

"What?" she asked with a smile on her dimpled face. "Why

are you looking at me like that?"

"Just wondering, that's all."

"About what?"

"You. I find it amazing how much we're alike." Miller could detect no nervousness on her part. If anything, she appeared totally at ease and sincere in her feelings. What he had to find out was whether she was a plant. He wouldn't put it past the government to try and frame him again.

"Careful, my friend. Say the right thing and I may fall in love with you."

Garrison Miller was skeptical. No woman had ever loved him, except for Taryn Weisser. But, she was a girl. Why would Cassie Davenport? He wished she were being honest with him. Imagine a woman who believed in his principles and ideals, and who loved the dominance and torture he loved to inflict. Having a woman like that would be the catch of a lifetime. And he'd love her and be committed to her like nothing else. But, this was all too fast, too curious for it to feel right. If he was being suspicious, there had to be a reason for it. He'd always trusted his instincts before. He had no reason to stop now.

She smiled at him in a seductive manner. If it's too good to be true, Miller thought, it probably is. After a few minutes of small talk, he decided to use Cassie Davenport as his alibi come inauguration morning. He worked it out in his mind. In bed, drugged, she'll wake up hours after the assassination, hear what happened, and awaken him to tell him about it. Of course, earlier he'd have left to do the deed, but she'd swear he was there asleep with her the whole time. Feeling his power rushing to his loins, Miller mounted her and forced himself into her. It was the only way: Fuck 'em before they fuck you!

Garrison Miller laughed. 'Daddy' had taught him well.

After ten minutes, Miller had had enough. For some reason

it wasn't fun anymore. Something was missing. Taryn flashed in his mind and he realized what was wrong. Cassie wasn't supplying the fear and loathing of pain that he fed upon.

Miller pushed himself off her, and said, "I gotta go. I'll drop by your place tomorrow." He walked out of the room half hard, picturing the fearful pleading he would find in Taryn's eyes.

Taryn's body stiffened when Garrison Miller entered the dungeon. Was this madman here to impose more pain on her? She began to shake.

"Well, well, well," he said, leering at her naked body on the bed. He reached over her head and tightened the straps attached to the metal rings in the wall. He did the same to the apparatus affixed to her ankles. "In medieval days, this rack was the ultimate device for torturing peasants." Miller's face was filled with excitement and hatred. He stared at her and slowly turned the winch.

Taryn felt her muscles begin to strain. She first felt it in her ankles, then her legs, until her taut body rose off the bed and she felt it stretching her arms. Her heart beat faster than ever before, her mind fearful of what he was going to do next. Hanging horizontally above the bed, facing the ceiling, she cried, "Please, Gary, I've been cooperative. Please don't hurt me anymore."

"Hurt you? I haven't begun to hurt you."

"But, why? Why are you doing this to me?"

"WHY? Because you know too much. Your release means my imprisonment, and I can't have that." He turned the winch one more full circle, careful not to tear her muscles. She screamed. "Also, it's about time someone else feels what I've felt all these years."

He didn't say anything else. Taryn knew she had to placate him. If not, his anger might get worse and he'd stretch her body until her joints separated. "What are you feeling, Gary. Tell me, because I don't understand."

"My father, goddamnit, was torn away from me when I was your age. Well, it's time someone else felt that pain." His eyes were miles away.

Taryn knew she had to be conciliatory. "I know what you're feeling, Gary. My father abandoned me, too."

He wasn't listening. "They killed him, even though they knew he was innocent." His eyes returned to Taryn, crazed. "Just like I never got to see my daddy again, you will never see your mother again." He turned the handle another revolution, and she screamed louder. She was stretched tight as piano wire.

Hanging between the ceiling and the bed, Taryn could no longer keep her head held up. She let it fall back. Everything was now upside down, and she became dizzy. After a minute or so, the muscles in her neck began to ache, adding to the pain she felt in every tautly stretched joint. Internally, she was raw and tender. He had stuck everything imaginable into her orifices, from himself to objects she had never before seen or imagined.

"Damn, that's beautiful," Miller commented.

"A masterpiece," the McKays agreed.

"I reckon I'll call it 'The Wench on the Winch.'" Garrison Miller laughed at the alliteration, and the McKays joined in.

Taryn rotated her head to uncramp the muscles. "Please, I'm begging you."

Miller lowered her body onto the bed. "Help me with her," he ordered the McKays.

Lonnie and Tommy undid Taryn's feet from the winch and retied them, with longer straps, through the rings on the ceiling and back to the winch at the foot of the bed. Miller freed her wrists from the rings on the wall.

Taryn felt her legs being pulled up to the ceiling, as the brothers turned the winch. Soon, she was hanging upside down, her feet spread apart and her head and arms dangling close to the bed. "Please?" she cried.

"Get used to it, Taryn, because this is your future."

"What do you mean?" Lonnie McKay asked.

"What do you mean what do I mean?" Miller retorted, annoyed at the insubordination.

"I mean she has no future. We're gonna have to kill her after you kill McBride."

"Are you telling me what I can or can't do? Who the fuck do you think you are?"

"What I reckon Lonnie means," his brother Tommy interrupted, "is that if we keep her here any longer than necessary, we're inviting trouble. We gotta get rid of her so nothing ties us in with McBride's murder."

Taryn felt the blood rushing to her head and down her arms to her fingertips. They were discussing her future, whether she lives or dies. If the future means more of this torture, she thought to herself, I'd rather die now.

"No! I'm going to keep her."

"But, Garrison."

Miller sat on the bed and looked into her face. "Ain't that right, Taryn? You're mine now," he whispered. "Forever!"

Taryn smelled the stench of beer overlaying the odor of decayed food on his breath. The crazed look on his inverted face, along with the laughter coming from it, caused her body to shake.

Without another word, Miller took the tube of K-Y and spread the slippery jelly all over his right hand and wrist.

* * * * *

Although the fighting around the country had escalated to obscene proportions, Washington, D.C. was hopping in preparation for the inauguration. The major networks glass-enclosed broadcast booths were already on top of the Department of Labor Building on Constitution Ave; technicians were laying miles of cable around the stands along Pennsylvania Avenue; and the white stone of the Capitol was patriotically draped in red and blue. On the platform and thrust, everyone was in place rehearsing every minute of the inauguration ceremonies. It was in ironic contrast to the riots taking place downtown.

Moses returned to the Watergate from the briefing and rehearsal for the Cabinet nominees. He changed his clothes and walked into Jane's suite through the adjoining door. On the other side of the living room, the door to her bedroom was open. He stopped just inside the threshold and stared at her still body lying there. Her eyes were open, but her mind was miles away. Moses felt for her. Her child was in the hands of Sayyid Kassim, and she was trying to cope with the extreme stress. How courageous she was. She had promised him she would refrain from drinking, and she'd been true to her promise. He admired her even more for that. Jane was as genuine and as honest as it gets.

The ringing from the telecomp inside his room disrupted his thoughts and Moses returned to answer it. He pushed the telecomp button on the table next to his bed and the wall screen opposite it lit up. Ray Jackson's picture appeared.

"Willie's been arrested."

"What? Why?" Moses asked, the alarm apparent in his voice.

"He just called me. Said he was checking out the sites along the parade route, seeing where we could place the evidence. All the time, the Fibbies were watching him. Because he seemed suspicious, they brought him in for questioning."

"Did they arrest him, or just bring him in for questioning?"

"I don't know," Ray said, "but, I think you should get down there immediately. He told me he wouldn't say anything until you arrive."

Moses grabbed his coat and thought about what to tell the FBI. And what not to. Whatever he said, he had to make sure it didn't involve Jane. He returned to her room and sat on the edge of her bed. It pained him to have to tell her there was a glitch in their plans.

"What's wrong?" she asked.

His face, he knew, betrayed his worry. He told her about Ray's call. "I have to go there and get Willie out. Damnit, this could ruin everything."

"Moses, just tell them he's one of your bodyguards doing a safety check for you. After all, you're president of the National African Caucus and a nominee for the Cabinet. Your safety, come Inauguration Day, is a major concern." She said it matter-of-factly, with no enthusiasm nor excitement, unlike her vocal and demonstrative self. This was spin, and spin, lying, had become Jane Weisser's life.

"I'll be back soon," he told her. Moses walked out of the Watergate Hotel. It troubled him to leave her alone with one more thing to worry about.

Jane looked up at the ceiling from her four-poster bed. Her only hope was Sam. She had to talk to him again. After all, he still loved her. She had to persuade him to talk to Sayyid about releasing Taryn. But, after deceiving him about her mother being ill and jetting off to London, how could she ask him for another favor?

Jane arrived at the Hart Senate Office Building without

any hindrance. No one had followed her. At least she didn't think so. To be honest, she didn't care anymore. Desperation, she realized, begets courage.

As always, Jackie allowed her entrance into Sam's office without question. He was alone, working behind his desk on his inaugural speech. Jane closed the door behind her, and he looked up. She stared into his suede gray eyes and felt her heart beat a little faster.

"I'm surprised to see you here, Jane."

She didn't say anything. Her throat was dry.

"But, for you to be here, there has to be a problem. What's wrong?"

"It's Taryn. My child's in the hands of people who may kill her, Sam. Please, you have to get her released. For me. For us. For all we've been to each other."

"I'm sorry, Jane, there's nothing I can do. Sayyid makes the rules and he wants you both dead. I'm telling you this not to scare you, but to warn you."

"I know you've been protecting me, Sam, and I appreciate it. But, I need you to do one more thing for me. Please, tell him to let her go." It sounded so simple. Just do it!

Sam stared at her. "As you said, I'm only a pawn in Sayyid's scheme."

Jane remembered saying that to him when she found out who Sam Howard really was that night at the cabin. Now, he was throwing it back at her. "You're more than that and you know it. You don't need Sayyid. You're going to be President of the United States in a few days. Leader of the free world. If anyone needs anyone right now, he needs you.

"Tell him I've already proven I'll remain silent. Look what happened in London: I never said anything, even after his men shot me. Please, I'm begging you. Imagine how you would feel if it were Adam or Bradley. What would you want *me* to do if the tables were turned?"

"Jane, I love Taryn like I love you. I'll do what I can."

Jane retrieved her car from the Hart garage and returned to the Watergate suite. She had played her trump card. Sam's love for her.

Moses returned to his Watergate room after straightening out the problem with the Capitol police. He was the future Housing and Urban Development Secretary and president of the NAC. His security was of national importance.

Moses walked into his room and gasped in disbelief. Someone had ransacked the place. Drawers were on the floor, empty, and papers were strewn everywhere. The bed was upside-down, and his clothes were inside-out. "Jane!" He turned and ran into her suite through the adjoining doors. On entering, he saw the same horrifying scene. Sofa cushions were sliced open, and, in every room, the furniture was overturned, drawers emptied. The place was a complete mess. Even worse, there was no sign of Jane. "Damnit, what's wrong with me? She had me move in here to protect her and I failed."

"What in the name of God?" Jane walked into her suite, her mouth agape.

Moses turned and yelled, "WHERE HAVE YOU BEEN?"

"I went to Sam and asked him to talk to Sayyid about releasing Taryn." She looked at the disheveled room. "What happened?" Before he could answer, she ran into his room. She returned with wide open eyes. "Someone suspects us."

Moses felt his stomach turn and the perspiration drip down his face. They had left nothing in their rooms that could incriminate them. They'd made sure of that. "But who?" he asked. "And what do they suspect?"

"I don't know, but we're going to have to be extra careful from now on."

Although Moses was carrying out the operation with his people, it was Jane who was in charge. Subterfuge, after all, was at the core of her profession. He felt confident with her decisions. "The big question is, can we still pull it off without being caught?"

Jane's eyes were deep in thought. "One thing's for certain," she answered, as if trying to convince herself more than Moses, "if we don't do it, the consequences will be worse than if we do it and are caught."

Moses looked at the chaos around the suite and tried to remain optimistic. He sorely missed the faith that was once the underpinning of confidence in his life.

"Hey, Gary, you ol' horndog," Cassie Davenport called out from her kitchen window. "Doing anything interesting tomorrow morning?"

Garrison Miller was shoveling the snow in her driveway from the previous night's two-inch fall. Tomorrow morning? Tomorrow was Inauguration Day, the day of Moses McBride execution. He had to answer carefully. "I got nothing scheduled so far, why?"

"How about my coming over your place and you can whip up something for breakfast?"

Miller laughed. She did have a great sense of humor. Too bad he had to use her for his alibi. "It's a date."

"Great. I'll be there for breakfast. I want to see how long I can take it."

Miller saw her seductive look as she turned away from the window. He went back to his shoveling, thinking: Exactly what I needed. With her initiating the invite, there'll be no proof I coerced her there as an alibi in some grand scheme. "Yes," he laughed under his breath, "everything is working out just fine."

After spending the morning and afternoon meeting with just about everyone, Sam was finally alone in his senate office. His speech was ready, and he was ready. Ready to be sworn in as President of the United States. He closed his heavy eyes, leaned his head against the leather chair, and imagined how Britney would feel if she were there to share in his success. Oh, how proud she would be of him right now. He also thought of his mother and of her belief in him. And of his father, who had pushed him through derision and humiliation and embarrassment. But, he had done so because he cared for and loved him. Wasn't that why? Sam opened his eyes and thought about Jane. He refused to believe he had lost her love for good.

Sam picked up his videophone and punched in the prescribed code on the key pad. His belief in their love made him feel omnipotent. Being the next President of the United States made him feel omnipotent. He *was* omnipotent! "We have to talk about the girl," he said to Sayyid Kassim when the Iraqi's picture appeared on the small screen in his hand. It was time to bring Taryn home. And let Sayyid know who needed whom.

"And the mother?" the leader of Al-Qiyamah asked.

"Jane will be no problem."

"Where is your loyalty, Sam? Al-Qiyamah comes first. It has been our passion, our reason for living."

"NO! SAM HOWARD COMES FIRST. MY ALLEGIANCE IS TO NO ONE." He had taken control, just like Jane had said he should. He waited for the man's reply.

There was silence, then Sayyid spoke calmly. "How do you plan on taking care of this problem, Sam. You've promised, you've interfered, you've done nothing, and you've done too much already. I'm afraid Dr. Weisser is going to land us all in prison."

"No, she won't. Jane will be indebted to me and remain quiet forever when I bring Taryn back to her." It felt good to finally be in control. "I want ..."

"So, you took the girl so you could make the mother think you saved her?" Sayyid was visibly impressed. "I must congratulate you on your ingenuity, Sam."

Sam couldn't believe what he'd just heard. Sayyid was under the impression that he was the one who had kidnapped Taryn. Which meant Sayyid didn't abduct her in London.

"But, there is another problem."

He had to think. "Someone's here. I'll call you back." Sam closed the videophone and thought out loud, "Who has her?" He remembered Taryn's relationship with Garrison Miller. "If he's behind this, then he probably had her brought back to him." Sam opened the portable again and called his men who were still tailing Jane. "Talbot, I want you to stake out Garrison Miller's home in New Carrollton. Stay there, no matter what, until you see Taryn Weisser. I have a picture here somewhere." He pulled out his wallet from his pocket. Inside was a graduation picture Taryn had given him last year. "I'll fax over a copy to your car. Whatever you do, don't barge in, or they may kill her on the spot. Wait for them to emerge with her. If my hunch is correct, Miller and the PWA are behind her kidnapping." Sam put the phone away and sat back. He couldn't call in the FBI; it would open too many cans of worms, too many questions and too many answers. He'd quietly bring Taryn back to Jane." He stood and stretched his arms over his head. Tomorrow was Inauguration Day. If luck was with him, he'd bring her back by then, unharmed. And then he would have everything: vindication, Jane's love, and soon thereafter - revenge.

His secretary disrupted his daydream to inform him of a meeting with the Secret Service. For the next forty-five minutes,

Director Morton outlined every move of the following day. When they left, and he was again alone, Sam picked up the videophone and called back Sayyid.

"As I was saying, Sam, although you may think you have taken care of the problem, there is another one. One you did not anticipate."

"What?" Sam asked, caution in his voice.

"Moses McBride has taken a room at the Watergate. And it adjoins Jane Weisser's suite. What do you make of that?"

Sam felt the bile in his stomach work its way up his chest.

"They have been meeting in her room, Sam. You talk about loyalty. How's *that* for your Yehoudi's loyalty?"

Sam didn't answer.

"Watch your back, Sam. A knife in yours means a knife in mine."

The bile reached Sam's throat.

"Just as sure as they killed your family, Sam, they will surely kill you. Only together will we remain safe."

Sayyid disconnected, and Sam sat there with the open videophone in his hand, thinking about Jane and Moses McBride.

Jane had removed all signs that someone was living in her adjoining room. With no traces that Moses had ever been there, and with it set up to look like a temporary office for TWO, the police responded to the manager's call about the robbery. Feigning ignorance to all their questions, the police left, the manager left, house cleaning came and left, and all was finally back to normal.

Moses returned later with his belongings, and he and Jane shared tea on the sofa in her suite. It was almost midnight, and they were worn and tired and scared.

Jane daydreamed of the cabin in Maryland and the long, solitary walks through the woods, drinking in the fresh air, feeling at peace.

"You're smiling. What're you thinking?" Moses asked.

"Oh, about a place not far from here, yet light years away from here. A place where I could be me, alone with my thoughts. I wish I was there right now."

"After what just happened here, maybe that's not such a bad idea."

Jane let out a little laugh, but it came out as a sigh. She told him about the cabin, its history, and why it would be impossible to ever go there again.

"You have to forget the past, Jane. The future is all that matters. With Taryn back, and with Sam and Sayyid defeated - and with you in control of your life again - I can tell your future is going to be wonderful."

"Thank you, Moses. You always know the right thing to say. But, reality can't be rooted in the future. We have to deal with the problems and the worries of the present. And the plain truth is - if we don't get away with it, we go to jail for the rest of our lives. And if we succeed, we could be signing our, and my daughter's, death certificates. Either way we lose."

"We can still back out. Just say so and it's off."

Jane saw the sincerity, and pain, in his eyes. Moses didn't want her to experience the same torment he'd been forced to live with the last few months.

"So, tell me," Moses asked, as he helped her off the floor, "do you want a drink right now?"

"Yes," she said in all honesty. "But, I don't want one. I want many. And I know I can't have just one, so I won't."

"That's how it works, Jane. Addiction is a disease of the personality. The desire to drink, or smoke, or whatever will wane with every small victory achieved by refusing to have 'just one'."

"When, because I can't seem to stop thinking about it."

"Everyone's addiction is different. Could be a month, could be a year. But, it will happen. Just believe it will."

"You mean have faith. Interesting coming from a man who's lost his." The psychologist stared at him and waited.

"You may get your daughter back, I won't. It's really hard for me to believe in God's great plan any longer. I've tried to renew my faith, but I wasn't the better for it."

"It's going to take time, Moses. One day, the need and the desire will return in you. Could be a month, could be a year. But, it will. All you have to do is believe."

Moses smiled at his own words reversed and reflected back to him. "Well, I truly hope time decreases your desires while it increases mine," he sighed.

Jane kissed Moses good night and agreed to be ready by 6 a.m. He left her suite, and she sat at the window, gazing out but seeing nothing but the hopeful visions of the future Moses had described. She thought about Taryn and prayed with the fervor of a child. She looked out toward the Potomac and found her thoughts returning to Moses. He was a real *mensch,* a good person, the kind of person she'd always strived to be. She debated his thoughtful offer of backing out. What if they did? The fighting around the country had lessened considerably the last few days. Maybe it was because Sam Howard, 'Uncle Sam,' was taking the oath of office tomorrow and everyone was filled with hope.

CHAPTER SIXTEEN

Inauguration Day

At six o'clock in the morning, Jane, with coffee in hand, looked up from the sofa and saw Moses walk in through the adjoining door. Before he could pour himself a cup, she said, "I'm going back to my house to see if there's any word on Taryn and to take care of some last minute business. I'll call you on your videophone the moment I leave for the Capitol. It should be sometime between 9:30 and 10. If you don't hear from me by then, you'll know something's wrong."

Moses poured a cup and sat next to her.

Jane continued: "The ceremonies will end about 12:30 to 12:45, then Sam and Bill will head off to Statuary Hall to have lunch with the leaders of both Houses, the committee chairs, and his new Cabinet. He should begin his walk up the Mall to the White House between 2:00 and 2:15."

"When do you figure he'll get to the first designated spot?"

"Sometime between 2:30 and 2:45." Jane looked at Moses and saw nervousness and uncertainty. That wasn't good. Today, of all days, he needed to be confident. "Moses, are you okay? Is something bothering you?"

"Ever since this place was torn apart, I feel like we're being watched."

"We probably are. But, no one knows what we're doing. If anyone did know, we would've been stopped by now."

"Sorry, I'm just a little paranoid today."

Jane took Moses by the hand to calm him. The roughness of his palm made her take notice. "What happened?"

Moses McBride's eyes welled up. "The day my apartment building was bombed, I ran inside the fire and found Jessie first. I lifted her in my arms to carry her out. When I reached the front door, I grabbed the knob and my skin burned onto it."

Jane cringed, but continued to hold his hand in hers for support.

"If only I hadn't left them in the first place, then maybe …"

"You can't second guess yourself, Moses. You did what you did, you did everything you could, and that's that. Heroes aren't heroes because of the success of their attempts, but rather for the attempts themselves. In my eyes, Moses, you're a hero."

"But, why was I chosen to live instead of my baby? She had a full life ahead of her. Damnit," he cried in anger, "if there's a God, why did he choose to take a child?"

"As a man of God, you must believe that Jessie and DaNell were sacrificed so others may live. Have faith, Moses, and you'll understand."

Moses nodded his head. "You'd make a great preacher, you know that?"

Jane kissed his hand. "There's nothing to worry about. If there was, we would've aborted the plan immediately."

"I know, but something tells me we're headed for a trap."

"Like you said to me, if you want to pull out and scrap the whole thing, just say so. If you don't think we can do it ..."

"No, no, we can do it," Moses told her without conviction.

Jane had to assure him. She had to put his mind into a self-fulfilling prophecy, convinced of success. "Yes, we can. And we will!" Jane's effort to restore Moses's confidence had had an uplifting effect on her own spirits.

A short while later, Jane walked out of the Watergate and got into her Mercedes, which the concierge had summoned up to the front entrance. She drove toward Foxhall Road, less than ten minutes away. It was a sunny, yet cold day. Good, she thought. If it was raining, Sam would have driven the parade route in the bubbletop limousine. So far, things were working in her favor. Although she was nervous, she was also confident they were going to get away with it. She hummed along with the radio. But, then, she thought about Taryn and got misty-eyed.

Jane unlocked the new door she'd had installed after the explosion. She entered the burned-out hallway and felt cold and frightened. Here was the place she loved most, the place where she'd made a life with her child. She looked at everything for the last time. Tonight, she would be in Honolulu starting a new life. Jane sighed and went from room to room, packing the things she couldn't leave behind: Photographs, valuables, papers. She then changed into her clothes for the inauguration.

At 9:25 she was ready to leave for the Capitol. She called Moses to inform him.

Jane packed her car with the few boxes she needed to take with her, then went back and checked the old Georgian house one last time. It pained her to have to abandon her home, but what else could she do? As she walked down the stone pathway, another car pulled into her driveway. Two men whom she didn't recognize got out.

"Dr. Weisser!"

Sam's men! They weren't Arabs, nor did they look like Garrison Miller's honchos. Sam was making sure she would be by his side.

"If you will come with us."

A black Lincoln pulled up behind them. Two men jumped out and approached her. Sayyid Kassim's men! "I'm sorry, gentlemen," one of the Arabs said, "but there's been a change in plans. Dr. Weisser is to come with us."

Jane saw one of Sam's men pull out a gun. Before he could do anything, the two Arabs had their own guns pointed. She began to shake. Who would she be safer with? Neither, she told herself. She tried to say something, but her throat was clamped shut.

Sam's man dropped his weapon and put his hands up. "The president-elect is expecting us to bring Dr. Weisser to him. If we don't, he'll have all of Washington out looking for her," the American told the other two.

"You tell him she will be in good hands. An old friend just wants to see her."

They escorted Jane to the black car and drove away, leaving Sam's men behind. At least there was no bloodshed. Maybe that meant she'd survive this new setback. Her abductor said, 'An old friend of his just wants to see her.' That could only be Sayyid! They were taking her to Sayyid. Jane read the passing signs. They were heading north toward Maryland. The cabin! Sayyid was the one who'd had their rooms ransacked. He was the one who suspected them of plotting something. And, now, he was stopping it from happening. She closed her eyes, and her chin fell to her chest. What made her think she could ever pull this off?

* * * * *

Garrison Miller was excited. Not because he was in bed fucking Cassie Davenport. That had become old hat. He was excited because today was the day he was going to personally snuff out Moses McBride's life. Yes, revenge was sweet, he thought as he lay underneath the petite woman, pumping his hips up into her. Today was payback time. He looked at the clock on the night stand to his right. It was 9:30. Just enough time to do it to her and get to Washington. He'd return to his bed a few hours later where she'd still be asleep, never knowing he'd come and gone. Miller laughed under his breath at the play on words. Glory fuckin' be, it felt good to be alive.

He had to concentrate. He had to fantasize about Taryn downstairs if he wanted to finish this boring sex. Cassie was grinding him real good, like a real whore. There were no whips involved, no pain nor suffering, no delightful foreplay. Cassie was unable to conceal a look of relief when he told her he wasn't in the mood for 'extras' this morning. Today, he would just fuck her before she had a chance to fuck him, if that's what she had planned. Ahh, good ol' America, Miller thought. The land of the free to screw you before you screw me. Miller inwardly laughed again. Jesus, it was as if he was high or something. Trying to focus, he looked at her on top of him. She was sweating, gyrating, moaning. His throat was dry, and he was finding it hard to maintain his erection. To keep himself excited, he thought about what he was about to do to her.

Before Cassie arrived, Miller had hid the hypodermic needle between the mattress and the box spring, to his right. He reached his hand over to get it, but he couldn't. He had to reposition himself to get closer without her knowing. He also had to concentrate on his fucking or else she'd suspect something. Miller grabbed her breasts and tweaked her nipples hard. Usually she smiled, but today she winced. He knew she didn't like it, even if she feigned pleasure like she had all the other times. She was a fake, someone who could destroy him. Only, he was too smart to allow that. No, he would destroy her first. He would destroy anyone who got in his way.

Cassie's hips pushed down on his erection even harder. She was about to come. He figured when she did, she'd never feel the slight prick of the needle in her ass. He tried to scoot over a little to grab the hypodermic. As his hand reached under the mattress to grasp it, Cassie stopped moving. His heart pounded and he became semi-soft. Did she see him reach for it?

"I'm thirsty, are you?" she asked.

Miller tried to swallow and noticed he couldn't. His lips, mouth, and throat were dry. Not a drop of wetness anywhere. It felt as if he'd eaten sand. No wonder it was so difficult to maintain his erection. "More than you can imagine, but I can wait." It was 9:35. He had to do it now. If he didn't, he'd get to the Capitol too late to meet McBride out front.

"Well, I can't come if I'm dry. Those eggs and bacon were too salty." Cassie got off of him, stared at his limp penis, and said with a mocking tone to her voice, "You need something to drink, too. Look at you, you're all dried out."

Miller's sudden impotence, and Cassie's recognition of it, embarrassed him. Her sarcasm, as if she was making fun of his manliness, made him angrier and more committed to what he had to do to her. He watched her leave the bedroom, then looked at the clock. "Shit! I gotta get outta here." Carl Block and Jimmy Siefert were already in position at the parade route. In case he failed, they would finish the job. Although Miller had wanted to do it personally, at least the nigger would be dead.

With Cassie out of the bedroom, he repositioned himself on the bed so his right hand could reach the hypodermic needle.

He felt for it, then brought his hand back to his cock. He had to get hard again if he was going to make her come, if he was going to knock her out. Garrison Miller closed his eyes and fantasized some more about Taryn tied in the dungeon underneath his house. It got him a little stiffer. He then fantasized about Moses McBride's dying eyes staring into his own, and again he was at attention.

Cassie walked in, with a glass of juice in hand, and saw him playing with himself. "Ah, the hand. Man's second favorite part of his body," she laughed.

It felt as if she were laughing at him, belittling him, and Miller got angry. He held it in, so as not to ruin the moment. Later that afternoon, when he returned from Washington and she was awake, he'd teach her a lesson she wouldn't soon forget. He knew of every torture known to man. He would make her pay. Damn right, you fuckin' whore!

"You want any of this orange juice?" she asked, holding the glass in front of her. "It's real cold."

Miller tried to swallow again. "Yeah." He sat up, and she walked to his side of the bed and handed it to him. The glass was wet, and it tasted good. It felt as if it went straight to his groin, rejuvenating him. He drank it all and put the empty glass on the night stand. "Just what I needed to go another round."

They resumed the sex, with Cassie on top, and Miller saw she was about to climax. He reached under the mattress with his right hand, felt the needle with his fingertip, and slid it out. For some reason, his head was spinning. He also noticed he couldn't feel his erection any longer. He couldn't feel anything. Sex was never like this. He wondered what was wrong.

"Are you okay?" she asked. The words came out of her mouth in slow motion.

"I ... I ..."

"Come," she said, looking into his eyes.

He lifted his arm from the side of the bed and brought it up behind her ass.

"I'm coming, Gary. Can you feel it?"

He concentrated on her orgasm, on Moses McBride's death, and he finally came. She screamed, and he used his last bit of strength to drive in the needle.

Cassie fell onto the bed beside him and saw him plunge a hypodermic into his own thigh. Cassie worried briefly that a combination of her drug and Miller's own might prove fatal to him. Not that she had any concerns for Miller, himself, but it would be hard to frame him if he was already dead.

She dressed, making sure to remove any evidence that she had been there. She also took the needle, for analysis, and left the drugged man asleep on his bed.

Cassie returned to her rented house next door to make sure there was no evidence left there either. Before getting into her beat-up old car she thought about Miller almost drugging her. She realized she had come close to blowing the mission.

Cassie Davenport felt cleansed as she drove away from New Carrollton, Maryland.

As was customary, Sam Howard and his sons, at the invitation of the president, had spent the night before at Blair House. At 7:30 a. m. they, along with Vice President-elect William S. Lawson and invited guests, including the Reverend Dr. Moses McBride, had attended services at Washington's Metropolitan AME Church. Sam and his sons returned to Blair House at 8:45 to re-freshen, and a short while later were driven to the north portico of the White House for breakfast. It was a bright, clear winter day, and President and Mrs. Price had welcomed the president-elect and his sons to their new home. Along with the vice-president and the vice-president-elect, members of the Joint Committee on Inaugural Ceremonies, and the leadership of the Senate and the House, they had coffee and assorted cakes in the Blue Room before leaving for the Capitol shortly after eleven.

As Sam and his sons drove away, he looked back through the rearview window at the majestic house. His new home for the next four - no, eight years.

"Pretty awesome, eh, Dad?"

Sam laughed. "Yes, Adam. It's pretty awesome."

Bradley added: "I can't believe I'm going to be living in the White House."

Sam turned away from the site and stared at his two boys, as the limousine drove past the crowds of cheering people barricaded along Pennsylvania Avenue. A long time ago, he was promised it by Sayyid Kassim. Now, it was his. He hoped his boys could adapt to being the sons of the most famous man in the world.

Sam's videophone rang and he removed it from his coat pocket. Because Adam and Bradley were in the car with him, he held it to his ear so they couldn't hear who was on the other end. Sam kept quiet and listened to his men detail Jane's kidnapping. Goddamnit! If Sayyid knew what was good for him, he wouldn't harm her.

Inside the Capitol rotunda, Moses was worried. It was 11:15, and Jane had yet to arrive. On a normal day, it would have taken her around thirty minutes to get to the Capitol from Georgetown, considering the traffic. Even today it should take no more than an hour. She had called at 9:25 to say she was leaving. But, she wasn't there yet, and she hadn't called again to tell him why. He had tried to call her on her videophone, but she wasn't answering.

The ceremonies were about to begin. Suddenly, there was a commotion inside the rotunda. The president-elect had arrived and was escorted into room EF100 of the Capitol. Where is she? Moses asked himself. He thought about the possibilities and his stomach tightened. Sayyid or Sam had evidently found out what they had planned and Jane was being held somewhere.

"Excuse me, reverend."

Someone Moses didn't know was standing next to him. His heart jumped and he turned, startled. "Yes?"

"We're ready to take our seats on the presidential platform," an aid to the Senate sergeant-at-arms told him.

"Fine." Moses couldn't very well leave. Sam Howard had personally requested he give the closing benediction. His leaving just before an assassination attempt, successful or not, would provoke unacceptable scrutiny.

"Doctah McBride," Senator John Calhoun of Mississippi said in a lazy, southern drawl, extending his hand. "Ah'm delighted to see ya." The man was much larger than Moses. His rotund stomach matched Moses's and kept their faces at some distance from each other. His long, silver hair was in disarray, and his eyes bulged out from their sockets.

"Good morning, Senator." Moses disliked the staunch conservative and his hypocritical stance on every issue. Out of respect for his office, he shook his hand.

"As a man of Gawd, ah know my colleagues and ah can count on yohr support come February when mah long overdue bill goes befoh Congress." U.S. Representative Josiah Hawkins of Oklahoma joined them. "Joe and ah sho' can use yohr help in persuadin' the President to sign the bill."

Moses didn't believe in the Calhoun-Hawkins Bill. He

considered it a ploy to give special preference to the Southern Baptist brand of Christianity. He looked around the circumference of the rotunda. Surrounded by the busts of America's great leaders: Washington, Jefferson, Lincoln, Grant, and Martin Luther King, Jr. he said, "I'm sorry, gentlemen, but I believe that mandating schools to provide time for prayer goes against the principles on which this nation was founded."

"Ah beg to diffah, reverend. You, above all, should know religion *is* the foundation of ahr great country. It is the cornerstone of ahr land. Freedom of religion promises us exactly what ahr bill is proposing. Look around you. Legally, we swear on the Bible; ahr currency reminds us that 'In Gawd We Trust;' and, today, the president will be inaugurated with the words 'So help me Gawd.'"

"And let's not forget, 'God Bless America,'" Representative Hawkins added.

Moses looked at the diminutive congressman. "You're talking about tradition."

"Do you want the right to pray taken away from ahr children, Doctah McBride? What would yohr followers say?"

"What I want, and what you should be fighting for, is equality for all, gentlemen. As a man of the cloth, and soon to be part of the administration which represents this country, I am obliged by consciousness and law to represent *all* people: Christians, Jews, Muslims, Atheists, everyone. Your bill will create more divisiveness around the country, not unity."

"Religion breeds morality, and morality breeds unity."

An aide came back to Moses to lead him to the ceremony. "And anything mandatory breeds contempt for the mandate and for those who mandate it. Even worse, all those who don't wish to follow it become the victims of that contempt," Moses stated. "No, what I believe in is our Constitution. There is a separation of church and state for a reason. Now, if you'll excuse me, gentlemen, it's time to take our places."

The aide escorted Moses down the blue carpeted steps at the West Front of the Capitol to his seat on the presidential platform. There had to be a half million people, at least, who had gathered there for the swearing in. He looked out over the crowd. They went as far west as 4th Street. To his right on Constitution Avenue, on top of the Department of Labor building, he saw the NBC and ABC broadcast booths. All the other buildings had people on top. Security was at its maximum. Moses looked around at those privileged enough to sit with the new administration: Invited members of the House and Senate, the new Cabinet, members of the Supreme Court, and friends and family of the new president and vice president. He took in a deep breath of the cold air and sat down. The day had come and there was no turning back. Again, he thought about Jane, but there was nothing he could do.

The Army Band began playing, and everyone stood. The last person to enter the presidential platform, escorted by the joint inaugural committee, was President-elect Sam Howard. He shook hands as he made his way to the twin leather recliners, one which Bill Lawson already occupied. The last person he shook hands with was Moses McBride.

Moses clasped his hand and looked into his eyes. There was something in them that bespoke fear and mistrust. Sayyid Kassim must have told Sam about him and Jane being together at the Watergate.

Senator McClarry, the chair of the joint committee, stepped up to the podium and spoke into the band of microphones. "Mr. President, Mr. Vice President, Mr. Speaker, Mr. Chief Justice, Mr. President-elect, and Mr. Vice President-elect, my colleagues and guests, welcome."

Moses looked at his watch again. There was still a few hours before the parade was to begin. Hopefully, he'd hear from her by then. If not, he would still carry out the plot. The wheels were in motion and could not be stopped.

Carl Block and Jimmy Siefert stood in the crowd and saw Moses McBride seated on the presidential platform. They looked at each other in shock and dismay. Garrison had failed. It was now up to them to kill McBride during the parade.

After Justice Reynolds swore in U.S. Representative William S. Lawson as Vice President of the United States, Senator Robert McClarry returned to the microphones. It was exactly noon, as required by law. "Ladies and gentlemen, the Chief Justice of the United States will now administer the Presidential oath of office to Samuel James Howard."

The Chief Justice approached the podium and asked Sam Howard to join him. Sam stood opposite him, with his two sons by his sides.

"Senator, are you ready to take the oath of office?"

"I am." There was a quiet among the almost half million people watching. History was in the making.

"Will you please raise your right hand and repeat after me?"

Sam did so and noticed he was shaking. He was about to speak the exact words spoken by every president since George Washington.

"I, Samuel James Howard, do solemnly swear ..."

"I, Samuel James Howard, do solemnly swear ..."

" ... that I will faithfully execute the office of President of the United States ..."

" ... that I will faithfully execute the office of President of the United States ..."

" ... and will, to the best of my ability, preserve, protect, and defend the constitution of the United States ..."

" ... and will, to the best of my ability, preserve, protect, and defend the constitution of the United States ..."

" ... so help me God."

" ... so help me God."

"Congratulations, Mr. President!"

Sam shook the Chief Justice's hand and hugged his sons as the United States Army Band played 'Hail To The Chief', a twenty-one-gun salute blasted from army cannons, and the crowd applauded exuberantly. He then stepped toward former President Charles Price and shook hands with him.

Senator McClarry announced for all to hear, "Ladies and gentlemen, I give you the President of the United States, Samuel James Howard."

The mass of people witnessing this great event shouted their approval, as their savior, 'Uncle Sam,' stood to address the country for the first time as president.

"I made it, Dad," Sam whispered to himself. He looked out at the crowd and felt a tear trickle down his cheek.

Jane occupied the cabin bed where she and Sam had made love so many times. The memories of them there flooded her mind, leaving her both angry and sad. Her captors had bound her wrists and ankles, with her back against the wall and her legs straight out. Thankfully, they had tied her hands on her lap, rather than behind her.

Jane watched Sam give his Inaugural Address. His proclamation of hope and optimism were nauseating. She wondered what Moses would do now that she hadn't shown up and he hadn't heard from her. He must have figured out what had happened. Had he called off the whole thing? And if not, would Sayyid Kassim realize she was behind the assassination? Jane didn't have to think about it for long. They had brought her there to stop her.

Jane worried about what would happen to her, and Taryn (if she were still alive), when Sayyid sees Sam's head blown apart later in the parade. It was foolish to think about; her death was a foregone conclusion. That realization made Jane feel even sicker than she felt from listening to Sam on the TC wall screen opposite their bed.

She prayed Taryn's death would be quick and painless.

Moses McBride listened halfheartedly to the speech. All he could think about was Jane and what he should do. She had told him during one of their many conversations at the Watergate about Sam's secret cabin deep in the woods of Burtonsville, Maryland. Could they have taken her there? He remembered her telling him that although Sayyid Kassim owned the place, he had listed it under the name ... damn, what was that name? He thought for awhile, then remembered: Harrington. He had to get out there, but he had to deliver the benediction at the end of the ceremony. He prayed that when he got there she would be there, alive. Moses was shocked to find himself praying again. If there is a God, he said to himself as Sam spoke, would He look over Jane and help her in her time of need? Jane had told him his belief was critical to their success. Maybe it was time to again put his trust in his faith. He prayed more fervently than ever and with increasing conviction.

Jane watched Sam give his speech, but she wasn't listening. There were too many other things on her mind. A short while later, the tumultuous applause from the wall screen disrupted her worries and she watched Senator McClarry return to the podium.

"Ladies and gentlemen, we have come to the end of today's presidential inauguration. As soon as the ceremony is over, my colleague on the Joint Congressional Committee on Inaugural Ceremonies, the distinguished senator from Illinois, Wendell Tyler, will form the presidential escort to the East Front of the Capitol. To conclude our program, will you please rise for the benediction by the Reverend Dr. Moses McBride, and then remain standing for the singing of our National Anthem."

Jane saw Moses approach the band of microphones, his purple shirt and black tie prominent, a white scarf around the shoulders of his long, gray overcoat. He looked calm and confident despite the enormous strain of her absence and the perilous plot about to be executed.

"Dear Lord, we thank you for your divine counsel, for guiding us today. Help us to be the best people we can be, to be the people whom you want us to be. Please watch over our elected officials, and over all those who have officiated in the past. Theirs is indeed a selfless calling for a noble cause. Please, dear Lord, help us to look toward the future, toward better days, with dignity, optimism, and courage. And, above all, please grant us your wisdom and your holy grace. We promise to respect and cherish our fellow man as your children. We promise to think with our hearts, not just our minds, and to feel with our minds, not just our hearts. With respect, compassion, honesty, and love, we can be the people whom you have created in your image and whom you have favored. Committed to working out our difficulties in a positive, constructive manner; to recognize and share our similarities and accept and appreciate our differences; to help our fellow man rather than hinder him; to live collectively as one in harmony or die separately alone in discord, we promise to live in your sacred light so we can be who we are - the children of the Lord. In the name of the Father, the Son, and the Holy

Spirit, we say thank you. And in the name of the Father, the Son, and the Holy Spirit, we say Amen."

Jane was deeply moved. In such few words, Moses had said so much. Did he really believe what he was saying? Did he truly have faith in the future? She prayed for him.

The National Anthem ended, and Senator Wendell Tyler escorted the President and Vice President to the East Front of the Capitol where they said good-bye to President Price and Vice President Fuller. Saluting, until the former leaders' helicopter was out of sight, the co-chairs of the inaugural committee ushered Sam and Bill into the President's Room inside the Capitol, just off the Senate Chamber. There, the president signed his first requests of the newly elected Congress: the nominations of his Cabinet and sub-Cabinet.

As they walked into Statuary Hall, Senator Tyler explained to Sam that, "Congress has hosted this inaugural luncheon every four years since President's McKinley was first inaugurated in 1897." Sam gave a cursory nod, but he wasn't listening; he was thinking about Jane in Sayyid Kassim's hands. If Sayyid felt it necessary to let him know who was in charge, he wouldn't put it past him to kill her.

Sam sat at the dais and listened to the leaders of both Houses make speeches and present him with gifts. He looked over to where his Cabinet was sitting and his eyes locked with Moses McBride's. Maybe Sayyid was wrong. Maybe Jane and Moses didn't have anything planned. After all, there he was, his nominee for HUD secretary, sitting and smiling at him. How he wished Jane was there.

How bitterly he now regretted his involvement with Al-Qiyamah.

* * * * *

They left Statuary Hall and exited the East Front of the Capitol to review the Military Services Honor Guard of the five different branches of the armed forces. Moses stood near the President and watched. He looked at his watch. It was 2:10, and his instructions were to proceed to his designated limousine for the start of the parade. Instead, he feigned illness and walked back into the Capitol rotunda.

Moses ran down the stairs, through the low-ceilinged corridors, until he was at the Capitol subway. He took the first available tram to the Dirksen Building where he'd parked his rental car. Trying to remain calm, he thought about Sam's secret cabin in Burtonsville, Maryland. As he disembarked and walked toward his car, he heard footsteps behind him. He looked back and his heart jumped. A Middle Eastern looking man was following him. Was he being paranoid? Not every Arab was involved in the plot, and he was in a secured area. Moses laughed at his foolishness, but his heart was still beating faster than usual. He wondered if this was what white folks felt like when they saw a black man approach them. Moses couldn't believe he was racist. Maybe it wasn't racism, but rather a natural fear of those who are different or those who have been perceived as threatening. If that be, he reasoned, then maybe white people weren't racist after all, just frightened. He knew he'd have to give that some more thought.

As Moses unlocked his car, the man stepped in behind him and pressed what felt like a gun in his back. "Get behind the wheel, reverend, and don't do anything that could get you killed. Do you understand?"

Moses nodded his head and got in as the man walked around to the other side of the car and did the same. "What do you want?"

"No questions, no small talk. Just do as I say and you won't get hurt." He pointed to the exit. "Pull out and head north on 50."

Moses did as the man ordered.

Fifteen minutes later, they made their way through the horrendous traffic and detours associated with Inauguration Day. Moses realized, from the signs he read, that they were heading toward Maryland. Maryland! Jane! He had wanted to get to the cabin to save her, and now he was being taken there at gunpoint.

It was 2:30, and Sam was inside the presidential limousine being taken from the Capitol up Pennsylvania Avenue to the viewing stand.

Jane lay tied on the king-sized bed. The two Arabs sat in chairs and watched, silently, with her. She felt her heart pounding. Would the plot continue? Had Moses called it off because she hadn't called or shown up? And why was Sam inside the limo? She made eye contact with one of her two kidnappers. She turned away from his gaze and watched the same scene being watched by hundreds of millions around the world. Sam had said he was going to walk the parade route.

By the National Archives at 7th Street, the limousine stopped and Sam got out, leaving Adam and Bradley inside to ride the rest of the route. A few cars behind the President, Bill Lawson did the same. The plans hadn't changed after all. Surrounded by Secret Service agents, Sam began the historical walk toward the White House. There, he would watch the rest of the parade with his sons and the Vice President from the glass-enclosed viewing stand.

He waved toward his admirers, smiling, enjoying his moment in the sun. Jane's chest tightened as Sam approached 10th Street, the spot where he would take his final step. Before he did, he veered off toward the crowd lining Pennsylvania Avenue. Jane saw him take an infant from a woman, hug the baby, and carry her back to the intersection of 10th. NO! she screamed to herself. Don't shoot him with a baby in his arms!

To Jane's relief, Sam walked back to the mother and handed her her child a moment later. Jane let out an audible sigh, and the two Arab men looked at her. She smiled, or tried to smile, and they turned their attention back to the TC.

Passing 10th Street, Sam walked back to the middle of Pennsylvania Avenue, but he was now well past the first designated spot. Their margin of error had now been reduced to zero. They had only one more opportunity to succeed.

At 3:20, Sam turned right onto 15th Street and followed the press truck on the narrower road that crossed between Sherman Park to the north and General Pershing Park to the south. He waved and threw kisses to the crowds in the stands lining both sides. Jane unconsciously threw him a kiss back and closed her eyes.

When she opened them, she saw Sam Howard for the last time. Two shots hit the President simultaneously, blowing his head into pieces, leaving only a body falling to the ground. A grisly shower of blood, bone and fragments of brain spattered the President's entourage. Nauseated by it, Jane watched the scene of chaos unfold. The Secret Service agents surrounded the fallen President. The federal and military police who lined the street swarmed over the area, guns drawn. Spectators pushed back and forth, as the desire to flee the scene contended with the desire to watch the horrendous, yet historical events taking place.

Jane sat there on the bed, numb. It was over. Sam Howard was no longer part of a world he was unfit to live in.

* * * * *

Ray Jackson, Moses McBride's right hand man, stared at the two marksmen who had shot the President. From the hill near the statue of General Pershing, which overlooked the stands and the parade, he signaled the man in the latex mask and the woman seated in the stands across the street to begin. Earlier, they had run there from 10th Street after it was clear the first spot was no longer workable. If it had been, he would've gone through the same routine then. The team at 10th Street disbanded as soon as they realized their opportunity had eluded them.

At the 15th Street site, the second team performed flawlessly in wake of the successful assassination. The man in the blond wig and latex 'Garrison Miller' mask appeared to be hiding a rifle under his long, green, winter coat. With the sawed-off metal barrel sticking out by his neck, he turned his head from right to left, as if trying to avoid being observed, but in truth giving the woman with the video camera a complete profile of his face. He then ran off in the direction of the Metro Center station.

While they were filming his man, Ray Jackson placed the spent cartridge shell with Garrison Miller's prints on it on the ground where the authorities would find it. He walked away in the opposite direction of the scene, wearing one of two matching pairs of boots taken from Garrison Miller's closet.

At 14th Street and Pennsylvania Avenue, Carl Block and Jimmy Siefert were confronted with the spreading edge of panic and confusion centered about the assassination scene. Block stopped a young Army private running in the opposite direction from where the entourage had turned onto 15th Street. "What's going on?" he shouted above the noise. Startled and confused, the wide-eyed soldier shouted back, "President ... shot ... dead." Block and Siefert looked at each other in astonishment, then in fear.

They jettisoned all thoughts about the PWA and their mission and immediately put their plans for escaping into effect. With one major alteration. There would be no rendezvous with Garrison Miller.

Outside of Garrison Miller's house in New Carrollton, Maryland, Talbot and Collins, the former Secret Service agents on Sam Howard's payroll, were in their car listening to the newscaster recount what had happened. "What do we do?" they asked each other. Sam was sure the Weisser girl was there. They agreed to wait it out. Sooner or later, Miller would emerge with her. They had their orders, and although the man who had given it to them had been assassinated, it was still a presidential order. Sam Howard may be dead, they reasoned, but that didn't mean an innocent girl had to die, too.

Jane watched the reactions of the two operatives guarding her. They were gesticulating wildly and shouting in their native tongue. One of them took out his videophone and made a call. Jane wondered if he was calling Sayyid Kassim.

The leader of Al-Qiyamah was livid. He screamed to his man, "KILL HER! THEN SET THE PLACE ON FIRE AND LEAVE AT ONCE!" Sayyid disconnected the call and ran his bony fingers through his long, gray beard. He paced the mansion, thinking about it. Sam had ruined it for himself by not killing the Yehoudi as ordered. Well, she would pay with her life, not only for what she knew about Sam and Al-Qiyamah, but also as Sayyid's revenge for her interference. Then, his men would take care of Moses McBride. And the truth about Sam Howard and the men of Al-Qiyamah would remain a secret.

* * * * *

The Iraqi closed the phone, said something to the other in Arabic, and pulled out his gun. There was a look of pleasure in his eyes, and Jane began to shake.

"Wait, Saleh," the other one said in English. He turned to his prisoner and smiled. "Why don't we have some fun before we kill her?"

The man called Saleh put his gun down on the dresser. He grabbed her breasts and squeezed them hard. Jane held in her screams. "How about you, Ismail?" Saleh asked. "What would you like?"

The short, thin Iraqi untied Jane's hands and legs, then ripped her dress from her body. Jane tried to resist him as he went for her undergarments, but every time she pulled away, he slapped her face. When he had her naked, he began to undress. The man called Saleh joined his friend in undressing.

Jane's mind raced. Yes, she was going to die, but she didn't have to be raped first. She needed time to think. "Please," she said as calmly as possible, trying to stall them, "if this is going to be enjoyable for you, it would be better if I empty my bladder first."

They didn't understand.

"Bathroom. I have to pee. Please?"

They laughed and spoke about it in Arabic. Saleh, the leader, said, "Yes. But, you must keep the door open so we can watch." He laughed at her again, and Ismail joined in.

Humiliated, Jane sat on the toilet and relieved herself. She had always been a fierce opponent of capital punishment. Death was just too easy for men like these. A life in prison, tortured daily and left to rot, was more just. She finished, and the two men returned to the bedroom without her. Jane knew there was no way out, except for the front door or the windows. But, they had guns. What did she have?

Suddenly, she remembered. Guns! Jane twisted her head and looked behind the toilet tank. The gun she had wondered about when she searched the cabin for incriminating evidence was still there. She took the weapon from its holster and checked to see if it was loaded. It was.

Jane knew she'd only be able to get off one shot before one of them returned fire. She raised her not-too-steady arm before her eyes and stepped back into the bedroom. The sound of tires on gravel filled the cabin, and the men turned to look outside. As they did, Ismail saw Jane from the corner of his eye. The time it took for him to raise his arm was enough time for Jane to get a round off. She pulled the trigger and saw his face implode as a fountain of blood gushed from his head. He had fired back at the last second, but the bullet had flown over her head as he went flying back. Her worry that the other would fire at her before she could get a second shot off was for naught. Earlier, Saleh had set his weapon on the dresser in preparation of violating her. Before he could react, Jane stepped toward him and shot him in the heart.

The reality of what she'd just done caused Jane to convulse uncontrollably, and she threw up on the floor in front of her. She then heard the sound of slamming car doors. There were more of them

She wasn't going to make it out alive.

The Iraqi jumped out of the car to see what had happened. Moses heard it, too. Although he couldn't be certain, Sam Howard was probably dead, and Sayyid's men had shot Jane. The bile in his stomach choked him. Jane was dead, and he was next. Moses got out of the car as his abductor ran into the cabin with his gun drawn in front of him. Before Moses could escape into the woods, another shot pierced the air and he saw the

Iraqi's body fly back out the door. Jane? He ran toward the body, jumped over it, and entered the cabin.

In shock from all the killing, from all the blood and guts all over the place, Jane stood there in stark nakedness, ready to shoot the next Arab who came through the door.

"JANE, IT'S MOSES! PUT DOWN THE GUN!"

Through her tears, and the ringing in her ears, Jane couldn't be sure who had called her name in that familiar voice. She held the gun straight in front of her, ready to squeeze the trigger.

"JANE!"

Jane kept the gun pointed at Moses until he came into focus. "Moses?" She lowered her arm until it was at her side. The weapon slid from her hand to the carpet at her feet.

"Jane, it's okay. You're safe now."

"Moses."

"Yes, Jane, it's Moses. You're all right. Trust me. Everything's going to be fine." He took off his overcoat, wrapped it around her, and held her close to him.

She couldn't stop shivering, even though the heat was on inside the cabin. "W ... What happened?"

"Shh, it's all over."

After she dressed, Moses walked her outside, away from that death chamber, and held onto her until she stopped shaking. He saw her staring at the third man crumbled in the bloody doorway. "How did you ... Who is ... Oh, God, forgive me."

"Shh, you've done nothing wrong. Matter of fact, you've done everything right." Moses told her about leaving before the parade began to look for her and how he was taken away at gunpoint and brought here.

"You saved my life, Moses."

At that moment, Moses realized that he again believed in his Lord. "No, Jane, you saved mine. Thank you."

"I'm sorry for acting like such a blubbering idiot. I guess I'm not as strong a person as I thought."

"No, you're stronger."

They looked at the body of the Iraqi laying inside the doorway. "We'd better get out of here," Jane said.

"Yes. But, first, get all the incriminating evidence you told me about and put it in my car. It may save us if this nightmare ever becomes known to the authorities. Or to our enemies." Jane went back inside the cabin to do what he said while Moses dragged the body of his abductor inside and placed him alongside the other two.

Fifteen minutes later, Jane and Moses set the cabin ablaze so no one would be able to identify the bodies. From what Jane would tell the FBI, they would assume they were three of Garrison Miller's cohorts. They'd also deduce that other members of the PWA torched the place to hide any incriminating evidence against them.

Moses looked at Jane and said a prayer for her. She stood there, expressionless, as she cremated her past and watched her memories flicker away in the flames.

The FBI and the Maryland State Police ascended on Garrison Miller's New Carrollton home a few hours later. The sun had set, and thirty-six officers jumped out of their cars and surrounded the modest four-room house.

"GARRISON MILLER!"

Miller awoke when he heard his name being called out on a megaphone. He sat up startled, yet foggy-headed. "What the fuck?"

"This is the FBI. Come out with your hands above your head!"

"WHAT THE FUCK!" His heart began racing.

"I repeat: Come out with your hands above your head!"

Miller looked at the windows. Once again federal agents surrounded his house. He turned to his side. Where was Cassie? Why was he asleep in bed? What happened? His head ached and he couldn't concentrate, couldn't make sense of what was going on.

Not waiting for his response, they smashed in the windows and crashed through the doors. Before Miller could stand, hands were grabbing him, throwing him out of bed to the floor. He watched his room being searched again, like it had been months before. "What do you want?" They forced him to dress, handcuffed his wrists behind his back, and read him his Miranda Rights. "Wait a minute. On what charges am I being arrested?"

"For the assassination of the President of the United States."

Shaking, he looked up at them and asked from his suddenly constricted throat, "What proof do you have?" knowing very well they had all the proof they needed.

A man in a suit next to him, the one giving orders to the others, said, "An eye witness at the parade came to FBI headquarters shortly after the assassination and told us they saw someone running from the scene, a rifle tucked under his coat. Luckily for us, or unlucky for you, she videotaped your escape."

"IMPOSSIBLE!" Miller screamed. "When my lawyers get done with you you'll never work in law enforcement again."

"We also found a spent cartridge shell, which we'll compare to this rifle we found in your closet. These muddy boots we found by your back door appear to be the same ones we saw on the videotape. When our labs test it with chemical samples of the earth taken at the scene, I'm sure it will also match."

"It's all coincidence," Miller told them. "I'm innocent."

"Save it for your trial, Miller."

"But, I'm not Garrison Miller. I'm Gary Walters. And I can prove I was nowhere near Washington today." Escorted outside to an FBI van, Miller looked at Cassie's house. "I was in bed all day with my neighbor. She can vouch for me. That's her house. Just ask her, she'll tell you the truth."

The agent holding Miller's elbow assigned a group to get the woman.

Miller felt a little better. This was all a mistake. However, what he couldn't understand was why he'd been asleep alone in bed.

The agents returned. There was no answer next door, and it appeared no one had lived there for some time. The house was empty.

Miller the Killer knew he was a dead man.

Lonnie McKay ran into the dungeon when he heard the commotion upstairs. "The FBI took Garrison away," he told his twin brother, Tommy.

"Ya think he'll talk?"

"What do you think? He'll say anything to save his ass."

"Jesus, we gotta get outta here."

The brothers paced back and forth, ignoring the teenaged girl tied to the bed. Although the dungeon below the basement was virtually soundproof, they taped Taryn's mouth shut, just in case. Obviously, the authorities had not yet found the camouflaged door inside the closet next to the washing machine and dryer. There was no reason for the Feds to suspect he was holding anyone hostage, no reason to suspect there might be an underground secret room. Damn! Moses McBride should now be dead and racial warfare ignited on all fronts. The niggers should be on their way to their final extermination. That was the plan. But, instead, someone had assassinated the President of the United States. And, again, the FBI was making Garrison their fall guy. The PWA was doomed. They were doomed. Now, their lives were at stake.

"So, what do we do, Lonnie?'

"Shut up and lemme think."

"Hurry, we gotta escape through the tunnel before anyone comes back and searches this place more thoroughly."

Lonnie McKay looked at Taryn. "Our lives are in danger if Garrison talks, Tommy, or if the girl talks. We gotta save ourselves, get rid of anyone who can identify us."

"What'd'ya mean'?"

"We gotta kill her."

Tommy McKay looked at Taryn. "Yeah, we gotta."

Taryn heard what they said and she began to tremble in fear. She hoped it wouldn't be painful, but with all the torture she'd gone through, how painful could death possibly be? She felt the tears running down her cheeks and urine soak the bed underneath her. Her eyes glazed over as Lonnie lifted the gun and pointed it at her head.

"Sorry, kid, but them's the breaks," he said. "At least it'll be quick."

The door leading down to the dungeon from the basement closet burst open with a loud bang. Taryn thought she was shot, yet she didn't feel anything. She forced her eyes open and saw Lonnie and Tommy spin around. Two men stormed in and fired their weapons, catching Lonnie and Tommy with a barrage to their heads and chests. Taryn's writhings and muffled screams continued until one of the men took hold of her shoulders and spoke directly to her face. "Don't be afraid. We've come to free you."

*****

Jane and Moses ditched the Arabs' car off the side of the road, somewhere between Laurel, Maryland and Washington, D.C. After telling the FBI the fabricated story about her and Taryn being kidnapped by the PWA, they returned in Moses's car to her Foxhall Road home. She couldn't very well tell them her daughter was in the hands of Sayyid Kassim and the men of Al-Qiyamah. That would reveal her and Moses's complicity. It was important to keep the story straight. Garrison Miller had to be accused of everything: the HOPE bombings, the kidnappings, and the assassination of President Howard. The terrible thing about the lie was that by protecting everyone involved in the counterplot, the authorities would have no lead to Taryn's whereabouts.

"Are you okay?" Moses asked her before they got out of his car. They had decided, after they left FBI headquarters, to retrieve her car from her home.

"Okay? I'll never be okay, Moses."

"Yes, you will."

Jane looked at her house and noticed the lights were on behind the closed draperies of her living room. "Dear God, someone's inside."

"Let's drive away and call the police."

"No, we can't. If it has something to do with Sam and Sayyid, then the FBI will know we were lying. Everything might unravel. I'm afraid we have to face this head on."

"But, it's too dangerous to go inside without knowing who's in there. What if it's Sayyid's men? The most important thing now is for them to silence us."

Jane mulled it over. Who was inside her house? She weighed the possibilities for a few seconds, then an idea came to her. She reached into her pocketbook, took out her videophone, and pressed in her home phone number. After one ring, an American male voice answered it. "Hello? Hello, who is this?" the voice asked.

Jane disconnected and turned to Moses. "Whoever it is isn't foreign. Maybe it's someone from the government."

"Then, how did they get inside? Did they break in? And why?"

"Enough questions! My life has been filled with them lately. I'm going in, Moses. After what we've been through, what else could happen?"

"After what we've been through," Moses said as he pulled out the gun he had taken from the cabin, "I'm not taking any chances." He checked to make sure it was loaded. "I'll be right behind you."

They got out of his car, quietly closed the doors, and walked up the front steps to the house. Rather than use the remote, which made a loud clicking sound when it unbolted the lock, Jane took out her key and slowly unlocked the door. Her heart was beating as fast as it had been at the cabin. Was she walking into a trap? At this point, she no longer cared. This nightmare had to end.

Jane walked into the charred hallway and looked into the living room. Taryn was sitting on the sofa, flanked by men in black suits. "TARYN!" She ran up to her baby and threw herself into her arms. "You're safe, you're safe! Oh, my God, I can't believe it!" Through her tears, she looked at the two men. "Who are you? And what are you doing in my house?"

"It's okay, Mom, these men saved me."

"My name's Dan Talbot, ma'am. This here is Jim Collins. Sam Howard assigned us to protect you. After your daughter's kidnapping in London, Sam realized it had to be Garrison Miller behind it because of his relationship with Taryn. He figured

Miller had her brought home to him, so he had us stake out his house." The former Secret Service agent told Jane the story about the FBI arresting Miller for the assassination of President Howard and how they had searched the house after he was taken away.

"If these men hadn't arrived when they had, Mom, Miller's men would've killed me. They showed up just in time."

Jane thought about what might have been and about all Taryn had been through. She hugged her and looked at the men smiling at them. "Thank you." She kissed her daughter again. "I'm so happy you're all right, baby. You are all right, aren't you?"

"I've been better."

To see her smile, to see her before her, safe, was all Jane needed. She went to the bar to get a drink, but she didn't take one. She stood there, instead, thinking about Sam. He had saved Taryn's life at the cost of his own. She had killed the one man who had loved her more than any man could love a woman. She spent a moment by herself to mourn her loss.

"Hi, Taryn, I'm Moses McBride."

The teenager embraced him with a gratitude that brought tears to Moses's eyes. He thought about DaNell, which made the reunion much more heartfelt for him. It was a positive thought, a feeling like … like he'd been reborn. Moses looked up to Heaven, and said, "Thank you, Lord." With Taryn still in his arms, he whispered, "Follow our lead." It was time to put the final nail in Miller the Killer's coffin. The nail that would deflect any suspicion from them.

Taryn pulled back and looked at him as if she didn't understand, but then her eyes let him know that she did.

"So, Garrison Miller kidnapped Taryn, after breaking into your telecomp, in case you figured out he was the one who tried to assassinate Sam in New York," Moses said to Jane. "If you talked, he wouldn't have been able to try again at the inauguration."

"That's right," Jane said, confirming the bogus story. "That's what Miller's men holding me hostage at the cabin in Maryland talked about. They cheered their great success when Sam was killed."

"That's exactly what happened with me," Taryn added as if it were true. "The two men holding me hostage, Lonnie and Tommy, kept talking about how white America was going to be now that they got Sam Howard out of the way. They also spoke about how the PWA was going to rule this country some day."

"So, then Garrison Miller was the mastermind behind the HOPE bombings and the assassination of the president who had built them, all because of the PWA's desire for an all-white America," Moses concluded for the benefit of their visitors.

"Miller and the PWA are some sick puppies," Dan Talbot said.

"They're mad dogs," Jim Collins added.

Jane, Moses, and Taryn looked into each other's eyes. As it had sounded convincing to the FBI, it now sounded even more convincing to them.

"I think we should all thank God it didn't happen," Moses said.

"Amen," Jane and Taryn responded.

"Amen," the two men concurred.

After Jane said good-bye to the men who had saved Taryn's life, she turned to Moses. Her own savior. "So, reverend, what now?"

Moses didn't have to think about it for long. "I'm going back to Harlem to rebuild my church. It's God's will," he said, then smiled.

Jane understood, and she returned the thank you. "You'll never know how much I've come to admire you, Moses. In the short time we've been together, you've taught me so much about myself."

"And what is that?"

"That I'm a strong person. And I don't have to prove it to anyone, as long as I know it myself."

"Remember that every time you feel the need to have a drink."

"I will. Thank you, Moses. For everything. For all your sacrifices, and for all your indulgences. I'll be forever grateful."

"As I will be to you." He took her hands in his. "You've made me believe again."

The two friends embraced and didn't let go of each other.

"Call me whenever you need to," he told her.

"Only if I can also call you when I don't need to."

They kissed, and Moses, with tears in his eyes, let go of her. Their fingers slipped away from each other, and he entered his car. He drove away with a smile on his face.

Jane turned to Taryn and said, "Let's go."

"Where?"

"To the hospital to have you checked out."

"Good idea. I'm not feeling all that well."

They drove to Georgetown University Hospital, just a few minutes away, where the doctor-on-duty examined Taryn from head to toe. They also gave her an internal exam. After filing a report with the police at the emergency room and receiving pain medication, they returned to the house on Foxhall Road. Jane, like she had done so weeks earlier, disguised Taryn. Twenty minutes later, the two women left Georgetown for the last time.

At Dulles International Airport, Jane watched Taryn's plane streak across the nighttime sky. With tears in her eyes, she blew her a kiss, promising to meet her in Honolulu the following day. At this point, it was better to be separate; two targets were still harder to hit than one. Sayyid Kassim wouldn't try to kill one unless he was sure he could kill both.

Jane drove out of the airport and headed for Fairfax. Although it was late, she had to see Adam and Bradley.

She spent some time with Sam's distraught boys and their grandparents. It was better this way, she told herself as she drove away. The only way it could be. If the truth ever surfaced, their lives wouldn't be worth living.

Jane arrived at the White House, and the Chief-of-Staff escorted her into the President's second floor study. He left, and Jane looked around. The carpeting beneath her feet was soft yellow. The walls were plastered, with tall bookcases on one and a white marble mantel on another. Tall triple windows, with sheer mesh curtains, looked out over the Tidal Basin to Jefferson's columned portico. James Monroe's desk, with its delicate tapered legs, sat before the windows, and one of Jack Kennedy's rocking chairs stood in a corner. Two flags, the country's and the President's, framed the door leading into the President's bedroom.

Jane and Bill sat on two yellow-covered arm chairs, with a small end table between them. She told him the story of her and Taryn's capture, ordeal, and rescue.

"Unbelievable!" the tall, elderly Texan said, his face expressing pain and disbelief. "But, tell me, Miss Jane, how were you able to shoot all three without them shooting you? And where did you get the gun?"

Dear God! It was the one thing they hadn't thought of for their alibi. Not knowing what to say, she told him the truth. "They were preparing to rape me and I feigned having to go to the bathroom. When I walked back into the room, they were undressing." The truth, Jane realized, sounded stranger than fiction. "Talk about stupid. They put the gun down on the dresser. With their shirts pulled over their heads, I grabbed it and shot them. My God, I can't believe I killed three men." It was a masterful performance, worthy of the master himself, Sam Howard.

President William S. Lawson took her hand in his to comfort her. "What else could you do, Miss Jane? It was self-defense." There was silence for a short time, until the President spoke again. "A few minutes before you arrived, I received word that the site in Burtonsville was burned to the ground. Nothing is left, not even the remains of your kidnappers. It's all been incinerated."

"Who would do that?" Jane asked. "Other members of the PWA?"

"Probably. Those involved wanted to be sure there would be no clues traceable back to them."

Satisfied that their alibi had been believed, Jane stood to leave.

Bill Lawson walked her to the door of the President's study. "So, what now, Miss Jane? A long vacation and then back to TWO?"

"No, I'm afraid not. I'm leaving Washington and politics for good."

"Then that will be Washington's loss. America's loss."

Jane didn't say anything. It was time to be selfish. Time to live for herself and Taryn.

"Where will you go?" the President asked.

Jane thought about what to tell him. "I don't know yet, Bill." She stood and hugged him, wished him good luck and Godspeed, and turned to leave. She walked out of the White House, knowing she could never trust anyone again.

Jane drove through the lit-up capital and looked at the city for the last time. She was sure she would never miss it. She drove north into Maryland, making sure she lost anyone who might be following her, and ended up an hour later at Baltimore International Airport. There, she met Rachel Porter, her college roommate, who took her car. Giving her Mercedes to Rich was the least she could do for her friend who had trusted her without question. She also asked Rich to quietly put her house on the market. She'd never be returning.

Twenty-five minutes later, Jane Weisser was in her first class seat under a different name. The American Airlines Airship 777 bolted up into the star-filled skies and headed for Hawaii. Jane let out her breath. The captain turned off the seat belt sign, and the stewardess came over and asked her if she would like a cocktail.

She declined.

The nightmare was over.

EPILOGUE

"O Iraqis! Yes, you triumphed when you stood with all this vigor against the armies of thirty states! You triumphed while emphasizing your ability to face the showdown and confrontation! You have recorded for Arabs and Muslims bright pages of glory that will be remembered for generations!"

- - Baghdad Radio, following the February 28, 1991 cease-fire

Sitting on the beach in Honolulu, Hawaii, Susan Winters (Jane Weisser) realized she was in Paradise. Not because of where she was, but because she was at peace. Chloe (Taryn) was safe and happy, and that was all that mattered. She watched the teenaged girl splashing in the water, and she thought about the future. The past was over.

With the waves crashing on the shore at her feet, Susan closed her eyes and soaked up the hot, January sun. She happily drifted asleep to the lullaby sounds of the ocean.

The twelve old men of Al-Qiyamah were also happy. The twenty-first century was theirs. The world was theirs. It had been there for the taking and they had taken it in the name of Allah and dedicated it to the memory of their sons who had died at the hands of the 'Great Satan,' America.

Sayyid Kassim sat at the head of the conference table inside his Baghdad home and looked at the victorious faces of the *ikhwan,* the brotherhood. "My brothers, let us speak Bi'-smi'llahi'r-Rahmani'r-Rahim," and they began reciting the Lord's Prayer. "Praise be to Allah, Lord of the Worlds, the Beneficent, the Merciful. Owner of the Day of Judgment, Thee we worship; Thee we ask for help. Show us the straight path, the path of those whom Thou hast favoured; Not of those who earn Thine anger, nor of those who go astray."

"Allah akbar!" God is good!

Sayyid pressed in a number on his telecomp and was connected to a private videophone in Washington. The men of Al-Qiyamah listened as he spoke to the man who had helped them carry out Saddam's brilliant revenge. "Sam was weak," Sayyid told the American on the other end. "If he had let us dispose of the Yehoudi like we wanted, he would be alive today. His weakness could have destroyed all that we worked for. She did us a favor by eliminating him."

Sayyid listened to the American tell him that the Jew had disappeared. He had no idea where she was, but it didn't matter; she wouldn't be causing any more problems.

"She believes she has saved her America," Sayyid said. "How simple-minded of her to think our plot would be so one-dimensional. The Americans have no subtlety and they never learn, do they?" Sayyid sipped his gawha while the American spoke. "Yes, that's the plan. We'll talk about it next week. Allah akbar!"

*****

Inside the Oval Office in Washington, President William S. Lawson sat behind his desk and thought about the position he was now in. He had the sole power to change the world. He would make it the place it was rightfully meant to be. It was something he was committed to do - so committed he had been willing to accept a standby role for perhaps the rest of his life. But now that had all changed. He swung his chair around and looked out at the new world. His world!

Sayyid Kassim looked at his men around the conference table inside his Baghdad home. A smile appeared on his face. From the murders of Sam Howard's family to this very moment, every eventuality had been anticipated. Saddam Hussein's multifaceted plot to destroy America and take political control of the United States had succeeded. Al-Qiyamah, the Rising of the Dead, was now complete. "Although with Sam Howard in the White House we could have exerted enough influence to regulate American foreign policy for sixteen years, we can still do a lot in the next eight." Sayyid smiled in triumph and raised his glass to the future. The old men of Al-Qiyamah followed suit. "My brothers," he said with joy, "to President William Sayyid Lawson and the third millennium." They drank in celebration. "Jerusalem is ours. Praise be to Allah."

"ALLAH AKBAR!"

Sayyid's friends left his palatial home after a few more drinks. Alone to ponder the future, he removed his kaffiyah from his head and sipped the glass of gawha in his hand. After all this time, it felt good to smile again.

A servant brought him his mail. One of the letters was postmarked 'Washington, D.C.' He opened it, wondering what it could be, and read it.

*****

To Sayyid Kassim: Baghdad, Iraq,

There is a sealed carton somewhere in this city with enough evidence against you and your men. If anything ever happens to my family, me, or my friends, or if anything ever happens to Moses McBride or his people, there are instructions to open that carton at once.

As long as we're safe - so are you.

Jane Weisser

Sayyid Kassim sat there for a long time, staring at the letter.

Acknowledgments

This is the part of the book where the author is supposed to thank everyone for their help. It's much like an awards show where you can't remember everyone, but you do remember there were many of them. So, I'll strive for brevity and at the same time accuracy.

I want to thank my wonderful family first: My late father always thought I was the most talented person in the world. I know if he were alive today he'd be in Heaven. My mother, after she read this book in one sitting, looked at me and said, "Promise me you'll never do anything but write." They were always there for me, knowing I could, and would, do it.

After I began writing the first chapter in 1991 after the Gulf War, where Saddam Hussein plots his revenge, I stopped because of the World Trade Center garage bombing and then the Murrow Federal Building bombing in Oklahoma City. I continued writing the book between 1994 and 1997 and every